THE REFUSED

THE REFUSED

A NOVEL

BY

RON SINGERTON

www.penmorepress.com

The Refused by Ron Singerton
Copyright © 2021 Ron Singerton

Published by Penmore Press LLC

ISBN-13: 978-1-950586-97-4(Paperback)
ISBN:-978-1-950586-98-1(e-book)

BISAC Subject Headings:
FIC002000 Fiction/ Action &Adventure
FIC014000 FICTION / Historical
FIC031020FICTION / Thrillers / Historical

The Book Cover Whisperer:
ProfessionalBookCoverDesign.com

Address all correspondence to:
Penmore Press LLC
920 N Javelina Pl
Tucson AZ 85748

STATEMENT OF APPRECIATION

This novel could not have been completed without the unstinting encouragement of my wife, Darla. Her suggestions (usually positive) as well as her computer and literary talents added enormously to this endeavor.

I also wish to thank my editor, Susan Wenger, whose thoughtful input in regard to character development, plot and historical detail was invaluable.

In addition, I owe deep gratitude to my publisher, Michael James, for the publication of this my fifth novel brought into existence by Penmore Press. Michael, having extensive military experience, offered me exacting information on the effects of heavy artillery which enhanced the credibility of this work.

CHAPTER 1

Albemarle County, Virginia
December 1859

The old mansion was deathly still as the sun peeked above the barren trees beyond the tobacco fields. Charlotte Stuart dressed and peered out the window. The only sign of life was wispy smoke rising from the half dozen slave shacks on the plantation. She was relieved that the "maintenance keeper" had not yet arrived, planting season now past.

Jerome would be awake and waiting anxiously for her in the carriage shed, their rendezvous for the previous three weeks.

She picked up her boots, her shawl, and a knitted satchel large enough for the blanket she folded and placed inside. She again listened for sounds and, hearing nothing, tiptoed downstairs to her father's study. The door was unlocked but she had found the key, just in case. The door creaked open. She stopped and listened; there was no other sound. Her father, in his own bedroom, would not rise for another hour, and her ailing mother might not stir until noon.

Charlotte brought a footstool to the bookcase that stretched from floor to ceiling. On the top shelf was a sturdy metal box with a solid lid. Partially hidden, it had escaped her notice until now. Beside it was a slender volume, one that Antonius Stuart would likely not miss. She read the title, *The Inheritance Laws of the Commonwealth of Virginia*, and flipped through the pages. Certainly it would be far too difficult for Jerome, and even she might not understand its complexities. But they would decipher enough.

She slid on her boots and replaced the key in the judge's drawer. Slipping the book into her bag, she braced against the wind, quickly crossed the colonnaded porch, and walked toward the barn.

A young dark woman nearing thirty, pretty and elegant in bearing, emerged from the nearby shacks and approached Charlotte. "I wants to thank you for the ointment."

"How is Ben? Does his heart still race, Eunice?"

"He hurts. I's worried for him. It be cold on the straw, but maybe he can sit outside today if Mr. Steuben allows."

"Yes, you mentioned that before." Charlotte tugged the blanket from the satchel. "I brought this for Ben."

The book, caught in the folds, fell to the ground, and Charlotte hastily picked it up and stuck it in the bag. Eunice saw it, said nothing, and accepted the blanket. "This will make my man happy. Jesus be with you, always will be." She looked toward the barn. "He there." Then, with a fleeting look into Charlotte's eyes, she said, "That boy in for trouble, Miss Charlotte. You knows what I mean."

"We'll be careful."

Eunice shook her head. "He wasting your time. No good will come of it. Only bad things."

***

"Did you get it?" asked Jerome. He crouched beside the brougham, a box-like carriage on four high wheels.

Jerome, with curly black hair and dark beige skin, was fourteen, two years younger than Charlotte. Holding his slate board and a McDuffey Reader, he searched her face with dark eyes.

"I have it, but I'm worried. Your mother's worried too. You must never tell anyone."

"I won't. I promise. But ever since you began to read to me, I wanted to know what those marks really meant, what things they said, and how to speak like you speak. Not slave talk."

"But you must never speak that way to anybody but me. You understand why, don't you?"

Charlotte pulled her shawl close about her and huddled with Jerome behind the coach with its high, spindly wheels. Together they toiled over the legalistic language, often resorting to a thumb-worn dictionary she'd given him as a birthday present. With her sixth-grade education she had taught him sums and words in French she'd learned from her Louisiana-born mother. His mind was quick, as sharp as hers, and he delighted in learning things he was forbidden to know.

Studiously, Jerome wrote the words on his slate board, repeated, then erased them and wrote again. An hour passed, then another.

A shadow fell over them from the opening door, and a walking stick thumped on the wooden floor. They froze as Cornelia opened the door of the sedan and laid her hand on a long white wrap. Frail, she steadied herself, and peered around the coach as if she'd heard something.

Turning to her daughter and Jerome, her hand went to her mouth.

"Charlotte, what in God's name are you doing? And that book! Certainly you aren't teaching him how to read?"

Speechless, Charlotte stared at her mother. Finally she nodded. "I am. Jerome is very smart and wants to read. Especially the law."

Cornelia leaned in close and hissed, "Law? You know it's illegal to teach a slave how to read. And even if he could, what good would it do? No colored man can plead in court—surely you know that."

She looked about, a frightened expression on her face. She coughed, spit into a cloth, and in a hoarse voice said, "I ventured in here to get my wrap. I just remembered where I'd left it. Your father wanted to fetch it for me, but I told him I needed to go outside. Thank God it wasn't he who found you."

She turned to Jerome with a stern look. "The judge would've beaten you to an inch of your life. Or, worse yet, you might have been sold, or lynched! And you, Charlotte, Lord knows what he would have done with you. I dare not even think upon it."

"But you won't tell him, will you?"

"Of course not. Now give me the book, I'll put it back."

"Mother, it's on the top shelf, too high for you to climb. And if it's not in its proper place he'll wonder why."

"I fear that you'll do this again, even if I tell you not to. So dangerous, so dangerous." Cornelia left the carriage barn, her cane thumping.

"Are you going to put the book back?" asked Jerome.

"No. You keep it, hide it. We must never meet here again."

"Where, then?"

"I don't know. I don't even know if we should."

Jerome was pensive for a moment. "We can meet in the tobacco shed, high up. No one goes there now, season's over."

Years before, when the boy was only ten, he and his mother had been assigned to clean the judge's study and dust all the bookshelves. Reaching to a high shelf, Jerome had toppled a half dozen law books and reached down to pick them up. One opened, and he peered at the print as the judge and Charlotte entered. With one swift motion Eunice had snatched the book from her son's hand. "Massa, the boy is just curious. He knows it's wrong and will never, never look at one again. I do promise, and I will keep a close eye on him."

***

"Good morning, Charlotte. You look pretty today. And you're up very early," said Antonius Stuart, with his peculiar smile and his arms crossed. He was the most learned judge of Albemarle County, a tall man with a white mane of wavy hair. He took her hand and gallantly kissed it.

"Father," Charlotte said with an impish grin, "I declare, you are such a romantic. Poor Randolph would be jealous."

"Well, our dear captain will have to abide with my affections. He and the senator will be here later. Mr. Mason has just returned from Washington and we'll have much to discuss."

"I would like to hear what you have to say," said Charlotte.

"Neither the judge nor Senator Mason may think that proper conversation for a young woman," said a lean, unsmiling man with a German accent and a saber scar running down his cheek.

Charlotte gave Hermann Steuben a long hard stare. "I hear what I want to, I say what I want to, and you, sir, can keep your Teutonic thoughts to yourself. I hardly need the advice of an overseer."

"Charlotte! That's no way to behave. Politics is a man's world—you know that," said her father.

Steuben pursed his lips and twisted his pointed moustache. He wore a drooping slouch hat, and the fingers of his left hand twitched in agitation while his other hand held his ubiquitous whip.

"In my country you would be—"

"This is not your country."

5

"Enough," said the judge. "My discussion with the senator and his son will be a private matter."

"I will take my leave, Mr. Stuart," Steuben said with smug satisfaction. "There are people who need special supervision." He looked toward the slaves.

Charlotte watched him go. "He is a vile man, Father."

"No worse than most of his kind." The judge cleared his throat. "In any event, there are things I must speak with you about. Serious things that will affect us all. Let's go inside."

Antonius Stuart ushered his daughter into the library and placed his hands gently upon her shoulders. His mood had changed.

"It is as we feared," he said. "Despite the fact that she occasionally hobbles about, your mother has a week, perhaps two."

"Is Dr. Levy sure?" Charlotte said softly.

Judge Stuart nodded. "The consumption is in its final stages. All we can do is make her as comfortable as possible."

Charlotte wiped away a tear.

Leaving the room, she climbed the elegant spiral staircase to Cornelia's sun-filled room. She waited at the door until her mother passed through another episode of her wracking cough and the bloody sputum that would most certainly follow. Upon entering, she dipped a cloth into a bowl of water and stood beside the bed as her mother wiped her face. With a shaky hand, Cornelia pointed to a chair.

"I'm sorry, Mama, that I upset you today."

Cornelia shook her head. "Do sit, my dear." She gave a wan smile and wistfully said, "There is so much you don't know about all of us—the judge, Jerome, me, and even Eunice. But I know things. *C'est vrai, n'est-ce pas?*"

"*Oui, maman.* It's true. Will I ever know them? The secrets?"

Cornelia did not answer but pointed to a crystal vase. "The sherry—please pour me a little into that glass." She sipped. "Perhaps the judge told you what the doctor said."

"Yes, but I don't know what I'm going to do without you."

"Nonsense. You are a strong girl. Willful beyond measure, in fact. But I don't fault you." She touched her daughter's hand. "I'm not afraid of dying. Life is an adventure, and I believe that the world beyond is one, too. And I don't mean just sitting in the clouds for eternity beside baby Jesus. That would bore me to death."

She laughed at her own pun and fell into a prolonged cough. Charlotte handed her another towel and waited. Her mother looked out the bedroom window toward the garden she'd helped Eunice plant seasons before. The flowers, a pretty mix of maiden's blush rose, Turk's cap lilies, and white lady banks roses, were now dormant. A sense of sadness descended upon the woman.

"I've always loved this room. It's been my sanctuary for the last fifteen years, ever since the judge chose not to share his bed with me."

Charlotte shook her head. "Chose not to. . .?"

"Ever since your father's trip to Georgia in '42. Everything between us changed after that."

Charlotte grasped for something to say. "Do you need anything, Mama?"

"I'm fine for now," Cornelia said. "But I do have one request. I wish to be buried by the oak tree down there, the one the judge and I planted the year you were born. That was a happy time, as I recall."

"I shall tell Father, and we'll make it a pretty place."

Charlotte wasn't quite certain when Cornelia began calling her father "the judge" instead of "husband" or "Antonius." Perhaps it was after that trip. Of course, everybody Albemarle County called him "Judge".

Cornelia sighed and said, "I have but one regret—I won't be here for the debutante ball and your introduction to all the beaux."

"I can't possibly attend a debutante ball just after—"

"Of course you can, and you must. I will be watching, you know," her mother said, a finger pointing upward. "And Captain Mason has already accepted the invitation, though it is still months away. I know that he favors you."

Charlotte smiled. The son of Senator Mason, the captain, always looked so dashing in his fine blue uniform with the red sash and gold braid.

"I do fancy him, but so do all the other belles."

"None can engage with him like you can. He is also a fine sculptor. I viewed his work at the capitol two years ago. Were he not running here and there in the army he could make a good living carving those stones. And he told me that he thinks you have great talent, too."

"I haven't done any carving yet."

"I'm sure he'll let you assist. Remember when you showed me your sketchbook? The drawings were so delicate, so precise. I was truly amazed. I think you will be a fine artist someday."

Charlotte smiled. "I'd love to attend an art school, but I doubt that they'd accept any girl."

"Yes, and righteous society says that some art may be inappropriate for a young lady. But those ideas are silly and invented by men. They can be so obtuse. What do they really know about women?"

"Mr. Steuben chastised me this morning for wanting to hear talk of politics. I spoke my mind about it, and he didn't take it kindly."

"I told the judge not to hire him. He has a dangerous past, Charlotte. Avoid him. Avoid him at all costs."

CHAPTER 2

A half moon barely shone through the dense fog that had blown in by seven that evening. The only other light came from oil lamps peeking out of the mansion as they cast a sallow glow over the snow-covered ground. Flurries grew in strength as a storm neared.

Eunice did not see him as he stood beside his horse and wagon, waiting for the right time.

She'd noticed him watching her for weeks. Ben had seen him, too, and cautioned her not to go out at night, but the pump was in the yard between the mansion and the shacks, and she needed water for cooking. Eunice tried to stay as far away from him as possible and never speak to him or acknowledge his presence. Like the other four women and eight men, she would steal sidelong glances at his pistol or the whip he'd menacingly caress when he thought one slow to jump to his commands.

The judge had warned him to use the lash sparingly—a badly beaten slave was of little use—but Hermann von Steuben marched to his own fife, and the whip too often carved deep into flesh.

Born into aristocracy, he had been expelled from university in Bavaria and, under questionable circumstances, fled in disrepute to Virginia. Having gambled away his inheritance, he found employment by extolling his aristocratic lineage. His money squandered, his living conditions had deteriorated until he could only afford the shack a mile up the road and across the creek from the Stuart plantation.

The kidnapping was done so swiftly that she had no time to cry out. He pried open her mouth and gagged her, then tied a rope around her hands and feet. It took little effort to toss her into his wagon.

No one was about as he flicked the reins and drove onto the road, the sound of the horse's hooves muffled by two inches of snow. It was fifteen minutes later when Ben ventured out, curious that Eunice had not returned. He called her name and inquired at the seven other shacks and at the firewood shed, but no one had seen her or anyone else.

"She not here, not anywhere," he said to Jerome, who came out wearing a heavy tattered coat.

"Wagon tracks and one horse," said Jerome as a flicker of moonlight passed over them. "See, they go to the road."

What had been a light dusting of snow had turned into a blizzard, making visibility hardly an arm's length as Jerome knocked on the door of the mansion. It was opened by Thomas, the footman, one of the only three slaves allowed in the house.

Curious as to who might be calling in such weather, the judge appeared at the door.

"Massa, Eunice gone, taken away," said Jerome.

"Taken away or run away?" said the Judge.

"No, sah, she no follow the drinkin' gourd. Would never leave without me," said Ben, shaking his bowed head.

"How do you know she's been taken away? Maybe she just went for firewood out back."

"Ben looked for her. Her bucket there by the pump, and water all over. Turned to ice now. And wagon tracks. We could follow them, see where they go."

Antonius stuck his head out the door and pulled his fur-lined coat close. "They'll be covered over by now, and I don't know who would possibly take her."

Charlotte appeared behind the judge. "Father, we must look for her. She'll freeze out there."

"I won't let you go out in this weather. The storm will likely clear by morning. Jerome, take the horse at first light and find her. But I suspect she'll be back in no time."

"I'll go with him," said Charlotte. "There will be patrollers out looking for runaways."

"No, you will stay here. I will write him a pass."

He brushed snow off his coat and looked at Ben and Jerome. "You two get along now. I told you what to do."

"I know who took her," Charlotte said as the judge closed the door, "and I think she'll be dead by morning."

"Do not defy me, Charlotte. Not this time." He ascended the stairs. "Cornelia's funeral is the only one I care to attend."

***

The storm ceased an hour before dawn. Jerome saddled the horse and led it out of the barn.

Ben held the reins. "I want to go with you."

"You should stay here in case she comes back. She'll worry otherwise."

"You have the pass?"

Jerome nodded and pointed to his pocket. "Miss Charlotte put it under the door."

"I didn't hear her. She come in the storm?"

"She did. Eunice special to her."

"Miss Charlotte special too."

Eunice lay beside the road, knees pulled up in a fetal position. Jerome dismounted and knelt beside her. Fearful, he touched her shoulder and said, "Mama?" He felt a slight shudder. A frozen shawl was wrapped about her shoulders as if it were a funeral shroud.

"Mama," Jerome repeated, lightly nudging her. She opened an eye and mouthed the word "cold."

Jerome sat her in the saddle, then draped a blanket over her. He looked about as the sun began to rise and saw that they were a half mile from the plantation. In the distance a wisp of smoke came from Steuben's house beyond the bridge.

Jerome took the reins and slowly walked the horse back to the plantation.

***

"She won't talk, not even to Ben. Won't leave the shack," Jerome told Charlotte. "He says that she's curled up on the straw beside the fire and moans every once in a while."

"I'll go to her," said Charlotte. "She might talk to me if menfolk aren't around."

"Should we tell Cornelia?"

"I will, later. I'm amazed that Eunice is still alive."

"She has a bad bruise. Steuben must have hit her."

"Did you see him?"

"No, but he must have thrown her out afterwards. She didn't get very far."

"Father will have to do something about this."

"I don't think he will, Miss Charlotte. No white man will be punished for doing what he did."

She knew he was right.

***

It was nearly dark three days later when Eunice appeared in front of her shack. Wrapped in a blanket, she slouched on a stool beside Ben, who sat in a throwaway rocker. A half-dozen slaves were shoveling snow in front of the mansion when von Steuben climbed off his wagon, tied his horse to a post, and approached Eunice and Ben. He stopped six feet from them and pointed to Ben. "Get a shovel and help them. Go on, now—do it."

Eunice stood. "He hurt bad. He can't do that work, not today."

"What? You are talking to me, nigger?"

"He cannot—"

The whip flashed and caught her on the cheek. She screamed, her hands reaching for the bloody gash. With fathomless rage and unbelievable force, Ben bolted forward and rammed a fist into von Steuben's face.

The man howled, fell back, and, regaining his footing, blocked a second swing. Seeing an opening, he launched a blow at Ben's chest just as Charlotte and the judge stepped onto the porch.

Ben stopped, uttered a cry, then collapsed face forward.

Blood flowing from her wound, Eunice dropped to her knees beside him as Charlotte joined her. One of the men dropped his shovel and helped Eunice turn Ben onto his back.

"Talk to me, talk to me," pleaded Eunice, but he stared up with lifeless eyes.

"He dead! He dead!" wailed Eunice. She pointed at von Steuben with savage resolve. "You killed my man! You killed my Ben!"

"He attacked me—you saw it!" blurted von Steuben as the judge walked down the steps.

Antonius Stuart leaned over and laid two fingers on Ben's neck. He closed the man's eyes and turned to his overseer.

"You have one hour to collect your things and get off my land. You hear? You get off my land."

His face narrow, the swelling on his face growing, von Steuben said, "I'll go, but you owe me twenty dollars, my salary for the month."

"And you owe me one thousand for the death of this man."

An hour later, von Steuben had loaded his wagon, and his horse plodded past the plantation gate.

Charlotte put her arm around Eunice, who said, "I wants to be with Ben tonight."

"Take him to her hut," the judge said. "I won't expect her to work this week."

Nobody saw the lone figure slip away and walk briskly down the road. With a hammer in hand the task took little more than twenty minutes. With moonrise on the cold, stark night there was no need for a lantern. Shortly thereafter, von Steuben mounted his horse and rode out without looking back. After watching from a copse of trees, the figure turned and disappeared from view.

***

At midnight, Charlotte and Jerome followed the cortege on their trek to the slave cemetery in a wooded area at the edge of the plantation. Just as his ancestors had been, Ben was carried in his coffin by pallbearers chanting an African language, one that was considered sacred and secret.

Torches illuminated the scarecrow trees, and Charlotte shivered as a wind rose. Women wearing white shrouds, kept hidden and only worn for funerals, followed the men.

"The words?" Charlotte asked Jerome.

"From the Bakongo tribes. They've been handed down for generations. Many of the people here have roots in Angola, others are from all over West Africa."

"I am the only white person here."

"You are the only one worthy of being here."

"Then I am honored. Ben was my friend. But I'm surprised that a man is carrying a cross."

"It's not entirely a Christian sign. Bakongo believe that the cross speaks to resurrection and the Four Moments: birth, life, death and what comes after, the unseen. Everyone here believes that those who've lived a godly life will live forever. So Ben will be with Eunice forever."

A variety of objects were placed on the coffin. One was Ben's walking stick; beside it was a bottle and his cup, both turned upside down with a hole punched in them. "It's to allow the power within to join the spirits of the dead," Jerome said when Charlotte gave a quizzical look.

She watched as Eunice knelt and placed her hands on the coffin. Bowing her head and swaying back and forth, she issued an incantation, then rose and began a high keening sound. Neither a lament nor a dirge, the cries were picked up and echoed in the night. But soon the mourners' voices changed from solemnity to exaltation. Chants rose ever louder and more stridently as they began a counterclockwise movement, the "plantation walk," around the gravesite.

"What does this mean?" asked Charlotte, trying to be heard over the shouting.

"He is no longer in bondage, no longer a slave to any master," said Jerome. "Ben is free and welcome in the world beyond."

Mesmerized by the intensity of it all, she realized how little she knew about these men and women, people she saw daily and had presumed to know. Gone now was the sullen, dispirited shuffle, the evading eyes taught to look away, the mincing deference to those who bought and sold them with callous indifference.

And there was Jerome, wild in the night. Suddenly she envisioned him running free in a world far across the sea. The scene before her could have transpired thousands of years earlier, and now it existed just below the surface.

"Come, come!" he shouted, taking her hand and joining in the dance as a chorus of joy and exaltation rose in the night.

"It was beautiful," she told him after the ceremony. "I never knew—could not even conceive of—the world that your ancestors came from."

"We have the blood of Africa, yet we will never know what it was truly like. There may have been great kings, armies, and civilization. But we can dream, Charlotte. And tonight you were with us. And maybe you saw how it might have been."

***

The next day Sheriff Whitcombe descended from his buggy and approached Antonius Stuart, who was smoking a cigar on the front porch. The sheriff tipped his hat and shook the judge's hand. He turned his attention to the men and women who went about their chores and said, "Are they all here? No runaways?"

"No runaways," replied Stuart. "Why do you ask?"

"You haven't heard? A man you employed, a Hermann von Steuben, was found dead this morning under the bridge down the road. Probably happened at night. Apparently, his horse dislodged some boards and fell, breaking a leg. It must have thrashed about, because the wagon and von Steuben rolled off. The wagon was smashed up. Von Steuben suffered a broken neck. The coroner said he died instantly."

The judge removed his cigar. "I had to dismiss him. He killed one of my people and likely raped a woman here, a colored. Whatever caused the accident, I think he had it coming.”

“But it’s still murder.”

“We’re talking about my property, sir.”

“Of course. But surely you have suspicions. Somebody, perhaps one of your slaves, an act of revenge? The woman, was she capable?”

“I doubt it. And even if one of them did, you would need proof. I’m not about to lynch someone without it.”

“I want to show you this,” said Whitcombe, lifting three warped boards from his buggy. “These were found on the rocks. You can see where nails were extracted. In fact, my deputy found a half dozen. Somebody must have had a tool, maybe a claw hammer, and removed them so that the horse would fall. So, I have to ask, who would have access to the tool? And who would want vengeance?”

“Almost everyone here could find a claw hammer. They do repair work and construction all the time.”

“Still, I would like to interrogate your people. Someone will know something.”

“I don’t like the word ‘interrogate,’ sir. I will question them, but they won’t tell me anything, even if they know.”

“Their code. I suppose you’re right. They are a mysterious people. We must keep a tight rein, Judge, lest things get bad. We don’t need no Nat Turner again. A lynching once in a while is not a bad thing.”

“Only if he’s proven guilty.”

“With a white man, yes. But a nigger?”

Antonius Stuart watched the sheriff climb into his buggy and drive off. The thought of a lynching rankled him. The murder could have been done by any of the men, but only one name truly stood out. And that one had complications. Hopefully, in time, the whole thing would be forgotten.

CHAPTER 3

February 1860

"Here they come," said Antonius Stuart as Randolph drove the buggy with his father onto the plantation.

Alighting, both the senator and Randolph kissed Charlotte's hand. She laughed as Randolph lifted her and swung her around.

"My Charlotte!" he exclaimed. "I declare, Father, is she not the prettiest lass in Albemarle County?"

"The county? Heavens, no, the prettiest in all of Virginia! But deportment, young man, deportment. Society, you know."

"Society be damned. I am truly and irrevocably in love."

"A notable but dangerous thing," said the judge.

The senator laughed. "As I mentioned in my note, Antonius, I'll be heading back to Washington shortly, but I wanted to speak with you first, get your take on the election and this Lincoln fellow."

"Then come on in. I have a good bottle of Tennessee whiskey. Yes, sir, important matters stirring. And not particularly good ones."

"Knowing you, Charlotte, I presume you want to hear everything my father and yours intend to discuss," said Randolph.

"I do, but I haven't seen you in weeks and I can't stand those cigars." She touched his coat. "You look so dashing in that uniform, captain's epaulets and all."

"Uniforms are made to impress pretty girls. One week in the field and the horses smell better than we do."

She became serious. "I was worried for you. We read about Harper's Ferry and John Brown. Your father wrote that you were there. It must have been awful."

"For Brown and his comrades. I wasn't in the fight—it was left to marines and a colonel. Lee, Robert E. Lee. Some of Brown's men were killed, and he was captured."

"What will they do with him?"

"That's up to the courts. But he attempted insurrection and tried to start a slave revolt like Turner's in '31. That's sedition, and if he's convicted, he'll be hanged."

"Do you think there will be uprisings by other abolitionists?"

Randolph took a deep breath. "I pray not, but the country is of two minds, and those minds are not talking to each other."

He turned and watched as a heavy wagon trundled onto the plantation. "Here's Charles. He has the marble I wrote you about. And, Miss Charlotte, I demand that you help me with it. Cornelia said that you did a magnificent sketch of an angel, and that's what it should be."

"And you trust me to work on it? That's courageous of you."

"Not at all. I will rough it out. You work on the hands."

Charles spied Jerome. "Boy, help me with this stone if it ain't too heavy for you."

Jerome crossed his arms and made a face. "You just a pile of bones, old man. You knows I can move it myself."

Charles grinned, his three teeth a contrast to skin dark as the night sky. "You no talk to your elders that way." Looking past Jerome, he said, "Miss Charlotte, where you want me and dis child to put da rock?"

"In the tobacco shed, Charles, and take care that Jerome doesn't hurt himself. He's not as strong as you are."

"You gets in da wagon, boy, hear?"

"They've been as close as father and son," Charlotte said as the wagon pulled away.

"I like Charles; he works hard and I don't have to reprimand him. But it doesn't mean I entirely trust him. Do you trust Jerome?" said Randolph, taking Charlotte's hand.

"I do. I think he'll defend me with his life if he has to."

"Very noble. And the murder of the overseer—is he innocent of that?"

"Yes, Randolph, I believe so, I truly do."

She turned and watched two riders come through the gate at a full gallop.

"Soldiers here?" she said as a corporal dismounted, saluted, and handed Randolph an envelope.

"From Charlottesville, sir," he said.

With a puzzled expression, Randolph opened it and scanned the hastily written message. "The mayor requests my presence at the capitol. They're forming a militia and want me to address the recruits. He asks that I come as soon as I can."

"A militia? Is that really necessary? Your company is only a few miles away."

"A company is only a few hundred men. Militias will necessary if there's real trouble. I don't know where this is heading, but I must go."

She gave him a hug. "Do be safe. You know I adore you. Come back as soon as you can."

***

Jerome closed the door of the three-story tobacco barn where late-harvested leaves dried on overhead racks. Tall narrow doors on hinges were open to allow in air, and a shaft of sunlight illuminated the stone.

In his island patois, Charles said, "Can't stay long—massa get suspicious. You tink about what I tol' you?"

Jerome nodded. "I want to help."

"I shows you how to get to da railroad," Charles said. "We walks at night, da station not far."

"Did your uncle go north?"

"He gone. You and Eunice go too. Others go during da war when men away."

"War?"

"You don' listen? You keep yo head in da sand? Every nigga know dat white folks goin' kill each other. An' it be soon, too. You see men goin' for soldiers, all fancied up, puttin' on dem pretty suits and marchin' roun', gravediggers goin' be busy, chile. Sho nuff. Noth'n be the same when da shootin' start."

"What will happen here?"

"I 'spect dis place goin' burn to da groun'. Others, too. 'Bout time. Matches easy to get." Charles raised his eyebrows and tilted his head in a curious way.

"I don't want this place to burn," said Jerome.

"Lordy works in mysterious ways," said Charles, his eyes burning with vengeance. "Yes'm, mysterious ways, boy. An dat's a fact."

***

With tea in her right hand, Charlotte raised her left to knock on her mother's door.

"I have things to say to you, things about Jerome," said Cornelia from behind the door, sounding irate.

Charlotte slowly lowered her hand and listened.

"Yes, Jerome," said the judge. "There are things you should know, and it concerns all of us. Troubling things. I thought that murder had been forgotten. But no, Whitcombe is hounding me. It's as if he has a personal vendetta and townsfolk are riled up about it. 'A white man murdered by a nigger,' they're saying. And just who do you think might have done it? Who besides Charlotte and Eunice cared so much for Ben?"

"You wouldn't dare accuse him," said Cornelia in a strained voice.

"I will if I have to. You know that."

"I know what you've tried to hide for all these years. You think I don't? It's as plain as day."

The coughing came again and Antonius said, "Do you want your sherry?"

"Not sherry, damn you. The whiskey—that bottle you gave me, if it isn't poisoned. Oh, it doesn't matter. I'll be dead in a few weeks anyway."

There was a moment of silence, and Charlotte almost stepped away. But there must be more. A revelation, a dying wish? Cornelia had said that her husband hadn't been in her room for years. What could now be so important that she hadn't said before?

"And just what do you know?" said Antonius sharply.

"About you and Eunice. I was here at the birthing when you were gallivanting around in one brothel or another. Of course, in our corner of the world a man can do whatever with his property and then happily deny it. As you have done, haven't you? And I know of the other three women you sold afterwards. But you didn't sell Eunice. No, she's pretty and you like the pretty ones, don't you?"

"Exactly what are accusing me of?"

"You and Eunice! Your son, damn it! Jerome, with his wavy hair, his expressions. The way he crosses his arms and gives that silly grin. I fear for him. I do, Antonius."

Charlotte dropped the teacup. She was about to turn away, but the door was already open.

"Father, I was just bringing Mother a cup of tea. Is she feeling any better?"

"I fear not," he said, anger still on his face. "Yes, bring her the tea. I'll be in my study. Don't disturb me today. Not at all."

***

Charlotte and Jerome sat at the edge of the tobacco field, it being warmer than usual and much of the snow having melted. In her mind, Ben's funeral had receded into a distant place, as had vague visions of Africa.

For days she'd turned the question over in her mind—what should she say to Jerome, if anything at all? Would he even want to know? Would Eunice want him to know? Most assuredly she'd said nothing about it. Was it her deepest secret, or was she just protecting her son from knowledge that would serve no purpose?

He seemed distant, pensive. But Jerome was far more mature than others his age.

"What do you know about your father?" she said, choosing not to look at him.

"My father? I never knew him. My mama said that he was a big man with kinky hair and an infectious laugh. But he was sold a few days after I was born and she never saw him again."

"And you believe that?"

Jerome shrugged. "Why not? And why do you ask?"

"Just curious. It's really none of my business."

"But you make it your business. I know you, Charlotte—you don't ask frivolous questions. You know something, don't you?"

"I think someday you should ask your mother about it. You were probably very young when she spoke of it."

Then, quite suddenly, she blurted, "I shouldn't have said anything. I am so sorry, forgive me, please forgive me."

Her hands flew to her face. With a moan she rose from the branch and hurried away. Behind her she heard Jerome call her name, but she shook her head and broke into a run.

How stupid. How much damage have I caused?

***

Randolph had roughed out the area where the hands of the sculpture would be, and Charlotte worked tirelessly, chipping and polishing delicate fingers that held a single rose. She had the unfinished marble placed by the oak tree as her mother watched from her invalid chair.

Moving closer, Cornelia peered at the completed hand and the rose with its white, luminous petals and murmured, "That alone is all that need be said. Life, like the stone, is never really finished. Your work is a thing of beauty, dear child."

"But I would really like to finish it."

"No, leave it as it is. I am pleased beyond tears."

Once back in her room, Cornelia sipped a glass of sherry. "In that drawer is a letter to the judge. You will present it to him if he ever attempts to sell Jerome."

"I'll do as you ask, Mama, but I don't think he will." Charlotte looked down at her feet. "I must admit something for which I am mortified. I was bringing you a cup of tea when you spoke to father about Jerome. I shouldn't have listened, but I did. I was going to keep it a secret from him."

"And you told him?"

"I told him he should speak to Eunice. I don't know if he did or not."

Cornelia stared out the window, then took Charlotte's hand. "She will have told him the truth. He is your half-brother, that is so. Don't blame yourself for indiscretion. I suspect he's known all along. But I ask you to protect each other—there may be dark days ahead." She coughed. "I have something else for you, Charlotte. I've kept it in a box in the closet. There was a period when your father had me do the accounting and the receipt of the tobacco money. I already knew of his infidelity and thought of leaving. I never did, but I took what I thought I might need anyway—enough for an emergency. Now it is yours."

The disease that afflicted and consumed her ceased three days later.

***

It was supposed to be a very private funeral, beside the oak tree and the unfinished stone. But dozens of carriages arrived with mourners, for Cornelia—a woman of integrity and forthrightness—was greatly respected, if not loved.

Following the eulogy, a large, stout man spied Charlotte and went over and put his arms around her. With red apple cheeks, a bushy black beard, and moustache, Gabriel Shelby III looked like a swashbuckling seventeenth-century pirate riding in on his great black horse. "My dearest, I should have come months ago. I am so sorry."

Charlotte felt like a small child in his embrace. "Cousin, no apologies are necessary. I'm so glad you're here. I know how much you adored my mother, and she spoke of you often. In fact, she insisted on reading your columns in the paper. She thought you wise and very, very funny."

"Annabelle wanted to come so badly, but she's taken sick and is confined to bed."

"Is it serious?"

"A temperature and chills; she'll survive. She extends her deepest condolences, as do I."

After the mourners departed, Shelby and Charlotte sat in the portico while Randolph, the senator, and her father repaired to the smoking room.

Shelby reached into his coat pocket and pulled out a copy of the *Richmond Dispatch*. "I know you're always curious about politics, so I thought I'd show you the article I wrote two days ago."

He pointed to the columns below the masthead. Charlotte read it.

"It's really that bad in Congress?"

"Afraid so. Not quite like Charles Sumner being caned by Preston Brooks in '56. Everyone's on a tightrope. The election, you know. The paper's sending me to Washington. There's lots of talk of secession."

"What will you do if it comes to that?"

"I might join up. I rather fancy cavalry—dashing and all."

"But cousin, doesn't the North have more people than we do?"

"Only twenty-two million to our nine. And," he said, taking a deep breath, "over four million of ours are slaves. But they can't ride like Shelby, so there's not much to worry about, is there?" He grinned and hugged her again.

"It sounds like a lot to worry about, Gabriel," said Charlotte.

Jerome passed the veranda leading a horse. Shelby waved and Jerome waved back.

"Has Jerome been behaving?"

"As well as Jerome can."

Shelby grinned then sighed. "Dangerous time, Miss Charlotte. Has been for a while. And just between you and me, I think it's going to get worse. Much worse indeed."

CHAPTER 4

Judge Antonius Stuart mopped his brow as he sat in his study with the distinguished Senator Mason.

"Damn hot," said the senator, holding up an empty glass. The judge looked over his shoulder at Jerome just outside the door. "Boy, fetch us two glasses of whiskey and open that window."

Moments later Jerome, wearing scarlet livery, returned with the drinks. The senator sipped. "Antonius, perhaps you can clarify a family matter I'm involved in. My cousin Rachael's husband, Wilbur, died a month ago. Her brother-in-law claims that he's entitled to the entire estate without any portion going to her. Is there merit to his argument?"

The judge pondered the question for a moment. "Well, he may have a claim there, but it would be better if it was in writing. The court might require that. I'll have to look into it. This part of the law isn't my specialty."

"I see," said the senator. "I do wish I had some clarity on it. Time is of the essence."

"Virginia intestacy law says that surviving widows are entitled to a dowry amounting to one-third of the real property," said Jerome, half to himself.

There was a stunned moment of silence.

"What did I just hear?" demanded the senator.

Jerome faced him. "Yes sir, it's true. In the book of inheritance. It's based on a Virginia law of 1785."

There was a moment of silence.

The slap sent Jerome across the room. "Uppity nigger!" The judge's face was crimson with rage. "Get out! I will deal with you later!"

Jerome slowly stood, shaking. He stared at the judge, rage building, and then the words came. "Yes, I can read the law. I damn well can! You call me 'boy' and 'nigger'! You are my father! My mother told me. You raped her just like you did the others."

Both men were on their feet.

"That is a lie!" shouted the judge. "A goddamn lie!" Grabbing Jerome by the collar, he threw him into the hallway. "You will pay for your insolence! Oh yes, you will pay dearly!"

Jerome stumbled back and sank to his knees. "You are my pa and I am your son. I am your—"

"You are nothing but a damn slave!"

Turning to the senator, the judge said, "This is blasphemy and it will be punished."

The senator nodded. "I'll keep my counsel. No one will know of this. But you might look into the statute the boy mentioned. And just to relieve yourself of future problems, you might consider selling him. My brother in Georgia needs a field hand."

***

Jerome had made up his mind.

"It's so dangerous, are you sure?" said Charlotte.

"I am, and I'm taking my mother with me. But I need Charles. Can you find a reason to go to the Masons and speak to him?

"I'll go with Father. He knows I want to see Randolph, and he wants to talk to the senator. But first I have something for you."

"What is this?" asked Jerome when Charlotte handed him a cloth bag. It felt heavy.

"The conductors won't charge anything, but others will. This should be enough for you and Eunice to board ship. Also, inside is the address of Annabelle. Tell her where you're staying. And don't stop in New York or Philadelphia. Bounty men are all about."

Two nights later, fearful for him and Eunice, Charlotte watched from her upstairs window as Charles led them and three men across the road and into dense woods.

***

"Make no sound," ordered Charles as he listened for hoof beats and whispers of men hidden along pathways.

There was a half moon and Charles moved slowly, picking his way past branches and snapped twigs, signposts of the railroad. It would be an eight-mile journey to the first station, near a cove beside the Chesapeake River.

"Da Quaker man will meet us and take us to one o' da houses."

"What then?" asked Jerome.

"He take us to a boat and speak to da captain. Den we sail away."

Clouds raced across the sky as they came to a break in the trees. It had rained the day before, and Jerome saw footprints of shoeless people and sliding marks, signs of struggle. No shoes meant runaways, and runaways meant patrols.

But all was quiet. "I tink we safe," said Charles, as they hugged a tree line that skirted the clearing. Jerome held

Eunice's hand, but the clouds broke and moonlight illuminated them.

"There they are!" The shout sounded as loud as a canon's blast. The baying of dogs and the pounding hoofs broke the silence.

"Run!" shouted Charles as he and the others dodged back into the trees.

The horsemen and dogs were nearly on them when Jerome pressed the purse into Eunice's hand and said, "Go! Go!"

"Not without you," she said, but he dashed toward the horsemen as fast as he could. Sensing their quarry, the dogs surrounded Jerome and lunged at him as the riders threw ropes around him and flung him to the ground.

"Got this one!" shouted one of the half-dozen men, all armed with knives, revolvers, and shotguns.

"Chain him," the leader shouted. "Chain him good, but don't beat him too bad. He's valuable."

"The others?"

"They'll be caught. I know where this one comes from. The judge will pay plenty for him."

***

Antonius Stuart fully expected that Eunice and the three men would be brought back in shackles the next day, but no patrol arrived with them in tow. It snowed again, and Mr. Bradshaw of South Carolina, the new overseer, was told to keep Jerome in chains outside the tobacco shed. Charlotte had put a blanket around him, but without breaking the lock there was no way for her to move him to shelter.

"I think Mama got away," Jerome said as Charlotte knelt beside him

"It was a brave thing you did, sacrificing yourself. I heard that the patrollers say that they were very angry when the dogs stopped for you. They couldn't find Eunice and the others without them."

"How long do you think he'll keep me in these chains?"

"I don't know. He's furious, having lost four people. I'm sure he's thinking about money, and you cost a great deal. He'll have to buy more slaves if he's going to plant tobacco."

Jerome slouched over, water dripping from an old hat. "What if he sells me?"

"I don't think he will."

"Why not?"

"Because."

***

"They'll be coming for him any minute," the judge said to Charlotte.

"Who's coming?"

"Senator Mason's men. I'm selling the boy."

"*Selling* him?!"

Antonius waved his hand dismissively. "He's my property, like that chicken there. And don't you interfere. You're damn close to being disowned—hear?"

"I hear, Father. But I have a surprise for you."

Returning from her room she handed him the letter. "I suggest you read this before doing anything rash."

He fairly ripped the envelope from her hand and marched into his study. He recognized the fluid penmanship, breathed with consternation, and read,

Dear husband,

These are my last words to you from beyond the grave. Failure to abide with my wishes will trouble my soul and yours for eternity. I have attempted to ignore and even tolerate your gambling, your adultery, and your

31

indifference toward me during these last dozen years. However, I know deep inside that you have a conscience and an awareness of right and wrong. You are, after all, a judge. And you have a son. He is not of our issue but I have come to adore him, and he has, with his kindness, become a son to me in all but name. Under no circumstances will you ever sell him. He is of your flesh and blood and, though now in bondage, will be made free. It is my desire, for his bondage is evil in the eyes of the Lord. Goodbye, Antonius. Do this for me and I will forgive all your sins.

Cornelia Stuart.

"But she didn't say when," mumbled the judge. "And 'in the eyes of the Lord,' it will not be soon."

Charlotte watched as her father spoke to the men at the plantation gate. The discussion was short, and the wagon and occupants trundled down the road.

By the time Antonius Stuart returned to Jerome, Charlotte, hammer and chisel in hand, was already pounding on the lock. It broke, and a cold and stiff Jerome stumbled into the shed.

"You knew, didn't you?" said the judge.

"Mama gave me the letter. I knew what it likely said."

"At one time I loved you, Charlotte, but I'm not so sure now."

"And you loved my mother once, too. But you abandoned her. I don't think you and I have anything to speak about anymore. And, if you wish, I will go away, I can take care of myself."

Antonius pursed his lips. "If that pleases you."

He began to walk away, then turned. "No, you should stay."

"Why?"

"Because," he said, his eyes staring skyward, "I need someone to cook for me."

"Then I suggest you hire a cook."

CHAPTER 5

Late December 1860

The air was chilled, but the sun shone in an azure sky as Charlotte and her cousin Annabelle strolled arm in arm beside the plantation.

"I am so excited," said Annabelle. "I just know that my beau will propose to me at the debutante ball. Of course, that won't be until July, but time will go by so fast. My mother and I will be going to Richmond in a few weeks. She's having me fitted for a very special gown."

"Is William a lieutenant now?"

"Yes, since he's graduated from West Point. He'll be in Randolph's regiment. Isn't that just grand? I can't wait for you and the judge to see him in his new uniform."

"I'm happy for you, but you know I'm not going. I wrote you about me and my father. I choose not to be in his company any more than necessary. And Randolph can propose to me any time, even right here."

"Oh, you are insufferable, and so stubborn! Of course you must go. It's the most magnificent event of the year. Everyone will be there, including Randolph. What if he wishes to propose to you then? What if he tells other officers that the senator intends to make the grand announcement? And what if Miss Charlotte is nowhere about because of an argument with her father? They will be stunned. Randolph may never want to see you again, and you will regret your decision for the rest of your life. Oh, no, Charlotte, you have to go."

"I'll consider it, for Randolph's sake. But I will commit to nothing more. At least not now."

***

For months the atmosphere between Charlotte and her father had been icy, but both looked forward to the visit of Randolph and the senator in mid-March. Both men kissed Charlotte's hand and complimented her as usual. The judge led them into his study where a fire glowed in the hearth. He poured them bourbon in crystal glasses and passed out cigars.

None cared to dissuade Charlotte from attending, certainly not her father, who had studiously avoided her. But he could hardly deny her the pleasure of seeing Randolph, who had been in Richmond for the last two months.

Though not wearing his officer's sword or pistol belt, Randolph still wore his blue uniform adorned with captain's bars. He took a seat on a divan and Charlotte sat beside him. The judge found his familiar high-backed chair, one that Cornelia had purchased in Charleston years before.

A light snow blanketed the fields, and there was a moment of silence as the men lit their cigars. Senator Mason, somber in his long black coat, pulled a newspaper sheet from his pocket and handed it to the judge. "The *Albemarle Southron*. It contains President Lincoln's inaugural address. Have you seen it?"

"I heard about it—haven't actually read it."

"Well, you may wish to."

"If you don't mind, sir, please read it aloud," said Randolph. "I haven't seen it, either."

"Of course." The judge adjusted his glasses. "'We are not enemies, but friends. We must not be enemies. Though passion may have strained, it must not break our bonds of affection ...'"

At the conclusion, he laid the paper on a table, shaking his head.

"That speech didn't inspire affection down here," the senator said. "I don't know when Virginia will join the other Confederate states, but I reckon we will, being the biggest toad in the puddle. Paper says that Jeff Davis'll be sworn in as president on the eighteenth."

"Secession," said Charlotte. "I still can't believe it's come to that."

"I can," said the senator. "New free states will be coming into the Union. The South could wake up one morning and find that the abolitionists have enough votes to outlaw slavery by afternoon."

Charlotte caught Randolph's eye, sighing. Of course the men thought she needed the issues of the day explained to her, as if she were a child, as if it weren't what everyone had been talking about for as long since she *was* a child. Randolph winked at her.

"We have to acknowledge the corn and face the facts," the senator continued, oblivious to the exchange. "There's no more land in the country to grow tobacco or cotton. Abolition of slavery means our way of life is over. No free labor, no economy, and that's the simple truth. It's time we just shuffled out of the Union and went our own way."

"Mr. Lincoln might not cotton to that," said Randolph.

"Well, we got into the Union voluntarily and there's no reason why we can't voluntarily skedaddle," said the judge. "But military men like you have to make a decision. Will you support the Union or switch to butternut gray?"

Randolph drew in a breath. "If Virginia secedes, I will go with it. But I'm fearful for the future. We don't have the industry, the railroads, or even the means to make artillery. And the bulk of the navy is up north. They could institute a blockade, and none of our cotton would get to Europe. We'd be cut off. That means no imports, no more guns."

"We'll get support from England and France," said the judge. "And, I declare, the North will pay dearly if it intends to invade the South. They won't get far, not by a full jug. No, sir."

"We have all the guns we need, and the war will be damn short," added the senator. "Damn short for sure."

Charlotte looked up from a smudge on her white gloves, dismay and consternation rising from within. "Sir, forgive me for speaking my mind, but this war you talk of will be ruinous! Cousin Shelby tells me that the North has twenty-two million people, and of our nine million only five are white. And over half of those are women and children."

She turned to Randolph. "My darling, I shudder to think of how many will perish. I don't want you hurt. I don't want you to die! This whole affair is over slavery, our 'peculiar institution.' And it is an abomination. Yes, an abomination, and we will be thoroughly destroyed! Do you hear me?" She rose to her feet, shaking with rage.

"Enough! That is treason!" shouted her father.

"Yes, treason it may be, but this war will be the end of us. I am so sorry for all of us. I truly am."

She strode out of the room and slammed the door.

Twenty minutes later, the senator and Randolph said their farewells to the judge. "I should say goodbye to Charlotte," Randolph said to his father.

"I counsel against it. And, to be quite honest, considering her attitude, she can't possibly support the South, war or not.

I regret that your lady is no longer one of us and will never be part of society. That is something you'll have to consider."

"I shall, Father, but, by God, I love her so."

***

In the three weeks before Charlotte received a short letter from Randolph, she realized that her remarks had been terribly chilling. She should have known the will of the South and the desire for independence. But to her mind the war was still an abstract thought. She could hardly imagine thousands of men intent on killing neighbors who lived across the Mason-Dixon line. It seemed the height of insanity. But not to Randolph, and now the damage was done.

She wished that Cornelia was still alive. Her mother always knew what should be done. Perhaps she'd counsel to not correspond, to let time play out and have events take their course. The war would draw them closer together, and if his love was real, he would marry her, society be damned. The debutante ball? "Of course," Cornelia would say. He would be there to sweep her off her feet as he always did. "You must go," she'd once said, yet that had been so long ago, and so much had changed.

It was with trepidation that Charlotte slid the letter from the envelope. Only three paragraphs long, it took only seconds to read.

Dear Charlotte,

I do hope this letter finds you and the judge well. As you will surely understand, I have been engaged with my unit in continuous drilling in anticipation of imminent action. Thus, it will be quite impossible for me to visit, even if I felt comfortable in doing so.

I fear that your dismissal of our cause is of concern. Certainly, you know that I adore you and always will. But I must ponder the efficacy of our future and our happiness together. I have been assigned to defend Richmond and will be there until August unless my battalion is ordered North before that time.

I wish that politics had not raised its ugly head, that we could remain as we were. I so badly want to hold you again, to hear your laugh, to see your beautiful visage. I pray that future circumstances will allow that.

With heartfelt devotion,
Randolph

It was late, and in the glow of a candle she folded the letter and returned it to its envelope. She blew out the flame and lay in the darkness. His words about holding her, listening to her laugh, his devotion to her despite her outburst gave her a semblance of hope. But there were other words too: "if I felt comfortable in doing so," and "the efficacy of our future and our happiness."

Was it all over? Had she destroyed the blissful union she had dreamed of year after year?

He'd said that he would be in Richmond until August, and the debutante ball was scheduled for July. *Perhaps, perhaps*, she thought. Yes, she would definitely go.

She breathed deeply and hugged her pillow. Rarely did she cry, but on that night she did.

***

After the fall of Fort Sumpter, enlistments on both sides swelled in gleeful anticipation of coming battle and glory. Companies, battalions, and divisions were formed, overwhelming administrative capacity. Lincoln called for the states to enlist seventy-five thousand, but so many rushed to Washington that thousands were sent home.

As Senator Mason had predicted, Virginia joined the Confederacy. Expectations of victory added to the excitement of the debutante ball, where officers would be wearing their new gray uniforms and golden epaulets.

On July 10th Charlotte wrote Annabelle saying that she had decided to attend the ball but had not received a letter from Randolph, even though she had written wishing him well.

Annabelle replied, overjoyed that Charlotte had decided to attend, and said she expected to see Charlotte there in the following week. Her letter included a copy of a thrilling report from William about the first battle against Union forces on the twenty-first.

Charlotte opened the letter from William hoping to learn something about Randolph as well.

Dearest Annabelle,

I had the honor of engaging the enemy with a battalion of the Nineteenth Virginia Infantry, many from Albemarle, at Manassas Junction here in Virginia. The battle was greatly contested with Federal victory in sight when General Jackson, now called "Stonewall" for his unwillingness to retreat, saved the day for our glorious

Southern nation. It was with great enjoyment that we witnessed terrified Union troops as well as distinguished civilians (including elegantly attired ladies) fleeing in panic back to Washington. One or two such victories must surely conclude this war. I am in the best of health and do hope to see you at the ball for which we have been promised leave. I am also being considered for promotion to captain, though the conflict may be settled before that can be done.

I so look forward to seeing you again.

With all my love, your Lt. William

There was no mention of Randolph. Surely he, too, would have been in battle since he was an officer with the Nineteenth Virginia. William could have extended a message from him regarding his condition. Perhaps, in the frenzy of it all, such a thought might not have come to mind. But she would learn much more in the next week, a time of hope, celebration, and joy.

***

On the train ride Charlotte exchanged a minimum of words with her father. He appeared pensive, and unusually dour. Sitting across from them was a matronly woman and her husband, a colonel of an Alabama regiment. The woman was chatty, oblivious to the judge's feigned interest.

"This is only the second time I will be in Richmond," said the woman, addressing Charlotte. She took her husband's hand. "Thomas and I met there twenty years ago at the debutante ball. May I presume that since you are wearing that beautiful evening dress you are meeting your beau there?"

Charlotte offered a fleeting smile. "Yes, I expect to. He's a captain and has been with his regiment."

"Well, he is most fortunate to win the hand of such a beautiful young lady. And I'm sure that you are very proud of him, defending our land from the Yankee invaders."

"Yes, yes I am," said Charlotte, ending a conversation she had no desire to continue.

The woman frowned and caught her husband's eye. He leaned toward her, and Charlotte was sure he whispered, "Something amiss. Bother her not."

Dozens of gas lamps illuminated the governor's mansion, and spritely waltz music filled its main hall. Debutantes from all Virginia as well as neighboring Confederate states had descended on the capitol. Young ladies were attired in elegant dresses covering a half dozen hoops and petticoats. They wore diamond broaches, emeralds, and sapphires bought from Tiffany of New York before the war.

Officers in uniforms of cavalry, infantry, and artillery escorted their ladies onto the dance floor as others watched from the winding staircase and the balcony above.

Charlotte, on her father's arm, entered the foyer trailing a gown of light blue, a corsage and a rosette of gold ribbon, full sleeves, a pearl necklace, and an aigrette in her hair.

Merriment and a swirl of activity was accompanied by tinkling glasses, laughter, and a Straus waltz. The entire scene was illuminated by gas lamps. Black boys in scarlet livery slipped through the crowd with silver trays, offering condiments and champagne.

Officers and wealthy men, along with their wives or sweethearts, greeted Charlotte and Antonius. There was a tap on her shoulder. Charlotte whirled around to find a beaming Annabelle.

"Oh, Charlotte," Annabelle said, "I am so glad that you and the judge have come. Isn't this wonderful? Nearly everybody is here. William will be along shortly. I'm told that he's on his way from a meeting with senior officers. I am just so excited!"

"This is truly a magnificent gathering, and you look lovely, my dear," said Antonius Stuart. "Have you by any chance seen Senator Mason or his son?"

"Not yet," replied Annabelle. "But surely they will be here. They won't dare miss this." She took Charlotte's hand. "I'm certain that Randolph can't wait to see you. My William told me that he is a spectacular leader and may be promoted to major. Aren't you thrilled?"

Charlotte nodded. Her eyes turned toward the entry of still more guests.

"There's William now!" exclaimed Annabelle. Her beau joined them and held Annabelle's hands. "You are absolutely beautiful and so wonderfully precious. My heart is pounding with joy!"

He shook the judge's hand and bussed Charlotte's cheek. "Please do excuse us for just a brief moment. There is something I must say to Annabelle."

She put a hand to her mouth, eyes wide with anticipation, and followed the lieutenant to an alcove. Five minutes later she returned, her eyes downcast.

"Charlotte, William has something to tell you, something important." Annabelle turned to the judge. "We'll be right back."

Charlotte glanced at her father, who stood alone, glass in hand. He nodded, stoic, lips pursed as if contemplating the sentence of one brought before him.

"Dear Charlotte," began William, holding tight his white gloves, his words coming slowly, "Randolph spoke to me less than an hour ago."

Annabelle held her cousin's hand as William handed Charlotte an envelope. It looked similar to the one she'd received months before.

Dear Charlotte,

I feel obligated to inform you that I will not be attending the ball this evening. I so deeply regret that I cannot consider matrimony between us. I have given lengthy thought to this decision and fear that our perspectives are too far apart. I cherish you more than you can imagine and will never find anyone as lovely or caring. But it would be terribly unfair for me to deny you the certainty of finding a gentleman of your persuasion.

You must know that this is the saddest decision I have ever made.

I fervently wish you the joy you so aptly deserve.

With everlasting affection,
Randolph

Charlotte handed the note to Annabelle. "It's as I thought. I do so cherish your friendship—and yours, William. If Randolph asks, tell him that I wish him well. But he never need concern himself with me again."

That said, she found the judge. "You may stay if you wish. I am leaving."

***

On the day they arrived at the mansion, she packed bare essentials, gathered up her money, and saddled her horse.

"I cannot remain here any longer," said Charlotte when she found Jerome.

"Where are you going?"

"Somewhere beyond the Confederacy. I will miss you, but there is nothing for me here."

"There's a war on, Charlotte. Traveling north is dangerous."

"I heard that ladies can go through the lines." She swallowed back tears. "I pray that someday you become free. I do with all my heart."

Jerome nodded. "I wish you well, sister. I hope to see you again."

***

The note she left for the judge was brief. He found it in his study, and it simply read, "I thank you for accompanying me to the ball. Nothing is as it should have been. Charlotte."

Two days later a man led Charlotte's horse to the plantation. When Antonius answered the door, the man said, "At the railroad your daughter entrusted me to return this mount. She has paid me for my time, so you owe me nothing."

"Do you know where she went?"

"I do not, except for the fact that the train was going toward the Virginia border. She wishes you well but says that she will not be coming back. That is all I have to report. Good day, sir."

CHAPTER 6

Mid-March 1861

The Pratt Street riot in Baltimore between the Sixth Massachusetts Infantry and Southern sympathizers occurred seven days after the firing on Fort Sumpter. Months had passed, and General Benjamin Butler's victorious troops placed the American flag on Federal Hill, the highest in Baltimore. The city, a railroad and industrial hub, had been saved for the Union.

Thousands of Federal soldiers were on the streets as Jack Volant and his brother Steven ascended the steps of Professor Jason Platt's Georgian Revival mansion. They were escorted through the elegant home of Italian design and led to a luncheon in a flower-lined patio behind the house.

There, the esteemed professor greeted other faculty members of the recently constructed University of Maryland as well as graduates, city officials, and military officers.

Women in fine summer dresses shaded themselves with silk parasols and exchanged gossip about the embarrassingly dreadful debacle at Bull Run and their relatives' frantic retreat to Washington only a week before. Several of the women spied the new arrivals, smiling and nodding in their direction. Both Jack and Steven returned a courtly bow and

Steven, recognizing one of the women, motioned that he would be in her company shortly.

Waiting for an appropriate opportunity, Steven, wearing the latest fashion of frock coat, vest, and perfectly tailored trousers, caught the professor's eye, stepped forward, and shook his hand.

"Sir, may I present my brother, Lieutenant Jack Volant, Union cavalry and a very fine artist as well. He is also a graduate of our fine university."

"Splendid," replied the professor. "And what were you studying before you joined the army?"

"Military science and art. Had it not been for the present conflict, I might have devoted myself entirely to painting. But my father says that the army pays and art does not."

The professor laughed. "I've always admired artists. In fact, I did some sketches of the great pyramids when I visited Egypt four years ago. Of course, they are most certainly amateurish in comparison to your work, but Egypt—ah, what a delight."

"I'm sure that your work is more than competent," replied Jack.

A major joined their little group and entered the conversation, eyeing Jack's dark blue uniform with a single row of gold buttons, a gold stripe running down his pant legs, and a gleaming saber at his side. "And what unit might you be with?"

Jack came to attention and saluted the senior officer, who returned the salute. "I'm temporarily assigned to General Butler's division here. I'd rather be with a cavalry regiment in the field, but orders are orders, sir."

"Yes, of course. I have a dear friend whose son recently graduated from West Point—George Armstrong Custer. I've known him since he was a toddler, a real firebrand, damn reckless, his father says. But young George is putting together a unit of Michigan troops. You might write to him. He's looking for talented officers."

"I will do so. I thank you for the suggestion, sir."

The major smiled. "Many students don't know it, but our esteemed professor here was a soldier in the war against Mexico."

"It was long time ago. I got a chance to fire a few rounds— lots of smoke and shouting. That was about it."

"He's being quite modest," said the major. "Everybody around here knows that he's a damn good shot. Probably still is."

"Well, you learn a few things in the army, don't you lieutenant?" said the professor.

"Yes sir, like not falling of a horse."

After the laughter died down, Jack addressed the professor. "My brother told me of the enlightening works you've written. I trust that he's read them and is doing well in your classes."

"He's doing very well, and I'm looking forward to his attendance next year." Professor Platt turned to the major. "Steven is quite a raconteur and has a pronounced interest in the land of the pharaohs. When he's not too distracted, that is." He smiled and raised his eyebrows, observing Steven assessing the comeliness of several young ladies.

"Isn't that right, Mr. Volant?"

"What? Oh yes. I greatly enjoyed your lessons on mummification," said Steven with a trace of impatience.

"That's good, very good," replied Platt.

Steven patted Jack's arm and pointed to a table laden with fruit, pastry, and lemonade. "Enjoy the luncheon, I'll be just a while."

Jack took his leave of the professor and joined a dozen others at the condiment table. He saw Steven, dashing at six feet with a mop of curly blond hair, engaging in pleasantries with the two women who'd noticed him earlier. They were laughing at his outlandish stories and impish grin, turning the heads of the more reserved guests.

Having renewed his flirtation with the two lovelies, he slipped through the throng and tipped his hat to a stately lady some years older than he. Radiant, with blond tresses and an hourglass waist, she delicately touched his arm and whispered behind her opened fan. She offered her hand, and Steven kissed it. Looking about, she tilted her lovely head toward an oak tree some distance away.

Neither she nor Steven saw the professor turn his eyes toward them. He watched for a brief, uncomfortable moment before turning back to the parents of a prospective student.

Jack and Steven left the gathering an hour later and walked toward their parents' house, two blocks from the family business.

"You know, Steven, I tend to notice things."

"As an artist?"

"That, and as a soldier. We look for danger, especially from places one might not expect."

"This sounds like another one of your prescient observations, all for my benefit."

"You have a demonstrably effective manner with women."

"How can I help it? They flock to me like moths to the flame. I can't help but love them, young or older."

"And married or not," said Jack tersely.

"Women pleased by their husbands do not look elsewhere. If it's not me filling that void, it will be somebody else. But I am careful, Jack, damn careful."

"So you say."

They walked quietly for a while.

"Will you be joining up after you graduate?"

Steven sighed. "You are a leader, Jack. And you have a combative side in spite of all your funny tricks. Oh, yes, I remember the time you tied a rock to my line when I wasn't watching. I thought I was bringing in one hell of a big fish. You laughed yourself silly."

"I thought it damn clever."

"Indeed. No, Jack, I might teach, might even help Father if we can stand each other. Despite the reversal at Bull Run, I don't see this war lasting long. It will likely be over before I graduate, and there are more volunteers every day. The army is just not me. Maybe that sounds a bit untoward, but I know I won't be any good at it. Does that bother you?"

"To be honest, I think you're making excuses. You'd be as good as anybody else, and they all start out green. I sure was. Think about it."

They walked a block further.

"I'm going back to the barracks," Jack said. "Stay out of trouble. And stay away from the professor's wife."

"She's in love with me. What can I say?"

"Say goodbye. It may save your life."

CHAPTER 7

December 1861

"I had a conversation with Father this morning. You know he's worried about you," said Jack as he and Steven walked down a muddy Baltimore street.

"He always is," said Steven. "He's been insistent that I join the colors."

"You're still of the same mind?"

"I am. Besides, there haven't been any big battles since Bull Run, and there may not be any more."

"I wouldn't bet on that. Armies rarely fight in winter, but it will begin again in the spring. You'll see."

Hoping to change the subject, Steven said, "So, where are we going? It's damn cold."

"I heard of a sculpture studio down this street. I thought we would take a look."

"You're interested in sculpture?"

"I'm interested in art. Sculpture is art."

With a crackling fire in a hearth, they stepped inside and passed two men completing work on a large marble bust of a Union officer.

"The major was killed at Bull Run," said a voice behind them.

Jack and Steven turned to see a short bearded man in a dusty smock. "His wife asked us to create this piece in his memory. We're working from a photograph. He was a civilian then, but adding the uniform isn't difficult," he said.

"It's a fine piece of work," said Jack.

"Name's Patrice Benoir, originally from Virginia but I'm a Lincoln man now."

"And you're the sculptor?" asked Jack after introducing himself and Steven.

"I did much of it, but we all have our specialties. Some do the rough carving, others the finishing work: nose, eyes, mouth, and such. Are you also an artist?"

"I'm a painter, or was before the war. I still dabble. Is there a piece in progress?"

"There is, as a matter of fact. Come."

They followed him to a back room in which tables were laden with hammers, chisels, and assorted polishing stones. Shards of white marble littered the floor. A woman perched on a high stool was chipping slender flakes from the bonnet of a life-size female figure. She turned toward the little party as they entered.

"Very nice, Charlotte," Benoir said. "Don't make the ribbons too thin. I know how delicate you like them, but this will be an outdoor piece. We must be mindful of the weather —ice and such. *Comprenez vous?*"

"*Oui, je comprends, parfaitement bien.*"

"Of course, she understands," said Benoir.

"How unusual—a woman sculptor?" said Jack.

"Unusual, yes. Actually, she's my second cousin on her mother's side. I was hesitant to take her on as an apprentice, but she was very persuasive. And, quite remarkably, she's the best details sculptor I have."

"Amazing," said Steven, starting toward Charlotte.

"Monsieur, please don't disturb her. She's very single-minded; even I don't intrude when she works."

He motioned them back to the front room. "She's a determined young lady. She lives with my sister, and I pay her well. But Margaret, she says that the girl's admitted to difficulty with her family in Virginia."

"Virginia ..." said Jack.

"Yes, so perhaps she also has constrained loyalties, living in Maryland with soldiers dressed like you."

"And she's not married, not engaged?" asked Steven.

"No, but according to Margaret there was someone. An officer with the rebellion. But we know nothing more. As for me, I'll be leaving for France in a few months. I have a cousin there who has connections to Eugénie, the empress. She's an art collector."

***

Steven Volant reread the note handed to him by a slender young man with a black goatee, bowler hat, and long frock coat.

Professor Jason Platt expects you to be at the north end of the cemetery at eight in the morning, two days hence. Failure to appear will be regarded as not only ungentlemanly but an act of cowardice. Pistols will be provided. Who your second might be is your decision. There will be no negotiation over this matter.

Having seen the demand read, the courier bowed curtly, turned, and strode away.

There was still a chill in the air, but it was fear that froze Jack's brother on the commons of the University of Maryland.

It had been so easy—the delectable seduction of the professor's wife at the conclusion of the previous semester. Most certainly, it was a delicious relationship, she being a true beauty. It could have gone on for months had she not relived it in her sleep. Interrogated by her jealous husband, she tearfully admitted the transgression, one which he'd suspected for a very long time. And though she feared for the life of the engaging and handsome seducer, there was nothing she could do about his certain demise.

Under no circumstances, thought Steven, would there be a duel. Though he had gotten into some unpleasant scrapes with the law, he'd never fired a weapon in his life. Nor had he any intention of doing so.

Steven didn't consider himself a coward, having been in more than a few fights in his twenty-three years. Robust and tall, he'd won most of them. But the sight of maimed youths returning from the front engendered revulsion as opposed to the patriotism that had infected Jack.

After retreating to a saloon for an encounter with several tots of whiskey, Steven took a carriage to the docks and perused the many ads for departing ships as well as ports of destination and the cost of passage. Exuberant broadsides proclaimed the magnificence of San Francisco by way of the Isthmus of Panama or around the tip of Tierra del Fuego. The latter, though a treacherous passage, would eliminate any possibility of malaria or yellow fever while being transported on the back of an Indian. Indeed, it was said that a traveler might feel fine in the morning and, due to one of those diseases, be dead by late afternoon. That prospect appeared quite unseemly to Steven. He would sail around the Horn.

He smiled at the sight of some comely ladies looking over the same poster. Yes, San Francisco would be an excellent refuge. An educated gentleman who was fluent in French,

Latin, and even a bit of Arabic should easily find employment as a lecturer in the academic world.

His father might be a problem, but he'd provide a partial explanation by telegram once in California.

He slipped into the family's splendid Victorian, gathered his savings, and packed a sturdy valise. A soft knock on the door was followed by his mother's euphonious voice.

"Dearest, your father requires your attendance. He says it's most important."

Steven steeled himself. His relation with Petain Volant was anything but cordial, especially after having made it clear that he would not join the Union army. To the senior Volant, defending the Union was a cause of holy import, second only to the uprising at the Paris barricades in 1848. To Monsieur Petain, Steven was a shirker with a checkered past. It was only his mother's intervention that allowed him to remain at the university, taking classes his father considered nonsensical.

Father was a man of little education and even less patience, but great drive. Having fled with wife and children during the year of revolt, he'd established himself as a savvy and, most importantly, reputable businessman. He was also known for his temper and pugnacity; few ventured to argue with him. Steven simply avoided the man. But now, as he walked deliberately into the study, he wondered how his father might complicate his flight.

"There is something you must do for me," said Petain without preamble.

Steven sighed. "I hope it won't take long, Papa. I'm leaving here."

"Leaving?" His father raised his eyebrows.

"I sail tonight with the tide. I'll be changing my name," he said with resolution, "and I won't be coming back."

"So, you are in trouble again," said Petain, with a look of disgust. "Did you rob someone and pawn the goods for illicit pleasure?"

"I didn't rob anybody. I never have. It has to do with a woman. And circumstances I care not to reveal."

A tense moment passed.

"I should have known. Come into the parlor. The thing you must do for me, for the family business—it will take you far away from here."

"Where?" Steven asked, suddenly wary.

"First Paris. From there, Alexandria." Petain handed his son a thick envelope.

"I'll need a passport, and I don't have time to get one at the French embassy," said Steven, his plans already in disarray.

"I know the American ambassador in Paris, a Mr. Elihu Washburne. I will telegraph him, and he will make the proper arrangements. Of course, I will have to leave unsaid the matter of your transgressions."

Steven's father tapped the envelope. "There is a great deal of money in this, enough for travel expenses, as well as mummies and their shipment from Egypt to France and then here. I require several thousand of them."

"Mummies? Egypt?"

"Precisely. With the war still raging, paper and linen is in very short supply. Our company can use wrappings, as can all other paper companies, not just here but in London and Paris as well. From what I have learned, ancient textiles are in abundance and, considering their age, very well made. My competitors are using the linens for bags, textiles, even bandages. We merely have to wash the wrappings. But I want dozens of actual mummies as well. They are quite valuable. There are collectors for that sort of antiquity."

The man became silent, his dark eyes riveted on his son. "A woman, you said. Is she with child?"

"I don't think so. She's married and has occasional relations with her husband. If any child results from my—"

"Enough! Yes, you will leave tonight. Normally I would have you face the consequences. This is hardly the first time. But I need the textiles, so, if asked, I will say that you left without telling me your destination. You say that you will have a new name."

"Marcel. Marcel Cheval."

"French. I approve." Petain nodded thoughtfully before returning to the business at hand.

"I'm told that there is a brisk business for mummies in Egypt. Do not spend much time in Paris before leaving for Alexandria. Be sure to bargain; that's what people expect in that part of the world." Petain's eyes narrowed. "I am trusting you, Steven, something I am hesitant, indeed reluctant, to do. If you succeed, you will gain my confidence. If you fail, well ..."

The man left the rest unsaid.

"I'm sorry that I won't be seeing Jack before I leave. Tell him that I wish him the best and that I will write."

"I suspect that he will want to know what becomes of you. I pray that you succeed. For your sake as well as mine."

The steam packet slipped out with the evening's tide, and the newly minted "Marcel" was certain that he would never see Maryland again.

CHAPTER 8

Alexandria, Egypt
July 1861

Obtaining the French passport, finding lodging, and taking ship from Le Havre took far longer than Marcel had planned.

The temperature had reached a scorching one hundred and twelve degrees when he arrived in Alexandria. It was a squalid shadow of what it must have been like when the Macedonian general arrived there and named the city after himself three hundred years before the birth of Jesus. But that city, later visited by Julius Caesar and Antony and then Octavian, who renamed himself Caesar Augustus, was no more. Its great library with its hundred thousand scrolls had become dust eons ago. Yet, thought Marcel, it was still Egypt where thirty dynasties had risen and fallen, and a haunting mystique lay hidden in the shadows. The very idea sent a shiver down his spine.

The docks overflowed with obsequious hawkers who descended like vultures upon new arrivals. A wave of babble assaulted him and a dozen Europeans in their heavy, stifling clothes. Like a determined phalanx, the foreigners shoved through the besieging crowd and hastily searched for their wooden trunks. Upon locating their valuables, they hailed small horse-drawn carriages and gratefully fled the chaos.

Scores of ships—steam-driven side-wheelers, clippers, and fast schooners—pushed their bowsprits over the docks as the bumper crop of Egyptian cotton was carried aboard by bent-backed stevedores in loose white *gallibayas*.

Wearing blinders, cattle and delicate Arab mares were led up ramps and into steamingholds. Carts filled with replicas of ancient pharaohs, stone columns topped with Ionic and Doric carvings, and bundles of desiccated mummies crowded the embarcadero.

Marcel approached one cart and, indicating the mummies, looked at its owner. With a combination of gestures and limited Arabic he said, "Where can I find these?"

The man gestured vaguely toward a conglomeration of mud-brick buildings, then hustled his cart into line.

Sweating profusely in top hat and frock coat, Marcel waved away hands dangling gold-plated chains, replicas of Old Kingdom necklaces, and recently carved scarabs while their vendors attested, in the name of Allah, the authenticity of their merchandise.

Only the call to prayer from a towering minaret halted the hubbub as men laid out their carpets and put their foreheads to the earth, chanting the sacred words of their faith. That respite gave Marcel time to dash for his hotel three blocks from the wharf. There, amongst bars, trading houses, tenements, and bordellos, he listened to men hoping to find ancient treasures worth a king's ransom.

For two oppressive days he wandered through narrow defiles and a labyrinth of passageways. Armed with a pen and ink illustration, he approached a boy. "Mummies, where can I find mummies?"

The child stared at the drawing. After holding his hand out for a coin, he led Marcel toward a dung-littered alley. The boy stopped and motioned him to wait. Women obscured in black cloth from head to toe leaned out windows to scrutinize the stranger. Then, like specters, they disappeared into the dimness of their disintegrating abode.

Wary of distrustful eyes, the boy hastily returned and beckoned him on. Marcel followed, nervously, looking right and left, then up at linens suspended between crumbling, sun-bleached walls. He passed stands shielded by tarpaulins upon which lay local produce. Men haggled, picked over merchandise, and turned to stare at him as flies and insects buzzed in the afternoon heat.

The boy led him through a labyrinth of narrow alleys to a shadowed souk, and Marcel spied a small human-shaped object wrapped in swaths of linen.

"Mummy," said the boy, tugging on Marcel's sleeve. An elderly man emerged from the door of the adjoining house and entered the souk. With a show of great reverence, he lifted the mummy as his eyes evaluated the cut and quality of Marcel's clothes.

"*Français*? Britisher?" he said through missing teeth.

"American."

"Ah," said the merchant, stroking a scraggly white beard. He gently raised the mummy. "Royal, a child, most sacred. Ancient, third dynasty of the Old Kingdom. Died during the time of Djoser, the builder of the first pyramid. Indeed, there are sacred scarabs in the wrappings. Here, you can see one barely covered. It is a treasure I would not even consider offering to most. But you look like a scholar, a respecter of our ancient and fabled land."

Marcel studied the mummified figure, not two feet in length, the wrappings tight and covered in a fine dust.

"Fifty dollars American, for you," said the man. The old vendor offered a toothless half smile, but it promptly vanished as a tall, gaunt, severe man with a prominently hooked nose silently placed himself beside Marcel. The vendor's eyes glinted like broken glass, and he made an upward motion with his chin, but the intruder did not move.

"It's a fake, worth a dollar at most," the man said in English. "You should stay away from this souk. The man is a charlatan."

The vendor, joined by two burly men, bristled. Then the gaunt man said, "Do you speak French?"

"I do," replied Marcel.

"*C'est bon.* We will speak in French."

"How do you know the mummy is fake? It looks real to me," said Marcel, taking in the man's erect military bearing.

"It is a mummy, for sure, but the manner of wrapping, the enticing fake scarab, tells me that the child probably died five or six months ago."

The man stopped and looked deeply into Marcel's eyes. Marcel stared back. "Who are you?"

"I won't reveal anything more here. What you are seeking is not in this slum. I think it best if you follow me; you have much to learn." He gestured toward four heavily built men who were steadily approaching. "This is not a safe place."

From inside his gallibaya he revealed a curved sheath knife, not unlike that carried by nomadic tribesmen of the Arabian desert. Seeing this, the advancing men stopped and slid into a nearby souk.

"You only unsheathe it when intending to draw blood," remarked Marcel.

"Then you understand," said the man. "And they know that I am quite capable of using it."

As Marcel and his stoic companion walked away, Marcel said, "I can trust you? With or without the knife?"

"I am not this Egyptian trash, monsieur. I am an Algerian, a former soldier in the war against France. But I go by an Egyptian name, Jabari Abraxas. It's the one I'm known by in Paris." He flashed a startling grin. "I am also an actor and a raconteur. There's a café not far from here, one of the few in Alexandria. We can talk there."

Marcel wasn't entirely certain how this austere Jabari Abraxas had found him and why he seemed protective of Marcel's money or his safety. But if he'd saved him from buying an expensive fake, he was thankful and willing to hear what the Algerian had to say.

They walked in silence for twenty minutes past centuries-old mud-brick buildings and ancient stone dwellings built with stones carved hundreds, if not thousands of years before, all removed from walls and Pharaonic monuments that once proliferated in Alexandria.

Jabari directed Marcel to a café, and over a cup of strong Turkish coffee, Marcel said, "You mentioned Paris. Do you have business there?"

"I do. In addition to what I've told you, I'm a skilled purveyor of antiquities: Egyptian, Babylonian, Sumerian, for certain clients."

"Real antiquities?"

Jabari appraised Marcel for a long moment, then smiled rakishly, white teeth appearing against a darkly bronzed face. "If they pay enough. For many, the appearance alone suffices. And, of course, they all look sufficiently ancient."

He stopped and cocked his head. "Now you know my name, monsieur. May I ask yours?"

"Marcel, just call me Marcel."

"Very well, Monsieur Marcel. Why do you want mummies?"

"I need them for my father's business. A large quantity— hundreds, to be shipped from here to France, and then to

America. There is a great shortage of linen due to a war there. You may have heard about it."

Jabari nodded. "I am a literate and learned man. Yes, of course, a civil war since April."

The Algerian sipped his coffee. "Then you don't need real mummies—I mean, those from the old, middle, or new kingdoms. Those can be quite expensive and a bit more difficult to obtain, being deep into the desert."

"What others are there?" asked Marcel with skepticism.

"Ah, that is where I might be of service and how I might make myself quite useful. So, let me say this, monsieur. Mummies—the unwrapping of them in a mystical, otherworldly macabre setting, harking back to the days of long-deceased pharaohs—is all the rage across cities of Europe. It's all about the afterlife, theirs as well as ours, since we all hope to exist forever in one form or another. Modern Egyptians know of this and cater to the fascination with it in the French and British salons. There are even artists who make paint called 'mummy brown,' oil mixed with the dust of ancients."

"How bizarre."

"Indeed. But, as I suggested, the truly ancient ones are now harder to obtain. Of course, there are still hundreds of thousands of real cats and exotic creatures that Egyptians mummified, but those don't have the same allure. No, Monsieur Marcel, an entire industry has arisen here to provide mummified bodies and parts of bodies to foreigners seeking them."

Marcel took another sip of the brackish coffee and looked intently at the hawk-eyed man across from him.

"And of course," Jabari continued, his voice low, "these recently mummified corpses look almost identical to those of two or three thousand years ago. Only a true expert could tell the difference between those recently made and the real thing. I am such an expert."

"I see. And these fakes are wrapped with the same linens?" asked Marcel.

"Of course. Egyptian cotton hasn't changed in four thousand years. Woven into cloth and bleached by the sun for three or four months around a mummified body, they have the look and same musty scent. And for those purchasers desiring to unwrap them in a performance, scarabs, jeweled amulets, and the eye of Horus can all be manufactured and set nicely inside the wrappings. When revealed, these pieces of apparent antiquity can have the most profound effect. Of this I personally know."

"And you can help procure these for me? Not just the wrappings, but the fake mummies as well?"

"I can do better, for I, too, am an actor, a chimera who adapts and changes based on the necessities of life. But you must trust me as I must trust you. I've had many adventures —some, unfortunately, less savory than others. But I know things that can make us rich."

"You say you're an Algerian, Monsieur Abraxas. But you choose to live in Paris. May I assume that you've had problems in Algeria? Perhaps the recent war, or something else?"

"I am a patriot of my homeland but ..."

"I see. But to continue our discussion. You said that you know things that can make us rich. I would like you to elaborate, since we're speaking of some sort of collaboration."

"Ah, that comes after we seal an agreement."

"And what would this agreement entail?"

"Something I've given great thought to, but a matter requiring a person of obvious repute. You seem like a well-schooled gentleman. And you're obviously interested in a profitable venture beyond simply procuring mummies," said Jabari, a finger touching his prominent nose. "So, are you also a showman? A raconteur who would spin ghostly tales of the ancient world while unwrapping these mummified beings?"

"Until now I hadn't considered it, but it does present interesting possibilities. So, yes, I'm interested if it's truly possible."

"Then," said Abraxas, "you might consider an expert assistant who's extensively traveled the ancient world and Egypt in particular."

"An assistant?"

"*Oui*, monsieur," said Abraxas with an ingratiating smile and hard eyes. "My presence will provide additional legitimacy and expertise. In Paris I have everything that will be required, including a sarcophagus and countless trinkets which can bring a fine price. I will do this for, say, thirty percent—a gracious offer. Look as you might, you will find no one who'll do it for less."

Marcel steepled his fingers and studied the peculiar Algerian. The offer represented a considerable departure from what he'd previously considered, a tutorial position or a sinecure as a lecturer at an obscure academic institution. But such employment would afford barely enough to live on. And Paris was not a city that valued the indigent.

"If I were to accept your offer, we'd require a place of business, one attended by those educated enough to have an interest in the ancient world. I'm speaking of a salon, perhaps, attended by the elite."

"Of course. I know of such a salon right in the heart of Paris. As I said, I'm an actor but not a European—someone accepted as a gentleman in French or British society. I would require one such as yourself to make my plan succeed, posing as a mystic, one of the cognoscenti of the afterlife."

"And away from Algeria and the authorities there."

"You are rather perceptive. And since I speak fluent French, I can slip into the shadows of Paris if necessary."

"So, you are a wanted man," said Marcel.

"Some people may have an interest in interrogating me. I'm not interested in speaking with them. Yet I am one who can detect foibles and frailties in others. Character has many shades of gray, and though you seem quite upstanding, your interest in acquiring and selling less than truly ancient artifacts speaks volumes. So, though I mean no insult, I suspect that you, monsieur, have an interesting tale of your own. One that you care not to reveal. So perhaps we are suited for one another."

Marcel looked hard into the Algerian's eyes. "Monsieur Jabari Abraxas, I think it's time to go to work."

"And then to Paris, Mr. Marcel."

CHAPTER 9

The South
Late May 1862

With growing anxiety, Annabelle entered the studio. She was met by Patrice Benoir, who removed a dusty pair of glasses.

"Charlotte, a visitor to see you." Patrice Benoir led Annabelle into the workroom. Turning from a large Revolutionary War sculpture, Charlotte removed her smock and descended her ladder.

Annabelle threw her arms about her. "I was so worried. I didn't know if you got my letter and if you would still be here."

"I did, and I'm so happy you came. How on earth did you get here?"

"I took a British ship. The blockaders wouldn't dare stop a ship flying the Union Jack."

Annabelle looked over her shoulder. Benoir had left the room. "I have never seen so many Yankees in all my life. There must be a whole army here. I feel like they're all watching me."

"I know. It's disconcerting, and I'm still not used to it. Probably never will be."

A sculptor entered, nodded to Annabelle, and rummaged through a toolbox.

"Is there somewhere we can talk?" asked Annabelle.

"Benoir's office. He won't mind if we talk there."

They entered a small room with a desk, two chairs, and a half dozen marble busts. Annabelle set down a large carpetbag and sat quietly for a minute, eyes tearing. She ran her hand over her dampened cheek. "My William is dead."

"Dead? Oh, my God! What happened? When, how?" said Charlotte kneeling beside her.

"On the fifth. There was a battle just outside Williamsburg. General Johnston's men were attacked. The Nineteenth Virginia tried to hold the line, but many were killed. I've been helping the doctors in our hospital; some of the wounded were brought there. One of them said that William fought very bravely but was slain late in the day. I had to see you—there is nobody else I could possibly be with. I am just weary, and so distraught."

"I'm so sorry. He was a wonderful man. What are you going to do? Are you going to stay here?"

"No, no, absolutely not. This is enemy territory and I'm already sick of this place. I'm going back, and I want you to come with me. We're needed at the hospital. There are so many wounded now. We need every woman who can help."

Charlotte exhaled slowly. "My work ..."

"This isn't a time for art. It is a time for sacrifice. You must come home, you must."

Annabelle cried, and Charlotte held her close.

"How will we get back?" asked Charlotte as a company of soldiers marched past the office window.

"Not by ship. The Yankees took Norfolk on May tenth and soldiers are stopping anybody thought to be secesh. But I brought these." Annabelle removed nun's habits from her satchel. We'll say that we're from the Baltimore church of the

Immaculate Conception, bringing medicines to Union captives. The Yankees won't bother nuns."

"I'll say goodbye to Monsieur Benoir. And then we will go home."

***

December was bitterly cold as Captain Randolph Mason looked down the hill toward the Union dead and slaves who were collecting the bodies. He leaned against the stone wall and reread the letter. It was the third he'd received from Charlotte since she'd returned from Maryland. She'd replied to each one of his, and in each she reiterated how much she still adored him. He couldn't help but be pleased.

It was only seventy-six miles from Fredericksburg to Albemarle County, but to Randolph it could have been a million miles. Charlotte filled his dreams every night, though he quickly put them away in the morning. There was no time for such longing as the Army of Northern Virginia marched and countermarched to flank the Union army.

He didn't wish to burden her with details, but he would answer her questions about his health and the war.

> Dearest Charlotte,
>
> A terrible battle here raged from the eleventh to the thirteenth when General Burnside threw his massed regiments against us. What brave men and what stupidity in their high command. We absolutely decimated them, particularly the indomitable Irish brigade, the Sixty-Ninth New York. Our men remained fairly safe behind a stone wall and fired into their lines. After thirteen assaults they finally saw the futility of it and withdrew, suffering even more losses.

69

I do believe that one more defeat will spell the end of the war, for surely their people must despair when they see the lists of dead and wounded.

I pray that when it's all over we might meet again and perhaps, my love, we can find a way of being together. By the by, I am being promoted to major due to the death of Major Scott, who perished due to pneumonia.

With greatest devotion,
Randolph

Charlotte replied three days later when the mail arrived along with more wounded men, many from the recent battle.

My dear Randolph,

I am so pleased to hear that you were unscathed during the terrible encounter at Fredericksburg and applaud your promotion. You say that it was due to the death of Major Scott, a sad thing in itself, but I strongly suspect that you would have been promoted regardless.

On another note, Jerome has been dividing his time between my father's plantation (the last overseer having been drafted) and the hospital where he is doing sundry chores. I encouraged him to work here since so many slaves are being requisitioned by the army.

I live at the Charlottesville General Hospital and have not returned to the mansion. Jerome tells me that all father's male slaves have been taken away or fled north, and only a few women are left.

We have received many casualties from the recent fighting, and unfortunately many have died of dysentery, pneumonia, measles, and typhoid. We don't know the names of many, especially those with debilitating head wounds.

Most distressing, we have had numerous deaths due to amputations. There have been days when severed arms and legs are piled up before they're carted away. There are five hundred beds and fifteen doctors, but supplies are running dangerously low.

I wish we had chloroform, but we don't, and the men suffer mightily during amputations. We have also cared for several Union wounded. One who has recovered begged to remain and help doing chores at the hospital. He is terribly fearful of being sent to a prison camp and has been allowed to remain. His name is Charlie. He is about the age of Jerome, and they have become friends. He's really a sweet boy, and I can't imagine that he was a soldier. He thinks I'm his protector and brings me tea all during the day.

I am saddened to burden you with all this but as you know, I have never shied away from reality. I do hope you forgive me for this indiscretion. I long to be in your arms.

With everlasting love,
Charlotte

***

"I am Antonius Stuart," said the judge as he approached an orderly. "Do you know where I might find my daughter, Charlotte?"

The orderly led him to an annex crowded with beds filled with wounded and dying soldiers. A corporal was being carried to a table beside which were saws, bandages, and bottles of alcohol. Three men, a doctor, and Charlotte followed. Terrified, the soldier babbled and pleaded as he was gingerly placed on the table.

"Hold him down when I begin, but, first, I must see where to remove the leg," said the doctor.

"Charlotte, I need to speak with you," said the judge, pushing forward. "It is truly important. I'm just returning from Richmond."

The doctor glanced at the judge and frowned. "Charlotte, who is this man?"

"He is my father and will be leaving immediately."

"But Charlotte—"

"Nothing you have to say to me is more important than saving this man's life. Perhaps you would like to comfort him while we cut off his leg. If not, then go. I have nothing to say to you now or ever. Goodbye."

***

In late June, Charlotte received another letter from Randolph.

> Dear Charlotte
> The entire army of Northern Virginia has for the first time entered Pennsylvania, and it's difficult to keep the men from falling out of line and eating all the apples and everything else they can pick. What beautiful country! Of course, we pay for everything we buy in their stores but they don't appreciate Confederate script. I just don't know why!
>
> We were marching north but have turned around. Apparently there is a Union force of some size that might desire to confront us. We are pleased to satisfy their wish. There are seventy thousand of us, and I am so proud to be part of this army. I do believe we are invincible.
>
> Your Randolph, with love

CHAPTER 10

Gettysburg, Pennsylvania
Early July 1863

Captain Jack Volant's mount, a coal-black mare, nervously pawed the sunbaked earth. Thousands of horses, hot and lathered, were held close-reined as they tossed their heads and took a pace forward or back, breaking the line. Snorts and whinnies merged with the steadying voices of riders and the flapping of unit standards. An order was given and companies moved into place, blue-uniformed riders boot to boot. There was silence in the ranks. Two years earlier, before they were veterans, there might have been bravado or anxious chatter. Not now. These survivors of dozens of engagements knew exactly what they faced and how they would act. It was never routine, but they were certain of what had to be done.

Each man slid the strap of the kepi beneath chin and adjusted the shoulder straps connecting the carbine to the leather loop at the bottom of the McClellan saddle. And they waited in the torpid summer sun.

From a hundred yards behind the cavalry, a line of Union twenty-four pounders belched another volley, and a mile away explosions blew apart the gun carriages of Jeb Stuart's artillery. Plumes of gray smoke from the Federal artillery drifted high in the still air. What remained of the flamboyant general's field pieces were quickly hitched to mules and driven off to the jeering of his cavalry.

On the opposite side of the field a ragged cheer went up from the Federal ranks. Union gunners had, after two years of bloodshed, become highly proficient with their "flying artillery." For Stuart there would be no more Confederate fire on this, the second day of July.

It was one in the afternoon and ninety degrees. Jack Volant, like all other men in the Fifth, Sixth, and Seventh Michigan Volunteer Cavalry, still wore the blue cotton jacket over a white shirt with only the top button undone. Regulations. Both hands were encased in leather gauntlets with the trigger finger cut away for ease of firing. Once white, the gauntlets were stained and frayed, age and wear taking their toll. Sweat rolled down his face and stung his eyes.

The Confederates in their tattered butternut had few such restrictions. The Union blockade had reduced them to men wearing a ragged assortment of clothing. But none of that diminished their pleasure in a good fight.

The army of Northern Virginia had driven the Federals out of the town of Gettysburg and up into Cemetery Ridge; two hills, known as Big and Little Round Top, lay three miles west of the massed cavalry. Jeb Stuart's assignment was to proceed around the hills and attack the Union rear, requiring Federal divisions to leave the line facing Robert E. Lee. But to do that they first had to destroy the Union cavalry defending that route.

In a hook-shape stretching three miles, ninety thousand Union troops and hundreds of artillery pieces awaited Lee's frontal attack. It was presaged by a Confederate bombardment, most of which passed harmlessly over the hills. But that would be an infantry battle. For the cavalry, it was a contest of other men's concern.

Jack removed his kepi with its crossed sabers and drank from his canteen. Although many troopers wore brogans, since they walked their horses as much as they rode, Jack still wore the high black cavalry boots, uncomfortable for walking as they were. In the army since before Bull Run, he had become somber, efficient and, except where it concerned the men under his command, distant and largely silent.

At five foot eleven he stood three inches taller than the average soldier. Lean and hardened, the pleasures of student days having drained away, he saw no joy or gallantry in the war. It was brutal, savage, and unrelenting. The excitement and fervor of "On to Richmond!" had ground down to bitter resolve.

The instant grin, the irreverent jest, the maddening tricks he'd used to his brother's dismay lay like the bleached bones of dead comrades strewn amongst the weeds and brambles of the fields of death. Now his smiles were fleeting and rare, the brittle wariness constant.

"Cap'n Volant," said a grizzled lieutenant on a rangy bay. The beefy man swathed in a luxurious gray beard and drooping broad-brimmed slouch hat was fifteen years Jack's senior. A veteran of the '47 war against Mexico, Brian McNally would have attained the rank of colonel had it not been for a pugnacious temperament which rearranged the face of a senior officer. War, attrition, and his indomitable spirit had returned him to the rank he'd held so many years earlier.

"Cap'n, we have some young 'uns," he said in a distinct South Carolina twang. "We have to keep a close eye on them."

"They'll be veterans after today, if they live. We were all fresh fish once."

The sound of artillery ceased and, except for a horse's whinny, quietude settled upon the massed brigades. Two companies distant, a major's horse reared high in the air, toppling the man to the ground. While a sergeant grabbed the mount's reins, the officer slowly rose to his feet while rubbing a bruised leg. He mounted again, but his metal canteen ruptured, causing its contents to cascade down his trousers.

"Oh, dear Lord," a corporal shouted. "The major's water has broken!"

With immediate concern, several hundred men took up the alarm, all bellowing, "Our commander's water has broken!" followed by "Send for the midwife" and "Is it a girl?"

Crimson-faced, the major wheeled his mount. "It's a boy, damn you! Maintain! I want decorum in the ranks!" Another peel of laughter rippled through the brigade.

"Well, that was entertaining," said the rumpled lieutenant, raising an ancient spyglass he had carried to Chapultepec and Mexico City. He scanned the Confederates a half mile away. "My, my, how purty."

With exacting expertise, the ranks of Confederate horsemen executed a left oblique, swinging the entire mass into a front line. Once that was complete, an order was given and the horses came to a halt.

The lieutenant handed Jack the glass. "Aren't those boys something? Cap'n? They are very, very good."

"I would prefer that they were very dead," replied Jack, half under his breath.

"Well, we will just have to assist them in that endeavor," said Brian. "You know, they learned a thing or two about Union cav at Brandy Station. Yes, sir, until then those Southern boys cut us to shreds on their daddies' fine horses. Our lads only knew a horse from the back of a plow, but at Brandy we gave them boys a real thwacking. Our lads earned their spurs, yessiree, Cap'n."

"Uh-huh."

"And just before that, Jeb Stuart paraded twelve thousand right in front of Bobby Lee. What a parade that must have been with those pretty southern belles all agog, waving their dainty little kerchiefs and blowing kisses. And then, you know what?"

"I'm sure you'll educate me, lieutenant."

"Well, I shall if you insist. Now you remember Colonel Grierson, the music teacher who hates horses. He up and led seventeen hundred Union cav right through the great Commonwealth of Virginny. Burned ties, twisted track, cut telegraph, tore up everything and came back unscathed."

"Is that the end of the saga?"

"No, sir, not at all. Jeb Stuart in his fancy plumed hat wasn't about to be outdone by a music teacher. So, he tried to do the same up north, but his people got all split up, some going one way, some going another. Now here he is with—what? —less than four thousand? Not enough, Cap'n. Not by any measure. I just reckon he's gonna feel Bobby Lee's wrath and that won't be purdy."

"I hope you're right. Now bring the companies to attention. I have a few words for them."

Wilting in the saddles, troopers straightened and nudged their mounts into line. Jack walked his horse to the front and for a long moment scanned the faces of the Seventh. He had learned to trust his men; they had fought and bled and would not shrink or falter. And they knew that their tight-lipped, no-nonsense captain, a scholar and, some said, an aspiring artist, would demand nothing he would not do himself.

"Within the next hour the brigades of Jeb Stuart will be destroyed. You will drive them from the field in utter disgrace." Jack saw a resolve pass through the ranks. "He will not pass. He and his men will suffer humiliation. We must do our duty; we shall have victory on this fateful day."

A welcome breeze filtered through sweat-drenched jackets and lifted red scarfs around men's necks. Hands reached for sabers, raising them slightly from scabbards, confirming that they would slide easily when drawn.

Unfastening the flap of his holster, Jack drew his Remington. "Check your pistols, make sure that there is a percussion cap on the nipple of each cylinder. No cap, no fire. Do it now."

As six-shot revolvers were drawn, he said, "We go in with pistols. Five rounds, close range. Save the sixth for the man coming directly at you. There will be plenty of time to bang sabers."

And there would be, since reloading a pistol while riding was virtually impossible. Jack turned to his irascible lieutenant. "Do you have a few words for them?"

"Yes sir, you know that for sure."

He leaned forward in the saddle and spat a wad of tobacco. "I am a son of the Old South, but I am a Union man to the core. I took an oath as did y'all. You are mostly Michigan lads, and I ask you, what is the mascot of Michigan?"

"Wolverines!" came the shout.

"Wolverines, indeed. Coming back from the Mexican War I chanced to be in Michigan and saw two wolverines tear into a bear. I felt sorry for the bear; in fact I cried." A ripple of laughter followed the lieutenant's words.

"The wolverine is a damned mean animal that doesn't give quarter, and neither will you. Now, the Seventh Mich has a pretty little song. It was sung by my people when they came from the old sod. When we go forward, we sing the Gerry Owens and we fight like Irishmen on this lovely day!"

"McNally," said Jack when the lieutenant wheeled his horse about, "if I go down, you take them in. Press them hard. Give Stuart a drubbing he won't forget."

"Cap'n, sir, you'll be just fine and I'll be with you all the way. And when it's over we'll share that flask you keep so nicely hidden."

"That would be a pleasure. For the Union, McNally, and for the old sod."

His eye caught Custer and his staff riding onto the field. Once again, the Union was about to be tested.

***

There wasn't the slightest breeze at Gettysburg that morning. But the short blast of a bugle across the field galvanized the regiment's attention. Amongst the long lines of butternut and gray, the stars and bars and unit flags unfurled, limp in the airless and torpid heat of the afternoon. Sweating in the dank humidity, horses were kept at the walk in perfect lines as they slowly advanced. Sabers were still in scabbards, pistols secured in holsters. But for an occasional order the only sounds were the soft tread of hoofs.

A hundred yards down the line, Custer spurred his mount and placed himself to the front of his three regiments. He nodded to his bugler, and rapid blasts were followed by the order "Forward at the walk."

Positioned in front of his company, Jack Volant ordered the swallow-shaped flag, red above white with the number seven stitched onto it, to move up to the national standard by his side. The command began the irreversible march. Minutes later came the shout "At the gallop," followed seconds later by "Draw pistols!"

They were moving now, horses' hoofs thudding on the hardened ground, flags standing out as hearts pounded, a grimness setting in as men prepared themselves for killing and death.

"Close rein, mind your position, hold your lines!" Jack shouted, lest the mounts, energized and spurred on, bolt forward, leaving gaps in the line. Men were no longer boot to boot, but only an arm's distance separated them as dust rose, making the rear ranks nearly invisible.

Commanding officers on opposing sides drew sabers that flashed in the sun. Shouts rang over the field as thousands of horses charged toward each other at a dead run.

The once orderly lines began to fray as horses dashed past one another. The distance between the barely controlled armies closed while Union batteries began a final barrage into Confederate ranks. Men were blasted off their mounts, and horses toppled over one another, but the rebel lines regrouped and the lines bolted forward.

"Charge! Charge! Charge!" came the commands as spurs dug into animals' flanks. Horses, wild-eyed, raged forward in a maddened and terrifying stampede. The ground became a blur as lines dissolved. With faces tight, screams and imprecations from thousands of desperate men filled the air as shots whistled around them.

A delirious, savage, mindless fury that propelled the need to engage, to close, was coupled with the near certainty of dismemberment and death.

Both sides, charging at twenty-five miles per hour, obliterated the distance between them. Ranks broke, meshed, and broke again. The collision of first and second ranks saw men somersault into the air only to be trampled by those behind. For the briefest of seconds everything seemed to stop. Then came a fusillade of shots and the sound of clashing sabers mingled with a cacophony of carbine and pistol shots. There were more screams, shouts, and orders as total mayhem ensued.

Brigades, companies, and squad formations dissolved into seven thousand individual contests, each a matter of life and death. Frustration and terror reigned as horses slammed into one another and maimed, unhorsed men were dragged by terrified mounts, their saddles flapping as they tried vainly to escape the carnage.

A rebel riding a monstrous horse loomed before Jack, his bearded face full and inflamed. The man, a Confederate sergeant, leveled and fired a shotgun just as Jack's pistol discharged twice, one shot striking the man in the left elbow, the other the horse's chest. Startled by the screaming mount, Jack's own horse reared and pawed the air, and the shotgun blast ripped open its belly. Steel pellets riddled Jack's leg as he toppled to the ground.

The Confederate was also unhorsed, and his bucking mount fell heavily over his lower body.

Jack tried desperately to dismount, but to no avail. Jack's bay swung its head and, with bulging eyes, collapsed, pinning him.

The men and their horses lay in a tangle of legs, saddles, and weaponry. The rebel's mount still thrashed about as it tried to rise. Raising himself on an elbow, Jack aimed and fired. His bullet pierced the animal's skull. Its head dropped, and all its movement ceased. Jack slumped back on the bloodstained ground. His bent saber, attached by a strap, lay on his left while his Sharp's carbine, still in its socket, bound him to his saddle. It was impossible to move. Twelve hundred pounds of his dead mount sprawled over his legs.

Something felt wrong. A warm stickiness oozed into his boot. The thought came to him that he would bleed to death, and he wondered how long that might take. He tried to pull his foot out of the boot but couldn't reach it, and he resigned himself to wait for the end.

He became conscious of a man lying an arm's distance from him. The Confederate issued a long moan, a fatalistic sigh, and then a deep, painful utterance. Jack ignored it, his eyes darting to the left and right as battle raged about him.

Rapid and incessant pistol shots were overwhelmed by the louder crack of carbines interspersed with the metal clank of sabers. More shouts, screams, and commands were punctuated by bugle calls. Sounds of struggle came in waves, some within mere feet of him.

A sudden blast toppled a man from his horse. The soldier's body drooped, lifeless, over Jack's dead mount, increasing the weight upon him. Seconds later a Union soldier was slashed by a saber, his hand flying past Jack's face. A fallen staff with the swallow flag of the Fifth Regiment was lifted from the ground, its steel tip thrust into a Confederate's chest. The dying man grasped it with both hands as he slid off the saddle, the standard having been pulled from his torso.

Another bugle call and an undulating wave of blue charged past. Shouts rose from it, calls to rally, to reform ranks, to push on. All assaulted Jack's ears as he glanced upward at the bellies of horses, their legs pounding the earth as riders furiously spurred them on.

Gradually the sounds became distant, the shots muffled as riderless horses ran past him. Then, but for the buzzing of insects, the world became eerily silent.

For some reason the flow of blood ceased. Perhaps the swelling had been constricted by his boot. Again, Jack tried to wiggle his foot, to free it from the weight pressing upon it, but it was useless. He lay motionless as the day's heat settled heavily upon him.

He swatted away flies and closed his eyes. His war was over, but the thought gave him no pleasure.

"Water, Billie, do you have any water? I fear my canteen's broken," said the other man hoarsely, the sound coming through blistered lips.

Jack turned his head and stared into tremulous eyes, those of a man likely hours from death.

"Canteen's on the saddle," said Jack.

"Oh," said the Confederate, resigned to his fate.

Rising on an elbow again, Jack leaned forward and wiggled the canteen until it fell from the saddle. Pulling out the cork, he took a long swig, then held it out.

"Don't drink too much, it will have to last. There may be no corpsmen all day, if at all."

The man drank and handed it back. "Wooden ones, we only have wooden ones. They hold more water but bust open or leak."

Jack didn't reply.

"Can't feel much below my elbow," the man said wistfully. "Kind of numb, you know. Bleeding still."

Jack lifted his head and untied the red cloth around his neck. He handed it to the man. "Tourniquet. Tie it around your arm above the elbow. You can do it with one hand and pull it tight."

"You think they'll cut off my arm? That's what they do. The bone just splinters, can't put it back together. Think they'll cut it off?" he repeated.

"I suspect they will."

"You know, Stonewall Jackson had his arm cut off after Chancellorsville. Died from infection a week later. Lee said that Jackson lost his left arm and he lost his right."

"So I heard."

"But the doctor cut off the whole arm, not just from the elbow down."

Jack didn't reply. He had no desire to talk. If gangrene set in, the man was as good as dead. Why talk to a dead man?

Twenty minutes passed in silence.

"What's your name?" the man asked without rancor as he watched a circling flock of crows.

"Jack. Jack Volant. Lieutenant," Jack said, wishing the rebel would simply be quiet.

"French name. My grandmother was French. Taught me the language as a child. I was in Paris before the war. You?"

Got to answer, thought Jack. A civil thing in an uncivilized time. "A student. An artist. Look, reb, I really don't feel like being social, no offense. It's not like we're having mint juleps on the veranda of your daddy's plantation."

The man let out a ragged laugh. "My daddy never had a plantation. No slaves, either. But he did have a black mistress, a pretty one too."

They lapsed into silence again, and finally Jack said, "Okay, since we're so neighborly here, what's your name?"

"Gabriel Jean-Louis Shelby the Third," he said. "Damn, I don't want to lose my arm. You could've just shot the horse."

"It crossed my mind. I also could have put a bullet through your head, you know. It might have saved you a lot of pain. For whatever reason I chose to only wound you since I knew you were going down. You should thank me, Gabriel Jean-Louis Shelby the Third."

"I guess." The man looked around at the battlefield, empty but for dead men, dead horses, and some distant wounded. "So, who won this? I don't see any of my men."

"Stuart's shredded. Your boys lost," said Jack sardonically. "Actually, you lost the day Fort Sumpter was fired upon. The North is an industrial giant. Guts and glory are no match for three million men and fifty thousand guns."

"I suspected that."

"Well, it's true. Thousands of immigrants get off the boat and don Union blue every day."

"So, this has all been for naught."

"Afraid so."

"But there's still a lot of fight in the Confederacy."

"I don't doubt that, and a lot of boys are going to die because of it."

Shelby sighed. "It hurts now. I think the bullet went clear through."

"Not much to stop it in the elbow."

"How's your leg?"

"Hurts."

"Do you speak French?"

"Yes, why?"

"Just curious. I'm going back to Paris if I live. You should go too if you still want to be an artist. That's where you find the best of them. Maybe we might even see each other there. Friendly-like."

"You're assuming one hell of a lot, considering that you shot me."

"And you shot me."

"*C'est la guerre.*"

"Yeah, c'est la guerre."

CHAPTER 11

Mid-July 1863

"Annabelle! Annabelle!" Charlotte hurried through the ward, holding a letter, and hugged her friend. "This just came from Randolph. It's two weeks old but such wonderful news."

"We won? Is the war over?"

"Oh, how I wish it was. No, Randolph has a wonderful idea. He says that as soon as the war *is* over, he'll resign his commission and marry me. And then we will travel to California and start a new life there. I am just thrilled!"

"That's wonderful. I'm happy, but I will miss you so."

"Nonsense, you'll come with us. I insist."

"Really?"

"Absolutely. Maybe we'll all go to San Francisco. It's supposed to be a great city now."

Annabelle frowned. "But California is a Union state."

"I've heard that there are thousands of Southerners in California. And the war shall be over anyway. The whole question of slavery will be of no consequence, never to be mentioned by me or Randolph again."

More excited than in years, she fairly skipped down the ward. Charlie, carrying her a cup of tea, said, "You look so happy. It must be good news."

"It is, it is. Thank you for the tea. You are a darling. Now go help Jerome ready those beds, there may be more wounded coming in."

***

Nine wagons from Gettysburg lumbered toward the Charlottesville General Hospital where nearly recovered soldiers were moved outdoors to make room for the seriously wounded who flooded into the wards. Upon hearing of their arrival, dozens of volunteers descended upon the facility to assist nurses and doctors in the disaster that had befallen the army. Charlotte, her nurse's apron smeared with blood, helped carry men to waiting beds and quickly assembled cots, many placed so close together that there were only inches between them.

Those with severe head injuries were cordoned off in a field beside the buildings. Nothing, it was determined, could be done for them except the bandaging of wounds. Late in the afternoon as wagons were unloaded with even more wounded, Charlotte prayed that Randolph would not be in one of them. Word spread that the Nineteenth Virginia had lost 60 percent of its men but retreated in good order as Union troops on the high ground shouted "Fredericksburg! Fredericksburg!"—a reference to the horrific Union defeat the year before.

Exhausted by the day's effort, she leaned against the wheel of a wagon and stared into the distance. Two orderlies emerged from the building and approached the wagon.

"There's a bed for the captain," one said. "We can bring him in now."

Charlotte rose to her feet and stared into the wagon. "Randolph!"

The orderlies carried him inside and laid him on the bed. Blood oozed from one leg and the ankle of the other as he lay half conscious. Oblivious to others around her, she pulled off his brogans and pants and peered at the wound. From the thigh down, one leg was shattered, bone protruding with skin hanging in shreds. The ankle was broken in two places, and three toes were missing.

"Oh, Randolph," she cried. She took his hand and kissed it as he turned his head toward her.

"Dear Charlotte, you see, I came back to you, but I fear that I will not be long for this world."

Some minutes later a doctor stood beside the bed, examined the wounds, and gently laid a hand on Randolph's forehead. "Rest easy," he said. Randolph issued a feeble smile.

"My men, how are they? Are any here?"

"Some are, Major. They're being attended to. Miss Charlotte will return in just a few minutes."

The doctor motioned her to follow. They walked to his office at the far end of the ward. "Please sit," he said, nodding toward a chair. He pulled his own from behind his desk and reached for her hand.

"Dear lady," he said in a very quiet voice, "you have, during this last year, become one of the finest nurses I have ever beheld. The Confederacy is honored to have you. Indeed, though I wouldn't say it in front of my colleagues, your understanding of medicine and hygiene is far more advanced than that of many of our young doctors. And you have seen countless wounds, helped with amputations, and comforted the sick and dying. You know what is a fatal wound and what is not, so I won't deceive you with false hope."

Charlotte put her hands to her face. Her entire body shook with despair. "And he has a fever, doesn't he?" she finally said, wiping her tears.

"I'm afraid so. It rained terribly on July fourth, and we don't know how long he lay in the field before being put into the wagon. The rough ride didn't help, and the wounds are from exploding cannon balls, not bullets."

"Amputation?" she said wistfully.

"We can do that, but, as you know, it will cause great pain, and there might be tetanus or gangrene already in his system. And the fever—well, I fear it's pneumonia. There's little more we can do for him. What I do suggest, dear nurse, is that you comfort him the best you can." The doctor sighed. "I am so sorry, it's a grievous war and you have seen so much suffering. More than any young lady should ever see. It is time for you to go home, Charlotte. It really is."

Charlotte nodded, not trusting herself to say anything. Returning to Randolph, she leaned over and kissed him.

He smiled wanly, grasped her hand, and whispered, "You'll meet a good man someday, my darling. But I'll always watch over you. I do love you so."

She shook her head. "I want no other man. Never, never, dear Randolph. I only want you."

He lingered for three hours, then sighed once before slipping away. Charlotte remained beside him as doctors and nurses stepped around her. Extreme sadness began to give way to rage against the people who'd caused her grief. She cried inconsolably as Charlie entered the ward with a cup of tea, wearing his blue Union kepi, saying words of consolation.

She stared at him as he approached. Suddenly she bolted up. "Get away from me. I hate you. I hate all you damn Yankees! I never want to see your kind again!"

"But, nurse Charlotte, I am your friend, please—"

"You are no friend of mine. Get out of my sight!"

Jerome put his hand on his friend's shoulder. "You'd best go. There's nothing more to be said."

***

It was Senator Mason who suggested that Randolph be buried on the judge's plantation, to which Charlotte had returned. Jerome built a fine coffin and dug a gravesite near the vegetable garden. Charlotte contemplated carving Randolph a stone, but didn't have the energy. For days she sat in a rocking chair on the veranda with Jerome.

The horrors of war continued, with battles edging ever closer to Albemarle County. A Union cavalry raid carried out by Generals Custer and Sheridan on the Lynchburg railroad line was accompanied by the burning of several plantations, along with the freeing of hundreds of slaves.

On occasion Charlotte visited the hospital to train new nurses, but she rarely stayed long. Once a nurse asked her to take a package to the post office, and while she was there the postmaster, whom she'd known for years, said, "Miss Charlotte, a letter for you."

Back on the veranda she looked at the bold print and smiled.

"Who's it from?" asked Jerome, now over six feet tall and powerfully built.

"From cousin Gabriel." She extracted two sheets from the envelope and read aloud.

Dear Charlotte,

I'm sorry for not having written earlier, but I was in a Union hospital in Maryland until recently. I suffered a serious wound at Gettysburg and was captured by Union forces. Unfortunately, my left arm had to be amputated below the elbow. I have very nearly recovered and now, as a noncombatant, will be allowed to sail for France to reenter my previous occupation.

I have applied and been accepted as a journalist for <u>The Messenger</u>, an English-language newspaper printed by a bookstore/café called Galignani's in Paris.

I learned that the Nineteenth Virginia was involved with Pickett's division in the assault upon the Round Tops at Gettysburg and suffered numerous casualties. I presume that Randolph was in that attack and I do hope that he is unscathed.

"Cousin Shelby doesn't know?" said Jerome.

"I'm afraid I didn't write. I just could not." She turned back to the letter.

Strangely enough, I have made a very good friend of a Yankee lieutenant who was in the cavalry battle at Gettysburg. We managed to shoot each other in that action but have attempted to put that behind us. He is a rather dour fellow and is having a very difficult time, especially with the bottle.

I do hope someday to see you in the City of Light. Say hello for me to that mischievous young man, Jerome.

With my very best wishes,

Your cousin Gabriel

"I can't imagine why he thinks I'm mischievous."

"I can," retorted Charlotte, almost smiling. Quickly she became serious again.

"I think you should carry this. It was Randolph's." Charlotte handed him a pistol. "An officer at the hospital gave it to me, but I have no desire to use it. I don't think Randolph would mind you having it since it's for our protection."

Jerome examined the Colt pistol. "Are you sure? He was a soldier and I am still a—"

"Hush. It doesn't matter. But maybe you should practice with it. Things are quite unsettled now."

***

There was hardly a word exchanged between Charlotte and the judge for over three months. On occasion Antonius would slowly walk through the weed-choked tobacco fields where no crop had been grown for two years. But usually he would seal himself in his study, a glass of whiskey in hand, and stare at the shelves of law books he no longer consulted.

From time to time, he spied Jerome and Charlotte beside the oak tree or tending the garden. He knew it would be useless to try to talk to her; she studiously ignored him. Once each week he drove his buggy into town to speak with Senator Mason, who'd resigned his position after the death of his son.

He always avoided the gaggle of people at the post office peering at the lists of dead, wounded, and missing, always hoping that a son, father, or boyfriend's name would not appear. Purchasing a newspaper, the judge instead returned to the mansion and read of the latest fighting.

The army had been knit back together after Gettysburg and was still a substantial force, but had never had a chance to relax since Grant had taken command of the Union army. He was dogged and seemingly had an inexhaustible supply of men. And after the Emancipation Proclamation both England and France turned against the Confederacy. To

92

make matters worse, Vicksburg had fallen, cutting the South in two. And now there was a dwindling supply of recruits and ever-increasing desertions.

The judge folded the paper, sipped his whiskey, and wondered if his world could return to what it had been, even if the South won the war.

Often, having drunk more than he would have previously done, he climbed the stairs to his bedroom and fell into a fitful sleep. Sometimes he thought he heard the voice of Cornelia or Charlotte. But with drink he was never really sure.

***

Of the sixteen hundred men who joined the Nineteenth Virginia, only thirty were left by March 1865. General Lee's army, relentlessly attacked by Grant's divisions, numbered less than thirty thousand.

From time to time Charlotte peered out her window and saw bands of men in tattered uniforms plodding beside the plantation. A few carried weapons, but most had left them on one battlefield or another, the once indomitable cause having been nearly lost.

Every once in a while, men asked for water. They went to the pump in the yard as directed, expressed their thanks, and moved on. But near dusk on the first of April, three armed men entered the property, all wearing bits and pieces of Confederate gray.

From the second story window Charlotte peered down and saw one man put a match to the wick of a lantern. Two moved slowly toward the veranda while the other walked stealthily to the side of the house, having slung a double-barreled shotgun over his shoulder. The one with the lantern approached the judge with kindly words as Antonius rose to greet him.

"How can I help you?" he asked as the man's comrade glanced up to the window.

"Maybe you might have some fixin's to spare. All we have is some hardtack, wormy and all. Have to smash the maggots before eatin', you know. Perhaps that lady up there can scrape somethin' together. And maybe y'all let us in, Grandpa. We won't stay long."

"Wait here. I'll ask my daughter if we have anything."

"Where is everyone? I see no niggers about."

"Not much reason for them to stay. Some followed the Yankees and some just lit out on their own. Headed north some months ago."

"That so?" Again the man glanced toward the window.

Judge Stuart turned and was moving toward the door when the man drew his pistol and fired.

Charlotte, still watching, screamed as the judge toppled forward.

"Still alive," one of them said.

"He's dyin', and I want him to die slow and painful," the other man said.

He opened the front door and they entered the house. The one outside with the shotgun turned toward the house but failed to see Jerome emerge from behind a shack. Drawing his Colt, Jerome pulled the hammer to full cock and fired. The man spun about, hands to his blood-soaked shirt, and collapsed, his shotgun tumbling beside him. Jerome approached and peering down at the soldier, fired again, and, after slinging the shotgun over his shoulder, he dragged the man around a bush and out of sight.

The man with the lantern walked back onto the porch. "Thomas, you there? Found you a nigger woman, maybe? We've got something nice in here. White, real purty-like. Come on, now."

That said, he leisurely reentered, a saber clanking by his side. Jerome stopped for a moment beside his father, then peered through the window and silently entered the parlor. He heard an upstairs door slam as the man with the lantern ascended the stairs. Silently Jerome followed.

"Little lady, come on down now. No sense hiding under the bed. All we want is some fixin's and maybe a bit of that silver you hid from the Yankees. We won't hurt you, promise." He laughed as the glow from the lantern illuminated the darkened stairs.

"Don't shoot—might hit her. Just kick the door in," said the other, sliding his pistol back into its holster.

He pushed open the door and, seeing Charlotte, gave a ragged smile. Suddenly she sprang aside as Jerome raised the shotgun and pulled the trigger. The eruption of flame and lead ripped into the Confederate's back. He screamed and fell. Jerome raced downstairs to confront the other man, who reached too late for his holstered pistol. Another blast issued from the shotgun and the man crumpled, dropping the lantern. Its glass panels shattered, oil spilling and igniting wallpaper, carpet, and wood. Flames shot to the ceiling as Jerome raced upstairs. Thick smoke and embers swirled about him.

"Charlotte, it's me. They're dead and everything's on fire!"

Flames devoured the stairs and raged along dry timbers. Choking on the smoke, Jerome and Charlotte raced through the parlor and reached the yard as the house went up like fireworks on Jeff Davis's inauguration day. Within twenty minutes the house was little more than ashes.

They carried the judge to the edge of the tobacco field, where Charlotte placed her shawl beneath his head. She knew the wound was fatal, and her animosity faded away.

She held his hand as she had held so those of so many others and was surprised to feel a tear run down her cheek.

Breathing heavily, Antonius said, "Charlotte, dear, I wish it had been different, I truly do. I wanted to apologize. I tried to tell you at the hospital but—"

"I was too stubborn, a terrible fault of mine. Despite everything, I do love you, Father. Always have."

Antonius coughed up blood. "It will be over with me soon. Please bury me beside Cornelia. I hope she doesn't mind. She and I had good times many years ago. I'd like to see her again."

"I have no doubt that you will, and I think she'd like to see you, too."

He coughed again, turning his head from side to side. "Where is Jerome? Where is my son?"

"Father," said Jerome, kneeling before him.

"I have always admired you. If the world was different, I would have tried to be a real father to you. Forgive me. I should have freed you years ago. But now I do."

Jerome peered into the dying man's eyes. "You do? You really do?"

"There's a metal box in my study with the papers; might've survived the fire. Find it, you'll see. I wrote it some time ago."

He closed his eyes, opened them again. "Charlotte, this old place, our world, is over. You and Jerome find a new one far, far away."

They stayed with him until he died an hour later. By lantern's light, they dug the grave and buried him beside Cornelia.

Charlotte and Jerome spent the night huddled together in a slave shack. At dawn, they searched through the still-smoldering ruins of the Judge's study, eventually finding the box amid charred shelves. It was the same box she'd seen when searching for a law book for Jerome before the war. With hammer and chisel she broke the lock and, to her astonishment, found three bags of twenty-dollar gold coins with the markings of the US mint. Beneath the bags was an envelope containing a signed letter of manumission.

"Do you think it would have made any real difference? I mean him giving me my freedom." said Jerome after she handed the letter to him.

"He might have treated you differently but would have had to acknowledge that you are his son. That would've been difficult for him. Cornelia insisted that he do it, and he finally did. It would've made her happy if it had happened before she died."

"So now I have been freed by my father and Mr. Lincoln. But Charlotte, in spirit I have always been free."

They stood there quietly for a time.

"What about the deserters?" Jerome said.

"Leave them to the buzzards. They have to eat too."

They were sitting together on a bench beside the tobacco field, watching eddies of smoke rise from the house, when a wagon turned onto the property. A stooped man in a frock coat and top hat brought the horse to a halt beside them and surveyed the smoking ruins. Turning to Charlotte he said, "I am with the Society of Friends and have been charged with delivering a box of remains. It is meant for a Jerome, in care of you. Postage has been paid by the congregation in Canada."

"Remains?" said Jerome.

"That is correct. Might you be Jerome?"

"I am."

The Quaker lifted a small box from the wagon. "Our congregation in Richmond received it two days ago." Handing the box to Jerome he repeated, "Shipped all the way from Canada. It's said that she was greatly loved but wished to come back here, to where her man is buried. Seeing the smoke, I was afraid that y'all had gone. I'm glad that you're still here."

Charlotte offered the Quaker a twenty-dollar coin, but he refused to take it. Tipping his hat, he solemnly climbed onto the wagon seat, flicked the reins, and drove away.

"Are you going to wait until midnight?" asked Charlotte.

"No, it won't be the same. There's only us, no women to sing or dance in the old way. My mother will understand. Ben'll understand, too. Africa is still here."

Jerome removed the urn from the box and carried it to the slave cemetery. He dug a hole and placed his mother's remains beside Ben's coffin and, as Charlotte watched, he knelt and gently covered it. He remained there for some minutes.

"They're all gone now," Jerome said. "We are the only ones left."

"I suppose so. No one will disturb them anymore. I hope they're pleased to be together again."

Early the next day Jerome said, "What are we going to do now?"

"As Father said, we have no reason to stay here, and I have no interest in rebuilding the house. I no longer want to live in this land. We should follow his advice and go far away."

"Up North?"

"I'll never go there."

"Where, then? I'm not going to stay here."

"Paris," Charlotte declared. "You'll come with me, won't you, Jerome? We'll take ship from Norfolk, now that we have money."

"It's a long walk," Jerome said, a lazy grin spreading across his face.

"We take the carriage, silly, and pretend we own the world."

"I feel like we do, sister. I really do. I'll hitch up the wagon and we'll start life all over again."

CHAPTER 12

New York Harbor
Summer 1866

"So, you've landed a job there," said Jack Volant as he and Shelby sat in a pub two blocks from the dock.

"Through some contacts, artist friends I made before the war. I submitted stories I wrote for newspapers in Richmond and got hired."

"What's it like, this Galignani's?"

"It's a reading room, café, and publisher all in one. It's also the only American bookstore in the city. There's ten thousand Americans in Paris now, so it's quite popular; many of them go there to meet other Americans." Gabriel peered into a second glass of whiskey, then downed it. "It pays well enough, and it'll be a good change. I won't go back home—Richmond and the rest of the South is still occupied country. Won't recover for years. Yankees everywhere, no particular offense, you see."

"Sure," said Jack, a glint in his eye as he stirred a cup of coffee.

"Well, I'm tired of writing about the 'lost cause' and how the damnyankees"—he always pronounced that as if it were one word—"and uncouth carpetbaggers have deflowered our fairer sex and polluted the land. Which of course they have."

"I own a very nice carpetbag, and 'damn Yankees' is two words, Shelby."

Gabriel Jean-Louis Shelby the third grinned. "Well, it should be one. Everybody down South knows that. Anyway, Paris is alive, vibrant, the place to be. People know how to live in the City of Light. And besides, most Americans aren't fluent in French, and they want to know what's going on in Louis Napoleon's Second Empire. I'll be given carte blanche to write for a hungry readership about art, politics, the economy, everything. And all the scandals."

"The scandals should be very interesting."

"They always have been. It's the syrup of intrigue and delight, especially when it involves some lofty aristocrat of impeccable credentials. The more important they are, the more delectable the story. We really have nothing here to compare with the scandals in Paris. No titled aristocracy. No emperors, princes, or kings reduced to utter ruin by a demimonde like La Païva."

"I've never heard of her," said Jack.

"I subscribe to *Le Monde* and try to keep up with Paris news since I'm going to be working there. I learned about her and a number of the other top courtesans who ply their trade in the city. Those that don't know about them know nothing about Paris."

"You seem well versed in all this," said Jack with a slip of a smile, "so you can educate me even though I don't see myself going to Paris or consorting with those women. What's a demimonde?"

"The highest-paid and most sought-after courtesan. These are women, often beautiful and always seductive, who frequent the finest salons, entice the richest and most important men, and are paid in diamonds, racehorses, and fine houses." Shelby sat back in his chair. "Sometimes they even have enough influence to change the direction of national policy. One, an Italian living in Paris named Castiglione, seduced Napoleon III. She's the one who convinced him that Italy should be independent of Austria and induced him to declare war."

Jack considered this. The French had beaten the Austrians in 1859, and Italy was now independent. That represented a great deal of influence indeed.

"It's said that her beauty stopped Strauss in the middle of a concert," Gabriel continued.

"And you're going to write about these people, a sort of gossip column?"

"Amongst other things. Why not? We writers and artists have very active, indeed lusty imaginations. That's what makes us unique." Shelby stroked his beard. "From what I understand, Paris is a world unto itself. Life there is tolerant of human frailties that would be roundly condemned in America. They have a different take on things, Jack."

"So they tolerate human frailties but still want to hear all about them."

"Oh, yes. There are two or three other demimondes that have tongues wagging. One is named Cora Pearl, née Emma Crouch, originally from London. She started out penniless, hated men, married anyway, moved to Paris, and sent her husband back to England. Then she roped in an Italian duke who showered her with one million francs, jewels, servants, and even her own chef. It's said that he bought her a racehorse, and that she rides about Paris, flaunting her beauty. She has her own chateau with a bronze bathtub and supposedly gives gala dinner parties. It's reported that once she asked her chef to bring her in on a platter. She was quite nude."

"That must have been quite interesting," said Jack.

"Apparently so. She appeared at a ball dressed as Eve some time later."

"I didn't know that Eve was dressed."

"There's fig leaves in the painting."

"Who else?"

"I see that you have a sudden interest in Paris fashions. Well, there is another demimonde, rather notorious, a Jewess from Moscow named La Païva, who is the rage."

"The one you mentioned before."

"The very one. Her real name is Esther Pauline Lachmann, and, like Pearl, she went from being a penniless woman of the evening to conquering Paris. She married a Portuguese marquis for one night, got his fortune and title, then sent him packing. He committed suicide the next year. She entertained one man for the length of time it took to burn ten thousand francs in her boudoir of onyx and gold. And then she seduced Emperor Napoleon III and Émile Zola, the greatest French writer of them all. Paris, Jack, is about excess—scandal, art, and lust."

"Particularly the latter?"

"Perhaps, but it's lust for life and all that that entails. And perhaps lust for itself."

"That's a lot of lusting. Do they do anything else?"

"Maybe in between. There's a mysterious woman whose doings I would investigate, a demimonde named Yvette Maillard."

"Is she also notorious?"

"It seems so. There have been several murders in Paris, some political. She may be involved, but it's a bit murky. I do know that she is the favorite of a Monsieur Étienne Daudet, one of France's most popular artists. As an investigative journalist, I want to find out."

"I'm sure you will. I guess Europe has a rather different set of ethics, or perhaps just more money lying around," said Jack.

"We certainly don't have as much money or opulence, but our nation had quite a time during the war."

"So I heard," said Jack. "I guess I missed it, being continuously in the field."

Shelby grinned. "Well, before Gettysburg, I knew a few soiled doves—'public women' as we called them. There were four hundred and fifty brothels in Washington, DC, alone, right on Constitution Avenue. It was called Hooker's Division, named after the general. There were hundreds more in New York and seventy-five in Alexandria. Nashville had a total of fifteen hundred prostitutes, all available to the boys fighting gloriously for the Confederacy. So perhaps we should go easy on Paris."

"Perhaps. But it's of no consequence to me. If I ever do go there, I won't be interested in some courtesan. I'll be there to paint."

"So you say." Shelby leaned his left elbow on the table, the bottom half of the coat sleeve pinned to his shoulder, and ordered another drink. "Do you still have pain in the leg?"

"Some. What about you? Does the arm still hurt?"

"Every once in a while, especially on cold days. Funny, I try to reach for something and forget that half of it's missing. Other times I can almost feel a tingle in my hand, even though it's been gone for years."

He stared at some point past Jack's shoulder for a moment. "I never really got a chance to thank you after Gettysburg."

"For shooting you?"

"Hell, no. That was totally unnecessary. For visiting me after the surgery. Damn fine sentiment considering that you, a damnyankee, were barely able to walk, even with that crutch."

"That's two—"

Shelby raised his other hand. "I know, I know. You have a real fixation about that, Jack."

"Actually, I was there when they took off your arm. It wasn't very pretty, but I thought that since we were such bosom buddies, I should say sweet and consoling things after the sawing was done."

"I don't remember that. They put some horrible stuff over my face to knock me out, though you kind of wake up when that saw slices into bone. But I thank you for the sentiments. You still use that crutch?"

"Not much anymore. I've been walking about, exercising. At least since I got off the bottle," Jack said, raising the cup of coffee.

"I didn't hear from you for a long time. I wrote but got nothing back. Finally, a girl you met found one of my letters and wrote for you."

"Clementine. She's a good woman. I'm sorry about not writing. Something happened after Gettysburg. I started getting nightmares, seeing the faces of dead friends. And the faces of men I shot. I went downhill, into an abyss. I had no desire to do anything, just sit and drink and stare into the distance. Scotch became my best friend, helped me forget. One day, in '65, I got so drunk that my pop took me to the army doctors. When I finally woke, I begged for the bottle and caused a ruckus. They chained me to the bed so I wouldn't hurt anybody. They said I raved at night and cursed during the day. And then a nurse came."

"Clementine?"

"Yes. I eventually let her hold my hand. She just sat there every day. Didn't really say much, but I sure couldn't curse or scream or do anything violent with her pretty eyes gazing at me. I never cried before, but I cried then. And I never drank hard liquor again."

"And you love her?"

"Most assuredly. I've been courting her but haven't proposed yet. I told her that I have to have a decent income, and that may take a few more years."

"You can work for your daddy. He has a profitable company. Paper makes money."

"The only paper I'm interested in is drawing paper, not the mummies my brother sent to the factory."

"Will your lady wait that long?"

"I hope so. She says she loves me, but she comes from a very traditional household. Her pop makes all the family decisions."

"So, you have to satisfy him," said Shelby.

"That's it. He likes the fact that I fought in the war; one of his sons did and was killed at Antietam. He asked me about my financial prospects."

"And you said?"

"I didn't. Well, not really. I mentioned a few options but said that I really like to paint and draw. He stayed quiet after that. But I've told Clementine that I won't marry her until I can afford to do so. I never want to have a wife living in poverty."

"Not much money in art, Jack. Not unless you get the right credentials, and you can't easily get them here."

"Where then?"

Shelby shrugged. "Some American artists of the Hudson River school sold well, but that was twenty, thirty years ago. A fellow named Catlin has made a name for himself with Indian portraits—even took the paintings and live Indians to Paris. They performed for Louis Napoleon. It's said that he was very impressed and gave them all medals. But I don't imagine that you'll be going out to Sioux and Crow country to paint. With the hostilities in the Dakotas, the Sioux would consider your scalp more valuable than your art."

Jack grinned. "I've been taking art classes at the university and in private studios. We mostly draw from plaster casts. It's not very inspiring, but I want to be an artist. I want to paint more than anything."

"I know of several artists in Paris. One is a fellow named Édouard Manet. He's even been accepted at the Salon, the big event held every year where they have the official exhibition. If you don't make it there you don't make it in Paris. But maybe your brother knows Manet, too." Shelby downed his whiskey. "Speaking of your brother, you said he's changed his name?"

"He calls himself Marcel now. You'll most likely run into him," said Jack, watching a half dozen sailors enter the bar.

"And he's an entertainer of sorts in a fancy salon."

"He wrote that Paris salons are obsessed with 'mummy mania.' I think it's quite bizarre, all that mystical nonsense, but he's performing for the elites who have little else to occupy their minds."

"I would like to meet him."

"He'll enthrall you with all kinds of tales. A few may even be true."

"Why'd he wind up so far from home?"

"To escape being shot."

"By you?"

"No. By the husband of the woman he seduced."

"Oh," said Shelby. "That's an even better story."

CHAPTER 13

Paris

Spring 1866

Elated and hardly believing her good fortune, Charlotte watched as Eugénie delicately caressed the black marble bust of a Negress, her hands held together in supplication with a chain binding her wrists.

"It's exquisite and pulls at one's heart," said the empress as they stood in a parlor of the Versailles Palace. "I have been a collector for years, especially since I married Louis. And I like unique pieces like those of Charles Cordier."

Charlotte looked to where Eugénie pointed and saw a polychromed bust in dark silver and bronze.

"It's entitled *Negro of the Sudan.* I think the name of yours, *Hope, Deliverance, and Prayer*, is quite fitting, since the woman is in bondage. I am a very religious woman and pray every day and night. In fact, when my husband first met me, he asked, 'What is the road to your heart?' and I said, 'Through the chapel, sire.'"

Charlotte nodded, seeing a determined woman who was said to be headstrong, well educated, and, in her younger years, an excellent rider and athlete.

"As an American of no social standing, I'm amazed to have been invited here," said Charlotte.

"Nonsense. Society thought me too low in status to marry Louis, and I have long supported women's causes. I even demanded that the Ministry of National Education award a baccalaureate to a female graduate. The first in France. And I do advise my husband on matters political."

"But you didn't know who I was," replied Charlotte.

"It was because of that clever Monsieur Benoir! I'll tell you what happened, but it's such a beautiful day, let's wander into the garden."

Sunlight illuminated Eugénie's red hair partially covered by a chapeau that she had designed, the rage of Paris. The brim, swooping upward, sported an ostrich plume that waved in the breeze.

"So, our dear friend came to me with your beautiful piece with the inscribed name, 'C. Stuart.' Of course, I thought it had been carved by a man, since there is hardly a woman sculptor in Paris. He was very circumspect about you. And *voilà!* You appear. How wonderfully surprised I am."

"He can be rather devious, Majesty. I worked for him in Maryland, and I gave him my Paris address. He came, saw the piece, and said, 'I must show it to someone,' but he didn't tell me who. Certainly, I was curious. And then I received one letter saying that there was another inside, which should only be opened by a footman at the Versailles. So, I waited outside, quite perplexed, until I was escorted in and there you were!"

"Well, I think you're a fine artist and have a great future. I do have connections, you know."

She laughed and pointed toward a manicured shrub. "This is where I desire another of your works, perhaps a woman holding a child. Yes, a Negress to complement the one I have purchased. And, of course, I will pay you for it."

"I am truly honored. Now I think it is time for me to go to work."

CHAPTER 14

Paris

October 1869

Inspector René Gustave, exceedingly tall and cadaverous with a black moustache and pointed goatee, laboriously sifted through files to be stored away, perhaps never to be seen again. Certainly there were more important things to do, especially in light of the last sensational murder. But any complaint would result in a rebuke by the chief inspector, Monsieur Ambroise Arseneau. And that he would avoid at all costs.

The door of the office flew open. Gustave jumped, dropping one of the files.

"Monsieur Inspector! There has been another murder, and we have been asked to investigate it," said inspector Gaspard Desvaux.

With a vexed expression, the chief inspector looked up from a sheaf of reports. At four foot ten with a pronounced paunch, a grey, unkempt beard extending to his stomach, and myopic eyes, the sixty-one-year-old inspector was an indefatigable autocrat. He was known as Le Terrier, but called Le Nain, the dwarf, behind his back. He gave the bearer of bad news, officer Gaspard Desvaux, a disgusted look.

"The victim, his name?" Arseneau commanded in his strident, imperious voice.

"A Monsieur Jacquet Lapieux, a wealthy and respected member of the aristocracy. He was a distant relative of Empress Eugénie. Perhaps she should be informed," said Desvaux.

"*Mon Dieu*, an important man in-in-indeed," said Rene Gustave, hoping to appear insightful.

If Arseneau heard Gustave's statement, he ignored it. "And where was the body of this Monsieur Lapieux found?"

"In the 13 e arrondissement in the Quartier du Vieux-Moulin, Monsieur Inspector," replied Desvaux. "He had been stabbed to death at approximately two in the morning. Apparently there was a witness who informed the police."

Arseneau meticulously cleaned his monocle and placed it over his right eye, making it appear far larger than the left. "That does not make sense," he said, adjusting the lens. "Why would a man of such esteem be snooping around in the poorest district of Paris so late at night? What was he doing there?"

"That's the mystery," replied Desvaux. "Perhaps he had an assignation with a prostitute or he was part of a government operation. He may have been an informer or an undercover agent."

Gustave nodded. The government had thousands of spies, and the area was inhabited by ragpickers and people of dubious reputation, many of whom were destitute and violently opposed the regime.

"So there might have been antigovernment activity going on. 'To the barricades,' eh?" said Gustave, raising his fist with a devilish grin.

Arseneau pursed his thick lips and stared at his assistant. "No barricades, Scarecrow!"

"No, of course not," replied Gustave, nodding vigorously. Arseneau's father had been an officer in the Grande Armée, a hero of the Old Guard, and a victim of the *Anglais* at Waterloo. Joking about insurrection in Arseneau's presence was a bad idea for anyone who desired career advancement. Not that such advancement was likely for Gustave as long as he remained the chief inspector's assistant.

As a young man, Gustave had studied under the enigmatic Eugène François Vidocq, the father of modern criminology. Vidocq had developed indelible ink, the use of plaster casts, recordkeeping, ballistics, and the study of comparative handwriting. Thus, Monsieur Gustave, an apt student, came with enviable credentials. But in Arseneau's eyes those credentials didn't begin to make up for his involvement in certain unfortunate events with the military twenty-two years earlier. Moreover, the chief inspector distrusted the value of Vidocq's investigative techniques and considered them at best irrelevant. What he valued was the element of fear and ruthless investigation.

"Gustave," said Arseneau with a quick wave of a stubby arm, "check the listing of government informants. The volume is on the shelf above my desk. Do it now, we have little time."

Arseneau turned back to Desvaux. "And why has the department of the thirteenth arrondissement asked us to handle this murder? Don't they know we are investigating a homicide barely two weeks old?"

"Oui, Monsieur Inspector. They are very much aware of it, but some of the circumstances are similar, and they know that you, Le Terrier, are the most proficient and dogged investigator in Paris."

"Indeed," said Arseneau nodding his bald head. "It would only make sense. Of course, I will give this case immediate attention. And I am certainly aware of Monsieur Jacquet

Lapieux. But not necessarily in the best sense. He had a questionable reputation—a gambler, continuously in debt. There was an incident with a courtesan that made the papers. And as I recall, he frequented some of the most questionable salons in Paris, especially Chez Chantilly on Rue Saint-Honoré in the first arrondissement."

"Ah, Monsieur Arseneau," said Gustave, peering at a handwritten page in a well-worn volume, "Monsieur Lapieux is listed as a gov-government agent, an-an informer. It's possible that he was assigned to a case in the 13e arrondissement and murdered for political reasons."

"But not by a ragpicker," said Desvaux. "They wouldn't want a police investigation in their sector. I believe, Monsieur Inspector, that he may have been murdered by someone from another part of Paris. Perhaps from the 18e arrondissement, Montmartre. That's a hotbed of anti-government sentiment. Monsieur Lapieux was a monarchist and had, through Empress Eugénie's influence with her husband, enacted very harsh measures against the poor. In fact, he was absolutely hated."

Arseneau walked to a wall displaying a large map of Paris. He drew a finger along Rue de Rivoli, one of the most magnificent streets of the city, then to Rue Saint-Honoré, a few blocks north, not far from the Palais Royal.

"True, but a man has been murdered and it's our responsibility to find the assailant. Indeed, there are many expressing the same views as Monsieur Lapieux, and they may also be in danger. And the previous murder victim, though a courtesan, was also an informer for the government."

"So, there is someone out there who has it in for the regime and murders with seeming impunity," said Desvaux.

"Not with impunity. There will be justice. But we must divide our force in order to carry out surveillance," said

Arseneau. "Monsieur Gustave, you will remain at the Café Martinique where you will have a good view of Chez d' Chantilly. If you see anything suspicious you will immediately contact me here. Is that clear?"

"Oui, monsieur, but how can I contact you without leaving my post?" said Gustave, perplexed.

"You will hail a gendarme on horseback and he will carry a message at a good clip. Has that not occurred to you?"

"But of course. And I will remain in the café all day and all night."

"Precisely!" Arseneau turned to Desvaux. "I presume that the corpse is still at the morgue. That's where we must immediately proceed."

"I just hope that it's still there, Monsieur Inspector. If the victim's body hasn't been returned to the family, it might have been taken by a university. Cadavers are in high demand."

"Those of the indigent, yes, but not those of men of stature. Not the corpse of a relative of Empress Eugénie. That is for certain."

***

"It may still be too early. Bodies aren't exposed until past one," said Gaspard Desvaux. At that hour it was customary for a curtain to be raised so that the public could view the corpses on the stone tables behind the glass. All were naked except for a cloth covering the genitals.

The Morgue lay at the extreme upper end of the Île de la Cité, just in back of the old church of Notre Dame. The doors of the morgue, once open, were a magnet for eyes incapable of looking away.

As they entered a dignified man in a bowler hat and short jacket approached them. "Inspectors, I was informed that you were coming. I am François Regnard, director of this establishment. I am also a doctor."

"We wish to view the body of a Monsieur Jacquet Lapieux," said Arseneau. "Is it here?"

"Most likely, monsieur. We received the corpse of a well-dressed gentleman early this morning. He had no identification, no wallet, but fortunately I'd seen a sketch of him at the racetrack in *Le Monde* a few weeks ago." Regnard looked pleased with himself. "I carried out the examination myself."

The curtain shielding the deceased from onlookers had already been raised, and bodies of men, women, and children lay on the slabs, one beside another. There was a great assortment: old men, pregnant women, children who'd died of starvation, and infants, many of whom had drowned. Several dozen people were jammed inside the morgue, all pressing against a restraining rail, all staring at the deceased.

Arseneau and Desvaux followed the superintendent down a long corridor. The three men entered a large hall with a partial glass ceiling that allowed sunlight to filter down. The clothes of each corpse were carefully hung on a line so that people might recognize the garments and thus identify the bodies. A stream of cold water from an overhead tap flowed over each body and a close, sickening smell permeated the room.

"Here we are," said Regnard. "I believe this is the subject of your investigation."

"It appears so," said Arseneau. "I request that you close the curtain, this being a police matter."

A sound of disappointment rose from the crowd, many hoping to witness a medical inquiry that might include a dissection. Arseneau ignored the rebuke and looked closely at the corpse. The face was drained, but there was a slit in the neck where blood had clotted.

"Is this the wound that killed him?" asked Desvaux.

"I don't believe so," said Regnard. "If you assist me in turning the body over, I will indicate the fatal wounds."

With the corpse lying on his stomach, the force of the killing blows became immediately obvious. It was clear that a sharp weapon had been plunged into the man's back, each time with enormous force.

Arseneau peered at the wounds. "They're very deep. I would think just one would have been fatal."

"Indeed," said the superintendent. "I inspected the wounds carefully and found them to be quite unique. They were not caused by a common knife, one that can be purchased in any local shop. No, Monsieur Inspector, these wounds are from a foreign instrument. The incisions are deep, with a distinct curvature. The kind of knife used in this murder isn't made anywhere in Europe."

Arseneau and Desvaux gave Dr. Regard a curious look. "Please explain," said Arseneau.

"I strongly suspect that the knife is a *jambiya*. It's used almost exclusively in the Near East. Many regional varieties exist. For instance, there is the Omani khanjar fighting knife, the Moroccan dagger knife, and even a Mughal Islamic jambiya. In addition, there are Persian and Ottoman knives of slightly different design as well as those from Turkey. Some have jeweled sheaths and are exquisitely decorated. But they have one thing in common. They are all quite deadly."

"You know a great deal about knives," said Desvaux.

"I learned about them when I was in the army some time ago. One does not forget. And as I was saying, it appears that the assailant was quite skilled."

"So, whoever used this knife may have been from one of those regions," said Desvaux. "I agree that it appears he was very skilled."

"But three stabbings in the back." Arseneau turned to Desvaux. "What does this tell you, Inspector?"

"It tells me that he was stabbed in the back." Averting the chief inspector's retort, he quickly raised his hand. "But it had to be a surprise. Monsieur Lapieux possibly had an encounter with an individual, then turned away, thinking that the matter was settled, only to be viciously attacked. But there had to be something unquenchably furious in the heart of the assailant. Why else would he repeat the stabbing three times? It had to be more than a simple argument or misunderstanding. It had to be an act of insanity."

"Indeed," said the doctor. "The wounds are extraordinarily unusual."

"And there is the matter of the cut to the throat. Why would that have been necessary?" asked Desvaux.

"Perhaps a final statement of contempt. A coup, not unlike those inflicted by the wild Indians of America who take a scalp whether the victim is dead or not," said Arseneau as he and Desvaux followed Regnard out of the gallery.

Regnard nodded to an assistant and the curtain was raised. Immediately dozens of pedestrians crowded the railing to stare at the corpses laid out on the tables.

***

"Monsieur Desvaux, you said this morning that there was a witness." Arseneau tapped his fingers on his desk. "What did the police in the thirteenth arrondissement say about that?"

"It was a young woman, likely a grisette who was out late at night. She refused to give her name; perhaps she didn't have a license to engage in her profession and was afraid of being arrested."

"I-I have something on my mind con-concerning this girl," said Gene Gustave hesitantly.

"And what could that possibly be?" said Arseneau.

"That this grisette might have had blood on her clothes."

The chief inspector gave Gustave a curious glance. "Continue."

"Well, why would she even approach the police? It would have been a natural thing for such a person to-to slink back into the shadows. But no, perhaps to establish her own innocence she boldly approaches an officer. But if she has blood on her clothing, then ..."

"Are you suggesting that she was the murderer?" said Arseneau.

Desvaux promptly opened his notebook and flipped through a half dozen pages. "Inspector, I neglected to tell you that the investigating officer mentioned that there was blood on the woman's clothing. But he assumed that she approached the victim after the assault, that is, after the man was dead and the assailant had disappeared."

"So, she possibly went to the victim to see if she could render aid and then soiled her clothing by touching Monsieur Lapieux's body?" said Arseneau. "Or are you suggesting that a young woman could carry out such a murder so effectively, so brutally?"

"Per-perhaps, Monsieur Inspector," replied Gustave. "Only if there was sufficient hatred. She may have been exceedingly strong and skilled in the art of assassination. It-it's not unheard of. And the policeman may have surprised her after she killed the man."

"The officer did say that he may have suddenly come upon her, and she did seem a bit unnerved," said Desvaux. "But wouldn't anybody other than a soldier or policeman be unsettled by the sight of such a murder?"

"Certainly, but what of the knife, the murder weapon? Surely he would have seen that?" said Arseneau.

"Perhaps not. Women wear voluminous clothing," said Desvaux. "How difficult would it have been for her to hide it in the folds of her dress or even inside her coat? After all, it was at two in the morning and very cold. The officer most certainly wouldn't have made her disrobe."

"I think it imperative that we find this woman, this grisette," said Arseneau. "We should follow up on Monsieur Gustave's suspicion. Yes, we must find her. It is most important."

"And what of the salon?" asked Desvaux.

"I want Chez d' Chantilly to be watched," said Arseneau to both junior detectives. "If our Monsieur Lapieux frequented that salon, someone there might have seen him leave, if indeed he was there at all that night. And if he was, perhaps he had an unpleasant encounter and somebody followed him. Somebody very angry. Somebody wanting to kill."

"So, we have two possible suspects," said Gustave.

"Perhaps more," said Arseneau. "There might have been accomplices. In either case, someone will eventually be tied in knots like a cat with a ball of string."

"I've heard that there are often exotic performances at Chez d' Chantilly. If there's an accomplice, he might have been noticed by others at the salon. I think we should speak to any who might have been there," said Desvaux.

"But if so, would he chance returning to the salon?"

"Only to prove by his attendance that he's innocent," said Desvaux.

"That's why it is so very important, Monsieur Gustave, that you keep a close eye on the salon. We must gather evidence in order to make an arrest. This is a capital crime. The head of the guilty party will roll beneath the blade of the guillotine," said Le Terrier. "And I will be there to witness it."

CHAPTER 15

Paris

November 1869

The gloomy weather made it extremely difficult for Inspector Gene Gustave to see anything from the Café Martinique's rain-streaked windows. But certainly he couldn't remain inconspicuous if he stood outside, getting drenched as he watched the cabs that discharged their elegantly dressed passengers at the door of Chez Chantilly. And if he did see someone of suspicious character, how was he going to find a gendarme on horseback in this weather?

An impossible assignment, and failure would only reduce him further in the myopic eyes of Le Nain.

In 1847, as a young police inspector attached to General Thomas-Robert Bugeaud's command, Gustave had been responsible for the interrogation of one Mustafa Hakim, a tribal chieftain who'd been captured by French forces. Hakim had been closely allied with the Algerian leader, Abd al-Qadir, during the final year of France's conquest of Algeria. The assignment was very important, as Hakim was privy to the strength and plans of Qadir. The intelligence to be gained had been of extraordinary value to General Bugeaud.

But Gustave had come under the spell of the wily and clever Hakim, who spoke fluent French and lulled him into complacency and presumed friendship. While officers on the general's staff mocked the young investigator's stutter, Hakim accorded him the greatest respect.

Thinking that the camaraderie he'd built with the Algerian would lead to the revelation of important information, Gene, without permission, had accompanied the prisoner to Algiers where they both enjoyed dinner at a prominent French café. Excusing himself, the Algerian, wearing his jambiya and flowing robes, simply walked out the rear exit and disappeared. It was said that the man had left Algeria and never returned.

Horrified and incensed by his own naïveté, Gustave reported the loss to General Bugeaud and was promptly dismissed, never again to be employed by the French army.

Despair hung over him for years until he achieved limited success in numerous police investigations. He'd made a great effort to gain valuable skills and was eventually promoted, finally arriving at the Prefecture of the Île de la Cité. But that did little to gain the appreciation of Le Terrier, the brusque chief inspector.

Gustave desperately needed a success, a magnificent breakthrough in a bewildering case. But for that, there would be little opportunity.

He envied Desvaux. The man was the epitome of the stalwart, unflappable cop. He never smiled. The cold gaze he leveled on those he interrogated was like a scythe, intimidating, eviscerating, leaving even the innocent feeling queasy and hoping that those hard, unblinking eyes would turn somewhere else.

Inspector Desvaux was tall and heavily built, upright and unbending. He wore a black top hat regardless of weather and steeled himself like armor in a long black frock coat. He frequently mentioned the acclaim he'd won during his own army service, a veiled rebuke of Gustave. Desvaux, with his muttonchop sideburns and twisted moustache, pointed at the ends like the emperor's, was Le Terrier's man.

Gustave shuddered, already bracing for Arseneau's look of contempt. "Failed again, eh?" he'd say, a reprimand cutting to the core.

He would have to do something to prove his worth; even an action contrary to orders on this dreary, cold night.

Carriages massed in front of the salon. Men in elaborate livery sat stoically holding the reins of horses, opening doors, and accepting the coins given them by the elite. With a nod and a mumbled *"Merci,"* each would climb onto the front seat of his rig and the carriage would move down the boulevard. The procession lasted well over an hour as aristocratic men, either alone or with a wife or courtesan, hurried to the door of Chez d' Chantilly and handed their umbrellas to a waiting doorman.

There was no sign of anyone conceivably suspicious. With an umbrella low over his head, Gustave departed the café and worked his way through the carriages. He felt foolish, peering at one potential suspect after another, each giving him a curious look. After the cabs departed, he trudged back to the café, thoroughly soaked. Feeling inept and ridiculous, he decided to wait an hour, maybe two, then retreat to his flat, where he resided alone. He wondered how many nights this would have to be repeated.

***

With shocking red hair piled high on her head, a rotund body, and a narrow face that thirty years earlier might have been appealing, Madame Marguerite Couture stood at the door of Chez Chantilly and regarded the woman before her with disdain. Eliza Breton shifted from one foot to the other, holding her possessions in a small stained sack.

With obvious disdain, Madame Couture bade her enter the hushed parlor, where Eliza begged her for employment.

"Dearest cousin, I have nowhere else to go, no one else to appeal to," said Eliza, wiping her eyes and nose with a soiled rag.

Eliza stood, her drawn face showing extreme fatigue, her gray-streaked hair hanging limply over her rounded shoulders. Before her, Marguerite sat imperiously on a gilded sofa.

"You couldn't find work in Bordeaux or Paris?" said Madame Couture with pursed lips, inspecting her manicured nails.

Eliza's head drooped. "I am an old woman with few skills, dear cousin. If I were young and pretty, I might find a man who would care for me. My own husband, bless his soul, perished at sea three years ago. But I will do the most menial chores with never a complaint. I only wish a bed, clean clothes, and perhaps a few coins. And," she said with a sudden glint in her eyes, "I can keep secrets. Oh yes, I have had many in my time, and I observe things no one might suspect. Soiled things, intimate things that would be of value to you. Yes, I do see things ..."

She let the sentence hang in the perfumed air. Marguerite evaluated the statement with a wary look. In her business in it was always good to have a spy. A mousy woman in service, virtually invisible to her soigné guests, all vying for the choicest courtesan or a tip on a fast horse, could be of inestimable value.

Madame Couture sighed. She had hoped that this supplicant in rough peasant clothes from the hovels of Bordeaux would never appeal to her charity, virtually nonexistent as it was. Eliza was from that underside of society, the class of eternally impoverished poor that Marguerite had fled at the age of fourteen. Working her way up from streetwalker to courtesan, through four marriages, each to an even wealthier man, had finally allowed her to comingle with those who sought out the discreet services she could provide.

"You will report to me each evening after my guests have departed," said Madame Couture. "I must know what you have learned. And I will tolerate no insubordination, no whimpering or wheedling. That you are kin is of no consequence to me. The chores will require diligent effort and, mark me, I do employ you with great hesitation. If I find anything missing, or hear the slightest complaint from one my guests, you will be dismissed without a letter of recommendation. Is that understood?"

"Indeed, madame," said Eliza, bowing her head and showing no inclination to use the word "cousin" or "dearest."

Eliza would be watched, but she would be watching. She couldn't have survived without the stealth and deceit that belied her innocent, fragile appearance. And this house had oh, so many secrets. Whispers in the night, assignations, chicanery, and perhaps even plots were more valuable than the few sous she would accept with fawning appreciation.

In her voluminous pink coral silk dress trimmed with flounces, an overskirt of lace, and a wreath of pink roses and pearl bracelets, Madame Couture pointed toward the unvarnished kitchen beyond the parlor and dismissed Eliza with a disparaging look.

It would be another three hours before guests arrived, plenty of time to remind the two live-in courtesans that she would brook no incivility between them. But she suspected that the rivalry between these young and appealing beauties would only become worse. Perhaps much worse.

***

"Monsieur Daudet, Madame Maillard, so good to see you again," said Madame Marguerite Couture with what sufficed for ingratiating charm. "I do hope that you are staying for the evening's performance." Sotto voce she added, "It will be extraordinarily mystical. We have not one but two experts in the arts and mysteries of the ancient world. Indeed, Monsieur Daudet, the Egyptian would be excellent subject matter for one of your exquisite paintings. And, of course, Mademoiselle Maillard would make the most magnificent subject of all."

Marguerite had pasted on her social face, fawning over her guests, hanging on their every word. She raised her heavily lidded eyes and gazed with unquestioning astonishment at their pronouncements no matter how banal. This face had been exactingly cultivated, even before a mirror, for several decades, and it rarely failed to make each who entered feel exceedingly special. Of course, most could detect a charade, but they well understood that the salon, with its attempt at ultimate discretion, was the epitome of charades.

"How sweet of you," said Yvette Maillard in her wispy voice. All heads had turned to watch her entry. Employing studied grace, the demimonde smiled demurely. With her arm wrapped around that of the famous artist, she said, "Monsieur Daudet and I will stay for at least part of it. Isn't that right, Étienne?"

"For a while, yes. I've been looking forward to the evening's performance and a reprieve from the studio."

"Do you know," continued Yvette, "my dearest artist is completing the most marvelous painting of *L'Empereur* on horseback during the war against Austria. It is positively romantic, and so highly detailed. One can see the serious yet masterful composure of our august leader. I'm sure Louis

Napoleon will purchase it. I can't wait to see it in the Salon des Arts."

"You are too kind," said Daudet, his eyes falling upon Marguerite's husband, who shook hands with important men and assessed the availability of the exquisitely dressed women in their company. Wending his way through the two dozen guests, he approached Daudet and clicked the heels of his thigh-high black boots. He nodded smartly with Prussian correctness while his left hand held tight to his gleaming saber.

"Oberst von Brandenburg, it is a distinct pleasure to see you again," said Étienne Daudet, assessing the imperious colonel who never failed to wear his full uniform, that of the Prussian cavalry. It was his objective to impress and to intimidate when the opportunity arose, especially when engaging members of the French military. But as an officer in Europe's strongest army he respected Daudet for not only his artistic skills but also his excellent swordsmanship. Daudet, easily offended if criticized either for his art or his imperialistic views, had engaged in numerous duels.

That Daudet invariably won was of consequence to the *oberst*. Indeed, Brandenburg proudly displayed the *Schmitte* bragging scar on his left cheek, inflicted by a saber while at Heidelberg University during his youth. The act of standing and taking the cut was considered a mark of honor and courage amongst the elite.

"I congratulate you on your latest dueling engagement," said Brandenburg, standing a foot taller than the artist. "Did the fellow who insulted you apologize following the wound?"

"He did, but the entire event has been given far too much press. The man was terribly inept with the rapier; a slice at the arm and the referee ended the duel. But blood had been spilt and, like a gentleman, he shook my hand once the wound was bandaged. In fact, he decided to buy one of my paintings. It was all quite satisfactory," said Daudet smugly.

"I saw it all," said Yvette Maillard. "Monsieur Daudet makes little of it but it was quite thrilling. I should not have been worried since Étienne is one of the finest fencers in France, but the sight of a sword pointed at him did make me pale. I have implored him to cease dueling but, well, men engage in such dangerous things." She shook her exquisite head.

Brandenburg offered a fleeting smile. "It's all about honor, my dear. A man, just like a nation, especially my Prussia, must maintain its dignity, its resolution. If that is lost," he said, raising his voice, "then there is nothing. Nothing at all."

The enormity of his statement resounded in the parlor and the polite, engaging chatter came to a sudden halt. Sensing the chilling effect, he stood quite erect, peered at the questioning crowd, and with a rare smile raised a glass of champagne. "*Vive la France.*"

With far stronger sentiment "*Vive la France!*" echoed as the attendees raised glasses and conversation resumed.

With that, the colonel and his wife panned their eyes over the room and saw Eliza Breton watching them. She turned away abruptly and busied herself fluffing up pillows and putting champagne into buckets of ice before scurrying out of the parlor.

"A bad choice, madame," said Brandenburg. "I give her less than a fortnight before she does something terribly foolish."

***

"Is that Camille Lapin? It's early for her to go to her room. I thought that she would want to see the performance," said demimonde Yvette Maillard, watching from the parlor as the courtesan climbed the spiral stairs.

127

"I suspect that she has an assignation this evening and wants to prepare for it," said Madame Couture.

"Does she live here?" asked Daudet.

"She rents a room. It was quite lucrative for me when she had many wealthy clients. But now she seems to entertain just one man, and he doesn't pay enough."

"Yet despite her appetite for that one lucky man, her presence attracts numerous men who wish to earn her favors," said Oberst von Brandenburg, watching Camille with appreciation.

More guests filtered in, talking excitedly. Others met in hushed groups, exchanging news of the murder of Jacquet Lapieux, who had frequented the salon only recently. Others spoke about the opera or the Salon des Arts or new works at the Louvre. Ivan Turgenev, the congenial author of *Fathers and Sons*, was surrounded by several of his avid readers. Cigar smoke, intermingled with expensive perfumes, drifted toward the chandeliers.

But for the murder, an air of complacency permeated the salon. Wealthy men commingled with sumptuously attired women in flowing, narrow-waisted *poult-de-soie* dresses held tight by satin corsets.

Smiles were exchanged as both men and women calculated who should be approached and who was on the cusp of a delicious scandal. It was a most delectable sport played out in every salon, as if the world of the Second Empire and its lascivious pleasures would never end.

A woman from Poland played the piano while gaslight bathed the room with an intimate radiance. Thick carpets muffled sound while gilt mirrors, rich dark paneling, plush sofas, and faux marble busts adorned tables. A large oblong table covered in draped satin had been placed at one end of the parlor. Only a single spray of flowers in an oriental vase adorned the table. It lay as if waiting for something to begin.

Madame Couture glanced up and saw Marcel Cheval walk quickly up the stairs toward the bedrooms. Her husband also saw the performer and said, "He hasn't much time."

"In some instances, it doesn't take much time."

"I guess it's less expensive that way," replied the colonel.

"Dear husband," said Marguerite with a sly glance, "I am surprised that you haven't attended to the young lady in question."

"*Nein*, my love. You have my entire attention. Of that you should have no doubt."

Madam Couture sniffed, turned away and thought, *Oui, my oberst, but for how long?*

CHAPTER 16

Paris
November 1869

The car rocked gently over the rails and Jack Volant, tired from the long journey from the port of Le Havre, slumbered in a fitful sleep. On occasion he would jerk or bark an order as old visions assaulted him. Once he gasped, and reached for a nonexistent revolver to the consternation of a man and his wife sitting across from him. When Jack moaned, the man reached across and touched his shoulder.

"Monsieur, monsieur, are you in pain? Do you require assistance?"

Waking with a start, Jack took a deep breath and shook his head. "No, monsieur, I must have had a bad dream." He issued a nervous smile. "I'm fine, but thank you for waking me."

"Of course, but you are safe now and we are nearly in Paris."

It was a mild and cloudless day, unusual for the city in November. Jack emerged from the Gare Saint-Lazare, the largest train station in Europe. Built of gray stone with statues and triumphal arches, it was a marvel of engineering that Jack, having just arrived, found imposing beyond measure.

"You look very dashing," said Jack, as his brother threw his arms around him.

"*Mais oui*! This is Paris!" Marcel tossed Jack's luggage into his one-horse tilbury, a light two-wheeled carriage with a top for winter.

Jack grinned. Whatever disdain he'd had for his brother had been largely consigned to the past. Marcel, to both Jack and his father's amazement, had delivered great numbers of mummies and ancient textiles to the business, gaining him considerable favor. That Marcel never asked for money only added to his status.

"As requested, I found you an inexpensive apartment in Montmartre. It's an interesting neighborhood, lots of artists —all poor, of course—a lot of immigrants—also poor—and some great cafés."

"I'm sure it will be just fine. Do you live there?" An armada of omnibuses, wagons, and elegant carriages swirled around them.

Marcel laughed. "No, but I have friends there."

"All women?"

"Mon Dieu, a round of canister already! Of course there are women. This is Paris, Jack, the greatest city in the world. To the French, to be in Paris is to have the world at your feet —'*Le monde à ses pieds*.'"

"I'll have to remember that. So, where we are going?"

"It's a magnificent morning. I thought we'd drive out to the Bois de Boulogne. It's the most beautiful park in France and a great place to see people. Especially those who make this city hum."

"This carriage looks like it's made of straw," said Jack, eyeing the large wheels and the dashboard mounted on an elaborate set of springs. "Is it safe?"

"It's a gentleman's carriage for famous people like me. And no, it's not safe."

Jack climbed in. "Are you famous?"

"In certain quarters. I know a lot of influential people and they know me. I get around."

He flicked the reins, and the tilbury darted off down the Rue de Clichy between the eighth and ninth arrondissements toward the grand Rue de Rivoli, then past the Jardin des Tuileries. Marcel turned onto the Avenue de l'Impératrice, the grand boulevard honoring Empress Eugénie, wife of the emperor, Louis Napoleon III.

As they passed men and women and a dozen styles of carriages, Marcel waved to those he recognized and they waved back. Cab drivers in livery, wearing top hats, black coats with gilt buttons, and butternut-hued pants, looked straight ahead while maneuvering their vehicles down the crowded boulevard. Jack admired one carriage in particular, the elegant *attelage A la d' Aumont*, the height of refinement. Other Parisians rode horseback along the bridal path beside the wide macadam road.

"Everyone goes to the Bois de Boulogne between two and four in the afternoon," said Marcel, "and there is a peculiar etiquette about it all. When you see somebody you know, you only wave the first time. The second time you simply nod, and the third time you ignore them. If you violate it, you're done, considered terribly gauche."

With a practiced military eye, Jack scanned the street. "Why all the soldiers?"

"The army? Oh, one hardly notices after a while. There are also five thousand police and three thousand municipal guards in the city. There's an undercurrent of unrest. Here on this boulevard are the wealthy and middle class, but half of the city is desperately poor. The emperor requires total control to prevent insurrection. Until last year there was complete censorship, though lately that's eased a bit."

"Is he popular now?" asked Jack, glancing back toward the Arc de Triomphe.

"The emperor, *Napoleon le Petit*? It depends on who you ask. The students hate him, but students are rarely satisfied with the status quo. Actually, Napoleon was quite popular when he came to power in '48. There was an election a few years later, and he won by a huge majority. That was before he staged a coup and named himself *l'empereur*. But he was still popular when France declared war on Austria. After France's victory, Louis, more popular than ever, decided to change Paris. Or should I say that he had Baron Georges-Eugène Haussmann, the 'demolition artist' change it completely? It took almost fifteen years."

"Change it how?" asked Jack as the Bois de Boulogne came into view.

"Before Haussmann, Paris was a city stuck in the Middle Ages. Stinking, narrow, dangerous streets, no sewers, smoke-stained buildings—all firetraps. And there was the endless clanking of wagons over cobblestones."

"Cobblestones are very useful for revolutions," observed Jack wryly.

"Precisely, and that's one reason why eighty-five miles of streets have been paved. Haussmann was given the title of Prefect of the Seine, and nothing was allowed to stand in his way. He made a lot of enemies. Wiped out entire neighborhoods. But he was supported by *l'empereur* and likely offered Louis his daughter in return. Another delicious scandal known only to the elite. The power of censorship, eh?"

"I heard that the emperor has a new woman every night," said Jack.

"Sometimes two, all brought to the Palais des Tuileries, stripped naked, and offered to him. *L'empereur* has an insatiable need. Eugénie is apparently an understanding woman, but it's widely known that she is frigid, maybe because of several miscarriages. The papers said that she recovered very slowly after the birth of their only son, Napoleon Eugène. In regard to things carnal, she was reported to say '*Sex? What filth.*" So, after six weeks Louis went back to his mistresses."

They continued down the Avenue de l'Impératrice.

"Now, as I was saying about the reconstruction, this avenue cuts a swath right through the richest neighborhoods, from the Arc de Triomphe to the Bois de Boulogne. Wanting to beautify Paris, Haussmann planted forty thousand trees. Everything's changed. He put in thirty-two thousand gas lamps, and rows of six-story buildings with iron balconies. And then he built the Théâtre de l'Opéra and a three-mile boulevard, the Rue Lafayette."

"Quite a building project," said Jack.

"Thousands were put to work. He made Paris the envy of the world, a city of one and a half million people. And he improved the city's defenses—not that anyone would consider invading Paris."

"I saw the walls coming in on the train."

"Yes, I'm sure you did. There are two. The old fortifications are close to the center. The city expanded beyond them, so newer ones extend farther out. They're rather substantial, and there are forts even beyond them." Marcel waved to a pretty young lady riding sidesaddle.

"The French have an expression about Paris," said Marcel, breathing in the invigorating air.

"And that is?"

They entered the wooded park with its fountains, waterfalls, lakes, and gardens waiting for spring.

"It's about walking these pathways, enjoying the ambiance of art, culture, and pleasure: '*L' essence de la vie dans la ville.*' One savors the essence of life in the city. At least until winter, when it becomes bleak, cold, and very dismal. They call it *la grisouille*. But in the cafés," Marcel said with a knowing grin, "there's always good food and plenty of wine. And, of course, plenty of courtesans."

Marcel slowed his tilbury while he waved and nodded to those who recognized him. They circled the lake and pulled off the path beside a waterfall. Polished carriages streamed past, along with equestrians and people on foot.

Jack watched as a smartly painted omnibus lumbered by, pulled by four horses. Fourteen people sat on the inside, and the same number had found benches on the roof. They waved gayly, taking in the languid afternoon.

"Who is that?" said Jack, diverting his brother's attention away from another pretty lady.

"What?"

"The one in that carriage with the man in the top hat and gray riding coat."

"That is Mademoiselle Yvette Maillard, one of the most admired and sought-after demimondes in all of Paris. She is stunning, is she not? Men would do almost anything to spend some time with her."

"I would do anything to paint her portrait. She's extraordinary."

"I think you'll have to paint her in your dreams. Her face is angelic and her figure, well ... No, Jack, she wouldn't consider sitting for an unknown artist. And you see the man who's escorting her? He is Étienne Daudet, 'the painter of France,' as he calls himself. Very pompous, very rich, and the most highly respected artist in Paris. His work is always in the Salon des Arts."

"I don't care about him," said Jack. "You said that you're known by important people. Does she know you?"

"Of course. She and Daudet attend the salon where I perform."

"That's where you do the mummy routine?"

"I do, and the 'mummy routine' is extremely popular—my primary source of income."

At that moment, the couple saw Marcel and offered a perfunctory wave.

"Then you can introduce me to her if she comes," Jack persisted.

"I don't know when she'll come. And though she will be polite, she may also be very condescending. You'll be setting yourself up for an embarrassing situation. Daudet will certainly be with her, and he can be an arrogant bastard. He isn't aristocracy, but he is the epitome of snobbishness."

"When's your next performance?" asked Jack, watching the elegant carriage drive back toward the boulevard.

"Tonight, at nine. You can accompany me if you want. But don't say I didn't warn you."

***

Marcel scanned the crowd. Most of the guests had yet to arrive—they'd be fashionably late as usual—but Étienne Daudet, accompanied by Yvette Maillard, had several appointments that night and had come early. The couple was greeted obsequiously by Madame Couture and Colonel Albrecht von Brandenburg. A few other guests, having arrived before the chill of the night, crowded around the demimonde and the artist, all wishing to bask in the glow of Daudet's company.

"Are you going to do me the honor?" Jack asked as the famous couple was offered glasses of champagne.

Marcel nodded, then motioned for Jack to follow.

"Monsieur Daudet, Mademoiselle Maillard," Marcel said, offering a slight bow, "may I introduce my brother, Jack, an artist and former officer of the United States Army."

Jack extended his hand and Daudet shook it stiffly. The lady gave a slight nod and gracefully extended hers.

"I am pleased to have the honor," said Jack, his eyes going from Daudet to Maillard. "I chanced to see you this morning in the Bois de Boulogne when I was riding with Marcel. Maybe you remember; I believe you waved to him."

Daudet shrugged. "Perhaps. We see so many people."

Jack turned to the demimonde. "I'm sure all of Paris agrees that you are a most striking and elegant lady. As an artist, I would like to paint your portrait. It would be a gift and, of course, I would charge nothing. I simply wish that it be shown to others. I have recently arrived, and if you are so willing, it may help to establish me here."

"My portrait? What a sweet idea, but you must understand that my time is extremely limited."

"Mademoiselle Maillard is being extraordinarily polite," said Daudet with a tight-lipped smile and raised eyebrows. He was once again joined by Oberst Brandenburg.

"What she actually means is that she will not have any time, lieutenant. None at all. And, may I ask, exactly where and by whom have you been trained? I imagine not in Paris or anywhere in France."

"I studied art at the University of Maryland for several years. I do not have the following or the formidable experience that you—"

"I am certain of that," said Daudet. "I do not mean to impugn your integrity, monsieur, but to be worthy of executing my lady's portrait would require my approval and, beyond that, years of study at the Salon des Arts or a similar institution. You would have to have been acclaimed as a portrait painter of renown, one who has executed numerous paintings of extremely worthy people or historical subjects. It's nothing less than an affront to Mademoiselle Maillard to have even considered making such a bizarre request."

"Oh, Étienne," said Yvette, "That is a bit harsh. The American gentleman is only trying to estab—"

"Mademoiselle," said Brandenburg, "I do believe that Monsieur Daudet is right. One cannot expect to simply come to France or even my Prussia, present himself as an accomplished artist, and demand your time and attention—"

"I am not demanding," said Jack with an edge he had not displayed in a very long time. "I was giving the lady an opportunity to have her portrait painted at no charge. And I consider your comments insulting, Herr Oberst, since neither you nor Monsieur Daudet have viewed my work."

A frozen silence ensued for a second until Madame Couture inserted herself. "Gentlemen, gentlemen, let us not cloud this beautiful evening with such dysphoria. I'm sure that Monsieur Volant meant no harm. Now, my dear colonel, it is almost time for the performance. I think you should offer some introductory remarks."

No one moved for a very long moment. Daudet glanced at Brandenburg, then back at Volant. Yvette Maillard's look of congenial indulgence turned to one of extreme discomfort.

"Jack," interjected Marcel, giving his brother a gentle tap on the shoulder, "I do need your help. Will you please come?"

"Mademoiselle." Jack gave a curt bow and abruptly turned away from Daudet, Brandenburg, and the demimonde.

"That was a dangerous and unnecessary encounter," hissed Marcel as they walked across the room.

"Really?" said Jack. "I rather enjoyed it."

"I'm sure, but you nearly destroyed my welcome here," said Marcel.

"You always land on your feet, Steven."

"'Marcel,' please."

"Sure, Monsieur Marcel. Now let's see this little charade of yours."

***

Yvette Maillard arranged her features into a mask of calmness. She had been approached by dozens of men, mostly wealthy, desiring her favors, but never by an aspiring artist who wanted nothing more than permission to paint her portrait. She wasn't at all sure she had the time or inclination to sit for a portrait, but the decision was hers to make. Étienne had no right to speak for her.

Another thought seeped into Yvette's mind like a threatening cloud on an otherwise placid day. The eyes of this man, this former soldier of the American war, had suddenly gone quite cold. He'd remained still, unflinching as he stared into Étienne's eyes.

Daudet removed a cigar from a gold case. "That man plays a dangerous game."

"Yes," said the demimonde, "but it would not be wise to play against him."

"Am I to be frightened? As you must know, I am an excellent shot."

"Of course, but he's likely had much more practice. And killed many more men."

Ignoring Étienne's harrumph of indignation, Yvette considered the pearl handle derringer she kept discreetly in her purse.

She was rather good, too.

CHAPTER 17

Paris

The same evening

What had been an invigorating, beautiful day had become cold and heavy. November clouds brought a steady drizzle. Police investigator Gene Gustave peered through the streaked window of the café. Having to once again return to this onerous and thankless task had made him despondent. Moreover, he was angry with himself for having left his window seat to relieve himself and finding, upon his return, that his table was taken. Showing his police credentials, he eventually recovered his seat, but time had been lost and carriages had already arrived outside the salon. Now he had no idea of who might have arrived, and lowered visibility only hampered things more.

Perhaps, given the dire circumstances, he would simply have to insinuate himself within Chez d' Chantilly and make his observations on the spot. But, no. Any violation of orders would bring down the wrath of Chief Inspector Ambroise Arseneau, and there was little that was worth that. Thus, like the night before, Detective Gustave sipped on his café au lait, sank into his chair, and watched the cabs crowd up and discharge their fares.

***

The tinkle of a small silver bell gradually silenced the guests. Jack watched Oberst von Brandenburg, left hand steadying the heavy Prussian saber at his side, walk decisively to the front of the parlor and stand beside his wife. Putting the bell on an elegant side table, she nodded to Albrecht.

"*Mesdames et Messieurs*, Madame Couture and I wish to welcome you to an extraordinary performance this evening," said Brandenburg in a clipped German accent. "It is one which you will see nowhere else in Paris. You will find it mysterious and mystifying, a spellbinding journey back in time to an age of the gilded pharaohs and the hereafter they so desperately sought."

The two dozen guests glanced at one another with anticipation, then observed a table elegantly covered in black satin.

Brandenburg looked to Marguerite. "But my lovely wife is far more conversant in the study of the ancient world than I. So it is with great pleasure that I have her introduce our esteemed and honored performers."

Delicate applause followed. His florid face having acquired its theater mask, the oberst fixed Marguerite with what he seemed to consider an adoring smile.

Jack had found a vantage point on the curved staircase leading to the second floor. With interest mixed with suspicion, he crossed his arms and found himself amused at the susceptibility of the jaded beau monde.

Suddenly Yvette Maillard walked by. She smiled at him and proceeded down the hall to a door which she opened and then shut. From where he stood, Jack could hear raised voices, but his attention shifted to the floor below.

All but a few of the gas lamps were extinguished, resulting in a sepulchral dimness. It was as if a spell had been cast, and the audience appeared to hold its breath. A small candle-lit lantern glowed on the table, emitting a spectral light. Incense wafted through the parlor as a door opened from a darkened adjacent antechamber. Two servants wearing loose white gallibayas reverently carried a sarcophagus into the hushed room and placed it on the table next to several glass jars and statues of the gods Horus, Maat and Anubis. They went back into the antechamber, then reappeared carrying four alabaster canopic jars, each crested with the head of a different Egyptian deity.

From the corner of his eye, Jack glimpsed a maid in nondescript clothing as she emerged from the hallway and slipped into a parlor closet, leaving the door cracked open only an inch.

The servants slipped back into the antechamber. A moment later, a somber-looking Marcel entered the room carrying a small black bag. He was followed by an equally somber-looking man who wore a gallibaya and a jeweled jambiya held at the waist by a gold-knotted cord. They stood on each side of the sarcophagus in absolute silence. From the bag Marcel produced a pair of scissors and scalpels and made a show of examining them both before laying them gently upon the table.

"We are honored this evening with the presence of two distinguished gentlemen, each having great expertise in the arts, mysteries, and dark secrets of the ancient world," said Madame Couture in a susurrous voice.

"Monsieur Marcel, an academician of exceeding repute, committed years of research into the long-deceased worlds of Mesopotamia, including the fabled cities of Babylon, Sumer, and Thebes. He traveled extensively throughout the Near East and even ventured into the tombs of long ex-animate but not-forgotten pharaohs. Often, he discovered what the grave robbers of the distant past had not. Indeed, this very sarcophagus on view was extracted at great risk from such a tomb."

Her eyes swept the audience.

"And to assist Monsieur Cheval is the renowned historian and fellow Egyptologist Jabari Abraxas. The lineage of Monsieur Abraxas has been extensively and diligently explored, and it can be said that he is distantly related to the Ptolemys, perhaps even to Cleopatra, the last Pharaoh of Egypt. Jabari Abraxas will add his knowledge to that of our eminent Monsieur Cheval as the sarcophagus is opened and the mysteries of the ancients begin."

There was a scattering of applause as Marcel nodded to Jabari and removed the lid of the coffin. Once again, the two servants appeared and carried the heavy lid into the antechamber.

With great care, both Marcel and his accomplice lifted a mummified body from its crypt and laid it on the table as the servants emerged from the shadows and returned the sarcophagus to the adjoining room. Gasps and murmurs arose as Jabari raised the lantern and held it over the mummy. A few tattered ends of cloth fell away, and a stone scarab toppled out and fell onto the table. Marcel picked it up and, looking into his assistant's eyes, said, "A royal, for certain."

"Indeed," replied Abraxas, "this mummy is sacred and so very ancient. We must take care, monsieur, not to disturb the ba, for according to the ancients, this person has been admitted to the underworld by the god Horus."

With solemnity Marcel, palm upward, indicated the falcon-headed god through whom the pharaoh had ruled Egypt.

A door closed upstairs. Jack watched as two courtesans silently walked downstairs to the parlor. One angrily whispered something and the other said, "Be quiet!"

From his vantage point he could see Madame Couture glare at the two women before composing herself and turning back to the performance.

With exquisite deliberation, Marcel began the unwrapping. "I do believe that this is a female from the Old Kingdom," he said conspiratorially to Abraxas. "Undoubtedly we will find a gold scarab amulet over the heart to cover the embalmer's incision. Now I will unwrap the linen, of which there may well be hundreds of yards."

"You see those canopic jars on the table?" said Abraxas to the men and women peering through the dimness. "They contain the stomach, lungs, liver, and intestines. But one thing, the most important thing, is missing. What, my dear friends, might that be?"

There was deathly silence until one man whispered the correct organ.

"Yes," said Abraxas, "the heart! That remains inside the body, for only it might ensure passage to the underworld. But"—he raised his hand—"only if it is judged honorable. For this to happen it must be weighed against an ostrich feather, the one inserted in the headband of Maat, goddess of truth and justice. Standing before the god Horus and awaiting judgment, the supplicant is represented by the goddess, who will hopefully say, 'Her heart is true, she has not sinned against any god or goddess, nor has she told lies.' And then the supplicant will say, 'Hail to you, august, great, and potent god. May you grant that I be among the living.'"

With infinite patience, Marcel unwrapped linen, revealing scarabs in the shape of the dung beetle, symbol of rebirth. He examined each and laid it on a silver tray.

"Precious, so precious," he intoned, gently handing a scarab to a man in a silk top hat. Inspecting it closely, the incredulous guest passed it to the lady beside him, who held it tightly in her hand as if it would grant her the wisdom of the ancients.

"As written in the Book of the Dead," continued Jabari, "the mummification process took seventy days, and there were many, many steps, each of which had to be carried out with meticulous care. The ba, the very soul of the deceased, must return to the body and breathe life into it. Then the reincarnated being proclaims, 'I am alive. I am strong. I have awakened. My body will not be destroyed in this eternal land.'"

As the unwrapping continued, the funerary mask of the mummy came into view. That was followed by the exposed torso with hands crossed over the chest, imitating Osiris, god of the deceased.

"Look here," said Marcel, waving people even closer, "see the mask painted with bright colors, still vivid after thirty-five hundred years. Oh, how beautiful she might have been in life." He lifted the mask to reveal a scrawny skull, the mouth open in an eternal scream. On the side of the skull there appeared a great gash.

"She was murdered!" exclaimed a man over the gasps of fellow audience members, his hand over his eyes.

"Yes," said Marcel, "but that horror would demand even greater deference and adoration. Hence even the addition of more expensive offerings, all of which will be made available tonight."

A woman fainted, but others crowded closer as Marcel, his voice rising, held aloft a curved pick. "With this instrument the brain would have been pulled through the nostrils and discarded, since ancient Egyptians knew nothing of its value. And here—see this scar? Oil of cedar trees was injected into the stomach to preserve it forever."

"Indeed," said Jabari. "And observe that she holds in her gnarled hands wheat and peas, symbols of food for the afterlife. And so, the soul with its renewed life force would be rejoined with the ka, the person's double, the ba, and the ankh, the transfigured spirit that survives death and spends its days in the lofty presence of the gods."

Following those words, delivered with haunting cadence, the gas lamps were relit.

Madame Couture stepped forward and took a glass jar filled with dun-colored dust. "This is powder of the ancient peas and wheat, and it is known to have medicinal properties for populations today. In fact, if spooned moderately into tea or wine, it will provide excellent vitality. Indeed, I consume a measure of it daily. And though precious, it is available at an amazingly low price, just like the amulets and scarabs found with this mummy. But now, to conclude our performance, I should like to read from a poem entitled 'On a Bulbous Root,' written by the Englishman Martin Tupper. It proclaims the beneficence of this marvelous substance, this ancient powder!"

The audience listened raptly as Marguerite extended her palm to the mummy as if in homage and in a low voice recited:

"What, wide awake, sweet stranger, wide awake?
And laughing coyly at an English sun,
And blessing him with smiles for having thawed
Thine icy chain, for having woke thee gently
From thy long slumber of three thousand years?...

What emblem liker, or more eloquent
Of immortality... than this dry root,
So full of living promise? -- Yes, I see
Nature's 'resurgam' sculptured there in words
That all of every clime may run and read:
I see the better hope of better times,
Hope against hope, wrapp'd in the dusky coats

Of a poor leek,-- I note glad tidings there
Of happier things; this undecaying corpse
A little longer, yet a little longer
Must slumber on, but shall awake at last;
A little longer, yet a little longer,--
And at the trumpet's voice, shall this dry shape
Start up, instinct with life, the same though changed,
And put on incorruption's glorious garb!"

Applause followed as Marcel, Jabari, and Madame Couture bowed and shook hands all around. A number of men and women in the audience spoke earnestly to Madame Couture about the price of the artifacts, and money was passed. Marcel and Jabari exchanged pleased looks as everything but the canopic jars and mummy were purchased by the adoring crowd.

***

It had become horrifically frustrating for Inspector Gene Gustave. Already several of the guests at Chez Chantilly were standing outside awaiting their carriages. The rain had not abated, and as Gustave peered through the café's streaked window, all hope of learning anything was quickly slipping away. He clenched his hands. Something had to be done. Anybody who might have had contact with Monsieur Lapieux would likely be in the salon, and to do nothing but watch the egress of a possible assailant would be the height of folly.

He had to have something to report. Something substantial and praiseworthy that would elevate him in the eyes of the chief inspector. With sudden determination he rose, threw three francs on the table, and dashed into the rain. Horses pulling cabs reared up as he sprinted across the wide boulevard. Men shouted and stared at the disheveled inspector, tall and ungainly, as he tore past astonished guests.

***

Jack was about to descend the stairs when the sound of furious knocking assailed the front door. The footman opened it and an inspector rushed into the parlor, clothes sopping wet.

"Police business!" he shouted as the guests stared with frowns and consternation.

"Police business? What police business might you possibly have?" demanded Madame Couture who angrily pushed her way forward.

Water poured off the inspector's coat as he rose to his full height. "An in-incident," he stammered.

There was a moment of total silence.

"And exactly who are you?" asked Oberst von Brandenburg, who had just joined his wife.

"I am inspector Gene Gustave of the Prefecture of Po-police of the Île de la Cité. I-I am investigating the case of a Monsieur Jacquet Lapieux who frequented this salon. He was murdered and last seen here."

"I hardly remember such a man. Was he even a guest here?" said Madame Couture, turning to her husband.

"Once, perhaps twice, but what does that have to do with this salon? Surely he was not murdered here," protested the colonel.

Seemingly oblivious to the scene before him, Étienne Daudet marched up to Madame Couture. "Excuse me, but I have been looking all over for Yvette. Have you seen her?"

"I last saw her with you," replied the madame.

"Well, she must be here. She couldn't have left on her own, certainly not without telling me. I insist that she be found. I am becoming quite worried."

"Find her if you wish, monsieur," said Gustave, who seemed frustrated by the sudden interruption. "But I must question anyone and everyone who might have seen Monsieur Lapieux leave this es-establishment. It is quite possible that someone followed him. He was a very important man. Indeed, a relative of the empress."

"I see," said Brandenburg. "But that hardly implicates anyone here. More importantly, we must locate Mademoiselle Maillard. Something may have happened to her and you, sir, are an impediment just now."

From his position on the second floor, Jack noticed that Jabari Abraxas was peering intently at Gene Gustave and exchanging words with Marcel. But that seemed of little consequence as the anxiety and commotion in the parlor grew. Curious about the alleged murder, Jack descended the stairs and stood within a few feet of Gene Gustave.

Angry voices spilled out of the second-floor hall. "The police, and now this!" Madame Couture hissed.

"And just how was this monsieur actually murdered?" her husband asked.

"With a knife, a very unusual instrument. It was a-a most vicious attack."

Inspector Gustave's eyes roved over the perplexed crowd and alighted on Marcel and Jabari. "There! Those knives!" He pointed at the jambiya on Marcel's hip, then the jambiya on Jabari's. "Are they not the same type that—"

"Nonsense!" shouted Madame Couture. "Those men are performers, guests. They had nothing to do with this alleged murder. Monsieur Gustave, I demand that you leave this salon! You have no right to barge in here and—"

There was a sudden shout as Yvette Maillard ran down the stairs, a shoe flying after her. Seconds later Camille Lapin followed. Another shoe sailed past, just missing the demimonde. With a sudden leap, Lapin lunged for Maillard.

Daudet tried to intercept, but Brandenburg was in the way, and quite suddenly the ranting courtesan was lifted off her feet. Clutching one arm, Jack pulled it high behind her back, and Lapin screamed as she was thrown to the floor.

"Arrest her! Someone get a rope and tie her up," shouted Daudet as people scrambled out of the way.

"An arrest is for the local police," replied Gustave, who had barely glanced at the catfight between two courtesans. "I am here to investigate a *murder*." He glanced back at the spot where Marcel and Jabari had stood, then cursed. They were both gone.

The inspector turned and ran down the street, his coat flapping in the downpour.

Only a half dozen people remained as the parlor became quiet. Jack lifted the sobbing Lapin from the floor. Putting her hands to her face, she hurried to her room.

Mademoiselle Maillard held tightly to Daudet and turned to Jack. "I must thank you. That was very brave." The demimonde extended her hand, and Jack lightly kissed it.

"I am pleased to have been of help," said Jack as Daudet stared at him.

"Yes," said Madame Couture, "I think you kept the situation from getting worse. I want this entire calamity to be settled, and I will speak quite sternly to Camille in the morning. If and when she comes to her senses. And my dear Yvette, I hope that you are not injured."

"I am not," replied Maillard, "but I will not return as long as my sister is in this house."

"Most assuredly, I believe it is time to go," said Daudet, his arm around Yvette as if claiming her as his possession.

Madam Couture looked about the disheveled room. "I do not see Monsieur Marcel or Monsieur Abraxas." She turned to Jack. "Do you know why they might have left or where they have gone? The mummy must be disposed of and the canopic jars put away. Neither I nor the servants are responsible for that."

"I have no idea where they might have gone, or why," said Jack. "I don't even know where my brother or his assistant lives. But I do think this was all a charade, and I suspect that your guests bought some very worthless baubles."

That said, Jack Volant walked past Madame Couture and closed the door behind him.

CHAPTER 18

Paris

The same night

Dashing out of the salon's backdoor, Abraxas disappeared into the shadows. Marcel attempted to follow, but Jabari turned and hissed, "Go back. Get away from me."

Perplexed, and worried, Marcel hailed an omnibus and sat inside the lumbering vehicle. He stared out the rain-streaked window as the four horses pulled the conveyance down the street. For a brief moment he glimpsed inspector Gene Gustave racing along the sidewalk, his cadaverous figure bent against the wind. The detective stopped at a street corner and peered into the gloom, studying each cab as it passed in the sallow light of the gas lamps.

Why did I run? thought Marcel, suddenly angry. Questions swirled in his head. Apparently there were things he didn't know about his assistant. Something was wrong, terribly wrong, and now, having run from the salon, he might be a suspect in someone else's crime.

What did Marcel know about Abraxas? Only what the man had told him. He'd hinted that he had taken part in the failed war against France. He'd alluded to being a fugitive and wanted for the murder of a French officer who had raped a woman. In addition, he'd said that for over ten years he had trafficked in exotic goods between Egypt and France. The war between Algeria and France had taken place two decades earlier, and, despite all his years in Paris, Jabari always seemed wary, avoiding government officialdom at all costs.

Still, Marcel was surprised that Jabari had recognized the inspector and bolted through a back door, disappearing with hardly a word. More disconcerting, Marcel had no idea whether or not he'd ever see the man again—they only met at the salon. And if Abraxas failed to show for the next performance, then a credible element of the act would be irretrievably gone. There was no one to replace him.

Another thought occurred to Marcel. Now that he'd run from the salon, would the detective be waiting if he returned? And if he didn't return, what would become of his enterprise? What would become of him?

No, he thought, going back would silence any suggestion of complicity in whatever crime might be leveled against him. And as for running, well, he would think of a plausible excuse.

But all that would be left for morning when he went to the salon to gather up the few relics he had stored in the anteroom. He breathed deeply. The next hours would be far more pleasant.

She would be there waiting for him, petulant if he arrived too early, for there were always "arrangements" she had to make before he came. Secrets, ever more secrets. Of course, he had some of his own, some that she was not privy to. Everyone did. But hers ...?

Yes, he thought, he would run his fingers through her long brown hair and feel the warmth of her young body. A terribly jealous girl of nineteen, a grisette, almost always wearing her gray worker's clothes, she could, if she chose to, be so very soothing. And that was something he desired on this unsettling night.

Two transfers later, Marcel alighted and walked to the Place Pigalle, the public square between the eighteenth and ninth arrondissements at the foot of Montmartre. Gas lamps glowed, and nightclubs and cafés still catered to late revelers. It was here on the Rue Pigalle that so many artists lived in their cramped ateliers.

But that was not Marcel's destination. Warily, he hurried as he neared the Rue Saint-Denis, a crime-infested, rundown patch of tenements where one could rent dilapidated rooms in the semi-industrialized neighborhood. Here the death rate soared from disease amongst the teeming population. They were the poor, living off theft and prostitution, largely displaced by Haussmann's demolition of their former housing.

It was in a one-room hovel that Jeanne Virot lived in at night and escaped from by day. It was also the one that Marcel ventured to when other women were not available.

Virot never asked him for money as she did other men. He'd offered to find her new and far better accommodations, but she'd refused. None of her other assignations ever occurred in this blemished part of the city. She knew in exactly which lonely parks and darkly lit cafés she would find vulnerable men for her nighttime endeavors.

With her slender figure, piercing dark eyes, and exotic looks, she had no difficulty attracting those who'd pay ten or even fifteen sous in an out-of-the-way cheap hotel for an hour of pleasure. Somehow she'd always escaped the police raids that would result in women arrested and transported to Saint-Lazare while their male clients were released with little more than an admonishment. And she never registered with the Prefecture of Police as did five thousand other prostitutes —only a fraction of the one hundred twenty thousand *filles insoumises*, "unruly women," who operated out of one hundred ninety legal brothels or walked the Rue Breda seeking desperate men.

Those men were a matter of survival. It was Marcel she truly adored, for he treated her kindly, not like the others who used her, then slinked away before dawn.

It had begun with a chance meeting years earlier. Though Marcel enjoyed the finest salons that wealthy women frequented, there was a darker thrill that he enjoyed in the late hours of the night. In dimly lit cafés he found destitute young women who lived on the grimy edge of existence. No haughty intellectual talk, no grand impressions needed to be made with them. The promise of less than a franc would lead to an hour or more of thrill devoid of any commitment.

But this girl seemed different than the others, most of whom had vacant eyes and emaciated bodies. In this one a fire raged. There was an intensity in her burning eyes. He could only guess what thoughts swirled in her mind. He was drawn to her and, following those moments of rabid lust, offered to take her away, to buy her fine clothes and introduce her to society. But she would have none of it. They spoke little, but it became evident that the world in which he existed could never be hers.

"Alien, a hypocritical fabrication," she said. "Horrifically false and not of the people. Not the real people of Paris."

He was tempted to say, "You can live with me on the Rue de Turbigo, a nice neighborhood in the third arrondissement. I'll take care of you."

But he knew it would never work. There were things she did. Things she did not want to tell him. And in truth, although he hungered for her more than any other, he had to have others. He always did.

He wouldn't debate it with her as, eyes blazing, she described a vacuous, indolent society living like a leech upon the backs of others. Someday, she insisted, they would be extinguished in a rampage of blood and carnage.

Marcel had shuddered. He wondered how such violent ideas could, like a cancer, flourish in a girl of seventeen. The overthrow of society, the regime, so enormous. It was the fantasy flung about by students and the underclass. And yet ...

There were nights when she held onto him so tightly that he could hardly breathe. Was it out of desperation or desire?

"Are there others? Other women? I hope not, I truly do. I am a possessive woman, very possessive," she'd said during their last encounter, her eyes so intense that he had to look away. Of course, she knew there were.

"But I've seen you in the cafés with other men."

"I don't ask for money from you, but I have to live. They mean nothing to me. Those men, married men, are maggots," she hissed. "They are the bourgeoisie, the ones who will be drowned in the Seine when it turns to blood."

"You are dangerous," said Marcel, pushing deep inside her.

"As a woman must be," she said. Her moans filled the tiny room.

But that was a week ago. Now there was no answer when he knocked on the door. Perhaps she was still involved with some "client" or an "arrangement" somewhere else. She had let him know that, in her case, the term "arrangement" had nothing to do with sex, but she would not allude to what it might be.

Upon first meeting with Marcel she had placed a key to the ancient door behind a loose brick. Now it was gone. Did she not want him to come? Perhaps he might wait for her to emerge from the one-room flat or come stealthily along the crooked lane not more than four or five feet wide. She knew these alleys, these dank passages, as well as the others who existed here. In fact, she was admired and treated with great courtesy, and not for her sexual favors. No one here could afford those. There was another reason—but, again, what that might be eluded him.

It was too dangerous in his elegant upper-class finery, complete with cape and top hat, to dally here. He knocked again, though not too hard. People listened and guarded this neighborhood. There was a code here, there were rules. He glanced about, saw suspicious shapes in the gloom, and hastened back toward the Pigalle.

***

Cold, wet, and dejected, Gene Gustave returned to the Café Martinique, across from Chez d' Chantilly, where the proprietor allowed him to get a few hours of sleep above the café. Gustave had weighed the prospect of returning to the police prefecture to announce his sighting of the Algerian, but that, he concluded, would be senseless since the man had fled. He could be anywhere in Paris or even on his way to Le Havre.

It had been over twenty years, and age would have changed his appearance, but Gustave had immediately recognized the man, and it was obvious that Jabari had recognized him. That he'd so easily escaped would, in the eyes of the chief inspector, only further diminish Gustave's dubious reputation.

Gustave would return to the salon in the morning and question Madam Couture and her husband, the Prussian colonel. He let out a long sigh before drifting into a fitful sleep.

***

The wind and rain kept up all night. A window shutter slammed again, waking Marguerite Couture. She turned over in the bed. "Albrecht, you must do something about that. It's most disturbing."

"I'll have a servant attend to it in the morning. The wind will subside. Go back to sleep."

But the wind turned into a gale and howled even louder. Infuriated with her husband's indifference, Marguerite rose and climbed to the third floor, where Eliza slept, and secured the shutter. Noticing lamplight from under the maid's door, she stopped. It was very late, and Eliza always went to bed as soon as her chores were done. Why she was still up puzzled Madame Couture, but the desire for sleep outweighed all else.

Once in bed, however, sleep eluded her. She petulantly lay next to her corpulent husband who, angered after being once again awakened, mumbled that he should return to Prussia where he maintained a country house complete with servants and a teenage courtesan.

Theirs had been a marriage of convenience, like so many others in Paris. She, a one-time lissette, a girl from a struggling family in Bordeaux, came to Paris at the age of twenty to escape the boredom of farm life. And, like so many young women with no city skills, she'd turned to prostitution. She had been attractive then, a busty woman with an hourglass figure and an enticing personality. Having established herself, she morphed into what Parisians called a cocotte, a higher-class courtesan. She drifted cunningly and seamlessly from one notable man to another before enticing the wealthy and once handsome Prussian oberst.

Brandenburg, with his Junker entitlements and aristocratic lineage, had risen quickly in the ranks of the Prussian army. But he'd decided to engage in the very lucrative business of supplying absinthe, the green liquor and poisonous addiction. Its largest market was Paris. But, being Prussian, he required the association of influential men of French nationality. He shunned cafés as too pedestrian; thus, the acquisition of a salon and an attractive woman became a priority.

In the beginning he and Marguerite enjoyed an intimate relationship, but that was long past. Now, at best, they tolerated one another, though none of their guests would have guessed.

Marguerite stared into the darkness, contemplating one fear after another. How would the intrusion of the disgusting investigator and its repercussions affect the popularity of her house? What strangeness had taken place with Marcel and Jabari Abraxas? Never before had they left without offering effusive appreciation. Had their disconcertingly abrupt departure to do with the murder, or the fakery? And then there was that American, the brother of Marcel. He was a strange one. Perhaps one she would not want to cross.

Tomorrow she'd settle everything to her satisfaction. She always did. But still, the murder rankled. After all, Monsieur Lapieux had been a very wealthy patron, a man with whom she had dallied and conspired, for there had been money to be made. His death and its subsequent investigation were threads being pulled from a complex tapestry. What else the inspector might find was unsettling indeed.

Closing the shutter did nothing to mitigate the storm. The branches of a tree tapped like a bony finger against the window and, adding to her disgust, there were angry noises in a room down the hall, the one rented by Camille Lapin. They were followed by a startled cry, the footsteps of somebody running, and another set of footsteps seconds later. There was a gasp as both sets rushed down the stairs, and a soft crack like the breaking of a small branch. Then all was silent.

A chill ran through Marguerite.

"Husband, something has happened," she said, shaking Brandenburg. "I heard a cry, then footsteps and another sound. We should go downstairs. I think it's serious."

"You've had this nightmare before—a storm, someone running, a shooting. You told me so. That's all it is. Too many mummies, too much absinthe. Don't wake me anymore. I was having a delicious dream, not a nightmare. For God's sake, don't wake me again!"

She sighed. Perhaps he was right; she had finally been drifting off. It was still quite dark, in any case, and there was nothing to be done until morning.

She lay back down, eyes open wide. Surely something had happened, but it wouldn't do to anger the oberst. He had a temper, and she could not forget the stinging slap that had ensued when she had last defied him. She became ever more determined to evict the young courtesan, Camille Lapin, the sister of the exquisite demimonde.

Though not as attractive nor engaging as Maillard, Lapin had to be enticing in bed. Monsieur Marcel spent many evenings with her. And yet, she was obviously jealous of Maillard. The two women argued continuously. Marguerite suspected it was over money and choice of men as well as status.

It was Yvette Maillard who, during a visitation to the salon months earlier, had asked Couture to take Camille in and rent her a room. Of course, Marguerite had agreed to the demimonde's request. Not to have done so would have been a slight, resulting in the loss of a highly desired guest who always left a heady donation following a performance.

The arrangement with Camille was only to be temporary, but the courtesan found patrons in the salon and gave Marguerite half the money she earned. Be that as it may, such a row could never be repeated. Yvette must be assured that her sister was persona non grata. Yes, thought

Marguerite, that would be the morning's first order of business.

Having made her decision, she closed her eyes and descended into a fitful slumber.

***

By seven in the morning, the night's downpour had abated, the rain turning into a cold mist. Inspector Gustave washed his face and went downstairs to the café, now filling with its usual morning customers. He looked through streaked windows and saw the milkwomen with their horse-drawn wagons set up their tables, cups, and saucers under a *porte cochère*. No Parisian would want to prepare food at home if they didn't have to, and seven was the hour when businessmen populated the streets and cafés. Had the milkwoman been here last night he would have questioned her; they were the repository of all gossip on the street.

But Gustave, his clothes wrinkled and damp, was totally unprepared for the sudden appearance of Chief Inspector Ambroise Arseneau. The portly man, his white beard set against a dark coat over his pronounced belly, emerged from a cab and strutted in, his small hooded eyes alighting on Gustave.

"Well," he said with an accusing tone, "what have you discovered? I expected a report by now. And why do you appear so slovenly? That is disgraceful. You are an officer of the constabulary. We must retain our comportment regardless of the hour or circumstances, Monsieur Gustave."

If Arseneau expected Gustave to be contrite and apologetic, he was entirely mistaken. Bitter and insulted, he rose to his full height, nearly two feet over the chief inspector.

"Monsieur, I am nearly sleepless from watching that house. I have been soaked chasing an Algerian fugitive, a murderer, I ha-have diligently tried to carry out an investigation in that sa-salon according to your orders. If I have been unsuccessful it has not been for lack of trying. And if that isn't good enough, I offer you my badge and—"

He suddenly stopped and stared out the window. A high-wheeled carriage halted in front of the salon. The man who had been conversing with the Algerian last night exited the vehicle, tied the horse to a hitching post, and quickly entered.

A moment later, another carriage stopped in front of Chez Chantilly. One of the women who'd interrupted Gustave's investigation with their fighting, disembarked. As they walked up the steps, a dowdy older maid ran out of the house screaming incoherently. She was followed by Daudet. The demimonde stopped abruptly, and the maid pointed to the open door. Sobbing uncontrollably, she blurted, "In there! Mon Dieu, in there!"

Gene Gustave swept past the chief inspector and dashed across the street. "Police! Don't go anywhere," he shouted to the maid as he followed Daudet and his companion into the salon.

Madame Couture hurried down the stairs wearing only a bathrobe, her husband following moments later. Bursting in, Gustave came to an immediate halt and stared at the bloody corpse sprawled across the Persian carpet.

The demimonde screamed and looked away while Marcel bent to touch the body.

"Stand back—no one touch her!" shouted Ambroise Arseneau. He turned to Gustave. "Have you questioned anybody here before?"

"Oui, Monsieur Inspector. I was here last night."

"And you saw these same people?"

"Indeed I did. But there was another man, the Algerian who—"

"Where is he?"

"I don't know. He ran from here."

"Very well, we will find him." Arseneau said. "Bring that maid back in here. She is most assuredly part of this." He turned his attention to those staring at the corpse. "Everyone here is under investigation. No one is innocent until I say so. You are all suspects in this murder."

"Monsieur Inspector, I am Marguerite Couture and this is my husband, Oberst Albrecht von Brandenburg. We are shocked, absolutely shocked over this horrible incident, but we have nothing to do with this—"

"This is your salon and I know precisely who you are, madame. What I want to know is the name of this young lady —and who killed her."

"Of course," said Colonel Badenburg. "She was a courtesan who rented a room."

"And her name?" demanded the chief inspector.

In just over a whisper, Madame Couture said, "Her name, monsieur, is Lapin. Camille Lapin."

CHAPTER 19

Paris
The following day

"I saw you here last night and I witnessed you darting out of the salon," said Inspector Gustave, singling out Marcel. "You knew that you were to remain and yet you ran. I have good reason to arrest you!"

"I had nothing to do with the murder. I left only to learn why Monsieur Abraxas departed so quickly."

"His name is not Abraxas. It is Mustafa Hakim, and he is a criminal and a felon. He murdered a Frenchman in Algeria during the war."

"He said that the man was a rapist and deserved to die," said Marcel. "And besides, it was a very long time ago."

"The man is still dead!" replied Gustave. "If indeed there was a rape, it is a matter for French justice. Not Hakim, whose escape you have abetted."

"This is insane," said Madame Couture. "Monsieur Abraxas, or whatever his name is, had nothing to do with the murder of Mademoiselle Lapin."

Gustave knelt by Lapin's body and examined her head and torso. He rose, glaring at Marcel.

"This murdered woman," said Gustave, "was killed with a knife like the one carried by your assistant. So, you, monsieur, are a coconspirator."

"It isn't unthinkable," said Oberst von Brandenburg. "Perhaps Monsieur Abraxas desired her favors and was turned down. Certainly he did not have enough money, and being an Algerian, well ..."

"He remains a suspect and, according to Inspector Gustave, is a fugitive." Arseneau took out a notebook and began writing in it.

Étienne Daudet peered over Arseneau's shoulder. "You're writing all our names? Surely you know who I am."

"Of course I do, but one's place in society is not an automatic exoneration and this is a most heinous crime," responded Arseneau. "It is not unheard of that popular people—indeed, famous people—perpetrate such acts while assuming that their status places them beyond suspicion."

"This is preposterous," said Daudet, who looked as though he might be about to have a stroke. "I am completely innocent of the murder and my credentials are impeccable. I am the best known artist in all of France. Even the emperor anxiously awaits the completion of my paintings."

"That is of little concern in this matter," said Inspector Gustave. "What does concern us is where you were last night after the salon closed."

"I escorted mademoiselle back to my estate, then went to the Café de la Nouvelle Athènes on Place Pigalle. I do a great deal of business there."

"And at what hour did you leave the café?" asked Gustave.

"Around midnight. Then I went directly home."

"And the mademoiselle was there, perhaps waiting for you?"

"Indeed she was."

"And she had been asleep since you'd taken her to your estate?"

"Of course. At least I presume so. She was very tired, it being a long day."

"I don't understand this line of questioning," said Brandenburg. "What has it to do with Mademoiselle Maillard?"

"That is what I intend to find out. Perhaps they detested one another, both competing for the same man. Then an argument, a prelude to murder."

"That is rubbish! Mademoiselle is hardly a murderer. I doubt that she even has a gun," said Daudet.

Arseneau gave Yvette a hard glance. "Mademoiselle, you were about to say something?"

"No, Monsieur Inspector. Except that it was a terribly stormy night and I was glad to be indoors. And, of course, I would not think of perpetrating such a heinous crime. My heart goes out to my half sister. She was a wonderful and loving person."

"So you say," said Arseneau, his ferret-like eyes again boring into Yvette.

"Madame Couture," said Gustave, "this incident must have occurred last night or very early this morning. Surely you must have heard something. A scream, people running, perhaps a shot?"

"I heard footsteps going past my room, but there was the storm. I might have heard other sounds, but I was half asleep and may have confused them with a dream. My husband says that I often have very disturbing dreams, even nightmares. So I cannot tell you what I really heard."

"Very well," said Gustave, once again kneeling over the body of Lapin and inspecting the wounds. "But this is most strange, something I do not understand. Her throat was slashed with a knife, and then she was shot. Apparently the knife attack did not kill her, but she had to have been seriously wounded. Why wouldn't the murderer simply employ the knife again? Surely another swipe and mademoiselle would have died."

"The question then," said Le Terrier, "is did the gun belong to the same person as the owner of the knife? If not, there had to be more than one assailant."

Arseneau turned to Marguerite Couture. "You think you heard footsteps hurrying down the hall. Did you hear a second person?"

"No, monsieur. I heard a hard tap and thought it to be a branch hitting the window, but then everything became quiet."

"Very peculiar," said Arseneau. "I would think that you would have investigated it, but, as you say, you might have perceived it as a nightmare, or an occurrence during a violent storm."

"Perhaps, but the reappearance here of Monsieur Daudet and mademoiselle does interest me," said Gustave, addressing the artist. "Just why have you both suddenly returned to the scene of the crime? It is most suspicious, is it not?"

"We did not return here to observe a murdered woman," retorted Daudet. "Neither of us had any knowledge of this. No, monsieur, I came here because of a crime perpetrated against me. Last night I was robbed. A pickpocket snatched my wallet during the performance, and I returned hoping that Madame Couture might know something about it."

"I do indeed," she said enthusiastically. "My servant found your wallet in the closet in a corner of the salon. I saw your *carte de visite* in it and was going to return it to you this morning. I have it in my bedroom and shall retrieve it. I'm sure the inspector will not object."

Arseneau didn't. A minute later the portly woman wobbled back down the stairs. "Here, Monsieur Daudet. At least we have solved that problem."

Daudet accepted the wallet and glanced inside. His brows knitted. "Gone! Nearly all the money is gone. Over one hundred and fifty francs! Madame, you have allowed a thief to enter your salon. The security of your house is your responsibility, and I require restitution. Yes," he said petulantly, looking at Arseneau for approval, "I do believe, madame, that you owe me one hundred and fifty francs."

"Surely you do not think that—"

"Enough!" said Arseneau.

Hunched and standing in the shadows, Eliza began to slip away as all eyes turned on her.

"Stop! You will remain here," said Gustave, grabbing the woman by her sleeve.

"I was just going to bring some tea," she remonstrated.

"I, too, want to know who she is," said Inspector Arseneau.

"My housemaid," said Madame Couture. "I doubt that she is in any way involved."

"Nonsense! That woman may well be the thief; she was trying to get away. I suspected her from the beginning." Brandenburg turned to his wife. "I told you to get rid of her. For all we know, she may have murdered Camille Lapin."

"I stole nothing and I did not murder the mademoiselle!" shrieked Eliza. "I did not. I did not!" Tears flowed down her ruddy cheeks.

"Check her room!" demanded Daudet. "That is where she has my money. I'm sure of it."

"The theft of your money is assuredly a crime," said Inspector Arseneau, annoyance creeping into his voice, "but Mademoiselle Lapin's death is of far greater importance."

"My money is my most important concern, not this dead woman. If you will not check her room, I will," Daudet said, his voice rising.

"I will do it," said Madame Couture, ascending the stairs quickly.

"Oh!" came her shout from the second floor. "It's here. The money is here!"

With a burst of energy, Daudet raced up the stairs as Madame Couture reappeared, money in hand.

Eliza Breton cringed as Desvaux spun around to face her. "You are under arrest!"

Daudet took the francs that Marguerite held out and counted the money. "Yes, it's here, madame." With a slight nod of contrition he added, "Perhaps I owe you an apology. I have been out of sorts for a while."

Now Madame Couture faced Eliza. "Why did you take that man's money?"

"I didn't take it all. No, no, and I am so sorry, but my granddaughter is ill, so ill. I only wanted the money for her, to pay the nurse and the doctor. I swear, it wasn't for me."

"It's still theft!" responded Daudet. "And that's capital punishment. The guillotine for sure."

"No!" shouted Eliza. I only—"

"Enough," Arseneau said for the second time that morning. "Madame Couture, you said that your maid could not have been involved, but servants know everything that takes place in a salon. Three people were involved in the murder of Mademoiselle Lapin. She was likely assaulted by two others, and one was probably not in this house prior to the murder."

"Which means that someone was allowed in during the night," said Daudet, pointing to Eliza.

"Were you awake? Was it you who unlocked the door?" said Desvaux.

"I did nothing!" said Eliza. "I was asleep—I was, I was."

"I don't believe her," said Brandenburg. "She must have opened the door and allowed someone in. And she did kitchen work, she had access to knives. Certainly, she was also one of the murderers. So there you have it, Monsieur Arseneau. Now you must find the one with the gun. I assure you, it is none of us here."

"That is a matter for further investigation," said the chief inspector.

Mademoiselle Maillard sat on a sofa. "I cannot believe Camille is really dead. Oh, how terrible. How utterly terrible."

Inspector Arseneau looked at her with curiosity. "Mademoiselle, may I ask, what sort of relationship had you with the deceased? I presume that you two argued last night."

"As Madame Couture knows, Camille and I had a contentious relationship since adolescence, but that does not mean I cared nothing for her. Quite the contrary, it was I who suggested that Madame Couture allow her to live here."

Yvette took a deep breath. "We shared the same mother but had different fathers. We were quite poor. My father was very handsome and hers was not. Hence, our appearances differed, as did our efforts to rise from our lowly status. I did all I could to employ my social and intellectual skills and, through those efforts, had the good fortune to meet Monsieur Daudet, a man of great distinction. Camille, always envious, was willful and promiscuous. I hesitate to say this, but she always thought that I owed her a great deal due to my position in society. I gave her money, but she insisted that it was never enough. In many ways I despised her, yet I felt sorry for her.

"I am truly saddened that she has died. But I had nothing to do with that, Inspector. You must believe me."

The chief inspector said nothing. Yvette attempted an ingratiating smile, perhaps hoping to charm him with her beautiful looks and mournful eyes, but such beguiling efforts were wasted on Ambroise Arseneau. He had little use for women, attractive or not. His dwarfish stature, paunch, and abruptness never gained him any truck with the fairer sex and, though he cast an eye every once and a while, the female of the species was of no value to him.

Turning his attention to Marcel, he said, "When was the last time you saw Mademoiselle Lapin alive?"

"Last night, before my performance. We spent about an hour together. We had a most pleasant conversation."

"A conversation? As in what the Japanese call 'pillow talk,' perhaps?" said Arseneau. "And following your performance, did you not see her again that night?"

"Not until she attacked Mademoiselle Maillard in the presence of Inspector Gustave."

"And you sought Mademoiselle Lapin's favors often?"

Marcel shrugged. "On occasions when I performed here, perhaps once or twice a month."

"Did you ever argue about money, payment for, should I say, services rendered?"

"Of course not. I always paid her what she wanted. And I was only one of her many suitors."

Ambroise Arseneau was silent for a moment, then knelt beside the corpse.

"There are three mysteries we must clear up," he said, examining the bullet's entry hole. "The first concerns the motive of the murderer. Why kill this woman? Was it over money or was it jealousy? Second is the matter of the weapons. Where are they and who owned them? And third, when and how did the assailant gain entry to the salon?"

"Madame Couture," said Inspector Gustave, "do you check your doors at night? They are locked, are they not?"

"Of course they're locked. I check them myself."

"In that case, I think we can establish that your maid let the killer in," said Arseneau.

"Unless Mademoiselle Lapin did it herself, thinking that perhaps it was another client," said Gustave.

"I don't think she would have," said Marcel. "She was extremely tired when I last saw her, and she said that she did not care to see anyone else that night. In fact, she admitted that she expected no visitors for perhaps two days."

"If that is truly the case," said Arseneau, "then there is only one other possibility, though she might have had accomplices."

He turned to Eliza Breton. "Mademoiselle Breton, I charge you as an accomplice to the murder of Camille Lapin."

Eliza sank to her knees. "She said she just wanted to speak to Mademoiselle Lapin. She said it was terribly important, a matter of life and death. She seemed so sweet, and—"

"Then you admit your guilt. Very well, who is the woman you allowed in?" demanded Arseneau.

"I don't know her name. I was woken up by the wind and heard a tapping at the front of the house. It sounded like twigs or branches, so I went down and looked through the window. She seemed sort of frantic, the storm and all. I let her in, and she told me to go to my room and stay there. She gave me five francs. I did as she said and—"

"Did you see a weapon?" said Gustave, peering into the old woman's eyes.

"No, monsieur, I did not."

"And you did not think it strange that she told you to go to your room and not come out?" said Arseneau.

"I—I just did what I was told. I always do what I am told."

"But surely you heard screams when Camille was killed," said Brandenburg. "Why didn't you alert Madame Couture or myself?"

"Because I was scared. I knew that I had done something wrong. I was shaking so, and I pulled the covers over my head and cried. I just cried."

Chief Inspector Arseneau sighed. "Inspector Gustave, take her away."

Turning to the stunned audience, Arseneau said, "This investigation is not finished. We have no motive as yet, and one of the assailants had a weapon of Near Eastern or Arab origin. How the murderer got that weapon, one not easily found in Paris, is yet to be determined. Until then, no one here is innocent. None of you will leave Paris until this is resolved."

CHAPTER 20

Paris

Two days later

"Oh, Lord, it's that damnyankee! Where did I put my gun?" blurted Gabriel Shelby, putting down his pen and rising to his feet.

"I told you at least fifty times, Shelby, 'damn Yankee' is two words, and the last time I saw your gun, it was in the hand attached to the arm I shot off," said Jack Volant, both hands on his hips.

Startled readers in Galignani's raised their heads as the two men stared at each other for a pregnant moment. With a laugh, Shelby turned to the patrons. "Well, folks, I shot him, too. And now here he is, grinning like a possum eatin' a sweet tater."

His audience, mostly American, laughed nervously.

Narrow and crammed with books, William Galignani's bookstore had opened in 1800, but the family printing business extended back to the early sixteenth century. It was the biggest English-language paper in Europe and possibly the first to use the printing press. With arched columns on its exterior, it resided on the elite Rue de Rivoli across from the Jardin des Tuileries. Now, as a noted journalist, Shelby could be found there virtually every day of the week.

"Well, Jack, now that we got past that drama, join me for coffee and tell me your woes." Shelby threw his one arm around Volant.

"Good to see you, Shelby," said Jack, drawing up a chair and glancing at his friend's scribbled sentences.

"Finally came to Paris, but I see you're alone. What happened to the sweet lady who brought you back to sanity?" said Shelby after ordering coffee.

"It's another chapter in the sad story of my life. I confessed that I wanted to be an artist, and her father said that Clementine would not live in poverty. But if I ever came to my senses before she found someone else, he wouldn't stand in the way."

"So, you didn't come to your senses and you left the little angel at the pier while you sailed off. My, my, my. I always suspected that you would show up, and, despite your error of judgement, I'm glad you're here."

Jack looked about. "So, this is your place of employment?"

Shelby nodded. "*The Messenger* is very popular with Americans, and sooner or later almost every one of them comes here. I get news of the States via telegraph, and I also delve into anything of interest in Paris as well as the rest of Europe. Most Americans speak atrocious French, and the French don't speak English. That makes my writing a valuable commodity for people from the States."

"What about censorship? Steven—or should I say, Marcel?—told me that the French government watches everything." Jack watched as an omnibus pulled up and several people speaking English disembarked.

"For sure, spies are everywhere, but Louis Napoleon isn't concerned about an American paper. And the French aren't interested in what goes on in the US except years ago during the damnyankee war."

"I think it's called the Civil War, Shelby, and that was over four years ago."

"Regretfully, not for the South. As Sam Clemens said, 'In the South the war is what AD is elsewhere: they date from it.'"

"I guess that's true. But still, I've always been surprised that the French didn't support the Union," said Jack, sipping his coffee.

"Well, they did not. Oh, they didn't cotton to slavery, though they had their own in the Caribbean for years, but when the Confederate raider *Alabama* fought the *Kearsarge* off Cherbourg, all France cheered for the rebs. The newspaper *Constitutionnel* said that there was profound regret when the *Alabama* went down. My friend Manet painted a picture of the battle. Not a bad piece of work."

"Maybe I'll see it someday."

"Nah. No one will buy it. With twenty thousand painters, art is a tough business here."

"But it's worth a try," said Jack. "So, you cover politics, art, fashions, and the like. That's quite a bit."

"Scandals, murders, and entertainment, too, which, interestingly enough, includes your brother and his little problem."

"It's that big a story?"

"Sure 'nuff," said Shelby. "In fact, I'm writing about it now."

"Care to tell me what you learned?" Jack glanced at the scribbled words on Shelby's pad.

"Well, things have developed rather quickly. When I heard about it yesterday evening, I hurried over to the salon where Marcel performs. The police were there, and they said the place is closed until the investigation is concluded. A number of people, including your brother, are considered suspects."

"For what?" asked Jack, remembering the argument between the two women.

"For the murder of Camille Lapin, the courtesan, on the night following Marcel's performance."

Jack was stunned. "I was supposed to meet Marcel at the Café Guerbois yesterday morning, but he didn't show up. I have no idea where he lives, he was quite vague about it."

"I think somewhere on the Rue de Turbigo, I don't know exactly where. He's rather elusive and I can see why, his sort of business and all. I suspect that he may have gone into hiding. The police may consider him a suspect, though I personally doubt his involvement. But this is not going to be easy for him. There have been three prominent murders, very bloody murders, in just a few weeks, and the investigators and the government are worried. Especially the chief inspector."

"Does he suspect me? I was there that night."

"Why would he? You just got to Paris and surely had no involvement with Camille Lapin."

"I only saw her the one time." Jack thought for a moment. "As I said, I don't know where Marcel went after the flare-up, but I doubt it was back to the salon to carry out a murder. He has no qualms about seducing women, especially married women, but he's no murderer." Jack sighed. "I don't know how to help him if he doesn't contact me."

"Right now, there's not much you can do. I think he'll surface eventually, but you came here for a specific purpose and, until Marcel shows up, I recommend that you pursue your own agenda."

"There was an artist at the salon named Étienne Daudet. Do you know him?"

"Of course, everyone in France knows Daudet. I interviewed him once—a real pompous ass. He has a demimonde who swoons over him. Rather pitiful. He was there, huh?"

"With his woman. I'd seen her earlier at the Bois de Boulogne. The lady is exquisite, and I foolishly suggested that I do a portrait of her. Daudet upbraided me for considering that she would even think of it. He was quite rude. He said that if I want to be an artist, I have to study painting here. But the only place I've heard of is the École des Beaux Arts."

"Manet says it's a worthless place. No one learns to paint there. They only teach geometry."

"Painting, monsieur? If you want to paint, you just paint!"

A strongly built man with a full beard and receding hair, golden in the morning's sun, strutted to Jack and Gabriel's table. Gripping a polished wooden cane in one hand while holding a top hat in the other, he peered at Jack, placed his hat on the table, and thrust out a hand. "Édouard Manet."

"I have heard of you, though I regret that I haven't seen your work," said Jack, shaking his hand and resisting the temptation to back away. Manet smelled as though he rarely bathed.

"He did a silly painting called *Le Déjeuner sur l'herbe*," said Shelby, glancing up from his writing. "A nude woman having lunch on the grass between two completely dressed men. What a ridiculous idea, Manet."

"I'm sure it's a fine piece of work," countered Jack, intrigued by the artist whose work had been scorned by society and the Salon.

"See," said Manet, "this man would know great art when he sees it. So, you want to learn the fine points of painting? You can practice at the Beaux Arts and copy the works of Raphael and Delacroix at the Louvre, but no one who studies there ever becomes famous or even mildly successful."

"That's true," said Shelby. "They remain penniless failures. As we say in the great commonwealth of Virginny, 'They're so poor, they can't afford to pay attention.' But the only thing Édouard's really good at is strutting about and impressing the ladies. They fawn over him like some Roman god."

Manet shrugged. "Adonis, for sure. They simply can't help it, and most fortunately there is no known cure."

Shelby rolled his eyes and went back to his writing.

A troop of cavalry passed. "They would make a fine subject, perhaps in a different setting," said Jack.

"Daudet paints heroic subjects. I paint ragpickers. Though I also did a portrait of Émile Zola, the writer. Of course, nearly all my works are rejected at the Salon." Manet shrugged. "The public and the juries can rip me to shreds, but I don't care."

"And you put up with my friend Shelby," said Jack.

"What he writes is refreshing, real, an objective view of Paris, just like my art. So, I come here when I'm not at the Café de Bade or Café Guerbois with Edgar Degas."

"I've seen a few of his works," said Jack. "*A Roman Beggar Woman* and *Portrait of an Italian*. Also one called *The Rape*, an interior scene. He did some self-portraits, sort of brooding, right? He doesn't seem like a bon vivant."

"That he's not," said Manet. "He's not French, he's Italian. Narrow face, downcast and sarcastic, but I like him. He talks a lot but never lets anybody see him paint. I met him at the Louvre in '63 but, like me, he was disgusted by the academic parameters. There was no freedom of expression, nothing spontaneous or inventive. So we both left and paint as we wish."

"If you're not painting today, why aren't you at the Café de Bade?" said Shelby.

"I got into an argument with that Monet." Turning to Jack he said, "You know, it really bothered me, his name being so close to mine. People got us confused. He is talented, but—"

"You're just jealous, Édouard. And I thought you two were friends. Didn't Bazille paint you, Monet, Renoir, and Sisley all standing together, friendly-like?" said Shelby.

"Yes, of course we are friends, but Monet is just too charming. Too nice. The 'sunny soul.' 'Oh, mademoiselle, how wonderful you look today and what a stunning dress. Surely it cost a fortune. Magnificent,'" parodied Manet in his cracked voice.

"I think you two have much in common. You shouldn't be so hard on him. The man's struggling just like you," said Shelby.

When Manet didn't respond, Shelby said, "Have you seen Cézanne lately? I want to interview him about his work for the Salon. I'm told he has a new piece. I mentioned you and he said that you wouldn't show your work anywhere near his."

"That's Cézanne. I saw him at Café Guerbois a few days ago. He was angry about something." To Jack he said, "He's usually depressed. He shuns us and sits in a corner. I think his mind is warped. He's hard to be around. You know, he never keeps a model more than a week."

"He made some obscene remarks about your attitude," said Shelby.

"That man is very jealous of me. I don't know why he displays his work at all. He despises money. He's a decent artist but has a terrible temper. I once heard him say that all of us artists are swine. I have no use for him."

Manet stopped long enough to pull out a chair, sit down, and order a glass of Bordeaux. He looked at Jack. "American? Yes, but you speak French well. That's refreshing. Most Americans can only say, 'I do not understand, *excusez-moi, je ne comprends pas,*'" he said with a grin.

"My parents are from Paris. I learned from them."

"I see. You know, there are several American artists here. The landscape artist Henry Bacon is one."

"I know of him. He was with a Massachusetts regiment in the war," said Jack.

"Second Battle of Bull Run," said Shelby. "I interviewed him, too. He was a war correspondent for *Harper's Weekly*."

"And Winslow Homer, the illustrator," said Manet. "You can find him at the Café Molière. He painted *Girl in White*, his mistress. It was rejected as too suggestive because her hair was not coiffured and she was posed standing on the fur of a wolf skin. How ridiculous."

Jack was surprised that Shelby could speak so casually of these artists. Few of them had been given attention in the American press. Not only were they, with the exception of Jean Frederic Bazille, virtually penniless, but none had been admitted to the Salon. Still, the life of these freethinkers piqued Jack's interest. "So, Édouard, what inspired you to paint as you do?"

"I was most fortunate to befriend the notorious writer Charles Baudelaire. Have you heard of him? He wrote *Les Fleurs du Mal*, a most erotic collection of poems. To its credit, it was promptly banned by the French authorities. It's a lovely work, just dripping with sensuous, delectable love. Yes, he encouraged me to paint what is real, life in the streets. But the French don't want to see reality, and that's why my work is refused by the Salon."

Jack said, "Refused. And you call your group *Les Refusés*. When did the name come about?"

"It was back in '63. The emperor was curious about what the Salon accepted. Renoir got a painting displayed but art by me, Sisley, and Monet was rejected along with three thousand other works. We were furious, and some of us met at the Café de Bade. Napoleon learned of it and, wanting to curry favor with the banned artists, came to another display at the Palais de l'Industrie. He wanted to see all the works, accepted and rejected."

"It didn't turn out too well," said Shelby.

"Unfortunately, true. He decided to let the public be the judge of quality, and seventy thousand people showed up on the first day. Our paintings were in a separate room. The public was very excited—should I say morbidly and sexually titillated?—by the new work. They crowded around the art laughing and howling their indignation."

"And, of course, all the paintings were rejected. Refused!" he added, his voice carrying across the café. "So, we began our own association."

"And you have been amazingly successful," said Jack with a very rare grin.

"*Mais oui!* We've made millions," said Manet expansively, slapping the table.

"But they all live in squalor," said Shelby, scribbling on his foolscap, now wine-splotched.

"Impudence!" said Manet in mock horror. He took out his pocket watch. "I'm going to meet with Renoir. At least he is respectful."

"Fine," said Shelby. "Just let me know when the emperor buys your next painting."

Manet tossed two francs on the table and finished his wine. "Good luck, Monsieur Volant. Come by my studio if you wish, but be wary of the Beaux Arts. The jurist's greatest joy is to tear asunder an aspiring artist."

"Quite a character," said Jack after Manet left, his walking stick clicking along the boulevard.

"They all are," said Shelby. "But he's right about the Beaux Arts and the jurists. Napoleon has a favorite, a Count Émilien de Nieuwerkerke, whom he put in charge of the Ministry of Fine Arts. He established a set of rules for submission in the Salon, and everything must conform to his standards."

"Which are?"

"Simply put, high emphasis on morality and religion, the glory of France, and absolutely no realism or commonplace by Manet and company. I see no change in sight. So, *Les Refusés* will be ignored and forgotten."

"A sad commentary," said Jack.

"Here in Paris they say, '*Plus ça change, plus c'est la même chose.*'"

"The more things change, the more they remain the same."

"You got it, *mon cher*," said Shelby. "Now, I have a favor to ask. There's a wagon behind the café with a rock on it. A fairly sizable one that I have to deliver to a sculptor, a friend of mine. It's rather difficult to do with one arm—thank you, lieutenant. So, I request your help. It will take about an hour of your time."

"If you insist," said Jack. "I'd hate to see you injure your other arm."

"You are so caring," said Shelby as they left the café.

CHAPTER 21

"So where are we going?" asked Jack as he drove the heavy wagon pulled by two stout horses.

"La Chapelle in the eighteenth arrondissement, just across the tracks of the Chemins de Fer du Nord."

Forty minutes later they halted as an engine chugged past, puffing thick black clouds while pulling six cars filled with an assortment of workers and travelers from north of Paris.

"We'll just drop off the stone and head back. I have an article to get out by morning, and that means a very late night. I don't have time to socialize," said Shelby.

"Sure. Is the article about the murder?" asked Jack. The wagon rumbled over the tracks after the train passed.

"In part. There are many unanswered questions, and the police aren't saying much. I'm inclined to believe that they have a number of suspects and aren't sure where to turn. But there's another issue I'm exploring, a much larger and more disturbing one." The wall surrounding the house emerged from behind a copse of trees.

"More disturbing than a series of murders?"

"Infinitely more. I'm thinking of writing a series of articles about French and Prussian armaments and military preparedness."

"With no sign of war and the emperor's adoration of Bismarck, it might not be of particular interest," said Jack. "The French feel quite secure. After all, they're the strongest military in Europe, beat the Austrians quite handily."

"That was a long time ago, and the Austrians aren't Germans. Personally, I think the French are deluding themselves. They're a study in complacency. And Louis Napoleon is no Bismarck."

"You actually think there's going to be war?" asked Jack.

"That I don't know, but I've heard it said that France is a country with an army and Prussia is an army with a country. And Prussia has expanded to more than half of Germany. You have to remember that Prussia defeated Austria in only seven weeks in '66 under Otto von Bismarck. Men who command armies don't like them to just sit around, do they?"

They arrived at a house that Jack would've called old if they had been back in the States. He opened the double doors in the six-foot wall, revealing a courtyard extending back to the house and a large shed with an overhang. Shafts of light streaked into the shed, illuminating numerous sculptures in various stages of completion. The yard was strewn with stone blocks in many different hues.

A dark-skinned young man with a mop of curly hair came forward and directed Jack to back the wagon to a large table in the middle of the yard. While Shelby held the reins, Jack climbed onto the wagon and, with the aid of the youth, manhandled the stone onto the table. Looking toward the shed, he could see the figure of what appeared to be a sculptor clothed in pants, a baggy shirt, and a large straw hat, entirely covered in marble dust.

The person stopped, waved, and returned to work on the stone. Shelby waved back and handed Jack the reins. With a click of his tongue, the horses moved forward and the doors of the compound were closed behind them. Since Shelby said nothing more about the delivery or the sculptor, Jack decided to let the lack of introductions pass. He enjoyed palling around with Shelby and that was good enough.

The day had turned cool. Jack stopped the wagon then reached back and pulled on a tattered Union army greatcoat, a garment Shelby thought fairly ridiculous. They crossed the tracks in near silence.

"I've had strange dreams lately, Jack. Things that I can't tell anybody else about. They likely wouldn't understand."

"Who is she?" asked Jack, seeing Shelby's discountenance.

"Regrettably, it's not a she. They're about the war. Nightmares—but strange that I'm having them after so many years. Sometimes I just wake up screaming. The neighbors rush over—none of them speak English—and I have to apologize profusely. I don't imagine that ever happens to you. I sometimes get the feeling that you put those feelings in a box and threw it down a well."

"Don't be so sure. Sometimes my entire world explodes. And it's not just when I'm asleep. I have to be careful—the temper, you know. There are times when I just want to kill. I can smell the blood, the fear, the rage building. It's the damn war all over again."

"What do you do about it?" Shelby took a cigar from his coat, stuck it in his mouth, and lit the match with his one hand. An aromatic plume wafted upward as he stared into Jack's hardened eyes.

"I run. I run away, Shelby. And I get the shakes."

"But you didn't run away in the war."

"My body didn't, but my soul did. As fast as it could."

"So, you're still a powder keg?"

"I try not to be. But, given the right circumstances, I think I can still kill."

***

"He's in the back room behind the printing press," said Shelby when Jack arrived early the next morning.

"I got us some coffee—American," said Marcel. "I think it's Shelby's private stash. So have a seat, brother. We have things to talk about."

"I think it's you who needs to do the talking." Jack sat at a rough table across from him. "It seems that you might be in trouble again."

"Indirectly. I certainly didn't kill that courtesan. I was nowhere near the Chantilly when Lapin was murdered," Marcel said, looking very tired.

"But perhaps you know who did it," said Jack, leaning back in his chair.

"I have some theories, some possibilities, no proof."

"Men or women?"

"Maybe both."

"What about your assistant, the Egyptian fellow, the one with the exotic knife?"

"Abraxas. It's possible. He does like knives. Sneaks them into Paris so he doesn't pay duty on them. And he does business other than fake artifacts—he's alluded to slicing up some competitors in the Near East and possibly France."

"Why would he tell you that?" asked Jack.

"A warning, perhaps. We were associates, not real friends. I always regarded him as cunning and edgy. He didn't encourage questions."

"Abraxas, is that an Algerian name?" asked Jack.

"More like Egyptian. He said that Abraxas was a god known for bravery."

"But he claims to be Algerian. The French are not very fond of his country."

"Oh, he's hardly a Francophile, for all the time he spends here. He's bitter about the conquest of Algeria. But he was a big help in buying mummies and playing the part of an Egyptian at the salon."

"I heard that there's an Algerian neighborhood in Paris," said Jack. "Does he have a woman there?"

"Not that I know of. He was quite circumspect about his associations with women. But he did say that a prostitute is an abomination and should be punished severely. Punished in the name of Allah."

"That would include Camille Lapin." Jack sighed. "Marcel, Steven, tell me the truth. Who do you think killed her?"

"I only have a vague idea, nothing concrete. No one I would care to implicate now."

"But you know the person," said Jack, put off by his brother's secrecy.

Marcel looked away for a moment. "Look, things might get complicated. I'm not really sure what I got myself into, and I'm worried. This person could be dangerous, very dangerous."

"I don't think you're just worried, I think you're terrified."

"That's why I'm leaving Paris."

"Where are you going?" asked Jack, not surprised by his brother's determination to flee.

"I have friends in the northeast, in Metz, close to the Moselle River. I can stay there until this blows over."

"Give me an address. I might have to get in touch with you." Jack slid a pencil and paper forward.

Marcel hesitated, then scratched out an address. "You know," he said, laughing, "they still use the guillotine in France. Right in front of the prison, La Roquette. Seems a bit archaic, shades of the French revolution. It's very exciting for the French; everybody wants to see a beheading."

"I have a hard time seeing your head in a basket," said Jack. "But I agree, if you don't want to hang around for the investigation, you might leave while you can. You should get out of France altogether."

"And go where? Not back to the States. I like it here. I'm quite popular as an entertainer."

"I watched. It was quite a carnival, all the hocus-pocus," said Jack, his fingers twitching in the air. "You could sell snake oil to boa constrictors. I had a hard time believing how those people were taken in."

"'Those people' are the bored elite who go to séances and talk to spirits. Egypt is the apex of their fantasies. I merely provided the aphrodisiac they lusted for."

"Why Egypt?"

"That place was obsessed with mummification and living forever. It had to be. Except for the upper classes, they only lived to their mid-thirties. Even the priests who purified themselves in the Nile died from water fouled by feces and dead animals. Even the wealthy had gum disease and rotted teeth from sand in their food. Ate away the enamel, like sandpaper."

"You make your charade seem so reasonable, Steven."

"I like Marcel better. I have no desire to remember my past life." He sighed. "I gave the Parisians what they paid for. I wasn't the one who deceived them. They deceived themselves and thoroughly enjoyed it. The sad thing is, I don't think I can do it anymore. That part of my life is over. So, I'm going away."

"Not for the first time," said Jack ruefully.

"I didn't want to tell you. I was reluctant to see you at all."

"I was wondering about that."

"Because I am ashamed, and you know it. You always did, even though you never said so. There's a word I'm thinking of that starts with the letter C."

"As in cowardice?"

"Yeah. Cowardice. I should have gone into the army, fought in the war like you did. Pop would've been proud of me."

"If you're looking for absolution, I can't give it to you. But I'll say this: six hundred and eighteen thousand men died in that war, and you could have been one of them. And even if you'd survived ..." Jack shook his head. "Everybody who fought left part of themselves on that bloody ground. I did. Shelby did. As for cowardice, I saw hundreds of men on both sides throw down their muskets and run for their lives. Bull Run, Antietam, Fredericksburg, the Bloody Angle, the Wilderness. Good men, honorable men, all ran. I can't fault them. They were scared and so was I. We will all live with those frailties for the rest of our lives. Perhaps you'll come to terms with yours if you think it necessary."

"How?"

"I don't know, brother. But I wish you good luck."

***

"So, your brother left last night," said Shelby, sitting with Jack at their usual window table as a cold fog swept past.

"By some back road, I imagine. I'm sure he thinks that there's a crime scene investigator at the station. I doubt that he'll be back in Paris for a very long time."

Jack, as usual, wore his heavy blue greatcoat, a cavalry relic of the war, which he favored for its warmth and its extra-long sleeves. Warming in Galignani's, he removed it and placed it over the back of the chair. His foreign dress was accentuated by a black slouch hat with a wide brim and a gold cord sporting two tassels, both frayed. He hung it on a rack behind him that supported a half dozen bowlers.

"Where did he go?" asked Shelby, composing a paragraph on his food-blotched pad.

"Metz. He said he has friends there. That probably means a woman. Likely somebody's wife."

Shelby grinned. "Maybe a good place to play, but not a good place to hide."

"Why not?"

"Because it's just across the river from Germany. That's why."

A tall, unaccompanied woman in her mid-twenties rose from a rear table and walked toward them. She was clothed in a simple day dress without hoops and wore no jewelry. Her face was tanned, and she wore her auburn hair piled atop her head. Deep green eyes were set in an unadorned but attractive face.

Jack followed Shelby's gaze. Both men stood as the woman halted beside their table. She looked oddly familiar, though Jack couldn't imagine where he would've encountered her before.

"Ah, so wonderful to see you again, Mademoiselle Stuart. I daresay, you look astonishingly beautiful and add radiance to this dreary day." Shelby bent to kiss her extended hand.

"You are an abominable flirt, Gabriel. 'This dreary day,' I declare!" the woman said with a lilting Southern accent. Her eyes went from Shelby, glowing in his rotundity, to Jack, who couldn't suppress a grin.

"My dear Charlotte, this gentleman is usually my best friend, Jack Volant. He's the fellow who helped me yesterday. Jack, I want to introduce you to my cousin, Miss Charlotte Stuart of the Old Dominion, the great state of Virginia."

"Delighted to meet you," said Jack, extending his hand. Turning to Shelby, he said, "You might have told me about her, Shelby. It would be nice to have a lady acquaintance. Especially a pretty one."

"You said that your world was all about art and you have no time for women," said Shelby defensively.

"Beautiful women are art," retorted Jack.

Charlotte laughed. "Oh my, a poet. Well, sir, I wish to thank you for delivering the stone. I regret that I didn't stop my work, but the angle of the sun was just right. It's a commissioned piece and must be delivered soon."

"I saw you wearing pants and naturally thought you were a man. But I'm quite impressed that as a woman you are tackling such demanding work," said Jack, hoping that he was saying the right thing.

"In a way that's a noble thought, but women are entirely capable of employing a hammer and chisel. I have always engaged in demanding work, whether here or in Virginia."

"I meant no disrespect," said Jack, seeing a challenging look in the woman's eyes.

"None taken. I realize that working in stone is an unusual profession for a lady, but I have always been a bit of a rebel."

"Charlotte has been sculpting since she came here," said Shelby. "Indeed, her work has even been purchased by the Empress."

"That is truly impressive," said Jack, wondering about the circumstances that had brought her to Paris and how devastating she might be to any man who crossed her. "I hope to improve my painting so that I might also display in the Salon des Arts, but I doubt it will be anytime soon."

Charlotte sighed. "I suspect that you are far better than what you admit to. I just have that sense." She turned to Shelby. "I once heard you mention Monsieur Volant, but I never learned how both of you met."

Shelby glanced at Jack as if to say, *I hoped I could have avoided this.*

"Ah, we met quite by accident. It was during the war and was not overwhelmingly pleasant at first. Opposing armies, you see. But all is well between us now."

Charlotte's eyes went from Shelby's ingratiating smile to Jack, who watched her every expression. Her smile slowly evaporated just as Jack was struck by a flash of memory.

"Miss Stuart," said Jack. "Were you ever sculpting in a studio in Maryland before the war? I believe it was owned by a Mr. Benoir."

"Yes, I was an apprentice there. How did you know?"

"I happened to visit the studio with my brother. You and I didn't speak to each other, but I thought you looked familiar even though it was many years ago. You only glanced toward us so I hardly think you would remember me. But I do remember you and the fine work you were doing."

"That's very kind of you. No, I don't remember you. I would've been quite intent on the sculpture." Charlotte looked into Jack's eyes, still unsmiling, and then the hat lying beside him. "Might I presume that you wore that during the late war, Mr. Volant?"

"I did."

"Jack was a lieutenant, and he was very solicitous of me after the amputation. More than I had any right to expect. We hurt each other, but it was a long time ago. We put it behind us."

"It's not something I can put behind me, nor do I care to, dear cousin. For me it was yesterday."

Shelby cleared his throat in lieu of a reply.

"I suppose that Monsieur Volant is your friend, but he cannot be mine. I have no use for Yankees. And, sir," she said, looking hard at Jack, "I really do not wish to speak with you or see you again."

"I understand, and I pledge to honor your demand," said Jack with a curt nod.

"Sir," she said, "there is a great deal you do not understand." The woman turned and quickly left the café.

"I don't want to antagonize her," said Jack, watching her leave. "If she comes here often, perhaps I should not."

"You have as much right to be here as she does."

"She's still hurting, isn't she?"

"And she will be for a very long time." The beginnings of a smile returned to Shelby's face. "At least she didn't say 'damnyankees.' That should warm the cockles of your heart."

"I might have forgiven her if she had. She is a pretty woman. A rather compelling one, too."

***

It was an extremely serious matter involving not only the police but the army as well. Detectives Ambroise Arseneau, Gaspard Desvaux, and Gene Gustave, accompanied by a colonel, arrived at the arsenal near Porte Chapelle Saint-Denis in the nineteenth arrondissement of La Villette at ten in the morning. The arsenal, a one-hundred-year-old stone building, stood alone only a hundred yards from the wall surrounding the enlarged city of Paris.

A captain strode forward to meet the inspectors and saluted the colonel. "The corporal of the guard is inside. He's still groggy, but he can speak."

"Was he the only one on guard?" asked the colonel.

"No, sir. There was a private, and unfortunately he was killed. We think he put up a struggle but was overpowered. His body has already been taken away."

"I will order the guard to be increased to six from now on," said the colonel. "This is intolerable."

The corporal, a bandage covering his forehead, attempted to stand and salute. The colonel waved him back down into his chair.

"Can you recall what happened last night?" he asked solicitously.

"It happened so quickly, Monsieur Colonel. Private Jacome said he heard a noise early in the morning. He was standing outside, and there was a terrible wind and a scattering of snow. He must have seen someone, because he called for me. I heard a shot fired—it must have been his— and a scream. I hurried out with my rifle and then ... then nothing. The first persons I saw when I woke were a corpsman and the captain."

The corporal pointed to blood on the bandage. "I don't know why they didn't kill me, too."

"Did you recognize your attackers?" asked the colonel.

"No, sir—the one I saw wore a cloth over his face," said the corporal. "He had a knife, a curved knife, sort of like the ones used by Arabs in the Near East."

"Private Jacome was slain with a knife," said the captain.

"A curved knife?" blurted Inspector Arseneau, his face showing surprise. "We've been investigating the murder of a member of the Assembly, also murdered by such a knife. Surely they aren't common in Paris. There may well be a link between these two attacks."

Addressing the major, the colonel said, "What was stolen from the arsenal?"

"Three barrels of gunpowder and four cases of rifles, about sixteen weapons in all."

"There are rev-revolutionary cells in the city, Chief Inspector. The theft of the rifles and the mur-murder of the conservative politician may be a precursor to an uprising," said Gustave. "It may very well involve the Algerian Mustafa

Hakim, known in Paris as Jabari Abraxas. To my mind, monsieur, he is still at war with France."

"Of that I am sure," said Arseneau.

"If that's so," said Desvaux, "then this isn't a simple matter of selling muskets on the black market, and it's not just about an uprising, either—it's about revolution. If that's the case, it must be crushed instantly."

"Indeed," said the colonel. "We must ascertain how many traitors there are and where they hide out. Once found, I'll have infantry exterminate them. We will employ artillery if necessary."

"This particular murder is still a police matter," said Arseneau in defense of his institution. "But we will call upon the army if needed."

"Then you must find this Mustafa Hakim quickly," said the colonel, "because the army will not suffer this again. I have the confidence of the emperor and three thousand troops under my command. I will use them against an entire neighborhood if I must. Of that you may be sure, Monsieur Inspector."

CHAPTER 22

Paris

December 1869

"Do you want me to drive you this morning? It'll take no time to hitch up the horse."

"No, Jerome, I'll take the omnibus. It's going to snow again, and I don't wish to see you get any worse. You should go back to bed and get over your cold."

"But it's a long walk to the omnibus. It's really no bother."

"You're being sweet, but the answer is no. Fix some hot tea and rest. No cleaning the yard, polishing my stone, or poring over that law book. The exam isn't for three weeks."

"I'll just check my wagon; the seat was loose. You know I have a furniture delivery to make. Monsieur Chenier expects help with moving Madame Richel's belongings to her new house, and I've already been paid. I'll rest for a few hours before I go."

"If you say so, but don't you dare take a sip of my Old Forester, you hear?"

"Oh, yes, ma'am, ah hears ya, ah hears ya," he said with faux humility, his dark eyes flashing.

"Don't give me that nonsense," said Charlotte. "Now get to bed."

Jerome waited until Charlotte left, then walked to the carriage barn where he stabled his horse and wagon. He secured the seat and climbed the stairs to the attic where he slept. Books were piled high on a desk. His clothes hung haphazardly in a closet in the corner. From a shelf he picked up a box and laid it on the bed. Lifting the lid, he took out a pistol, an old Colt cap and ball. He checked the copper percussion caps, determining that they were properly fitted over the cylinder nipples. Satisfied that they were secure, he shoved six cartridges into the cylinder, returned the weapon to the box, and placed it back on the shelf.

He'd never used the pistol since leaving the States, but there was danger where he ventured, even if the woman said he had nothing to fear.

Jerome lay back on his bed and considered the hour he should leave that night. By using the rear gate, he wouldn't wake Charlotte, who lived in the ancient house across the yard. He would never involve her. He loved her too much. But a thrill ran through him, for this was the night that he would acquire the prize possession. The man had promised to have it with him. Already Jerome had counted the francs he'd pay. He blew his nose and closed his eyes. Night couldn't come soon enough.

***

Despite Manet's foreboding comments, Jack was excited as he lugged his easel, paint box, and canvas to the Grande Galerie on the second floor of the Louvre, which, at over thirteen hundred feet, was the longest room in the world. Seemingly half of Paris was climbing up and down the museum's marble stairs and across its polished floors. Parisians and *étrangers* crowded into the elegant building, originally constructed in the sixteenth century as a royal palace for Catherine de' Medici.

The exhibit at the Salon des Beaux Arts wasn't until May. Surely he would finish at least two paintings for submission by then. He hoped that at least one would be accepted. That would give him a degree of recognition. It was an exciting prospect, and he was impatient to get started.

Off the main hall were numerous galleries to which hundreds of artists toted their stools and set up easels close to masterworks displayed on the walls. Gazing at the art were women in elegant hooped skirts and men wearing top hats and fashionable coats. Others attempted to squeeze past without brushing against a pallet or a student's wet painting.

Cigar and pipe smoke rose to the high ceiling as enthusiastic patrons clustered around paintings of sterile nudes or partially clothed women in scenes exalting religion and morality.

Jack, still wearing his greatcoat, looked into one packed room after another, amazed at the density of the crowd. He collided with a girl carrying several guidebooks and stooped to pick them up as they toppled from her hand. A woman, seeing an artist encumbered with easel and canvas, came to his aid. Together they collected the books and handed them to the girl. Jack straightened and said, "Merci" as the woman rearranged the delicate folds of her dress.

Charlotte smiled at the girl, then looked at Jack with some surprise as her smile vanished.

Never before had Jack felt like a pariah after the war. Even former Confederate soldiers had been civil. But it was entirely apparent that Charlotte still wanted nothing to do with him, and there was nothing that he could do about it.

He put two fingers to the brim of his hat and said, "Good day." She didn't reply. With a touch of sadness, he watched her disappear into the crowd. Gathering up his easel, paint box, and canvas, he turned and pushed his way into a gallery.

Forty artists sat on stools or stood pressed close to the walls as they peered at the great paintings, many poorly illuminated. The combined scent of oil paints, solvents, tightly packed bodies, and damp clothing mingled with perfumes and colognes. Men, women, and children, wearing their Sunday best, crowded around the artists and asked questions regarding their technique or offering critiques, desired or not.

The room was stifling and noisy. Onlookers peered intently, only inches from the wet canvases, accidentally nudging artists whose brushes made erratic strokes.

Jack had hoped to paint the military landscape *An Episode from the Russian Campaign* by Nicholas Toussaint Charlet, a dark depiction of French forces retreating from Moscow, but there was no space in front of the work. He moved along until a frustrated artist gathered up his easel and canvas.

"You may have my stool," said the painter. "I can't take the Sunday crowd; a child nearly knocked over my easel."

The man left in a huff, and Jack found himself in front of two works by Eugène Delacroix. Jack studied the paintings, one beside the other.

"I would paint *The Entry of the Crusaders in Constantinople*," said a young man, employing minute strokes to the mane of a horse on his canvas. "Look at all the people in it and the great Christian symbolism. A true masterpiece."

But the painting didn't excite Jack. The work seemed a conglomeration of figures all bunched together. There was nothing dramatic about it. Further, Jack had no intention of painting anything giving credence to the destruction of a city by a bloodthirsty, marauding army of zealots and looters.

Instead, he looked at the other painting, entitled *Mademoiselle Rose*, a lackluster female nude gazing down, her genitalia covered by a cloth. She sat atop red and yellow cushions over a wooden box. He considered leaving the room to find another work, but thought that the painting might be interesting if only he changed the colors, the brushstrokes, and the facial expression. Of course, it wouldn't be the same painting, but that didn't matter—no copy would be accepted by the Salon.

As he set up his easel and squeezed paint onto his palette, he took note of other artists, many of whom held magnifying glasses and stood within inches of art adorning the walls. He watched them return to their own work, attempting to replicate each brushstroke no matter how subtle or minute. He carried no magnifying glass, nor did he have any intention of doing so.

"Are you from Paris?" inquired the artist beside him.

"America," Jack replied.

The man peered intently at each addition to his work. "Well, you've come to the right place. If you can't make it in Paris, in the Salon, you might as well throw away your brushes. There are a number of jurists here today. Perhaps they will approve of your work. As a matter of fact, Monsieur Nieuwerkerke and his lover Mathilde, the Spanish countess, may come by. It's said that she's the one who actually decides the awards."

"I've heard of Nieuwerkerke but not his woman."

"You can't miss them; they're always followed by a crowd. An approving nod from either is a ticket to the Salon."

Jack finished sketching out the figure. After quickly painting in the soft background, he used bold strokes to block in the female form. It would be the first coat on the canvas, hardly more than a primer, but instead of bland pigments, he employed striking colors and large brush strokes. Cadmium yellows were mixed with flesh pinks and deep orange hues to give the figure depth and boldness.

Vibrant colors emphasized arms, breasts, torso, and legs. Ignoring minuscule details, scooping up paint with a palette knife, he attacked the canvas without reservation.

The face no longer had a down-looking cast but an inquiring look, one of pleasure, as if aware of being admired for her seductive body. Colors flashed upon the canvas with abandon; stroke followed stroke as the figure took shape. Exhilaration, a sense of freedom, came over Jack, oblivious to the ever-increasing number of people who slowed or stopped to watch him.

The comments seemed far away, of no real concern. When a woman giggled, he merely smiled, assuming that she was embarrassed by the lustrous color of the figure with only the barest covering. The remarks became more intrusive, however, and Jack began to notice titters followed by derisive remarks. He chose to ignore them, enraptured by what was emerging on the canvas.

He glanced to the side and saw the frowning artist beside him. Perhaps the man was upset by the attention he was receiving. There were ribald comments followed by raucous laughter.

"What is that? Certainly not art," said a rotund man to his mistress, who held a hand over her face.

"If you can't paint you shouldn't be here," chided another. A tall, gaunt man leaned over Jack's shoulder and with venom said, "You are defiling the work of a French master. Your colors are ridiculous, the brushstrokes madness, an affront to the public and to God. You should be ashamed!"

People, hearing the commotion, began to enter from other galleries. "Look at his clothing, certainly not French," Jack heard.

"An American, most likely. Do they paint in America?"

A woman entered and, working her way closer, glanced at the painting. Jack saw her and looked away. The crowd, the insults, became menacing, and the nonchalance Jack hoped to display was replaced by seething anger. When one man touched the canvas, Jack slapped his hand away. In the close, overheated room, tension built within him.

Quite suddenly he rose and smashed his stool to the ground. His brushes flew as the crowd reared back. Daubs of red paint became images of exploding blood; the cacophony of shouts and taunts mutated into a hellishness of pain and bottomless fury.

He was back there again as screams erupted from armless men, as canisters exploded, ripping away heads and faces. Everything blurred before him. Riderless horses, chaos, the terror and utter madness of impossible struggle descended upon him like a howling specter, blind and gnashing in its moment of death.

"Get back! Get away from me!" He swung his paint box against the wall. There were screams as people drew back, imprecations and shouts of alarm.

He heard someone say, "Call the police, he is mad! The man is insane, someone get him!"

A twisted face appeared, and a hand reached for his collar. Jack's arm shot out and a man tumbled back.

"Kill! Kill the bastards! Kill them all!" Jack screamed.

The woman's face, appalled, suddenly appeared before him, but she didn't matter, nothing mattered. He had to get out. Pushing past horrified patrons, he bolted out of the gallery. Behind him he heard shouts and a woman's voice calling, "Monsieur Volant, Monsieur Volant!"

Rain pelted down. The Louvre became a blur in the fog as he ran, heedless of astounded looks. The words "Fool, fool!" assaulted his mind. What was he doing here, what was he thinking? What stupidity! Hadn't Manet warned him? The whole thing was a monstrous joke. "No! No!" he shrieked, the insanity of it a bayonet into his soul.

He slowed a quarter mile later. His greatcoat was streaked with dark red paint. He gripped his coat and buttoned it. The paint smeared his hand. It was the color of blood. It should have been blood. Panting, he slowed and saw a woman hurrying toward him. Waving a hand in the dense fog, she appeared to be little more than a shadow, a specter.

He would not countenance anyone now. Pulling his hat low, he hurried on. His paints, easel, and canvas had likely been trampled and tossed in the trash. It didn't matter. He heard the whistle of a train. He would leave this wretched place, these fossilized minds. He didn't need Paris, didn't need the contempt, the ostracism.

Again he heard the woman call his name, but he couldn't face her, couldn't fathom the horror that had befallen him or the scene he'd created. He had become an object of ridicule, a sickening, scandalous joke in the morning paper. *An American who thought he could be an artist.* He felt small and craven, like a voyeur caught in the act. He began to run, the wind blessedly ripping away the woman's plea, the sound of his name.

CHAPTER 23

The lantern's glow was shaded three times before being extinguished. The heavy clouds of the evening storm had fled; a half moon illuminated the field. Jerome flicked the reins, and the horse plodded through the mud and silvery snow toward a copse of trees with branches like gnarled hands. Three men approached, loaded long boxes onto the wagon, and covered with them with bales of hay.

"This is the amount you wanted," said Jerome, handing Jabari Abraxas a wad of francs. The Algerian didn't count it.

"You show no one this knife and you do not remove it from the scabbard in the presence of anyone. If you are ever questioned, you tell them that you bought it from a foreign traveler, an Englishman who lost all his money in a game of chance. Do you understand?"

Jerome nodded vigorously and slipped the sheathed jambiya into a pocket of his coat.

"You know the back roads, the route I showed you," said Jabari. "She will be waiting along with several others. Don't stop, don't speak to anyone, not even her. Do nothing to bring attention. Now go."

Jerome drove past ancient houses and through dark, narrow streets where ragpickers emerged, then disappeared like ghosts. Those who spied the wagon watched in wary silence. The moon was high when Jerome reined the horse behind a dilapidated dwelling with a disintegrating roof. Figures emerged, one a slender woman who directed four men to unload and stow the crates in the cellar.

"You did well tonight," said the woman, handing Jerome five francs.

He stuffed the money into his pocket. "Will there be another shipment?"

"Perhaps soon. But remember, say nothing." Her dark, unblinking eyes met his. "A word to anybody is a death sentence. Understand?"

"I do. But when will the guns be used?"

"When the time is right, not a day before. Now get home. Be there before dawn. And Jerome ..."

"Yes?"

"You never saw me; you do not know who I am."

"Quite truthfully, madame, I don't even know your name."

The storm that had abated returned in full force as Jerome approached the house. Thunder rumbled across the blotted sky, and lightning illuminated bare trees bent in the wind.

Jerome's horse, a sixteen-hand bay, was one he loved to ride to the Bois de Boulogne on Sundays while wearing his finest attire. But she was a skittish animal that required a firm hand, even when pulling the wagon. Startled by a thunderclap, she rose up on her hind legs. With eyes wide, she threw her head from side to side. Fearing that the wagon would topple, Jerome sprang from the seat and grabbed the reins while attempting to calm the horse. But it was to no avail.

He had left the rear gate unlocked, and a blast of wind swung it open. At a dead run, the horse bolted through the open gate. Jerome, still holding the reins, tried desperately to avoid the churning wheels. The wagon careened wildly through the yard and tore past the house and shed until it collided with a large stone and toppled, sending Jerome ten feet into the air.

The mare, suddenly freed, stampeded around the yard, pulling its traces until they looped over another stone, bringing her to a halt. Stunned, Jerome slowly rose to his feet and approached his horse. It stood, its flanks quivering as water rained down.

Charlotte stepped outside, carrying a lantern whose glow barely penetrated the deluge. "Are you hurt?" she asked as she hurried forward, pulling a coat around her.

"I think I'm intact," he answered, still calming the horse.

"What are you doing out at this hour?"

She stared at the horse and the wagon with its broken wheel. "Put her in the barn and come into the house. I think we have to talk."

"I'll put the horse up, but I don't want to talk tonight. Please, Charlotte, I just want to lie down." Jerome took the reins and led the horse away.

"There is something going on, and it worries me," Charlotte said, trudging back to the house. "And that cold is only going to get worse."

Jerome removed the traces and wiped the horse down before climbing the stairs to his room above the shed. Removing his wet clothes, he sat on the edge of his bed in utter despair. Charlotte would want answers. What could he tell her? Certainly not that he'd been delivering rifles and gunpowder to those intent on destroying the regime.

No matter what story he concocted, he'd broken her trust. He wouldn't repeat the folly of tonight, but what would

Jabari and the strange, secretive woman think when he no longer showed up? Jabari, he knew, was a dangerous man, especially if he suspected a double cross.

Revolution! Power to the working people, he had been told by those who stole food in the middle of the night. Half of Paris, the forever impoverished, never had enough to eat, or a decent place in which to sleep. Revolution! The fever and excitement had ensnared him.

Living a double life, sharing food with the impoverished who scuttled from one barrel of discarded scraps to another, set fire to his imagination. He, who lived comfortably and could squire young ladies in the Bois de Boulogne and cafés, was enthralled. He regaled them with tales of how he had been freed from enslavement. He spoke of how he'd helped lead slaves to freedom on the Underground Railway. They listened to the youth who had seen great armies rip away the chains of bondage.

It had been months earlier when he had made a dreadfully wrong turn and found himself in their midst. Glares, murmured threats had only been appeased with a bottle of wine and a sack of lentils. He recognized what he had seen in their eyes, for they lived no better than serfs had a thousand years before. He returned with more food and found gratitude and admiration. He, a black youth who handed out food to bone-tired children, was welcomed, protected, and anticipated in the underworld of Paris. It became a thrilling thing, a saintly thing.

Through them he had met Jabari Abraxas, the man with searing eyes who, like a ghost, moved in the shadows. Revolution, the Algerian told him, was only a word, a hollow word, without the means to make it happen. Revolution required guns. From that, the rest followed.

Again, the rain abated. It was becoming light, but he still had time to catch some sleep. He would think of what he'd say to Charlotte in the morning. He would hide the knife, but not near the gun. She knew about that. Fortunately, she rarely climbed to the attic. She respected his privacy, especially when he entertained young women.

Rising from the bed, he lifted his coat and reached inside his pocket for the knife. It wasn't there.

***

Jerome didn't remember having slept at all. He dressed quickly and hurried outside. The storm had played havoc with everything in the yard. Blown off pedestals, tools had been buried in the mud. Workbenches lay scattered about, and the wagon, a wheel shattered, lay against the table on which the new stone had been placed. The table lay on its side, the stone having slid to rest at a precarious angle.

Charlotte was already up. She went about tidying the work shed and removing a canvas extension ripped by the wind. Jerome had hoped to avoid her, had hoped to find the jambiya and hide it before she noticed it. He scurried to where the wagon lay and looked about. A large hammer and shards of stone stuck out of the mud. Grabbing a number of thick wooden planks, he managed to right the wagon, but nothing lay beneath it. He was about to kneel and get a better look when Charlotte appeared. "What are you looking for?"

"I think I lost a few francs."

"I can give you money if you need it," she said, looking at the broken wheel. "I'm still concerned about your activities last night, but I have an errand for you, a letter for my cousin at Galignani's. I would like you to deliver it this morning. It's important. In fact, I'll give you four francs for the favor."

Jerome nodded and accepted the envelope. "I'll saddle my horse."

"And Jerome, you may have dropped the money on the road. I don't see anything here."

"I probably did. Don't bother looking for it. It's not that important."

"Then do go to the café. Gabriel is always there in the morning but often leaves in the afternoon."

"I'm on my way," said Jerome, hoping to find the knife on the road before someone else did.

***

It was midmorning before Jack appeared at Galignani's bookstore.

"I was hoping that you would be back, but I wasn't sure," said Shelby, sitting across from him. "You must have slept under a rock; you look like shit. You know that, don't you?"

Jack nodded and waved away a flask Shelby offered him.

"A detective, Monsieur Gene Gustave, came by here yesterday. He said that he read my story about Chez Chantilly and asked if I knew anything that could help his investigation beyond what I wrote. Particularly if it included anything you might have knowledge of."

"What did you tell him?"

"Nothing he didn't already know."

"But why ask you? He could ask me."

"Because he doesn't know how to find you. He also doesn't know how to find Marcel. Perhaps he thinks that you're hiding him. Just a hypothesis, of course. He was very insistent that I inform him if I learned anything. I told him that I would."

"Did you tell him that Marcel might have gone to Metz?" asked Jack.

"No, I wanted to talk to you before I say anything. I thought it only right considering that Marcel says he's innocent. I left him out of the column I wrote except to say that there had been a performance at the salon earlier in the evening. Same stuff as was said in *Le Monde*."

Jack nodded. "Marcel can be accused of many things, but not murder. I appreciate you not mentioning his name." He looked down at the table. "What about my adventure at the Louvre? Did you write about that?"

"No. I wasn't about to compound your disaster. We'll just let it dissipate. It's not like it resulted in a duel, and that's quite a popular thing here. Daudet has been in a few with rapiers."

"I know how to use a saber, but I would prefer pistols if I ever had to engage in that."

"Yeah, you do pretty well with a pistol," said Shelby, making a face.

Jack sighed and formed a lopsided grin. "I didn't mean to ruffle your feathers, Shelby. But swords are pretty antiquated."

"So is dueling," said Shelby, "but the French are all about *honneur*. They would go to war over it."

Jack ordered a café au lait. "I guess I made quite a scene. I suspect I won't be welcomed back, not that I ever intend to go there again."

"Persona non grata. But what do the Jews say? 'This too shall pass.'"

"I'm still thinking of leaving. I don't fit in here, and I'll never get into the Salon. That's death for an artist in France."

"So, you don't get into the Salon, who cares? Neither do people like Pissarro, Monet, Degas, or my idiot friend Manet. But they all paint. Don't you dare run away!" Shelby thumped his fist on the table loudly enough to make people stare. "Who knows, maybe you invented a whole new style of art. I mean, look at Peter Paul Rubens and his voluptuous females, and the way Rembrandt used light—they all broke the mold. So did Donatello and his nude. I imagine that he was damn near excommunicated on the grounds of obscenity. Hell, Jack, there's a scandal a day in Paris. Your adventure into public insanity will be null and void next week. Besides, there's something you can do for me."

"What's that?"

"I can't leave here; I have a paper to get out. So, I need you to—"

A young man tapped Shelby on the shoulder. "Bonjour, monsieur, I have a note from Mademoiselle Charlotte. She said it's quite important and gave me four francs to deliver it."

"That much? And she entrusted you? My, my, my. So, Master Jerome, are you staying out of trouble?" Shelby took the note from its envelope.

"Yes sir, of course, why do you ask?"

"You look a bit nervous, somber, not your usual devil-may-care self. Were you jilted by one of your girlfriends last night?"

"I'm afraid so," said Jerome with an uncertain smile. "You're very perceptive, but I guess that's your business, a journalist, I mean."

"Goes with the territory, young man."

Jerome glanced at Jack, and Shelby said, "I want you to meet my very good friend, Mr. Jack Volant, a fine artist and a former soldier of the Union army."

Jerome held out his hand and Jack shook it. With a grin, Shelby said, "Jerome is studying French law, but he's a mischievous fellow. I'm sure he's into all kinds of nefarious things. But he has, with questionable intent, also ingratiated himself with the beautiful ladies of Paris, haven't you, Jerome?"

"*Mais oui*, there are so many in Paris, it's impossible not to fall in love." His dark eyes glanced from Shelby to Jack.

"Well, there is truth to that." Shelby sighed. "And, Jack, it is with dubious honor I admit that Monsieur Jerome is also a relation, my cousin Charlotte's half brother.

"I thought I recognized you from when we delivered the stone," said Jack. "Well, it is a pleasure to meet you."

"And you, monsieur," said Jerome. "Perhaps we'll meet again, but I have to be getting back. A big evening tonight."

"Just don't put her in what we delicately refer to as 'a family way,'" said Shelby.

"Oh no, sir. We just discuss Descartes, John Adams, and the finer points of the Peloponnesian conflict," said Jerome with a fleeting smile.

"I'm sure the Greek wars leave them spellbound," said Shelby.

"Very interesting," said Jack as the youth mounted his horse and galloped down the road.

"Quite a story there," said Shelby. "Born in slavery, you know. He's a smart lad, very sure of himself here in Paris, but he worries me. Something I can't put my finger on, something, well, dangerous."

"For someone, as you say, so self-assured, he seemed ill at ease."

"Seems that way. But youth—who knows? Maybe he's already made a girl pregnant. That won't please Charlotte. Not at all."

"And he's her half brother?"

"Most assuredly. Her daddy just loved his women slaves. Concubines all. Loved them a lot in the biblical sense."

"Surely a common practice and one sorely missed by the former plantation men of substance," said Jack.

"One of the unspoken things in polite southern society. Oh, yes: 'Look away, look away, look away, Dixie Land,'" said Shelby. "Jerome was only one of many children born to colored women on her daddy's plantation. Most died within a few days, didn't live long enough to even be named. But Jerome lived—and he's thrived, largely due to Charlotte. She cares intensely for him. They are close, and that would be considered unseemly at home."

"Then it's good he's in Paris. I suspect he's a bit of a novelty here."

"There are plenty of dark-skinned folks here, but most are from Algeria and other French colonies. Jerome is unusual, coming from America."

"He speaks quite well," said Jack. "He wouldn't dare speak correct English down South."

"No, he'd be strung up faster than I can spit at a snake. Charlotte brought him with her when she came to Paris. Taught him good English and French in Virginny. Damn dangerous back then. He's accepted in Paris—different history, you see."

Shelby opened the envelope Jerome had given him and started reading. "Well, I'll be damned!" he exclaimed. "It's from Charlotte, and it's about you."

Jack frowned. "Why would she write about me?"

"You're asking me? To quote Miguel de Cervantes, 'What man knows thoroughly the riddle of a woman's mind?' I sure as hell don't."

"Not what I wanted to hear, Shelby."

Shelby read the rest of the letter, then handed it to Jack.

Dearest Cousin Gabriel,

I would be greatly appreciative if, upon seeing Mr. Volant, you give him this note. I wish to extend an invitation for him to visit me at my residence if he still remains in Paris. I will be prepared to meet him in the morning two days hence. I do request that if he has departed France you do notify me.

With love and devotion,

Your adoring cousin, Charlotte.

"She must think you fled France posthaste," said Shelby.

"I can see why she would. I saw her at the Louvre. Or at least I think I did."

"I know, she told me."

"She spoke to you about it? About the—"

"The day after. She said that she called your name, but you wouldn't stop. Kept on running. I guess she felt badly about how you were treated. She wants to console you, I suspect."

"I don't know why. She made it quite clear that she despises Yankees, and I won't wear Confederate gray to please her."

"Dear Lord, no! But it would be honorable to accept her invitation."

"What could I possibly say to her? And what could she say to me? I degenerated into madness. I went berserk, Shelby, there's no other explanation. I can't remember what I said, but I saw people look at me in horror and back away. And I hit one man, hit him very hard. I could have been arrested for assault."

"But you weren't, and my cousin is being extraordinarily gracious. The gentlemanly thing would be to accept. See what she has to say. She is an extraordinary woman."

"Tell me about her."

"No, that's not for me to do. She's gone through her share of hardships, and it's her story to share if she chooses. Allah be praised, she might even want to hear yours. Oh, and by the way," Shelby said with a mischievous grin, "she knows that I shot you, too."

"Even Steven."

"Ain't it, though."

CHAPTER 24

Paris

Two days later

"I didn't think you were coming," said Charlotte, sitting at a table in the sculpture yard.

"I didn't think I was, either." Jack stood warily as he looked at the woman who wore the hoopless dress of an artisan and appraised him with deep unblinking eyes.

"I suggest that we talk out here. I don't allow men in my house, except for Mr. Shelby and Jerome," she said stiffly.

"This is fine," said Jack, taking in her deep green eyes.

"Then have a seat and I'll bring some warm tea. It will just take a few minutes."

Jack nodded and watched her walk across the yard. Her stature was erect, determined, but quite elegant. It was as if she had been trained for presentation to society with all the winsome gifts of a beautiful Southern belle. But he saw nothing seductive or charming in her demeanor today.

The visit would probably end quickly, following the tea and a few non-combative words. That would satisfy the invitation, and he'd be on his way, suffering as little pain as possible.

He had a moment to look about. There had been little time to see any of her sculptures when delivering the stone, and now he studied one in black polished marble, nearly six feet tall. In its perfection it could have been a Michelangelo woman in anguish, her head back, mouth open as if in a silent scream. In her arms lay a child, its limbs hanging down, a study in death and despair. On closer inspection he saw that the woman was a Negress.

Perplexed, Jack wondered if he should say anything about it, beyond mentioning the quality of the work. He decided not to. One rarely discussed niceties in the first minutes of a truce.

A short distance away was the table on which he and Shelby had laid the stone days before. But the table had fallen and the stone had slid off. Getting it righted would take two or three men. Beside the stone was a wagon, its front right corner held up by a half-dozen wooden blocks. Spokes of the missing wheel littered the ground.

Jack stood when Charlotte returned carrying a tray with two cups of tea and crackers.

"Jerome, my half brother, crashed his wagon," she said, seeing him inspecting the damage. "He uses it to carry furniture, a business of his."

"There was a storm two nights ago," said Jack, sitting back down. "Not a good night to be out."

"The horse spooked," said Charlotte. "Surprising it didn't kill him."

A piece of metal, partially covered by mud, glinted beside the stone, but Jack took little notice. A number of tools still lay about. Some reflected the morning light, all blown helter-skelter by the storm.

"Jerome usually keeps this yard pretty clean, but he's been out of sorts lately."

They sipped tea in silence until Jack said, "I appreciate the invite, Miss Stuart, but quite honestly I don't know why you asked me to come. In fact, based on your comments at Galignani's I don't know why you want to meet me at all."

"It's certainly not to extend friendship or sympathy, if that's what you think," she said in a quiet but determined voice.

"I expect not. I do not ask for sympathy, never did, Miss Stuart," he replied coolly.

"So, why did I consider inviting you, Mr. Volant? Or do you still prefer 'Lieutenant?'"

"'Mister' is fine," said Jack evenly.

"Art is a creation, an expression of the soul. It is a manifestation of our approach to life, including its triumphs and tragedies. That sculpture over there, the one you were appraising, represents a tragedy I personally witnessed, but its meaning would be lost on all except a woman who has lost a child."

"It's a beautiful piece of work," ventured Jack. "And I suspect that the story behind it is stark and quite painful."

She looked at him for a very long moment. "Yes, it was a slave's child on our plantation. The baby died at birth."

"But it doesn't appear to have the mother's features," said Jack, regretting the words as soon as they were spoken.

"The seed was planted by my father just as was that of Jerome, if that explanation pleases you."

"That suffices," said Jack, "but you haven't answered my question."

"I witnessed the gawkers, and the obtuse, ignorant, and obscene shouts of derision heaped upon you at the Louvre. Their insults fed off one another with mindless stupidity and arrogance. In that claustrophobic gallery, facing those taunts, any artist would have packed up and left. But I saw something they did not. I saw your art and your determination. I saw boldness in color, a disregard for convention, a complete rejection of the banal, uninspired work the copyists were slaving over."

Jack frowned. "I didn't expect that. I presume that you are being honest with me."

"I would not say this otherwise. You have talent, inventiveness, and an eye for dynamic expression. Don't run away from it. Embrace it, develop it just like my friends Manet, Renoir, Degas, and the rest. Those are the people and the direction you should embrace. That's why I asked you to come here. The only reason."

"I thank you for that, Miss Stuart. I've already met Monsieur Manet, and he warned me about the Salon. But I thought I would conform to what was expected of a struggling artist in Paris. I was wrong. I don't wish to make a fool of myself again. I will soon be leaving France. This has been a great mistake, and I'm embarrassed by my own naïveté."

"That would be a shame," she said. "You'd be running away from yourself and probably never pick up a brush again. Your life would be spent doing something onerous. You'd regret the decision for as long as you live."

She said it matter-of-factly, without the slightest emotion. A statement of truth not to be contradicted or equivocated. Jack studied her unbending countenance. "Again, I appreciate your candor. I thank you for the tea, and I believe it's time for me to leave, Miss Stuart."

He stood and held out his hand. She looked at it and slowly shook her head. "Shaking your hand would mean goodbye, Mr. Volant. I think there is more to be said unless you are leaving with the afternoon train."

He looked at her curiously. "What more do you wish to say? I suspect that you have a deep contempt for my past actions even though they took place seven years ago. You made that quite plain. Shelby refused to tell me anything about you, and I doubt that there's anything you would want me to know. You are the daughter of a slave owner and still loyal to a slavocracy I gladly helped destroy. Is that what you want to talk about? I doubt it."

Charlotte bit her lip and looked down at her hands. "I have never defended slavery, Mr. Volant. I thought it repulsive. But I grew up amid the mentality of the South. I knew no other life, knew no one from the North, and thought of that region as an alien world. A world that wanted to destroy us, and indeed they—you—did exactly that.

"I was a nurse during the war and cared for soldiers, both Confederate and Yankee. They screamed the same when their arms and legs were amputated, bled the same, and died side by side, often calling each other 'comrade.' I cried with them and never became inured to their suffering. But eventually something inside you dies, does it not?

"There was nothing left for me in the South after the surrender. Shelby wrote and said that I should come here, pursue art as I had done before the war. I did, and I brought Jerome with me. I wanted to put the war behind me and I thought I had until I saw you and that damn Union coat and hat you insist on wearing. Then it all came back, Mr. Volant. It came back like the sickening, tortured screams of men on amputation tables with limbs thrown into piles five feet high."

"And you will blame me and the Union for the rest of your life." Jack rose from his seat, holding his hat. "I can do nothing about that, no more than I can stop my own nightmares. You tended to men, many of whom died. My job was to make them die. I never enjoyed doing that—and I presume that you never killed anybody, so you won't know how that is."

"Don't presume, Mr. Volant. If I did it was for good reason, and very long ago. And I do not wish to discuss it."

"As you wish." Jack gazed into Charlotte's implacable face. "I fear that we are damned, and will have to live with all our memories and all the hates. But slavery is over, and the nation is whole. That pleases me. I bid you goodbye, Miss Stuart."

He did not again offer his hand. He turned to go.

"The man I loved, the man I was to marry, was mortally wounded at Gettysburg!" Charlotte bolted up out of her own seat. "I held him in my arms as he died. You think I have no reason to hate? Damn you, Mr. Volant!"

Quite suddenly she burst into tears, swept the teacups from the table, and ran into the house.

Jack watched her go. A dam had broken, and a profound sadness came over him. He should leave, but there was a gaping wound and something more, something perhaps undefinable. Had she extended her invitation simply to tell him that he could still be an artist?

In the still air he heard sobs, unquenchable grief that had raged within her for years. If he remained in Paris, he would surely see her, and the pain would return again and again. Not sure of exactly what to do, he bent to pick up the teacups that hadn't shattered. Perhaps he would take them to her, a sign of empathy, a truce on the road to possible redemption.

Jack's eyes strayed to the metal reflecting the morning light. The part not covered by mud didn't seem to be a tool, for it was elaborately engraved. With growing curiosity, he pulled it from the clinging mud.

He stared at it and glimpsed the woman standing by the window. She was staring at him, perhaps wondering why he had not yet gone. The door opened and she stood on the porch, bewilderment on her face.

"Charlotte! Charlotte!" Jack shouted, grasping the jambiya and holding it over his head as he darted for the house. Ignoring every accusation that had come before, he halted five feet in front of her. "This knife, where did it come from? How did it get here? You've got to tell me!"

Incredulity appeared on her face. She stared at the weapon and slowly shook her head.

"It was here? You found it here?" she said, her voice strangely weak.

"By the wagon, under the stone. I was going to bring the teacups to you and found this. Do you know how it got here?"

"I have no idea. I've never seen it before. Perhaps Jerome will know. He might have had it when the wagon crashed during the storm."

"Jerome might have had it?" Jack repeated. "Where is he? It's very important."

"He sleeps in the room over the shed. I think he's still there. But why—"

"Come with me. I'll need a witness."

"A witness? For what?" she said, trailing after him as he made for the shed.

"For a murder that occurred at a salon. One my brother may be accused of, Miss Stuart, that's what!"

CHAPTER 25

Paris

The same day

Jack raced up the stairs with Charlotte close behind him. He pounded on the door. When there was no answer Charlotte said, "Wake up. Open it."

Jerome opened the door, bare to the waist and wearing a ragged pair of pants, and bolted back when he saw Jack. Stepping into the small, cramped room Jack held up the knife. "Where did you get this? I need an answer and I need it right now!"

Jerome reached for the sheathed knife, but Jack drew it away. "Where, and when?" he demanded.

Jerome looked from Jack's face to Charlotte's, his eyes wide.

"This is Mr. Volant, Jerome. He's a ... a visitor. We're very concerned. He found this knife in the yard near your wagon. You must tell us if it's yours and, if so, how you got it."

Jerome, still appearing stunned by the onslaught, raised his hands. "I bought it yesterday. I was riding near the lake at the Bois de Boulogne, and I started talking to an Englishman. He said he'd lost nearly all his money at cards and showed me the knife. He said he'd sell it for only five francs. I'd wanted a knife like that for a long time. I don't know what the problem is."

"The problem," said Jack, "is that this knife may be a murder weapon, and the police are looking for anyone who has one. If the authorities see you carrying it, they may charge you with the crime—the murder of a courtesan."

"Murder? I didn't murder anyone!" Jerome blurted, his eyes wild.

"We aren't accusing you of murder," said Charlotte, tossing Jerome a shirt. "But as I said before, there are some questions I want answered."

"Like what?"

"Like why were you out at night in the storm? You never go out in weather like that."

"The rain wasn't too bad at first, just a light sprinkle. I didn't know what time it was—you know I lost my pocket watch—and I had to pick up furniture in the morning. I didn't want to wake you, so I just hitched the horse to the wagon and set out. I thought it was almost dawn, and I would wait outside, then load everything up. Of course, I had the knife with me for protection. It's not a good neighborhood. And then the storm came, and I was told that I should go home. I was to pick up the furniture when the storm passed and was near our house when the horse bolted, and ..."

Total silence followed the soliloquy. Jack tossed the knife onto the bed, crossed his arms, and stared at the youth.

"I've been around a while, and I've dealt with a lot of men, Jerome. People who are used to telling lies are usually good at it. Those who don't, not so much. I want to believe that you are essentially an honest man. Honesty is a mark of character. It's not a light or transient thing. I think you'd better work on your story."

Silence settled over the room.

"You said that a courtesan was murdered," said Jerome. "Who was she? Someone you knew?"

"Her name was Camille Lapin, and I only saw her once. I wasn't one of her admirers. She plied her occupation at a salon, one in which my brother entertained. A man who assisted him carried the same kind of knife. Now that man and my brother are considered suspects. But owning this knife could also implicate you."

"Your brother? I don't know your brother or his assistant. I don't go to the salons. And there are other knives like this in Paris. I saw one on ..."

"On whom?" said Jack, when Jerome suddenly stopped. Charlotte stepped into the room as Jack pressed on. "Was he an Arab? Perhaps an Algerian?"

Charlotte looked at Jack quizzically. "An Algerian?"

"My brother, Marcel, unwrapped mummies in the salon where Mademoiselle Lapin was murdered. His assistant poses as an Egyptian during the performance. He carried a knife, a jambiya like the one Jerome says he bought from an Englishman. Someone who's wealthy enough to play at the tables and suddenly appears at the Bois de Boulogne to sell a unique knife for only five francs. A bit strange, don't you think? He could get more at a pawn shop. I witnessed the performance my brother gave, and I saw his assistant with the knife in his belt. So, tell me Jerome, what is his name?"

"Name? I don't know. He never told me."

"So, you know him?" said Charlotte.

Jack moved closer and peered directly at Jerome. In a quiet but searing voice, he said, "His name is Jabari Abraxas, and I suspect that he is extremely dangerous. I don't doubt that it was he who sold you the knife."

"Are you sure?" asked Charlotte.

"Marcel told me that the man sneaks them into France and sells them. My brother didn't kill the courtesan, but

Abraxas may have. The detectives think he might have approached her for her favors, only to be scorned. Perhaps, for that reason, it was he who killed Lapin, and he sold the knife to shift the blame." Jack thought for a second. "Jerome, did he give you his own knife or another one?"

"Not his own. I don't think he would sell that."

Charlotte exhaled slowly. "I don't remember you ever lying to me before, Jerome. And I think the story about the furniture is also untrue. I think you were doing something exceedingly dangerous and you don't want to talk about it."

"Or you're afraid to talk about it," added Jack.

Jerome lowered his head and covered his face. "I'm sorry. I did lie to you. I think it's best if I go away. I don't want you to be involved in any of this."

"But you are involved—we are involved," said Charlotte. "And I don't want you to go, I need you here."

"I'm scared, really scared."

"You have good reason to be," said Jack. "But whatever you do, say nothing about that knife, and show it to no one. And stay away from Jabari Abraxas."

"One more thing," said Jerome. "There's a woman I encountered. She's involved with Abraxas, and I think she's dangerous. But I really don't know anything more about her."

Back in the yard, Charlotte said, "I don't know whether to thank you or not, Jack Volant. This entire incident with the knife might have just gone away if you hadn't found it."

"That's what you think? I doubt it. Things like this tend to spiral out of control, especially when unsavory people are involved. I would keep the gate closed and a pistol close at hand if I were you."

"I don't own a pistol and wouldn't use one if I had."

"I think you should reconsider. But keep an eye out. I'm usually with Shelby at Galignani's."

When she didn't reply, he walked to the gate. "I bid you good day, Miss Stuart."

***

The clock on the mantle chimed three in the morning when Charlotte woke. A fog had blown in, and wind tore through the bare oak beside the house. But it was not the chimes or the wind that had interrupted her sleep. It was the horse as it trotted out of the courtyard, toward the front gate. Springing out of bed, she ran onto the porch. "Jerome, where are you going? You heard what Jack said!"

But he was already past the gate. She could hear the pounding of hoofbeats as the mount was spurred on. She felt drained, as if something terrible was going to happen.

Charlotte climbed the stairs and sat on the edge of her bed. It was still dark, impossible for anyone to see more than four feet in front of him. Dashing out on such a terrible night was an act of desperation The thought that Jerome might encounter Abraxas was too frightening to consider. And yet why else would he do it?

She lay back on her bed, but sleep would not come. If it weren't so late and she knew where he lived, she'd contact Jack. He seemed to care about what happened to Jerome.

And to her?

No, of course not. Nor would she wish him to. The damnyankee. He was an anathema, a bitter reminder of the extirpation of a world in which she'd once glowed.

Then she remembered his face as he spoke of his fear of damnation, and he seemed none of those things. Just a strange, troubled person, a caged man, haunted by his past.

Loneliness settled over Charlotte like a blanket of snow. She shivered as if she could shake it off. She had convinced herself so many times that there was a distinct difference between being alone and being lonely. Sculpting was a solitary endeavor, one she enjoyed. But it was a daytime thing. The cold stone provided no comfort during long winter nights. Bitterness was gnawing upon her, defining who she was and who she would become: a brittle, scarred old woman with only the barest essence of the lovely belle from so long before.

Damnyankee, she thought again. How dare he etch his name into the granite of her mind?

What did he think of her? Would he, in fact, think of her at all? If he had inscribed his mark upon her mind, then surely she had scorched any interest for her in his. It would be unseemly for her to invite him again, even if she wanted to—which was far from resolved. More to the point, would he even consider coming? Except for the matter of Jerome, they had said all that there was to say. Anything else would be superfluous, mindless, and banal.

No, let it lie. Let things return to normal. Chipping away on the stone, one day after the next, provided a sense of constancy that brooked no intervention. That's why she had come to Paris. Not because it was the "City of Light," the most dynamic and artful place in the world. It was a sanctuary for a recluse, a place where she could hide behind a six-foot wall.

The wall. Charlotte sat up with a start and looked out her window. Jerome hadn't closed the gate. She couldn't see it through the fog. She considered going out and bolting it, but decided against it. He would do that when he returned—although that would not likely be anytime soon.

Another thought came to Charlotte, and all consideration of sleep vanished. She dressed hastily, ran downstairs, threw on a coat, and bolted for Jerome's room above the shed. The knife, where was the knife? She pulled out the drawers from a rough wooden chest, but it wasn't there, nor was it in the closet or secreted in any of the boxes of assorted tools or knickknacks he collected from the pawnbrokers' establishments on Rue des Blancs-Manteaux.

With a mixture of anger and despondency, she returned to her favorite chair and stared out the window. If he didn't return by eight o'clock, she would go to Galignani's. Perhaps Jack would be there.

***

The fog came in great gasps, breaking and roiling up again. At one moment moonlight broke through and Jerome could perceive the field, trees bare, with twisted branches like arthritic limbs. On occasion a house came into view, its windows still dark. A dog barked upon hearing the clop, clop of the horse's shod hoofs. Jerome turned away. He didn't want to be seen.

He had fashioned a loop on a belt into which the sheathed knife was secured. Though he had never used a knife in anger, still it was a weapon, and that was of some comfort. He just hoped that there would be no reason to draw it out tonight.

The cluster of dilapidated shacks appeared through a dense growth of trees. He halted the horse and considered dismounting and walking the rest of the way. There would be no reason for the Algerian to be in the vicinity; the delivery was still two nights hence. A chill coursed through him, and not because of the cold. He admitted to himself that he was scared. Except for the first time he had ventured here, he hadn't experienced any real fear. He'd achieved a rapport of sorts. Though they considered him an outsider, they tacitly accepted him for his veracity, generosity, and allegiance to the cause.

But this night would be different, and his reception potentially perilous. A horse whinnied somewhere in the distance. The sound was followed by another whinny, not that far away. Jerome nudged his mount on at a walk. Twigs broke under its hoofs, and he hoped his horse wouldn't whinny in return. He remained in the shadows, the fleeting moon illuminating patches of ground like a lamp show when not obscured by heavy cloud.

Several hundred yards off the dirt road lay the remains of an old barn. Its roof looked like a swayback horse and part of the rear wall was gone. He had investigated it a year before and found that it had a serviceable loft and doors that could be shuttered against a piercing wind or prying eyes, not that anyone would venture there. After a hasty cleaning, he'd once brought a girl there, anticipating a rapturous evening. Though the *amourette* was briefer than expected, largely due to an invasion of mice, that did little to dissuade him from the idea of using it in the future. It loomed darkly in the night, and Jerome passed it without another thought.

As if she had been awaiting him, the petite woman was there, head covered in a large drooping hat, shoulders wrapped in a heavy shawl, and arms crossed over her chest. Her dress was plain, no hoops or adornment, but she wore a three-inch-wide belt, and tucked into it was an unholstered revolver. She seemed more attractive than before, but no less determined.

"No need to dismount," she said in a voice dry and devoid of inflection.

Jerome had halted ten feet in front of her and had no intention of dismounting.

"You should not be here, not for two more days. But you have come to tell me something I don't want to hear. Is that not true?"

"The wagon is ruined, broken, and cannot be repaired. I will not be able to assist you anymore."

"We can find another wagon. That's not difficult. But I see fear in your eyes. Are you cowardly? I thought not. Perhaps I was wrong."

"I am not a coward," replied Jerome. "A situation has arisen over which I have no control. I will say nothing about the delivery or your presence. Or the others," he hastily added.

She stared at him for what seemed an eternity. "That is a wise decision. Anything less would prove rather distasteful."

A strange phraseology. Perhaps she was more literate than he'd thought. But that wasn't his concern, not now.

"You should go," she said, her voice barely audible over the wind.

Jerome touched the brim of his hat, turned his horse about, and rode past the distant cluster of trees. A swelling of heavy clouds covered the moon. He turned his horse again, quickly rode amongst the trees, and waited.

The woman remained where he'd found her as a rider approached. Although it was impossible to hear the exchanged words, he could see her pointing. Jerome turned his mount once again and quickly left the grove.

It could have been anyone, a simple traveler, perhaps lost and asking for directions. But rarely would one be out this early in the morning. It could only be one person, and that man would resolutely follow him. Follow him home.

Jerome slipped from one cluster of trees to another until he reached the barn. Quickly dismounting, he opened a sagging door and led the horse in. Some minutes later a rider appeared in the distance. He halted his mount, surveyed all that was around him, and moved on.

There was time to think now. Should he have spoken to Charlotte about this? He had always confided in her. He told her almost everything except about the girls. He grinned, thinking that she undoubtedly knew. But this was different, chillingly so. He had just been hunted and could have been killed. He could only imagine what would she have said:

"Jerome, this is idiocy! You are collaborating to destroy the government that gave us sanctuary? For what?"

"For the poor, the wretched poor who are despised and condemned as subhuman. Just like the slave I used to be."

"But you're studying law, French law. If they allow you to practice, you can defend them in court. You may even become famous, a Negro lawyer speaking for the poor. You might even change the laws, become a statesman. You are so bright and have so many possibilities."

"But that will take decades. They cannot wait. They will not wait, and I can do something."

"What? Insurrection? Revolution? Have you any idea of the consequences? Of the deaths of so many? Do you think that a handful of insurrectionists will bring down the government? And when the authorities hunt you down, they'll come to me. Yes, Jerome. They will say, 'Aren't you a friend of the Empress?' What should I say? What would she say? And how might I defend you if you are still alive?"

"You don't have to defend me. The people will. The oppressed will. Just like slaves who rose up against their masters. There is always bloodshed in the cause of justice."

"But you will die, Jerome. And what will become of me?"

He sighed. What could he possibly tell her? That he adored her but would die for a hopeless cause? A fantasy? What had he been thinking? He lay his head on the saddle and closed his eyes. He would say nothing and all would be well. It would remain his secret, but he would be careful. Very careful indeed.

Jerome woke as the morning light streaked in from the roof, through the drooping timbers that had been assailed by countless storms. Cautiously he peered out and, when satisfied that no one was watching, saddled his horse and hurried toward home.

Only for the briefest instant did he see a shadowed figure on horseback. Like a phantasmagoric illusion it seemed to float from one clump of trees to the next. For a moment Jerome reined in his mount. Thinking it was only a flutter of birds, he spurred his horse and halted at the gate. It was closed. Charlotte had closed it. Had she seen him leave? He hoped not.

Rain commenced again. Jerome felt drained. He closed the gate behind him and saw that the storm had toppled a tree and broken a three-foot-wide section of wall. He would repair it later that day. Right now, he wanted another hour of sleep. After that he would talk to Charlotte. The options were few, he realized, and none particularly good.

CHAPTER 26

Paris

Two days later

It was another cold day, made even more uncomfortable by sitting on the top level of the omnibus. When it stopped in front of the old bookstore, Jack climbed down and wormed his way through a half dozen horses tied to hitching posts. One, a seven-year-old gray mare, belonged to Shelby. It was a spirited animal, which surprised him considering Shelby's ponderous condition, and it sported a McClellan-style saddle of Austrian design, nearly the same version used by North and South in the Civil War. He patted the mare's neck; it was a fine horse.

"It would seem that you had an interesting visit with Charlotte and Jerome," said Shelby when Jack joined him.

"Nothing like I expected. If it hadn't been for the incident with Jerome, I would have left after Charlotte excoriated me. She told me of how she lost the man she loved. It was as if she blamed me for his death. She ran into the house, tears and all. It would have been the end, and a very bitter one, too. I thought I would never see her again."

"But now you will?"

"Perhaps. She's concerned about Jerome, and now I'm involved. I wasn't expecting to be—not with the murder or anything else Jerome's implicated in."

"He didn't tell you?"

"No. He came up with a story, but I don't believe it and neither does Charlotte."

"And you think he's in something over his head."

"I do," said Jack. "I think that's why he said that he would leave Paris. Charlotte asked him to stay, but I think leaving is a good idea. He might go to Metz. My brother could find him lodging," said Jack.

"What about you? Are you leaving Paris?"

"I'll stay. At least for a while. I still want to be an artist; maybe I'll talk to Manet."

"And there is Charlotte." A smile played on Shelby's lips. "Despite that chain mail she wears, I think she's a lonely woman."

"Lonely is a far distance from liking or anything more, if I take your meaning. I think she may tolerate me until all this is over. After that? She's a magnificent-looking woman and a fine artist. She'll find somebody if she wishes. Or he'll find her."

"Such a pessimist."

Jack merely shook his head. "Tell me about Jerome. Maybe I should know more about him, considering that I'm now part of this little drama."

"Well, you're already aware that he's Charlotte's half brother. They're very close. He saved her life, you know."

"I didn't."

"There were three deserters, riff-raff, the slime that followed the armies," said Shelby. "They watched the house and saw Charlotte and her father but not Jerome. They came at dusk expecting a fine time."

"What happened?" said Jack, wondering what the boy could possibly have done.

For the next five minutes Shelby described how Jerome had killed the deserters and saved Charlotte.

"And then what?" asked Jack.

"The man Jerome shot dropped the lantern and the whole place went up in flames."

"They lost everything?" said Jack.

"Except for their lives and the money her father had put in that box. Charlotte and Jerome had enough for passage and left for Paris shortly after."

Jack sipped his coffee and sat back in his chair. "That explains a lot," he finally said. "Apparently Jerome's got a backbone. Do you still think he has the pistol?"

"I suppose so. I doubt he told customs about it." Shelby looked past Jack's shoulder. "There's that scarecrow inspector. Wonder what he wants."

Gene Gustave, seemingly more emaciated than ever, walked stiffly to their table and leaned in close. "This is not for publication, monsieur, but more rifles have been stolen from the arsenal. If you learn anything, you are advised to inform us without hesitation. The army is extremely concerned. They are watching the roads."

With that, Gustave turned and quickly left the café.

Jack met Shelby's eyes and slapped the table. "Guns, that's it. Jerome must have been running guns. Why else would he be out at night in a storm?"

"But who was he taking them to?" asked Shelby, his coarse eyebrows narrowing.

"I don't know, but I intend to find out."

"You said that his wagon is broken. If there's to be another theft, if someone is awaiting another shipment and he can't deliver ..."

"He doesn't suspect that we know about the guns," said Jack.

"I don't know if he's more scared of not delivering or of being caught by the police or the army."

"He won't be able to deliver anything until he repairs the wagon." Jack bolted from his chair. "I need to borrow your horse."

"I'm going with you. We'll take my carriage."

"Too slow."

"If he's caught ..." said Shelby.

"Then he's dead."

***

Jack was surprised to see Charlotte's front gate open and a black gelding half hidden in trees across the road. Did she have a guest? No, she would have shut the gate. Something didn't seem right.

A stiff wind tore at the wide collar of his greatcoat as he dismounted Shelby's horse and walked around to the back of the house. Gray stones had toppled from the wall; Jack clambered over them to gain access to the yard. Fog drifted over the ground, which appeared devoid of life. He waited, his ears tuned to any sound other than the wind and the tapping of branches.

The figure was faint, close to the work shed and at a distance from the house. The mist lifted. A figure rose off the ground, then fell back. A shawl fluttered, followed by the hem of a dress.

"Charlotte," Jack said, running toward her. A purple bruise spread across her forehead.

"There's a man in there," she said, vaguely pointing toward the house. "He has a knife and a gun. I threw a rock at him, but—"

"Stay here. Don't try to get up." Jack started for the house. Behind him, Charlotte rose determinedly and followed.

The front door was ajar. Jack peered through a window. Chairs had been overturned, and shards of a vase littered the floor. There was a sudden shout, the sound of a pistol shot, and an anguished moan. Another shot, this one shattering a window on the second floor. A moment later Jerome ran out, blood staining his right shoulder. Stumbling forward, he fell. Jabari, pursuing, tripped over him and fell flat. The pistol fell from his hand.

Recovering his balance and straddling Jerome's supine body, the Algerian drew his jambiya and raised it high. Charlotte screamed.

Concentrating on his intended victim and ignoring to Charlotte, Jabari didn't see the booted foot that slammed into his head. He toppled over, but still managed to slash right and left while deftly rolling away.

Jack retrieved the gun and fired, but the bullet went wide. The Algerian swung about and kicked Jack in the face. The pistol flew from his hand as he pitched backward. Jabari again raised the knife, but this time he flew at Jack, who glimpsed a raised revolver from the corner of his eye.

With a roar and eruption of smoke, the round caught Jabari in his shoulder and spun him around, but he recovered and stumbled toward the gate. Jack slowly rose and saw Charlotte, shaking, the weapon held down by her side.

"Give it to me!" he said, lurching forward. But Jabari Abraxas had already flung himself onto his horse and lay low over the saddle as it pounded away.

Jack knelt beside Jerome. "He's hurt bad, but alive." Gathering his strength, he lifted the youth and carried him into the house.

"On the sofa," said Charlotte. She sought a medical bag, drew out a thick bandage, and began to staunch the wound with it. Jerome's eyes sought hers, then Jack's. His breath was shallow, but he raised a hand and weakly held Jack's wrist.

"I tried to talk to him, reason with him, but..." he murmured before releasing his grip.

"Jack, I'm going to extract the bullet. I have chloroform, but he'll still feel pain. You'll have to hold him down. I have a bottle of whiskey in the pantry; please get it."

"For Jerome?"

"For the scalpel." She considered the bottle as he handed it to her. "For all of us."

Charlotte worked quickly. Within five minutes she held the bullet aloft, then wrapped it in a handkerchief on a table.

"He's lost a lot of blood, but he'll recover," said Charlotte after cleaning her instruments and carefully placing them in her bag.

They carried Jerome to the upstairs bed, the chloroform having taken its effect. He lay semiconscious, his shoulder swathed in bandages. From time to time he winced, murmuring delirious words, but his breathing was steady. Charlotte checked the bandages and said, "Jack, I want us to talk. Let's go downstairs. He won't wake for another hour, and I'll tend to him then."

They sat across from one another in the ancient kitchen, a white tablecloth covering a rough table. Dark wooden beams stretched across the smoke-stained ceiling, and along the walls hung copper kettles. A bucket of coal sat beside a great iron stove that radiated warmth through the close room.

She poured steaming tea into two large ceramic cups. "I trust this will satisfy? I detest those ridiculous demitasse cups the effete hold with their pinky sticking out."

"I never took you for a shrinking violet." Jack peered at the swelling on her forehead, a deep dioxide purple with a tinge of rose around it.

"You should have a cold compress on that." He found a cloth and doused it from the pump at the sink. She allowed him to wrap it around the darkening bruise and took a deep breath.

"It's strange how quickly circumstances can change the way we perceive things, perceive people. I never thought that I would be thanking you. But I am."

"That's not at all necessary. Shelby and I put it together and I knew that I had to be here."

"Put what together?" Charlotte asked, sipping her tea.

"A detective came by Galignani's and told Shelby that there had been another theft at an arsenal."

"Guns?" said Charlotte, her eyes wide. "Was Jerome involved in that?"

"There's a strong possibility, but I wouldn't want to accuse him until we have the facts. I just hope he's willing to give us a straight answer."

"Now I think he will have good reason to do so."

Time seemed to stand still.

"I'm mightily impressed with your surgical skills," said Jack. "I haven't seen a doctor do any better. And rarely have I seen one clean their instruments or even wash their hands as you did before removing that bullet. I truly commend you."

"That's very kind, but I've had a lot of practice. Regretfully, I even did an amputation when our doctor was summoned onto the field. That gave me nightmares for a very long time."

She put a hand to the swelling and picked up an old mirror. "Not much of a beauty mark, is it?"

"I don't think you need any, Mrs. Stuart. Some women might, but not you." Jack felt himself flush.

Charlotte frowned, cocked her head to one side, and took a deep breath. "I am amazed that you came back, and eternally grateful. Without your timely arrival, both Jerome and I would have been killed. I believe that, I do indeed. And considering your magnanimous assistance, Monsieur Volant, I believe you have earned the right to call me Charlotte."

Jack studied her and smiled. "That is indeed a privilege, Lady Charlotte."

She laughed. "Lady Charlotte? How quaint."

"Charlotte, my name is Jack. And I am a very simple man."

"Simple, I doubt." Then, with a thin smile she said, "Very well, Jack. Other than being a damnyankee, I think you are a fine, decent, and caring man. Those, especially in Paris, are a rarity."

"Damn Yankee, as I've told Monsieur Shelby several dozen times, is two words," said Jack with a twinkle in his eye.

"Oh, my, that will be a challenge to master, Monsieur Jack," she replied playfully. Then her smile faded. "Who was that man? The one who attacked us?"

"The one I mentioned before, who goes by the name Jabari Abraxas. He posed as an Egyptian, but Egyptian he is not."

"A stage name?" queried Charlotte.

"He, along with my brother, Steven—or Marcel, as he calls himself—were performers in the Salon d' Chantilly."

"I am aware of the place. Detestable, a den of pompous arrogant dandies and their vapid, hollow paramours. Deprive them of their money and they'll sink into the mud."

"Devastating, but a fair description," said Jack. "I was there, invited by my brother for one of his evening performances. That morning he'd driven me to the Bois de Boulogne and I saw a lady, a demimonde, whose portrait I desperately wanted to paint. Marcel said that she frequented the salon where he unwraps mummies. So, hoping to be introduced, I attended the performance."

"She must have been quite flattered. Did she agree to your proposal?"

"Flattered, perhaps, but no, she did not. Her suitor, a man named Étienne Daudet, was quite insulting and forbade her to agree."

"I have heard of Monsieur Daudet. He is a fine artist but a narcissistic fool who glories in the old regime. But the demimonde, she must be quite beautiful. Does she haunt your dreams?"

Jack took a sip of his tea. "Only as an artist."

"I see," said Charlotte, raising her eyebrows.

"I have no interest in courtesans or life in the salons. I came here to become an artist, something I now question. As for the demimonde, I doubt that I will ever see her again, nor will I make any effort to, if that answers your female curiosity."

"I think it's far too early to infer that I harbor jealousy, Jack," Charlotte said, again with a raised eyebrow and a fleeting smile.

"Of course. But to answer your question about Abraxas, he carried the same sort of knife I found in the yard. He also had one much like it during the performance at the salon. I've encountered numerous dangerous men, but he would be near the top of the list."

"And he got away."

They sipped their tea. "What induced you to return on this terribly cold winter day?" Charlotte said.

"A concern for you and Jerome."

Charlotte peered at him closely. "After everything I said to you? That astounds and impresses me."

"It seemed the right thing to do."

"Few men would have done it."

"As I said, I was with Shelby at the café when a detective came in. I believe his name is Gene Gustave. Apparently he knows that Shelby acquires a lot of information."

"Gabriel knows a lot of people. That's his business," said Charlotte.

"Apparently so. This Gustave told him about the army's stolen rifles—"

"Dear Lord!" said Charlotte, bounding from her chair. "Guns, so it's true."

"I saw fear in his eyes when we confronted him about the knife. He didn't want to tell us what he was really up to, but we knew that his excuse was bogus. He wasn't delivering furniture, Charlotte. I suspect was running guns to Abraxas, and he was scared."

"Oh my God," she said, slumping back down. "And he went out again last night even though you warned him not to. He left in a terrible hurry. I thought it quite strange and ran outside to stop him, but he kept going as if chased by banshees."

"And you had no idea of where," said Jack.

She shook her head, a worried look on her face.

"Whatever transpired, he ran back here, followed by Abraxas, who was intent on murder. But he also found you."

"Why didn't he kill me? He could have done so very easily," Charlotte said.

"Because you didn't know who he was and would never see him again. Jerome was his target. You were already unconscious. No need to waste time."

Charlotte wrapped her arms about herself. "So, he came here thinking Jerome might give away secrets?"

"Very likely. In fact, he might have thought Jerome would go to the police, tell them where the guns were hidden."

"And not implicate himself? I'd think he would be more cagey. They would have found that he delivered them."

"Then he would have been charged and put in prison," Jack said. Her hand touched his. "Or beheaded."

"So what do we do?" she asked.

"I wish I had a good answer. I don't. But for his own protection, he should leave Paris when he recovers."

"And what about Abraxas? His wound isn't fatal. Do you think he'll come back?"

"Not for a while. Perhaps not at all. He's too smart, too wary, especially if he thinks that I'll be around. For all I know, Marcel might have told him about me. About my past."

She seemed pensive. Quietly she said, "And will you be nearby, Monsieur Lieutenant?"

"Of that there is a strong likelihood, mademoiselle. A strong likelihood indeed."

CHAPTER 27

Paris

Four days later

"She fancies you, Jack," said Shelby, sitting at his usual table littered with notes and the malodorous ash of a twice-smoked cigar. "Quite amazing, actually. Except for Monet, Pissarro, Renoir, and on occasion Manet, she doesn't think much of anybody."

"You're speaking of Charlotte, I presume."

"Who else? I saw her two days ago, and I think she's smitten in a quiet sort of way. Charlotte is not particularly demonstrative. Unless she's having a hissy, and then you better find a hole in the ground. But considering the peril you saved her from, I got the impression that she might have been receptive to a little romance."

"The situation would hardly have been accommodating with Jerome, half delirious, moaning, begging for attention."

"After she patched him up, then," said Shelby. "I don't know how you might regard Charlotte, but if it were I, hesitation would not be on the agenda. She is a most handsome woman with a quick mind and biting wit. You could do much worse if you were considering a female companion."

"She's beautiful and certainly intelligent, but romance would be a complication," said Jack, waving away the cigar smoke.

"Horse dung! You need direction, motivation, and someone to keep you from going over the abyss, mister. She's your Clara Barton, your Florence Nightingale."

"You think I'm doing that poorly? That I need saving?"

"I think you have lost your way. You are disintegrating, though you might dispute it, and that pains me. If you intend to be an artist then be an artist. If not, find a purpose in life. At least before the next war."

"War? What war?"

"The one no Frenchman wants to think about except General Ducrot and Baron Stoffel, the military attaché in Berlin. I know Stoffel, interviewed him last year, and he's writing again in *Le Monde*, but no one is paying attention." Shelby pointed to the article. "The paper gave him half a column on the back page. So, I have a job for you, Jack. I would do it myself if I weren't as busy as a three-legged cat in a sandbox. I was going to tell you about it before you rushed off to save Jerome."

"Is this to give me purpose in life?" said Jack dryly.

"It's to obtain information, and it's damn important. I need you to meet with Baron Stoffel in Berlin. You can take the train through Metz. I'll give you a letter of introduction and say you're a journalist recently hired by Galignani's."

"And what exactly do you want to know?"

"Everything he knows about Prussian armaments, preparations, and intent. Especially their leadership under Prince William, Bismarck, and Moltke. It shouldn't take you more than a week but it's vital to me. The French have to wake up."

"I'm still worried for Charlotte. I don't want to leave her alone."

"You won't be gone long, and she can stay at my place until you return. I'll keep her safe, you can be sure."

***

"As an American, Monsieur Volant, you may learn far more than I can," said the French military attaché, after warmly greeting Jack in his Berlin office. "Indeed, the Prussians are so fervently righteous and confident, they will welcome inspection of their forces. Especially by a former cavalry officer who fought at Gettysburg. I can put you in touch with one of their propagandists, a Colonel Albrecht von Brandenburg, recently from Paris."

"I have met him. Arrogant, pompous."

"I believe that's the dictionary definition of Prussian, Monsieur Volant," said Baron Stoffel with a barely concealed grin.

"So, what makes the Prussians feel so righteous?"

"It's simple. Louis XIV was all-powerful. "*L'état, c'est moi*," as he famously said. He took the province of Alsace from the Germans and they want it back, along with Lorraine if they can get it."

"Can they?"

"It comes down to self-deception—ours, not theirs. The French army conducts itself according to the phrase '*On se débrouillera toujours*': we'll always somehow work our way through it. This stupidity is the result of thirty years of war against poorly armed, disorganized tribes in Africa. And in the last two years the politicians have gutted the military budget. They believe that war is unthinkable, a relic of the past."

Jack removed a notebook from his pocket. "I'd like to take some notes if you don't mind."

The attaché nodded.

"So, how does the army find its recruits? Train its men?"

247

"It's a truly scandalous system and would be a joke were it not so serious. We have no trained reservists. Conscription proceeds by picking names out of a box. But a youth from a wealthy family can pay for a substitute to take his place. Thus, only the poorest classes, the least educated, are inducted."

"We had substitutes during our civil war," said Jack. "They were paid three hundred dollars to take another man's place."

"But your Federal draft was only for two years, and men from all classes volunteered to fight—on both sides. Many of them were disciplined, trained, well equipped. Here the security of France depends on the Garde Nationale, whose most important responsibility is to defend the wealthy class and maintain the status quo. Worse yet, the men train only two weeks each year and must be allowed to return home every night!"

"But France has a regular army besides the Garde," said Jack.

"Yes, yes, a considerable force, but not trained for a major war. Certainly not against the Prussians."

The military attaché shook his head, his frustration growing visibly. "Yes! Do write about this travesty, monsieur. We are a nation only a river away from Europe's greatest threat. What the French army has become is a disgrace. Nothing but bravado and cries of *Vive la France!*" That is the basis of our strategy. Unlike Prussia, we have no general staff, and no military university. We have no plans for an offensive, no organization to get men to the front, feed them, or assign them specific orders. On paper we have a formidable force, nearly nine hundred thousand men, but nothing, absolutely nothing, is in readiness. Our men have to go to the depots, collect their weapons and uniforms, then report to their units and hope that someone is in charge."

"But the French army has some very advanced weapons," said Jack. "I've heard of the chassepot, your breech-loading rifle. It's supposed to be of excellent quality."

"Indeed, a fine weapon, and we have a million of them. It's far better than the Prussian needle gun, better range, more accurate, but will it be enough? I doubt it."

"What of the mitrailleuse?" Jack had heard of this weapon, a Gatling gun with twenty-five barrels.

Stoffel raised his eyebrows. "Another excellent weapon, but kept so secret that hardly anyone has been trained to use it. Trust me, it will sit in the warehouse or be poorly used to the end of the war."

The man sighed. "I sound like a pessimist, a defeatist, do I not? Well, perhaps I am. And who knows, there may be a miracle, the resurrection of Jeanne d'Arc, a Napoleon Bonaparte, but wars are rarely won through miracles or valor, monsieur. Prussia has universal conscription! Total readiness—every train, regiment, division on a strict timetable. All are ready on six rail lines, four added in just the last few years and directly aimed at our two defensive positions."

"And where are those?" asked Jack

"Metz and Strasbourg. As it stands now, we have to divide our armies. One wing is at Strasbourg, if and when we should ever cross the Rhine. The other's at Metz, a defensive barrier guarding the French interior. In my view, neither is capable of succeeding."

The attaché looked weary, his heavy white moustache drooping over a deeply-lined face. He sat back in his chair. "Monsieur Shelby wrote me that you were a soldier in your Civil War. So, I ask you, what was the most lethal killer on the battlefield? What created the greatest carnage?"

"Artillery. Massed firepower. Be it solid shot or canister. A few sacks of iron balls could mow down two hundred men. Arms, legs, heads, blown completely away."

"Yes, that is so. The artillery of your war was made up of muzzle-loaders just like most of our guns, rifled twelve-pounders. These are obsolete weapons, as outdated as swords against muskets. Perhaps Oberst Brandenburg will graciously show you what Prussia will use against us. A monstrous cannon. It was displayed at the Paris exhibition a few years back. Of course, we French did our best to ignore the thing. Oh, yes, Monsieur Volant, he will want to impress an American very much. He may even let you pull the lanyard and fire the damned thing."

***

"A pleasure to see you again," said Oberst Albrecht von Brandenburg, shaking Jack's hand. "That was a rather unseemly incident at my wife's salon, but it is all in the past." The Prussian cleaned his monocle. "So, my dear friend Baron Stoffel tells me that you are a former cavalry officer. In such case, you will appreciate the ingenious progress of Prussian arms. Ja, Herr Volant. It is my distinct privilege to show a fellow man of arms our weaponry, of which we are extremely proud."

It was a miserably chilly day, and Brandenburg's stout body was sheathed in a thick gray coat, which fitted him snuggly. The coat was adorned with a gleaming medal, the Knight's Cross of the Hohenzollern House Order, an iron cross topped by a crown and crossed swords. He wore a steel helmet with a gold spike and thigh-high black boots.

Jack, wearing a civilian coat and brown bowler hat, his leg aching in the cold, tried to keep up with the colonel, who strode purposefully across the muddy field. Quite suddenly Brandenburg turned and said, "There's something I thought of, something that you might have some knowledge of. There is an American, a Monsieur Marcel Cheval. Perhaps you've heard of him."

"I might have, but there are thousands of Americans in Paris."

"Well, it was in all the papers and, as a journalist I should think you would have heard of him. This fellow and a potential accomplice are being sought by the police. Of course, I would have lent my assistance to the detectives but I knew no more about it than anyone else. And my time was limited—my martial duties here, you see."

"And how long have you known this Monsieur Cheval, if I may ask?" said Jack.

"Some time now. My wife invites him every few weeks to unwrap mummies, a silly thing, a carnival for infantile and irrational people, gullible, with a shallow understanding of the world, of realpolitik, ja? This Cheval struck me as a debauched and shady character. An untrustworthy sort, not suitable for proper Prussian society. Of course, in Paris ..."

The oberst shrugged, raising one palm while the other hand steadied his heavy saber. He stared at Jack while twirling his once-blond moustache.

Jack stared back. "And how soon, Oberst, did you return to Berlin after this murder?"

"Only a matter of days. I was ordered back to my regiment, the hussars, but I am also assigned to the general staff and hence have this opportunity to meet with you."

"I deeply appreciate your assistance," said Jack. "Certain French officials believe that Prussia has every intention of going to war, of invading France. Do you think this is true?"

The colonel considered the question for a long moment. "Allow me to say this, Monsieur Volant; all nations have plans to defend themselves, particularly against a traditional aggressor. For a number of centuries, that has been France.

All of Europe has been terrorized by her rapacious armies. French kings have shed our Prussian blood, as well as that of the British, the Belgians, the Spanish and yes, the Russians. Never again, monsieur! Never again! But as for now, I have no knowledge of any belligerent intent toward Paris. We are at peace, and I hope that prevails. But in case it doesn't ..."

He let the sentence hang in the air, resuming his destination.

"Americans should know that the king of Prussia controls the North German Confederation and its entire army. Until recently, Germany consisted of many states, almost medieval in their desire for supremacy. But that has all changed thanks to Otto von Bismarck. It was his genius that helped Prussia defeat Austria in '66. It was he who developed our modern army."

"So, how large is it?" asked Jack as they approached a half dozen gray field guns with gaping barrels that stared back at them like cyclopes.

"We have twenty-two thousand magnificently trained officers of all ranks. They engage in war games, outdoor maneuvers, and map exercises, all intimately connected to their troops. And we have one million, one hundred and eighty thousand men under their command. It's the largest fighting force Europe has ever seen."

Jack nodded and made a notation in his book. "And weapons, of course," he continued as they trod over rain-soaked ground.

"Ja, we have thousands of rapid-fire, breech-loading field guns made of steel. They are far superior to the French brass muzzle-loaders. Not only is the range greater, but we can reload and fire many times faster. But it is this, Monsieur Volant, that I must show you." Brandenburg, pointed to the behemoths that sat like hippos in their riveted steel carriages.

"Every day a new crew trains with live munitions. The training is constant, no expense is spared. They will fire ten, fifteen, twenty rounds in a single morning. And if they miss their targets they fire again. They fire until they learn," said the oberst. "We are a hardworking, organized, determined, and disciplined people. We are not the French, monsieur."

"The French aren't disciplined?"

Brandenburg shook his head. "Herr Volant, war is not for children or untrained masses. As a former soldier you certainly understand this. If some foreign nation forces the North German Federation to fight, then they will suffer the consequences. But," he reiterated, "we only fight for what is right, for what is just. We do not make war for light or transient reasons. No, monsieur, Prussia is an honorable nation, but"—he waved a finger in front of Jack— "now let us meet the captain of that gun."

At over eight feet in height, the siege gun had a segmented barrel of four sections, each one greater in diameter until it merged with a massive center cylinder that could be elevated or lowered by a series of gears. Loading the enormous weapon was accomplished by swinging open a massive breech. A conical shell was raised by a hoist from a caisson and mechanically rammed home.

The overall appearance was one of profound lethality and stubbiness.

"The shell from this weapon has the weight and force to smash through any fortification," boasted the colonel as they approached the officer of the gun. Upon seeing the oberst, the captain sprang to attention and smartly saluted. The gun crew stood stiffly in their positions until Brandenburg returned the salute. "Do continue, Herr Capitan. We want to show this American journalist the power of our weaponry. Is this Krupp gun ready to fire?"

"It is, Mein Herr. The entire battery will be engaged. This gun will be fired first at targets by the tree line in the distance. That's nearly three and a half kilometers from here. We fire upon your command, Herr Oberst."

Brandenburg turned to Jack. "I give you the honor of firing the cannon. But I caution you, it makes quite a loud noise. Do not be surprised."

"I have no desire to fire the gun, and I've heard very loud noises before." Turning to the captain, Jack said, "Fire when ready."

The gun captain glanced at Brandenburg for confirmation.

"*Jawohl. Feuer!*" ordered the oberst, and the gun belched smoke and flame as the shell hurled toward the distant target. The blast was ear-shattering, louder than anything Jack had ever heard before. The air was sucked out of him and the concussion shook the ground. Stunned, his senses paralyzed, he nearly lost his balance and could hear nothing. He worked his jaw to clear his ears and stared at the beast recovering from its recoil.

Within seconds, five more rounds flew from the artillery as crews immediately began reloading. At a distance beyond the range of any other field piece, a series of explosions erupted, sending geysers of dirt, tree trunks, and boulders high in the air. Dark, acrid smoke hung in the sodden sky as orders rang out along the line.

The smoke blew away, and involuntarily, Jack shivered. He had seen the effects of massed gunnery, but this was utter devastation. Sadness descended upon him. To Brandenburg's triumphant smirk, Jack only nodded and walked away.

***

"The French might as well arm themselves with trebuchets, slings, and crossbows," said Jack as he sat with Shelby at Galignani's two days later.

"That bad?"

"As we used to say, they're going to see the elephant. I saw those siege guns, Shelby."

"The French are aware of them."

"But they haven't see what they can do. They haven't see them fired," said Jack. "I did, and it's the most monstrous thing I ever beheld. An entire forest was blown into the air. These are siege guns of incalculable power. They can decimate any fortification. Tell your readers that no matter what, they must negotiate with the Germans. On no account should they even consider going to war."

"I'm as alarmed as you are. But no one sees cause for war with Prussia. In fact, Bismarck was hosted at the Paris Opera just a few days ago. Louis and Empress Eugénie invited him to join them in their box—they greatly admire him. Most French assume that having an army is not the same as using it."

"All they need is an excuse. Even an inconsequential one. Something French honor cannot ignore. That, to my mind, is exactly what Moltke, Bismarck, and Prince William are waiting for."

"Very well, Jack. I'll write up what you told me. Who knows, maybe somebody in the French Parliament will read it," said Shelby. "Was there anything else that surprised you?"

"About Prussia? Nothing, really. I was already aware of their militaristic mentality." Jack looked down at his tea. "But there was something else, pertaining to our situation here at home."

"To Jerome?"

Jack nodded. "It was when I returned to Paris. The platform was crowded as usual—women, men, children, and their dogs. I was gathering my belongings when I glanced out the window and saw Jabari Abraxas in the company of a woman. Another train had just come in from Metz, but I don't know if they'd been on it. I doubt that they were on my train since it came straight from Berlin."

"So, he is still alive and recovered from his wound," said Shelby. "Did you recognize the woman?"

"No, I never saw her before, but Jerome mentioned something about a woman when I questioned him the day after he crashed his wagon. There may be a connection."

"Marcel is in Metz. Do you think they were meeting with him?"

"It's possible, but my brother made it clear that he wants nothing to do with Abraxas."

"Did the woman look Near Eastern, Arab?" said Shelby, jotting a note on a slip of paper.

"No, she was petite, European, and looked very serious. They were in a hurry, as if they had to get away before somebody saw them."

"And they didn't see you?"

"No. I was tempted to follow, but they got into a cab and rushed off," said Jack.

"Maybe it's time to question Jerome again, or perhaps Marcel. Something is going on. Oh, I nearly forgot to mention. Manet has invited you to paint with him, Monet, and Degas at Alfred Sisley's. Maybe Pissarro will show up, too. It's a plein air event for the presentation of works at the Salon des Arts in April. Every artist in Paris is hoping to get in. It's a great opportunity."

"But I'm an unknown. Why would they want me to paint with them?"

Shelby was already scribbling away and rolled his eyes. "Because, you dolt, Charlotte has arranged it. She is your savior, in case you forgot."

"Well, I do need saving."

"Damn straight! Now in the words of Oliver Cromwell, 'Be gone from this house!' Get your paints and report to Manet. That's an order, Jack Volant."

With a haphazard salute and a silly grin Jack rose from the table. "They'll only laugh at my work."

"Then you'll be in good company, 'Les Refusés'! The bunch who can't afford a good bottle of Merlot. Paint something the emperor can't do without."

"I've heard he's afflicted with piles. Maybe I'll paint them in flaming color."

"That will sell. It will most definitely sell."

CHAPTER 28

Paris

February 1870

Jack felt invigorated to be recognized as a fellow artist by those he regarded so highly. He especially liked Monet, not only for his sense of humor but also for the spontaneity and color he applied to his canvas.

"Vitality, *mon ami.* Show the world the joy of art and life," said Monet.

"I want to see your newest creation. Pissarro says it's inspiring," replied Jack.

"Pissarro is too kind. But you must see Cézanne's latest work." Monet shook his head. "He strives to paint the truth about society, all well and good, but this one is a monstrosity. You be the judge."

"So, who's here?" asked Jack as they arrived outside Bazille's studio, at Rue de la Condamine in the seventeenth arrondissement.

"All of our criminals," said Monet with a grin. "Renoir, Pissarro, Cézanne and Degas. And Manet, who still demands that I change my name, arguing that it is too close to his! Cézanne and Degas are sometimes hard to take but they're fine artists. *Refusés* all."

"Do you always meet here?"

"Bazille has the only house big enough. Too bad—he keeps it too neat, too clean. I like a place that looks lived in. But he's also the only one with money. And he has helped most of us. I told all of them that you were coming, and they're expecting you. An American artist with a unique outlook is refreshing."

"And they know about my disaster at the Louvre?" said Jack as they entered the studio.

"Does a cannon make noise? Of course they do, but don't worry, we've all had our moments, and for us, rejection is a badge of honor. Come! Let us enter!"

Here indeed were men after Jack's heart. They were not merely talking about art, they were making it. The large room was crowded with easels. Édouard Manet was holding forth in full glory, extolling the splendor of brash color, his brush never stopping. With fast strokes he slapped paint onto his canvas and waved the brush toward Jack. "See, that's how you paint a landscape! Strong, with dynamic color. No need to show every tiny detail. You want to create an impression, a mood, a feeling that captures the essence of the place. If you want minutiae, you take a photograph!"

He turned to Paul Cézanne and removed his monocle. "You know that the jury will scream when they see this. Even if accepted, they will consign it to the rubbish dump annex at the back of the salon."

"And you'll have fine company," said a tall man wearing a long coat and plaid trousers. "All our work will be thrown in there. It's happened before."

"Is that so, Bazille?" said Cézanne. "Then I will submit a pot of shit!"

Manet laughed. "Yes, we've heard you say that before."

"And I will repeat it. You all can grovel before the jury, but I will not. I paint for my own enjoyment and refuse to debase myself before them."

Jack, having set up his easel, glanced at Cézanne's painting propped against the wall, a large canvas of somber grays.

"He calls it *The Temptation of Saint Anthony*," said Monet.

The canvas depicted the clothed saint appraising four unappealing naked women contorting before him.

It was one of the strangest pieces of art Jack had ever seen, reminiscent of a medieval work of damnation. Then again, Jack had viewed a few of Cézanne's other works; meticulously executed, they were somehow bizarre, ghastly, shocking.

"Is the painting still in one piece?" asked Manet.

"Why wouldn't it be?"

"Because Paul is mad. If his work is rejected, or isn't perfect, he slashes the canvas to shreds. Some shreds are quite interesting."

Monet added paint to a light, spritely scene of a windy seaside boardwalk with a fluttering white-and-red-striped flag and sturdy beige buildings. Dabs of rough paint for people added movement to the whole. Looking pleased with the results, he put down his brushes, stood beside Jack, and studied Cézanne's work. "Very bold, provocative, but not the way I or Renoir would paint."

"I paint life as I see it, and I don't see the joy you do," said Cézanne. "I can't help but look at the underside, a mirror of society. People can be reduced to caricatures."

"Like the one you did of Louis Napoleon," said Monet. "A masterpiece."

"A masterpiece indeed. Louis should have bought it," said a solitary figure standing in the back of the room.

Monet laughed. "Perhaps that's too much to hope for, Edgar." He turned to Jack. "Cézanne depicted him sitting sadly, nostalgically, on his throne with long hands that look like the tentacles of a cuttlefish and those little skinny legs."

"Is that not an accurate rendering? The man is a monstrosity," said Edgar Degas, brushing a stray hair from his narrow face. "He'll be swept away like all the rest of the vermin, won't he, Camille?"

Pissarro, who with his white beard reminded Jack of a wise patriarch stepping out of the Old Testament, nodded sagaciously. "We shall see. They all live in decadence, and the pendulum swings. The common man will revolt sooner or later."

Jack admired Pissarro's softly lit landscape featuring a peasant man and woman in a barren field on the other side of a narrow river on a cool, cloudy day. In the distance were whitewashed houses with muted trees. The scene conveyed quietude, much like the man himself.

"But in the meantime, why should Napoleon be different from anybody else?" Degas said, studying his work in progress with brooding eyes. "Parisians refuse to look in the mirror. They want pretty pictures. Cézanne is right, paintings should reflect real life."

"I like joyous paintings," said Renoir. "There is nothing wrong with the reflection of vivacious life."

"Paint your pretty pictures. I will paint reality."

"What you really need is a wife," said Manet teasingly. "Someone to make you smile once or twice a year and who has intelligent opinions."

Degas sniffed. "What would I want a wife for? Someone to say, 'Oh what a nice painting that is'? I'd rather keep a hundred sheep than one outspoken girl."

"He doesn't know what he's missing." Manet slapped more paint on his canvas and winked at Jack. "You know, I was once jealous of Monet. He is the favorite of Parisian women. They can't get enough of him." He turned to Monet. "I heard you were screwing Madame La Cross. Is that true?"

"Certainly not. I only sleep with duchesses or maids."

Manet glanced at Jack. "We need to emulate writers like my friend Émile Zola, or Charles Baudelaire, the one who wrote *Les Fleurs du Mal*. They engage our imaginations. Lusty, scandalous, but insightful. That's what makes them—us—unique. That's what makes me put paint to canvas and revel in life. The Paris of life and pleasure. Despite our trials, Jack, that's what it's all about. I know about your crisis at the Louvre, but you must try again."

Jack looked around the room at the assorted paintings, then at his own blank canvas. They had less than a month to complete their works; the Salon des Arts would open to the public on May 1st. Until the very last moment, painters would be feverishly completing their canvases, and the entire gallery would reek with the smell of solvents and oil paint.

***

The demimondes were not yet awake, but the flower markets already bustled with activity, the gutters had been cleaned, and milk women driving their little horses found their usual sites and awaited their customers. Jack and Charlotte waved away peddlers with their licenses hanging about their necks. Although begging was unlawful, they gave a few sous to men without arms or legs and women with pleading faces and desperate children who soulfully sang chansons with Italian lyrics.

They passed the Madeleine, the great church in the eighth arrondissement built to honor Napoleon's army. Its white columns and frieze, reminiscent of a Greek temple, lay north of the Place de la Concorde.

"I read Gabriel's article about Prussia," said Charlotte. "It was quite ominous. He credited you for getting so much information. Is it as dangerous as you said it is? I mean, will there be war?"

"I can't say. But if it comes to that, I think you should leave. The French won't be able to stop them."

"I won't leave as long as Jerome is still recovering. And even then, I'll likely stay. As Gabriel said, the Prussians have no reason to go to war against France."

"The Prussians don't see it that way. There's the matter of Alsace and Lorraine."

They walked in silence for several minutes.

"Gabriel told me that Inspector Gustave came by Galignani's again," said Charlotte. "Apparently one of the guards at the armory remembered that one of his assailants was of very dark complexion. Perhaps a Negro. He asked Gabriel if he'd heard of anyone who fit the description. The police are searching everywhere."

"The Algerian has dark skin," said Jack. "Perhaps the soldier was confused."

"Not according to the inspector. And he said that the dark man was quite young, not more than twenty. Abraxas is more than twice that age."

"Jerome had best stay hidden until he fully recovers. Then he should get out of Paris," replied Jack. "Did Shelby tell you that I saw Abraxas at the station here in Paris?"

Charlotte shook her head. "Then Abraxas is alive."

"Yes, but as I said before, I doubt that he will come back to your house."

"I'm still worried. Especially for Jerome. Would you mind staying with me, at least until he recovers?"

They stopped, and Jack looked at her for any sign of hesitation. "Of course, Charlotte. But you needn't concern yourself with any closeness, physical, I mean, if you don't wish to."

"That's very noble of you, Monsieur Volant. But I am not alarmed by the idea. I confess, Jack, I have come to like you. I like you very much."

A smile spread across Jack's face. He put his arms around her and kissed her deeply.

"Oh!" said Charlotte. Two elderly ladies put hands over their mouths and giggled as they passed.

"No breach in the line should ever be ignored," said Jack, a twinkle in his eye.

"Just be careful, soldier, the breach may be a trap."

"Then I shall surrender and raise the white flag."

"My, my. A prisoner of my own. How delightful."

Charlotte tucked her arm under Jack's, and they continued along a quiet back street until they stopped before a pastry shop with an American coat of arms over its door.

"This is it," said Charlotte. "For us Americans it's the most popular place in Paris."

Jack gazed at the carved eagle in blazing color with arrows in its talons.

"See," said Charlotte, pointing to the array of pies, doughnuts, and gingerbread displayed behind the window, "this just mystifies the French. It's totally foreign to them. But the shop's been here for years. It's owned by Madame Busque, who has learned to bake the pies, and it's the only place in Paris you can find them. It's really quite amazing."

Charlotte and Jack sat at one of the tables surrounded by American bric-a-brac and Hudson River paintings. "One more thing about the inspector," Charlotte said. "Monsieur Gustave read Gabriel's article, and he was quite surprised to learn that Colonel Brandenburg was back in Prussia."

"Why should that surprise him?" asked Jack, glancing at a gaggle of Americans inspecting the selection of pies.

"Because, according to Gabriel, Brandenburg is still a suspect. But he's untouchable in Prussia, which truly vexes the inspector. The case, as far as he's concerned, is far from solved."

"Well, I suspect the next time anyone sees the oberst, it will be over the barrel of a cannon. That man will not come back to testify under any circumstances."

"Do you think he's the murderer?" asked Charlotte.

"I really don't know. He left Paris in a hurry and he brushed of the incident. But I think Abraxas is the one the police should be looking for. Suspicious or not, I don't think Brandenburg is the guilty one."

"Well, the case should keep the detective busy, and away from Jerome. I truly hope that he had nothing to do with the assault on the depot. I adore Jerome, but I'd hate to think that I'm harboring a fugitive."

"I think that you aren't."

Charlotte smiled at him. "I'm glad that I have your support in this dangerous time."

"The real danger may still be months away."

They listened to the hubbub of American voices around them, not common in Paris. Charlotte dug into a slice of mince pie. "So, tell me about it, your day of painting with the Refusés. It must have been quite exciting. Were they all there?"

"Most were, including Degas and Cézanne, whom I hadn't met before. Rather strange men."

"What about Baudelaire and Zola? They're favorites of Manet."

"Neither came by," said Jack, munching on a chocolate doughnut. "They said Baudelaire's case of syphilis has worsened and he's resting at home."

"That's so sad."

Jack nodded. " I really admire Monet and Pissarro. They're fine painters and true gentlemen. And of course,

Manet is the center of attention. Apparently he's the only one of the Refusés who's known to Paris."

"What of Renoir? I love his art."

"He showed up but didn't bring a canvas. He's hoping to get into the Salon this year."

"I'll tell you something that Gabriel told me," said Charlotte. "You know Émilien de Nieuwerkerke, the man who supposedly gives out the awards? It's a little-known fact that he's under the spell of a woman named Princess Mathilde, a Spanish countess. She tells him who to honor. No one dares contradict her."

"I think I've heard that someplace before," said Jack. "In any event, I don't think any of us are in line for medals. For the Refusés, displaying one's work will be honor enough."

"You know, Jack, I'm really quite proud of you."

"Why's that?"

"For having the courage to submit your paintings. I mean, it's a brave thing considering what you went through at the Louvre."

"I know what to expect. I know that my work will be rejected. But I'll be in good company, and I really don't give a damn what the jury says."

"As a jury of one, I like your paintings," said Charlotte. "I would give all of them medals."

"Then make some. Really big ones with lots of color, and they must say 'USA.'"

"And just where do you want me to pin them, Monsieur Volant?"

"You know, Lady Stuart, you do have a dangerous streak."

***

All was frantic and bustling as dozens of artists streamed toward the Palais de l'Industrie carrying canvases, many of them barely dry. Artists called out, *"Dépêchez-vous! Dépêchez-vous!"* encouraging each other to hurry lest they miss possible admirers or a nod from a judge. When all was in place, the two-hundred-fifty-yard-long site would display, from floor to ceiling, two thousand works of work.

Jack, Charlotte, and Shelby entered the great exhibition hall and found Manet and Pissarro.

"They did it again!" fumed Manet.

"Did what?" asked Jack.

"We're all in the junk room. Monet, Sisley, Bazille. I'll show you."

Pushing through hundreds of artists, they retreated to a nearly deserted anteroom where over a dozen works had been placed on walls by the hanging committee. Others, not yet hung, lay against a wall in the far corner.

"Look for the mark on the back of the canvas," said Manet. "If it has the letter *A* it means '*admis.*' The letter *R* means rejected."

Glancing about, Jack saw Sisley pick up one of his works. "Refused!" he said. "This is detestable."

Tucking the painting under his arm, he stalked out. "Never again, I swear, never again!"

Charlotte shook her head and scanned the wall. "Look, Jack, up there. One of your landscapes has been accepted. How wonderful!"

Jack craned his neck until he spotted it. "Yes, but it's too high up. No one will see it."

"The hanging committee decides the viewing levels," said Pissarro. "They stand around in a bunch and raise their umbrellas to vote on where each painting goes. They assign a number one if the work is to be at eye level. Number two goes up higher, and number three is almost out of sight, where the lighting is nonexistent. At least yours is a number two. Some people will see it."

"I guess..." said Jack dubiously.

Shelby picked through a half dozen canvases not yet hung. "Here's one of yours, Jack." He looked at the back. "An *R*. Too bad, it's a fine piece of work."

"But at least you're accepted," said Charlotte, beaming. That's really quite wonderful."

At ten in the morning, the exhibition opened to the public and thousands streamed into the enormous hall. Dozens of people were exulting over works of the masters, crowding around paintings of chaste nudes in biblical settings, all evoking a moral dictum. Medals had already been awarded, and Louis Napoleon and his wife Eugénie were in the hall along with other glittering personalities.

By midmorning the crowd had drifted toward the rear of the building and many, out of curiosity or a desire to be entertained, ventured into the annex. Charlotte stood beside Jack as several looked closely at his landscape. Many, shaking their heads, muttered their disapproval while passing on to examine other works.

"Do not mind them, Jack," said Charlotte, squeezing Jack's hand. "They aren't artists. You are."

Amongst laughter and derision another group entered, all talking at once. To Jack's surprise, the most assertive comments came from Étienne Daudet, on whose arm clung Yvette Maillard. Dressed in a fashionable gown studded with pearls, she doted on his lofty declarations. It was well known that the emperor had purchased one of his most recent works, a realistic painting glorifying French chasseurs during the Napoleonic wars.

Accompanied by Nieuwerkerke and a gaggle of jurists, Daudet employed his umbrella to point at various works of the Refusés while making scornful and snide comments to the enjoyment of his audience.

Wearing their stylish short jackets, frilly shirts, and buff-colored vests, men and women congregated before Jack's landscape, awaiting Daudet's pronouncement. But Daudet gave the painting only the barest glance.

"You look somewhat familiar," Daudet said to Jack. "Do I know you?"

"I think we had a chance encounter on one occasion."

Daudet's eyes flitted back to the painting. "Ah, yes, at the Salon d' Chantilly," he recalled, pursing his lips in disapproval.

Yvette glanced at Charlotte, gave the briefest of smiles, then pointed to Jack's work. "Étienne, it looks like rain coming down over the hills. I think it's rather romantic, like a place we should spend an afternoon."

"A place that I would never go," said Daudet. "The work is not developed; it's garish, with undefined lines and rough bits of color. What does it really say? I certainly don't know. It's an amateurish piece with no historic appeal. Were it any good, it would not be in the junk room. It's only suitable for the middle class. Perhaps over their wallpaper."

"Étienne, you're being far too harsh, darling. It's a daring piece of work, and I think this artist has a great future," said Yvette with a boldness that surprised Jack.

"I'm afraid, my dear, that you know nothing about art. Indeed, you have certain qualities for which I have rewarded you, but of art you are woefully ignorant." Then with red-faced vehemence, he said, "And you will never contradict me in public—and certainly not in front of the jurists!"

There was an awkward, silent moment followed by a gasp as the demimonde delivered a stinging slap. Daudet recoiled, his face even more crimson, before he raised his umbrella and slashed it downward. It abruptly halted inches from the woman's face.

"A gentleman, as you pretend to be, never, ever, strikes a woman," said Jack, eyeing Étienne with cool disdain.

Enraged, Daudet stared at Jack, spittle collecting on his lips. "You bastard! How dare you interfere in my affairs. For this, this insolence, there will be punishment. Punishment indeed! Yes, a duel tomorrow morning in the forest of Saint-Germain. We will use rapiers."

"It sounds like a pleasant way to start the day," replied Jack, staring into Daudet's eyes.

"This is ridiculous!" said Charlotte. "Jack! Surely, you're not going to consider such madness. This stupid, conceited man is not worth it."

"I'm afraid there is a lesson to be taught, Charlotte. So, I accept. But according to longstanding tradition, the one who is challenged has choice of weapon. And the weapon, Monsieur Daudet, is modern pistols, a Colt or perhaps a Remington. Only one round each. Tomorrow at nine."

"I will be his second," said Shelby, standing within inches of Daudet.

Yvette backed away, looking horrified. "Monsieur Daudet, you are a damn fool!" she said, and stormed out of the pavilion.

Charlotte released her hand from Jack's and looked at him with sad eyes. "I cannot, will not stand by and see you killed or maimed. I have seen too many men die. I'm going home."

"I'll go with you, wait. I don't want to be here any longer."

"No, Jack, I want to be alone. Just alone."

***

Two formally dressed men in frock coats and top hats inspected the pistols, ensuring that each had only one round in the cylinder, and that it would be fired with a single pull of the trigger. One of the adjudicators checked his pocket watch and glanced toward the sun, paled by mist and streaming clouds. The man approached Daudet, deferentially asked him if he wanted to proceed, and reminded him that, though common, dueling was in violation of French law.

Jack, standing forty feet away saw Daudet vigorously shake his head. The referee nodded and walked toward Jack, who waved him away.

Three minutes later, each was handed a loaded pistol and the etiquette of dueling was recited.

"Gabriel, this isn't your fight," Jack said. "I appreciate your courage and loyalty, but I don't want you to duel. Regardless of the outcome—walk away."

"Ah, that's hardly fun. Besides, this will give me something to write about. 'Aging Confederate engages in duel to avenge the death of his old enemy.' Aside from a good salacious scandal, there's little better than an old-fashioned duel. But Jack," said Shelby, looking gallant in top hat and tails, "just for the hell of it, don't miss the son of a bitch!"

Jack shed his tattered Union greatcoat but refused to remove his large-brimmed slouch hat. From the corner of his eye he saw a woman standing across the field, a coat wrapped tightly around her. He glanced at Shelby, who looked toward the distant figure.

"It might be her. Too hard to tell from here," said Shelby as a pistol was handed to each dueler.

"You may engage when I say '*tirer*,'" stated the referee.

Shelby, Daudet's second, and the adjudicators stood silently as a stiff wind blew leaves across the ground. Daudet carefully raised his weapon.

"Tirer!"

There was a sudden flash and a whiff of black powder as Daudet pulled the trigger. All eyes turned to Jack as the bullet tore away his hat.

Daudet lowered the weapon and appeared to sag as he peered at his opponent. Stooping, Jack retrieved his hat, examined the brim, and placed it back on his head. For a long moment he looked at Daudet, then raised his weapon. First he aimed at the man's head, but the barrel descended to the midriff.

Daudet's body quivered, and then his eyes widened as Jack lowered the pistol.

Another moment passed, and the attendants exchanged curious glances. Daudet raised both hands, the pistol in the right, and smirked. "What is this? The man is afraid to shoot?"

In an instant, Jack raised his Remington and fired. There was a sudden cry as the round tore through Daudet's trigger guard and ripped away two fingers. The shot, not at the body mass was entirely intentional.

Daudet's pistol, covered in blood, fell away as he clutched the remains of his hand. Bending over, he screamed as his second ran to him, a white cloth in hand.

The referee approached the second. "Do you wish to continue the duel?"

Glancing at Jack, the man shook his head. "Non, monsieur, there has been enough blood shed today."

Jack handed his weapon to the referee and looked toward the distant field. He saw a woman turn and walk away.

Shelby handed Jack his coat. "It's cold. I could use a hot cup of coffee or maybe something stronger."

Jack stared at Daudet, still grasping his damaged hand with his good one.

"That man won't be painting for a very long time," said Shelby. "And who knows, maybe Charlotte will talk to you someday."

"Perhaps, but it won't be soon," said Jack, despondency coming over him once again.

CHAPTER 29

Paris

Two days later

"Has the detective come yet?" asked Jack as Shelby ushered him into the back room of Galignani's.

"No, you might have an hour, perhaps less. Marcel is waiting. He won't stay more than a few minutes."

Marcel rose and gave Jack a brotherly hug. "I came as quickly as I could, but I was hoping that you would go to Metz."

"I can't leave Paris. Your old friend is back here and I'm worried about Charlotte." Jack sat, and the other two joined him at a back table.

"Abraxas is hardly my friend. We parted company when I found out what he's really up to."

"Running guns for the revolution," said Shelby.

"That's right. He tried to involve me. I told him that the whole idea is suicidal. The government will execute him for treason."

"And attempted murder," added Jack.

"Do you know Jerome, Charlotte's half brother?" Shelby asked Marcel.

"Of course. He was also involved."

"But not now. Abraxas tried to kill him and may try again," said Jack.

"I don't think he will. He's running scared. He's also a voracious reader; I'm sure he read the article about the duel, the shot that ended Daudet's career as an artist."

"I saw Abraxas at the Gare du Nord. He was with a woman, a French woman perhaps," said Jack.

"Petite, dark eyes, assertive?" asked Marcel.

"That's a good description. Do you know her?"

Marcel looked away. "I knew her at one time. We were, well, rather close. You know what I mean. That was before I learned about her and Abraxas."

"But you don't see her anymore?" asked Shelby.

"No, absolutely not. She is very possessive, dangerous."

"How did you meet her?" asked Jack.

"Like many other women, in a café. She is or was a grisette, a rather beguiling and alluring one. And very smart, not some empty-headed girl. She had me read Baudelaire to her before our sessions. She was always quite secretive. In fact, I don't even know her real name. She was rarely home at night, and I don't know where she went or who else she was with."

"Did she talk about revolution, arming the underclass?" asked Shelby.

"She hates the aristocracy. I'm sure that she would lead any uprising. But as I said, she gave no details, only vague references to the coming revolution."

"Where did you meet when you were bedding her?" asked Jack.

"In a part of town where the ragpickers live. A dangerous area. I never felt comfortable there, but she did." Marcel plucked at a thread on his shirt. "Look, I'm not involved in anything against the government and I am innocent of the murder in the salon. I'm going back to Metz. I'm sure the police will find the real murderer, and then I'll return to Paris."

"Why not leave France entirely? Go to England for six months, a year?" asked Shelby.

"I love France, and Metz is a large, safe place."

"And close to Germany," said Jack.

Marcel shrugged. "It's well protected. The French have strong fortifications there and a substantial force. I'm not worried."

"I would be."

Marcel sighed and glanced at his pocket watch. "I have to go. Please say nothing about me having come here. I'm still at the same address. I'll write if I learn anything more."

***

It was late in the afternoon when Charlotte opened the door. Jack picked her up, swung her around, and kissed her fervently. "Oh, Jack," she said, "I was terribly afraid of losing you."

"You were there, by the woods during the duel. I thought I saw you. I wanted to be with you afterwards but I—"

"Yes, I was there. I couldn't stay away. I was so scared. He nearly killed you."

"But he missed and I did not."

"You are alive and with me again."

"Of course with you, silly girl."

He embraced and kissed her again. "And I have wonderful news. Yesterday I went back to the Palais de l'Industrie to retrieve my painting, the one that was refused, and meet Manet, Pissarro, and Monet. They shook my hand jubilantly. I thought it was because I'd survived the duel. I looked about but couldn't find the painting. When I asked Manet where it was, he said, 'It's gone. Gone!' Then he dug into his pocket and handed me forty francs."

"Oh!" said Charlotte, beaming at him.

Jack grinned back. "Apparently a Scottish lord saw it. He thought it was quite dramatic; it reminded him of a strikingly beautiful place on the Isle of Mull called Penmore. The man bought it right there and then, and Manet says he wants three more. So, my dear, we are going to dinner and a stroll along the magnificent Avenue de Clichy."

"That sounds truly delightful. I haven't been escorted around Paris at night since I got here. Yes," she effused, "just the two of us, a night on the town."

"Poor Jerome." Jack laughed. "Here all by himself, probably bemoaning his fate."

"He's not here. He left for Metz two days ago. I think he was going to meet Marcel. Now that he's recovered, he's off to a new adventure."

"Wasn't he in school?" Jack said.

"He still intends to study law when he returns. He said he'll feel safe in Metz, and he expects to be quite popular there."

"I'm sure he'll meet plenty of girls, but safe? I'm not so sure," said Jack.

After disembarking from the omnibus they strolled toward the Café Guerbois on Avenue de Clichy at the base of Montmartre, where they might run into Manet, Renoir, and the artist Henri Fantin-Latour, together known as the Batignolles group for the location of the café. It was a warm evening, and Charlotte had decided that the occasion called for an evening dress in floral pink with three flounces, an overskirt of dainty lace, and a wreath of spring roses and leaves in her hair. To add a sparkle, she adorned herself with a pearl bracelet and a necklace of pink coral beads and matching earrings.

Conceding to fashion, Jack held his gloves in his hand and even donned a bowler he'd bought the day before. Assuming the look of a Frenchman, he wore a black frock coat and carried the requisite umbrella. But under the coat was a barely noticeable bulge.

"You look terribly dashing," said Charlotte, gazing up at him. "And I must say, I've never seen you so happy. It's quite a change from the dour man I was introduced to."

"I've never been happier. I guess your company does that, Miss Charlotte."

Charlotte flushed.

"And somehow I rather detect a change in you."

"*C'est possible.*" She laughed and entwined her arm around his. Then a more somber thought came to her. "I didn't know if you would come back."

"I didn't know if you wanted me back."

"Of course I did." She shuddered. "That man, Daudet, has a violent reputation."

"But in contrast, I am a peaceful, unassuming fellow. A true *bon ami* to all mankind."

She laughed again. "Dear Lord, no! But I saw your hat shot off, and I didn't know if you were stooping to retrieve it or if perhaps you had been hit. Then I saw you straighten up and put it back on. And then there was that curious moment when you lowered your pistol. I thought that perhaps you weren't going to shoot, that you had a change of heart. And then ..."

"He is a bully, and killing him would have been gratifying. Certainly, I thought of it. But that would have been too easy, too final. He values wealth, recognition. To deprive him of that nobility would be far more satisfying. I wanted him to contend with being a onetime artist for the rest of his life."

"That is rather profound. But what if he's ambidextrous?"

"I should have thought of that," said Jack with a grin. "But painting with the left hand, well that's a distinct disadvantage. The work will never be the same."

"You told me that you're ambidextrous. You could teach him," Charlotte said, her eyes flashing.

"What a splendid idea! Perhaps Manet will assist. I'm sure all the Refusés will welcome him with open arms."

"You should send him a get-well card and tell him that. He probably needs cheering up."

Cafés and restaurants were lit up by gas lamps. Looking through the plate-glass windows, Charlotte and Jack gazed at frescoes and mirrors that seemingly enlarged interiors and multiplied the crowd. Sidewalks were filled with scores of tables covered by white tablecloths and platters of cheese and wine. On the streets were the "coco" merchants ringing tiny bells, bellowing their cheap prices while offering cups of a pallid drink of licorice and water. The mixture was thoroughly enjoyed by the French but apparently no one else.

"There are so many things for us to do, Jack," said Charlotte. "We must go to the Jardin des Plantes. It has the only giraffe in France, nearly twelve feet tall. And the Grand Opéra, not quite as stuffy as the Théâtre Italien and much less expensive."

"I'm afraid I don't speak Italian," said Jack.

"There's a new music hall called the Folies Bergère. A fellow named Offenbach revised an old song and dance called the cancan. It's a bit naughty but it might be fun."

"There's also the Latin Quarter where the students and Bohemians live," said Jack. "Degas goes there to do sketches of the ragpickers."

"It's an exciting but sad place," said Charlotte. "There are masses of homeless people and the police keep them walking all night. Those who survive eat from enormous kettles, *hazard de la fourchette*, scraps given by the hotels for two sous. They aren't allowed to beg or even ask for charity."

"I've heard of them eating from the kettles. The person uses a harpoon and stabs into the pot one time to see what he can bring up. Not very appetizing," said Jack

A half dozen working men wearing wooden shoes moved with tired despondency through the otherwise joyous crowd. In their hands was black bread, the staple of their diet.

High over the city, a fireworks display began. Jack tensed at the sound of crackling explosions, and Charlotte reached for his hand.

"It's Louis Napoleon's version of bread and circuses," she said. "Masked balls for the wealthy and opulence for those in the aristocracy."

Ten minutes later they reached the Café Guerbois. It was filled with revelers, including Manet, Monet, Degas, and Renoir.

Monet greeted Jack and stooped to kiss Charlotte's hand.

Jack watched the lorettes titillate patrons with their low-cut blouses and flirtatious whispers. Bartenders wearing long white aprons hustled between tables as Manet ordered still another bottle of wine.

"I think someday I will paint that," said Degas, nodding to three people sitting by themselves with glasses of green liquor.

"They don't look very happy," said Jack.

"They're not. Some people call it the green hour, which is usually four o'clock, but time matters little to them once they're addicted to absinthe," said Degas with great disapproval.

"I don't understand the appeal of a drink that contains a poisonous herb," said Charlotte.

"It also erases memory and causes hallucinations, nightmares, hair loss, insanity, and eventually death," said

Degas. "But the despair, the distant gaze of lost souls, that is the reality of so many. Yes, someday I shall paint that and let Paris look in the mirror."

"Why doesn't the government ban it?" asked Jack.

"The army and navy have, but it's an epidemic, and a profitable one," said Manet. "Right now, it's just part of life."

"And death," added Degas.

***

It was nearly midnight when Jack hired a cab for the trip back to Charlotte's house. There was a full moon, and the clip-clop of the horse on the two-mile ride lulled Charlotte into a dreamy repose. She leaned back against Jack and said, "If I were to venture a guess I would think that you love me."

"More than you can ever imagine. I have been deeply infatuated but never truly in love before."

She sniffed the night air. "It has been so long since I was in love."

"Are you now?"

"What do you think?" said Charlotte, wrapping her arms around him.

"Somehow I don't think you loved me at first," said Jack.

"Mmm, well, maybe not right away. But you stuck in my mind like a hog in a mud hole, and I could not tug you out, try as I might."

"An apt description, Miss Charlotte. I'll never look at a hog the same way again. But I certainly won't propose to one."

"Are you going to propose?" she said, snuggling against him.

He put his arm around her and kissed her. "It's a matter being considered by the general staff. I think they'll vote in my favor."

The lights of Paris were dimming in the background, and Charlotte felt as if she were floating. Jack put a blanket about them to ward off the chilled air as the vehicle swayed beneath a billion stars.

"Do you think we'll be happy together?" asked Charlotte, wondering what it might be like to wake up in the morning beside a man for whom she had so many questions.

"I do believe so, but as an artist I will never be wealthy."

"What has that got to do with anything?"

"I want to make you happy, and regretfully that requires a worthy income. We shall marry, but it might not be right away. Our life will be a frugal one, unless of course you become a famous sculptor. That is quite possible."

"I'm not interested in fame, Jack, but good company is priceless."

They stared at a meteor streaking across the sky.

"Will you stay with me tonight?" said Charlotte. "I really don't want to be alone."

"Tonight, and every night if you wish. I wouldn't want to be anywhere else."

Deposited at the front gate, Jack paid the driver, who touched his top hat, thanked him, and bid him a good night. He turned the cab about and, at a leisurely pace, headed back to the center of Paris. Closing the gate behind him, Jack glanced at the old stone wall. "I will repair that tomorrow."

After looking in on his horse and Jerome's, Jack closed the barn door and joined Charlotte in the parlor. She poured two glasses of wine, and they settled on the sofa at the bottom of the stairs.

"That was a beautiful evening," she said dreamily. "The talk, the ambiance, the comradery of our friends, there's little better than that."

"Well, perhaps one thing," said Jack, placing his glass on the table and kissing her again.

"Mmm, well, perhaps, Monsieur Jack Volant. Are you a tender and considerate lover?"

"You will just have to find out, Miss Charlotte. But I will do everything to make you happy."

"Then perhaps we should peregrinate upstairs."

***

She was a remarkably beautiful woman with deep penetrating eyes. And to Jack's surprise, devoid of the Victorian constraints that inhibited so many American and British women. Perhaps it was the mystique and ardor of Paris, or the possibility that she had not enjoyed male companionship for many years. Once in bed, their coupling, born out of desire and love, was instantaneous.

Jack marveled at her caresses, her response to his every move. She glowed in the light of a half-dozen candles and held him closer than he had even thought possible.

She sighed after their first coupling, slipped her fingers through his dark, lanky hair and pressed herself against him, desire building once again. Magical, thought Jack as he held her, their bodies, souls, and hopes becoming one.

They drifted off as all but one candle sputtered out. It stood on a vanity table near the window, its light casting shadows in the darkened room. Jack considered blowing it out but didn't want to wake Charlotte. The wick would last only a short while longer anyway. He closed his eyes, and took in the scent of his woman's hair, and marveled at the warmth of her body against his.

The sound at first seemed far away. Maybe the neighing of a horse. Perhaps a fragment of a dream. Jack turned over and snuggled closer to Charlotte, but the horse whinnied again. Within seconds he was totally awake. His horse and Jerome's were in the barn behind the house. This sound was just outside the wall. Charlotte opened her eyes as he slipped out of bed.

"Why are you getting up?"

"I heard something. Stay in bed. I'm going downstairs. If it's nothing I'll be back in a few minutes."

He blew out the sputtering candle and glanced out the bedroom window. At first he saw nothing. The moon was high, and a stiff wind raised leaves, scattering them across the yard. Then came the light of a lantern, giving off a dull glow as a figure stealthily crossed the yard.

"Someone's down there, a man, inside the wall."

Charlotte sat up in bed. "At this hour? Is it Jerome?"

"I don't think so. He's taller. Stay right here. Don't come down."

Jack stepped into his trousers, picked up his revolver, and descended the stairs. The house was utterly still. Slipping to the front door, he undid the latch, then retreated to a position behind the sofa. He listened to the soft tread of footsteps that ascended the front steps. Intermittent flickers of moonlight pierced the front window as a hand twisted the doorknob. All remained still for a moment, as though the intruder questioned why the entrance would be unlocked. But it might not be unusual, the old house was remote and behind a gated wall.

The man pushed the door open—it made no noise—and he extinguished the lantern as he stepped inside.

Now a silhouette, the man stood there, eyeing the disposition of chairs, a sofa, and two wine glasses on a table. When he saw the unfinished bottle, he straightened and looked upstairs. He would likely assume that the occupants were asleep.

The man's jambiya slid from its ornate sheaf. He held it in one hand as he took cautious steps toward the stairs. Then he stopped. Sucking in a breath, he stared into the muzzle of the revolver. Two quick blasts flung him into the front window. He screamed as glass shattered. The knife spun away, and the man gurgled, his body twitching with eyes already vacant. Jack pulled the trigger one more time, and all movement ceased.

"Jack!" screamed Charlotte, racing downstairs.

"It's over, he's dead."

She stood transfixed, staring at the body that lay halfway out of the window. "Who ...?"

"Abraxas. I was wrong, he came back. I should have known when I saw him at the station. I'm sure he was looking for Jerome. Not finding him in the shed, he probably thought he might be in the house."

She moved toward the body and felt for a pulse. "What are we going to do with him?"

"I'll deal with it. You might scare up some coffee; I don't think we'll get much more sleep tonight."

The rope that secured the Algerian to the saddle also bound his legs. Jack shoved the jambiya into its sheath as the man's bloodstained shirt flapped in the wind. A swift slap on the rump sent the horse down the road toward Paris. It would be at least a mile before the body toppled and Abraxas was dragged ever farther down the road.

CHAPTER 30

Paris
The following day

The body lay on a drainage table, away from the curious public.

"It's hardly recognizable," said Gaspard Desvaux.

"He was still tied to his horse and likely dragged for some distance before he was found by the farmer who discovered him," said François Regnard, chief of the Paris morgue.

"What motivated you to send for us?" asked Arseneau, adjusting his monocle and peering into the face of the corpse.

"The knife, Monsieur Inspector," said Regnard. "Like so many Parisians, I read the account of the theft at the arsenal, and the soldier who recalled the exotic weapon. This"—Regnard handed the knife to Le Terrier—"might be the instrument in question. If true, I assumed that the body would be of great interest to you."

"Of course," said Arseneau.

"So, the death of this man solves two concerns," said Desvaux. "That is, the theft of the weapons and the murder of the courtesan at Chez d' Chantilly."

"Perhaps the theft in the armory, but only if he acted alone," said Gene Gustave. "I question whether Abraxas was really the murderer of Camille Lapin."

Desvaux glared at Gustave. "Who else could it be?"

"Possibly someone we know nothing about," replied Gustave, undaunted. "Besides that, there is Marcel Cheval, who has apparently fled Paris; Eliza Breton, who is in prison, perhaps awaiting the guillotine; and Colonel Albrecht von Badenburg, who has returned to Prussia to rejoin their army."

"The death of Camille Lapin is not my immediate concern," said Arseneau. "What I am looking at is a man shot dead; a murder, for certain. Does that not pique your interest? Three shots in the chest, all in close proximity. It appears that there are no other wounds, only abrasions and broken bones from being dragged by the horse. This man was killed last night. Somebody shot him, tied him to his horse, and made certain that it ran toward Paris. The farmer said that he saw hoofprints coming from the direction of La Chapelle."

"But who in the eighteenth arrondissement would wish to kill Jabari Abraxas?" said Desvaux.

"Someone who wanted him identified, hence the well-sheathed jambiya that might have otherwise fallen out," said Gustave.

"So, the question is, was the killing a matter of revenge, a rift between revolutionaries, or a random murder?" poised Arseneau.

"Does it really matter who killed him?" interjected Desvaux. "The criminal is dead. Our search for him is over."

"It matters in that we have lost an interrogation," said the chief inspector. "It was the duty of the state to apprehend him. Now we won't know his accomplices."

"Perhaps we should set a trap for them," said Gustave. "We can announce in the paper that new weapons are being shipped to the arsenal and have troops ready to respond to a robbery."

Ambroise Arseneau sniffed. "Ah, finally I hear an intelligent idea, Monsieur Inspector."

"Might I add one more thought?" said Gustave. "In the case of the courtesan, I think we are chasing shadows—that none of our suspects are the real murderer."

"No? Who then?"

"A woman, a grisette. One not yet identified but who is also involved in revolutionary activities. I believe there is a connection. That's the person we should be looking for."

The detectives turned to go. "How should I dispose of the body?" said Regnard.

"In a simple grave," said Arseneau. "But do have him face east, toward Mecca. Perhaps Allah might care to have a word with him."

***

"You just missed him."

Jack took a seat across from Shelby at Galignani's. "Missed who?"

"The detective, Gene Gustave," said Shelby, one hand twirling his ever-present pencil. "He said that the department wouldn't release any details of the killing of Jabari Abraxas until they had more information. At this point he doesn't want me or any other journalist to write about it. All he told me was that Abraxas was shot three times and found in a field. It's quite a mystery as to who shot him and why."

"It's no mystery to me," said Jack, tracking the coming and going of a dozen American and English patrons, all enjoying their morning coffee.

"Why's that?"

"Because I shot him."

"Why would I doubt that?" said Shelby, a bemused look on his face. "You're getting a lot of practice with that cannon you carry. So, tell me more, *mon* lieutenant.

287

Jack summed up the events of the previous night. Shelby stared at him for ten long seconds, then ran his fingers through his blond beard. "I presume that knowledge of who sent Abraxas to paradise is just between you, me, and Charlotte."

"I think that's best. There are many unsolved killings in Paris. This is just another one. The police can scratch their heads all they want. I did them a favor, let's leave it at that."

"Let's suppose that Gustave knows the connection between Charlotte and Jerome. What if the inspector pays her a visit? He would assume she knows where he is as well as his revolutionary activities."

"He has the authority to visit, I can't do much about that. She knows he's in Metz, but that's a damn big city."

"He'll be with Marcel, right?"

"Probably, but Charlotte doesn't know Marcel's address. If I tell her, she may feel obligated to reveal it. So, for now I won't. She won't put Jerome in danger. That you can count on."

"Well, damnation and all. You are a very smooth character, Jack. Cool as a bull with his harem of cows."

"I assumed you'd find the exact metaphor," said Jack, watching customers gathered around a copy of *The Messenger*.

"So, having saved Charlotte, you're her true hero."

"I adore her. She's become the center of my universe. And I think she likes me."

"Well, stranger things have happened. So, are you going to marry the lady?"

"When I can afford to support her. I sold a few of my paintings, but that's hardly enough."

"A damnyankee and a Southern belle. Ain't that just the sweetest thing I ever heard? I can see the little figures on the wedding cake now. You in a Federal uniform, she in a pretty dress, a brass cannon, and rebel flag right in between." Shelby stopped twirling the pencil for a moment. "But she had a close brush with death. How is she coping?"

"It was a frightening thing, Abraxas coming back. But she's experienced danger before. She knows how to deal with it, and I try to comfort her."

"That doesn't surprise me, either."

Jack just shook his head, then gestured toward the cluster of readers. "What's going on there? What are they reading about?"

"Probably an article I wrote about the succession to the Spanish throne. Something no Frenchman gave a damn about a week ago. Now they're having a conniption fit."

"I haven't heard anything about it. Why the interest in Spain?"

"Two years ago, Queen Isabella was deposed, and no one knew who would take the throne. Paris wants a monarch who'll support Napoleon and French interests in Europe." Shelby lit the stub of a cigar.

"And there's a problem?"

"Sure 'nuff. I've been cogitating upon it. Otto von Bismarck persuaded a Prussian relative, Prince Leopold of Hohenzollern-Sigmaringen, to take the throne. This portends a link between Prussia and Spain—which, you may have noticed, shares a long border with France. At first Leopold declined, but Bismarck was insistent, hoping that France would go rabidly insane and declare war."

"That's what the Prussians have wanted for a long time."

"Well, the French minister wrote to Chancellor Wilhelm demanding that he guarantee the sanctity of French interests," said Shelby. "Presumably the letter wasn't particularly diplomatic, and Wilhelm showed it to Bismarck. Apparently they felt insulted and only agreed to discuss the matter with Paris."

"And the Prussians haven't budged on this Leopold fellow?"

"Not at all. It's all about who's going to be dominant in Europe. The French don't want that to be Prussia."

"And Bismarck sees war as a unifier of Germany under Prussian control," said Jack.

"Exactly. And then there's the matter of Alsace and Lorraine, which the Prussians say France stole from them."

"So, France is considering war?"

"I heard that Louis doesn't want it. He knows that the army is weak and disorganized. But Eugénie is the power behind the throne. She said that this will be her war, and if there isn't one, her son will never be emperor."

"And Louis needs a victory to prop up his regime," said Jack. "This whole thing can go up in flames."

"Flames, yes."

"Indeed. So, where do things stand now?"

"The French ambassador met with William, the Prussian chancellor, and they came to an acceptable agreement. But in a telegram, Bismarck, determined to have his war, apparently misconstrued the facts, thereby baiting the French. I learned this from the *London Times*. Of course, the French were furious, just as Bismarck hoped. Now the threat of Spain in the pocket of Prussia has Parliament clamoring for war."

"That's damn near catastrophic," said Jack, thinking of Marcel and Jerome so close to the German border.

The readers, mostly American, folded *The Messenger* and quickly departed. "They're in a big hurry," Jack said.

"Booking passage? France may not be comfortable in a few months. The American ambassador might be very busy. Have you ever met him?"

"No, never had reason to."

"Well, I interviewed him. He could be helpful in a pinch. Elihu's a fine fellow even though he doesn't drink or smoke. Everybody has some faults. But he's scrupulously honest and intolerant of people who play with the truth."

"Good to know."

"Moreover, I suspect he reads my columns in *The Messenger*. I really like people who read my stories, Jack."

"I'll try to remember that."

***

Paris

July, 1870

"Even the minister of war says it would be a walk in the park," said Manet loudly as he entered the Café Guerbois with Cézanne, followed by Degas, Renoir, and Bazille.

"Where have I heard that before?" muttered Shelby as the artists joined him and Jack at their table by the window.

Four days earlier the deputies of the French Parliament had insisted on hostilities with Prussia. The vote was two hundred and forty-five to ten. But it would be left up to the emperor to actually declare war. He hadn't.

"Walk in the park or not, you can get a replacement if you're called up," Cézanne said to Renoir. "You are a pacifist, and you're traumatized by gunfire. What can you possibly be thinking?"

"I'm thinking that if the fellow replacing me were killed, it would haunt me for the rest of my life."

"Well, I'm not staying here," said Cézanne. "I'm going to Aix. My parents are there."

"That's hardly patriotic," said Bazille.

"Maybe, but this talk of war is sheer stupidity. Even Zola thinks so." Cézanne turned to Jack and Shelby. "He's gone to Provence, and Monet is in Trouville. Neither of them intend to get killed in a senseless war." He shifted back to Bazille.

291

"Renoir told me that you envision yourself on a magnificent horse galloping about a battlefield. Yes, heroic, dodging bullets and carrying messages spelling victory for France."

"I'm not looking for glory, but I will enlist," said Bazille in a quiet voice.

"You'll be killed for sure. You are a damn fine artist. Stick to that!"

Bazille shook his head. "I see it as a duty. As a Frenchman I can't turn away from it any more than I can lay down my paints and never pick them up again. This will be a quick war, and I will be able to look at myself in the mirror when it is over. You do as you wish, Paul."

Jack looked out the window. On the street, citizens in the thousands, some wearing costumes reminiscent of the 1789 Revolution, marched past while an opera singer, outfitted as angelic France, belted out "La Marseillaise." The entire city was awash in patriotic fervor. Cries of "*Vive la guerre!*" resounded as mobs roamed the streets, assailing anyone who opposed crushing arrogant Prussia in months if not weeks.

"What are you going to do, Shelby?" Jack asked as the debates swirled around them.

"I'll stay here and put my thoughts in *The Messenger*. I'm not about to go to the front. I've done that before and it wasn't nice. What about you?"

"If Charlotte decides to leave Paris, I go with her. If she stays, I stay."

Holding aloft a telegram, a courier dashed into the café. "It's war! At the Reichstag, Bismarck just declared war on France!"

"What about Louis?" asked Shelby, rising to his feet and stubbing out his cigar.

"It's done! The emperor has declared war on Prussia."

An instantaneous cheer erupted in the café. More drinks were ordered as people shook hands and shouted, *"Vive la France!* On to Berlin!"

Manet snatched the telegram from the courier's hand, read it, and handed it to Degas. "Tomorrow we join up!" he said to Bazille.

"The recruitment offices in Paris are already overwhelmed—they've had to send men home. They're not so crowded in Lyon or Strasbourg. We can take the train in the morning."

"You don't have to go that far," said Renoir. "We can enlist at the Hotel des Invalides. I hope to join General du Barrail's cavalry. I've heard he's taking his division to Munich."

"Ah, buxom women and lots of beer," said Manet.

"I'm going to Montpellier where the Third Regiment of Zouaves is forming up," said Bazille. "It's a crack unit and should be in the thick of it."

"What about you?" Bazille asked Manet. "Infantry, cavalry, artillery?"

"National Guard. I'll do whatever they want me to. Maybe just defending Paris on the wall at Rond Point de Villiers."

"Then you won't see any action," said Bazille. "The Prussians won't get past Metz. That's where you should be. Then you'll have something to tell your grandchildren about."

***

It was nearly dark when Jack entered the parlor of Charlotte's house. He sat heavily on the sofa as she handed him a glass of wine.

"It's bad?" she said, sitting on a chair across from him.

He nodded and took a sip. "It's war. The regiments are being called up. All of Paris wants to fight. None of them have ever seen war. It's all about the glory of France."

"Can they win?" asked Charlotte.

"With divine intervention. They haven't seen what I have in Prussia, but I don't think it would make any difference. They're all fired up. We'll see what happens in a month or two. It's not going to be pretty."

"What are we going to do?" Charlotte reached for his hand.

"Whatever you want to do. We could leave and go to Le Havre or England. Or even back to the States."

"I'm not so sure we should leave France. I don't even want to leave this house."

"We may have to. Paris has fortifications, but it isn't invulnerable. No city is anymore. Shelby said that I should meet Washburne, the American ambassador. I think we should both do it sooner than later."

"What could he possibly do? There are so many Americans in Paris."

"Most will be on a ship to London or New York by tomorrow night. Knowing the ambassador might be quite useful."

"But won't he be leaving Paris? I'm sure that the embassies will close if the city's in danger."

"If Shelby pegged Washburne right, he won't be going anywhere," said Jack.

"We've both seen war. I don't think we need to see it again."

CHAPTER 31

Paris

The first week of July

Jack checked the address on the invitation. "This must be the place. There's an American flag on the pole."

"What a dingy building," said Charlotte as she and Jack ascended the stairs to the second floor of the seven-floor apartment on Rue de Chaillot. "I thought it would be on the Champs-Élysées or Avenue de l'Impératrice."

"I doubt that the State Department lavishes money on embassies, and Washburne, according to Shelby, isn't one to indulge in pomp and circumstance or aristocratic surroundings."

"But it's so bare, so disheartening. Maybe you should paint a picture for it. Anything will help."

"What about the Siege of Vicksburg? Lots of color, things blowing up," said Jack teasingly as they entered the sterile office.

A young man stood beside the only desk, wearing a formal long coat, the room cool despite the warm day. He welcomed them and indicated two chairs as a clock struck the morning hour of eight.

"Gratiot Washburne," he said. "My father is expecting you and will be along shortly. He's likely in the storeroom. A shipment from New York came in an hour ago."

Jack and Charlotte sat silently, the only sound being the tick-tock of the tall mahogany timepiece.

"It's good you got here early," said Gratiot. "A lot of Americans will be here soon, and they'll have a thousand questions. Of course, many have already left Paris. I'm afraid it's going to be a very long day."

A serious-looking man of large proportions, in shirt sleeves and wearing a dark vest and cravat, entered a side door carrying a stout wooden box.

"Ah, the American artists. It's an honor to meet you, Miss Stuart," said Washburne, shaking Charlotte's hand. To Jack, he said, "I saw your paintings at the Palais de l'Industrie. Very impressive, Mr. Volant. I think you have a great career ahead, but regretfully we are heading into difficult times."

He laid the box on his desk and picked up a tin marked "Sardines."

Jack grinned. "Lunch, Mr. Ambassador?"

"The French won't touch canned food. They think it's absolutely barbaric," said Washburne in a feigned voice of horror. "But it's perfectly safe." He gestured at the box. "I sent for the fruitcake. It's actually quite tasty. And you never know, this all might come in handy if things get tight."

He turned to his son. "I know you want something to do while awaiting an invitation from l'empereur on the subject of invasion but, in the meantime, you might attend to the rest of those crates. I'll inform you if the invite comes in."

The youth smiled at Jack. "Yes, Mr. Ambassador. I know exactly what to tell Monsieur Louis Napoleon."

"Diplomacy, Gratiot," said Washburne, wagging a finger. "And put those sardines where I can find them, not behind the peaches."

A smile briefly appeared on Washburne's rugged face. He lifted a sheet of paper and handed it to Jack. "I'm sending this on to Washington. I think it pretty well describes the mood here."

Charlotte looked over Jack's shoulder as he scanned the telegram.

> The government here is clamoring for war. No language can measure the probable consequences and results. Everything is brought to a standstill, and ordinary people stand aghast with amazement. But the great crowds are mad with excitement and things are rushed as in a giddy whirl.

"That sums it up," said Jack.

"London papers expect France to invade Prussia within a matter of weeks," said Washburne. The French minister of war said it will be 'a mere stroll, walking stick in hand.'"

"No war is a mere stroll," said Jack.

"Well, as Robbie Burns said,

> 'The best laid schemes o' Mice and Men
> Gang aft agley,
> An' lea'e us nought but grief and pain,
> For promised joy!'"

Washburne looked from Jack to Charlotte. "So, are you planning to leave Paris?"

"We're not entirely sure," said Charlotte. "Through your dispatches, you certainly have a better understanding of the situation than we do. If there is war, do you think Paris will be invaded? Will we be in danger?"

The ambassador steepled his fingers. "If French armies are defeated, the Prussians will take their surrender on the field of battle. There'd be no need to invade Paris, and to do so would cost them thousands of casualties. No, I don't think Parisians will be in danger."

"That's reassuring. We're also concerned about Jack's brother and my brother. They're still in France as well."

"Where?"

Charlotte glanced at Jack. "Metz, we last heard."

"That should be safe enough." Washburne regarded Jack. "Mr. Volant, our mutual friend and journalist Gabriel Shelby tells me that you have already provided him with valuable information regarding the Prussian military. I, too, am desperately in need of intelligence. That's really why I asked you to come here. Plenty of people, including General Sheridan, will be observers and guests of the Prussians if war breaks out. But we in Paris will be dependent on French government and military dispatches. Most of these will be propagandist, particularly if French forces are stymied. We are neutral, of course, but Sheridan and President Grant are concerned about American interests here. We could use unbiased and credible information."

"It sounds like you need someone snooping around," said Jack.

"In so many words. You were a soldier and know that efficient preparations are essential for a victorious campaign. I would be greatly appreciative if you might gather some intelligence on French mobilization. Of course, you would be compensated for your efforts."

"I'll be happy to," said Jack. "Do you want me to go to Metz?"

"That won't be necessary. The depots are in and around Paris. I don't think it will take more than a few days to assess the situation. I'll ask Gratiot to go with you."

"Sir, I would rather go alone. I know what to look for, and I can make myself very inconspicuous. When do you want me to start?"

"As soon as you can."

***

The French forces were to have been divided into three armies based at Metz, Strasbourg, and Châlons, in command of generals who'd had experience in numerous campaigns. However, before the start of hostilities, Louis Napoleon's wife told him that he and he alone should lead the army. To this, he acquiesced. That required a complete reorganization, which left officers and men scrambling to merge entire divisions into eight entirely new corps.

Complicating the perilous situation even more, Empress Eugénie was in charge of the powerful Council of Regency where she could oversee the conduct of the war and further advise her husband.

And to the further dismay of the French, both Italy and Austria, previously considered allies, declared their neutrality. French ministers demanded that the two nations reverse their decisions, to no avail. Thus, France would go to war with no foreign military support and with very little encouragement from other powers.

It took Jack only a few days to assess the preparedness of the army. Despite the numerous wars the nation had engaged in, it quickly became apparent that a major mobilization hadn't been planned for since the time of Napoleon Bonaparte. All was in disarray. Depots containing uniforms, ammunition, and weapons were rarely near barracks or recruitment centers. Instead, they were positioned in a multitude of insecure places across the country. Even more disturbing, with the army's realignment men were to be led by officers they had never before seen.

Upon arriving on the field on July twenty-ninth, Louis Napoleon issued an order of the day to his troops: "Whatever may be the road we take beyond our frontiers, we shall come across the glorious tracks of our fathers. We shall prove worthy of them. All France follows you with its fervent prayers, and the eyes of the world are upon you. On our success hangs the fate of liberty and civilization."

By then, Jack had seen enough.

"I spoke with a French colonel two days ago," said Washburne after Jack trekked back to the American embassy. He set aside a stack of official passes. "He told me that General Leboeuf—the advisor to the emperor—said that within three weeks of mobilization, he expected to have three hundred thousand men and over nine hundred guns ready. But that time has passed and only half the troops are available."

It was warm in the office, and Jack sat beside a window from which he could see a column of soldiers on the street below. "I'm sure there was disorganization and a degree of ineptness in the Union army during the early days of our civil war. It took some time for the irregulars to be equipped, trained, and led onto the field. But the French don't have time to do that if they expect to invade Prussia. And from what I've seen, the Prussians have no such problems. They are the epitome of organization."

"So, what did you find?" asked Washburne.

"A rather alarming situation. Virtually nothing is prepared. I saw thousands of men, mostly new recruits, lolling around, totally disorganized. Many were drunk, even insubordinate, with only a kepi and a coat, perhaps a canteen. They're not being paid, and there's a lack of basic supplies, including food."

"Napoleon said that an army marches on its stomach," replied Washburne. "A hungry army resorts to pillage, whether in its own nation or someone else's."

"I've seen it before. And there is another matter having to do with preparation," said Jack. "They have no maps of Prussia. None. I heard that some officers went to schools to find some, but those would be of a general nature. The army isn't aware of specific roads, fields, bridges, or geographic elevations; it knows nothing of choke points where you can put your guns or marshal divisions."

"I suspect things would be very different if you were a general."

"Thank God I'm not. I want nothing to do with their war. But I would have some stinging advice for them."

"I'm sure you would, starting with the stupidity of doing it at all," said Washburne.

***

Within the following weeks, the Garde Mobile, a force only on paper, was expected to mobilize two hundred and fifty battalions of infantry and one hundred and twenty-five artillery units. But no such development occurred. By early August, all recruitment for the organization was halted.

Still, thousands of men answered the call and were sent to the front. Their supplies, in countless wagons, clogged the roads, and no provision had been made for disbursing them. This was compounded by the fact that only two major rail lines led out of Paris, as a result, much of the army's equipment never reached the front.

Units that reached Metz received ominous reports of a massive Prussian buildup. As the days slipped away it became apparent that the invading force wasn't going to be La Grande Armée. French generals concluded that with only two hundred of the expected three hundred and eighty-five thousand, an attempt to reach Berlin would be completely unrealistic. But in France this reversal was not the focus of conversation.

"You would think that they already won the war," said Shelby over the joyous din on August fourth.

Outside of Galignani's, Jack watched thousands of Parisians laughing, marching, and raising bottles of champagne in celebration of their first victory against Prussia.

"All the French papers have printed jubilant headlines about the action at Saarbrüken," said Shelby, glancing at *L'Opinion nationale* and the *Courrier des électeurs*. "What have you heard?"

"I was at the American Ambulance this morning with Charlotte. A few French wounded arrived there from the battle two days ago. I spoke to a sergeant in one of the tents, and he said that the French had six divisions against one Prussian infantry division and a few squadrons of cavalry. The Prussian fire was effective, but there was little they could do over such overwhelming force. They abandoned their position, and the French took it."

"But it was a relatively small action," said Shelby.

"Six divisions against one. I think all the celebration is a bit premature."

***

Although there was conflict in the Prussian high command over strategy, Moltke understood that the French army had run out of steam. Early in August and with rapid advancement, his well-organized armies won victories in the border regions of Spicheren, Wissembourg, and Froeschwiller. On August fourteenth the Prussians overran the city of Nancy on the Moselle River and faced the French fortress of Metz.

Overwhelming massed infantry supported by field guns decimated the brave but obsolete French cavalry and made it possible to envelop the French forces. Louis Napoleon ordered and counter-ordered major battlefield decisions and began to contemplate the disaster of total defeat.

In Paris the early jubilation had turned to rage and contempt for the emperor as the defeats mounted. Angry mobs surged through the streets, but no one had any legitimate strategy for reversing the course of the war.

"The French army has been split in two, one half in Metz and the other in Châlons, and neither can support the another," said Shelby, sitting across from Jack at Café Bade.

"What do you know about Metz?" asked Jack.

Shelby stood to observe the crowd through the narrow windows as the commotion outside escalated. "I was there once. It would have been impressive in the eighteenth century. But its battlements, walls, and general fortifications are in disrepair. Since the time of Bonaparte, over fifty years ago, nobody has expected that it would be attacked. There are other forts around it, but from what I've seen they're not going to stop the Prussians."

"And the town itself?" said Jack

"It's medieval. Like most towns built centuries ago it has narrow streets, houses tightly packed, and the cathedral dominates the city. There are hills around it and woods that might allow for a defense. The *Nationale* reports that three Prussian armies face it on a fifty-mile front. The French have thrown together one hundred and eighty thousand men to defend the city, but three armies are a lot of people."

"Metz will be surrounded if the Prussians get around their flanks," said Jack.

***

"I just received a letter from Jerome," said Charlotte.

Jack closed the door behind him and kissed Charlotte softly. "Is he with Marcel?"

"Yes, but they can't stay in his house. He says the Prussians are already attacking. The town has been shelled. The French are fighting in the hills, but casualties are mounting."

"Did he say where they're staying?" said Jack, already pulling his revolver from a parlor drawer.

"In a house by the cathedral." Charlotte watched Jack as he checked the cylinders. "What are you thinking?"

"I'm thinking that they're going to need all the help they can get. If the Prussians take Metz, they'll be murdering everybody in their way, soldiers and civilians. Soldiers aren't very particular when they're being shot at."

"But Jack, how will you get there? I heard that not even artillery can get through. And Metz is over two hundred miles from here."

"Trains are still running, and, if necessary, I can get a fast horse. The city will hold out for at least a week, maybe longer."

"I should go with you," said Charlotte. "They may have been wounded."

"No, go to the American Ambulance, it's the best hospital in Paris. That's where I'll bring them if they're hurt. There will likely be chaos around Metz, and thousands of refugees will be on the road. I can't take a chance of you being captured by the Prussians or some drunken troops of a broken French regiment."

"But what if you're hurt?" Charlotte asked, throwing her arms tightly around him.

He kissed her forehead. "Didn't I tell you that I'm indestructible?"

"I don't recall that."

"I'm sure I mentioned it on numerous occasions."

"You'd just better come back."

She kissed him, watched him mount his horse, and wondered if it was the last time she would ever see him alive.

CHAPTER 32

Metz
August 15, 1870

Metz was on fire.

The journey had taken longer than expected. Jack entered the stricken city and found a captain giving frantic orders to his men. Stating that he was an American journalist attached to the Metz sector, he asked the infantry officer for any information he might provide.

"Monsieur, I tell you this because you are an American and in extreme danger. Only one division of the Second Corps will remain here to protect the city, but two corps are to retreat on the road to Verdun. Then they must proceed to Mars-la-Tour on the right flank of Metz while two other corps head for Vernéville. As for my own unit, cavalry is to protect our flanks. We hope to reach the town of Gravelotte before the Prussians cut us off. That's where we will make our stand. This area isn't secure; I suggest that you leave at once."

The narrow, byzantine lane where Marcel and Jerome lived was little more than rubble. The walls of three-hundred-year-old houses still stood, but their roofs had fallen in. Splintered furnishings, cooking implements, clothing, and shattered windows littered the street's paving stones. Smoldering ruins sent acrid clouds skyward as still more shells fell upon the city.

A dog stood shaking beside the remains of what had been his master's house. It gazed with big brown eyes at Jack, then followed him, head down, until it collapsed on a charred blanket.

Jack peered into one abandoned dwelling after another. All the occupants had fled, leaving everything behind. A dead horse lay beside a toppled wagon, its driver hurled into the street. Still alive, he looked beseechingly at Jack and pointed to the cathedral across the street.

"Take me there, please, monsieur. It's a sanctuary, yes?"

"It is for now."

Jack helped the man to his feet and half carried him to the cathedral. He pushed open a door to Saint Étienne de Metz, an enormous structure completed three hundred years before. With flying buttresses and a huge expanse of stained glass, its spire reached one hundred and thirty-five feet into the smoke-blotched air. One of the Renaissance doors was partially open, a shell fragment having torn off its elaborate carving. Peering into the four-hundred-foot-long interior, he saw a priest carrying a box of silver candlesticks and a rolled-up tapestry.

"Father, this man is hurt," said Jack as the victim slumped to the floor.

The priest laid down the box, studied the man, and made the sign of the cross. "I'll get some bandages and water, but the cathedral is hardly safe."

"Safer than in the street."

"Yes, if they don't shell the roof and if it doesn't catch fire. But we will pray."

Jack was nearly out the door when he turned back. "Father, has a young man, an American Negro, come to the cathedral in the last month or two?"

"Such a person did. He brought along another man, very dapper. But I haven't seen them since the shelling began. I imagine they fled like everyone else."

***

Jack hurried to catch up with the civilians who, along with one hundred and sixty thousand troops, tramped up the single road leading to a steep incline toward the Gravelotte plateau. The soldiers, sweating in their heavy coats, baggy red pants, and dust-coated spats remained in column as they pushed past exhausted civilians who stood forlornly to the side. In between companies and divisions were teams of horses pulling pontoon bridges. Clouds of dust rose from wagons carrying every assortment of military essentials.

The August heat, the stench of the plodding masses and defecating horses, made him think of struggling populations fleeing the onslaught of Vikings who once pushed inexorably toward Paris. There had always been refugees in desperate flight.

I am no longer a soldier, he told himself. But gazing at the endless column of humanity, he knew he was one of them. A refugee as helpless as the rest.

Children screamed and wailed as Prussian shells exploded only twenty yards from the surging mass. Another blast sheared through a squad of soldiers, killing or maiming them all. Jack moved through the pall of smoke and found a rifle still operable and a pair of field binoculars. He took both, as well as the man's bayonet. Slinging the chassepot over his shoulder, he tagged behind a company of wounded soldiers.

Reports came in from the town of Saint-Privat of a fierce defense put up by French troops who savaged a Prussian corps led by the impetuous Prince Augustus of Wurttemberg. The royal lost eight thousand men in a frontal attack against a dug-in line of infantry. It was a stunning victory, but French forces retreated when enemy artillery silenced their guns. Only temporary disorganization within the Prussian lines allowed for an organized retreat.

Exhausted troops and civilians collapsed in the fields and along the roadway as darkness descended upon them. They slept fitfully, occasional shells erupting throughout the night. Jack pushed on past huddled groups, some still awake and talking in hushed, tremulous tones of what the next day might bring. The night was cold, and Jack had liberated a coat from a dead soldier. Sometime before dawn he found a squad of soldiers sitting around a banked fire. Most were wounded; some had been carried on stretchers by their comrades. They made room for him.

"Where are you coming from?" asked a private, taking a stubby pipe from his mouth.

Jack warmed his hands over the embers. "Metz, like almost everybody else."

"You have the coat and chassepot, and you look like a soldier, but you are not," said a corporal, glancing at Jack's shoes and pants.

"You're right. I'm an American," he said. "I'm looking for my brother. He was in Metz, but I don't know where he is now."

"Could be anywhere," said the private. "But wearing a French uniform could put you in danger, maybe get you shot if you don't follow orders, if you don't go into battle."

"I'm not concerned. I've been in a lot of battles."

"So, you will fight for the French?" asked the corporal.

"If necessary."

The man grunted appreciatively. "I'm Claude. This is Patrice, our corporal. We were in many battles too, mostly in Algeria, but it wasn't like this. We never faced artillery, only muskets."

"But now most of you are wounded. Where are they leading you?"

"Maybe Beaumont or Sedan, perhaps Paris," said Claude.

"No. There's a train a mile up. We're all taking it to Châlons in the morning," said the corporal.

"Well, that's better than walking," said Claude. "Most of us can still shoot, but we're not going to be in any assault, that's for damn sure. There's a new army forming up at Châlons, maybe half a million, and Louis is supposed to be there."

"Châlons? That doesn't make sense," said Jack. "It's a hell of a long way from Paris and not very defensible."

Claude shrugged. "I'm a private, what do I know? Only that there's going to be a lot of widows before this is over."

With dawn, Jack secreted himself in the ranks that hobbled to the siding where the train waited. Several of the eight cars were already crowded with wounded, and the others were rapidly filling.

"We're going to head north to Thionville, then northwest toward Sedan," said a medical orderly when Jack questioned him about their exact destination.

"Not Châlons?"

"Not this one. With all of the wounded, we've been rerouted."

"How long will it take?"

"We should get to Sedan in two days if we're not cut off and if the tracks aren't clogged with other trains. Of course, traffic to Châlons gets priority. But I've heard it's a real debacle. The artillery can't get through, and without that ..."

The orderly was right. Hours later the train pulled onto a siding to take on coal and was joined by another from Châlons. Senior officers from both met and entered into an intense conversation. They seemed quite indifferent when

Jack and a number of soldiers stepped off their train and listened in.

"The army at Châlons is commanded by very competent officers," stated a colonel. "It has a great quantity of artillery, infantry, and cavalry. All first class, and they should be able to inflict serious damage on the Prussians. But I was at the conference called by the emperor before ordered back to Paris, and I must say that I'm a bit concerned."

"About the Prussians?" asked a major.

"Them, of course, but the emperor seemed completely disinterested in what the generals had to say. It was as if he were in a different realm. Totally dejected. I actually heard him say, 'I seem to have abdicated.' His son replied, quite tartly, 'You abdicated the government at Paris; at Metz you have now abdicated the command of the army!'"

"So, what's he going to do?" asked the major.

"It's assumed that the emperor will be heading to Sedan to continue the fight. But if it were up to me, I'd take the whole army back to Paris where our defenses are strongest."

A cavalry patrol galloped up to the train. A captain, upon finding the colonel, dismounted, saluted, and handed him a message. "Sir. I'm sorry it has arrived late. The Prussians have cut the telegraph wires, and the only communication with Châlons is by horseback."

"So, we are back to the eighteenth century," said the colonel. He read the dispatch, then handed it to the major.

"This is most alarming," said the staff officer, staring at the message. "The Guard Mobile in Paris is on the verge of mutiny. Could that possibly be?"

"They've been unreliable since the first defeat. I just hope they don't oppose our troops in the field, the entire army of Versailles" replied the colonel.

"If that is so, then our forces must evacuate Châlons as fast as possible," said the major.

"I just hope that's realized by intelligent minds. Fighting the Prussians is one thing, having to deal with the Guard is an entirely different matter," said the colonel.

They sat idle for the remainder of the day. By late afternoon it was reported that the track was completely blocked. When it became apparent that food supplies were nearly exhausted, Jack slipped out and started toward Beaumont, only six miles from Sedan. He was still one hundred miles from the city. With congested roads and the possibility of enemy patrols, the journey would be protracted, but it was better to be on the march than on a train going nowhere.

Then again, where was he marching? Marcel and Jerome could have left Metz days before the Prussian advance on the city. If so, they might have already reached Sedan, or perhaps Paris. He was searching in vain.

It was already dusk when, dispirited and exhausted, Jack lay down amid a copse of trees. But for the buzzing of insects the night was still, and a soft breeze caressed the leaves of summer. He lay the chassepot in the high grass and considered that it might be the subject for a landscape. But moments later he put that thought out of his mind. There were others about, hungry and impoverished. It wasn't a time to take chances. He had to reach Paris and Charlotte. Everything else paled. She was what mattered.

A terrible loneliness seeped into Jack as the night grew colder. He wanted to listen to Charlotte's stories of the Old South, to make her laugh and sigh with their loving. He wanted to sit with her on the porch of the ancient house and watch shooting stars stream across the sky. He wanted to share a bottle of wine and spin half-truths about him and Shelby, knowing that she knew the real story. And he wanted to hold her again.

He hated this damn war as he did the last. But he'd somehow known the last one would end in victory, bloody as it was. This one, he feared, would not end well.

With his old cavalry in the field Jack had rested his head against the McClellan saddle, pulled the horse blanket over himself, and slumbered, still aware of the snorting and stomping of horses on the picket line. But now there was no saddle to lie upon, no horses to trouble the night. It took him a long time to doze off.

The whinnying of horses, guttural foreign voices, and the double blast of a bugle woke him instantly. A troop of uhlans sped past at a gallop not fifty yards away. Jack quickly slipped into the trees and watched them churn up dust as they rode in column, little triangular flags fluttering from lances tightly held.

It was time to go. No longer could he trudge along mindlessly. Danger was all about, and he could already be within Prussian lines. On foot, it would take many days before he reached Sedan, a place of possible sanctuary if it had not already fallen.

***

By dawn on the thirtieth of August, Jack had reached the small settlement of Beaumont-en-Argonne, a town of less than four hundred souls. Two miles west of the Meuse, it was there that the French army had come to rest. In the hills south of the still-sleeping village he heard the hoofbeats of cavalry, the groan of caissons, and occasional commands. An army was on the march, enveloping the town on the south and the west.

He couldn't believe what lay before him. Not a picket had been placed, not a cavalry mount saddled. No guns were loaded or manned for any possible action. Thousands of troops, exhausted from steady fighting, slumbered in the fields, on the streets, and in doorways. No officers were awake, no one stirred as the sun began to rise. It was an invitation for a massacre.

With silent steps he approached an artillery captain snoring amidst six of his crew. Jack poked him with the toe of his boot and leaned forward. "Monsieur, wake up. I believe there are Prussians in the hills. Perhaps several corps."

The officer opened one eye. "I don't hear anything. Don't disturb my men. You are a civilian, leave us alone."

"As you wish." Jack left the man and hurried past thousands of troops. Only at Chancellorsville had a Union army been so negligent. And they'd paid the price when Stonewall Jackson's screaming hordes descended upon Fighting Joe Hooker's army with devastating results.

Jack wondered if he should pick up a bugle and deliver a resounding blast, but he dismissed the thought. Surely within minutes the camp would be awake, orders given, and artillery sighted.

The road led four and a half miles north to the town of Mouzon on the banks of the Meuse River. That would be a good place to stop after the night's march.

Jack was only a half mile beyond the town when the entire world erupted in a barrage of artillery. Screams and shouts resounded as Prussian fire descended upon Beaumont and the French army. From a slight elevation he could see thousands of startled blue-coated men waking up, grabbing their chassepots, and running madly in every direction.

Officers, wild-eyed, buckling on rapiers, ordered panicked, disorganized drivers to harness horses to wagons and infantry to establish lines of fire. Meanwhile, masses of frenzied soldiers and terrified civilians dodged through hundreds of supply wagons littering the streets.

Several regiments mounted a counterattack, sending a battalion of Prussians scurrying back into the hills. But as the Germans pushed their forces both east and west, it became apparent that only a frantic retreat would save the army from total envelopment and capitulation.

Shells erupted around Jack as artillery fire ripped into the streaming masses. Several French gun positions had been quickly put into service, their shells falling into Prussian positions, but soon the artillery was silenced by effective return fire. From his vantage point north of the fleeing troops he could see the house-to-house fighting as French troops and civilians, with furious intensity, attempted to repel the invaders. But they were overwhelmed with savage reprisal.

A glorious charge by French cavalry, a determined fusillade of artillery, and the desperate fire from regiments of infantry slowed the Prussians, but it was only a momentary delay and they pressed on until dusk.

Jack, still shouldering his chassepot, stood in a field as a troop of French cavalry tore past in full retreat. A sudden eruption of shells tore a man off his mare, blew his horsehair helmet off his head, and ripped his arm off. A torrent of blood gushed from his body.

The rider's mount screamed and dashed into the field, empty saddle flapping against its flanks. Rushing forward, Jack grabbed the reins. The horse spun around, its frantic eyes wide, its body lathered in sweat.

The patrol didn't slow. Jack led the mare toward a stand of trees beyond the sight of terrified civilians lumbering up the road.

The guns stopped with the coming of darkness. The retreating army lit their campfires and settled in for the night. This time, thought Jack, they would post pickets and remain vigilant, since their abject neglect had cost them thousands at Beaumont.

Tired as he was, he refused to sleep. He mounted the horse and nudged it forward, having little doubt of what the morning would bring.

CHAPTER 33

Sedan

September first, 1870

The town of Sedan sat along the Meuse River, only seven miles from the Belgian border. By early morning it was already being shelled by Prussian guns. But the French had established major units in the woods and in villages around the settlement. Sedan featured two-hundred-year-old fortifications, including a moat and stone walls, most in disrepair. While hardly capable of stemming an attack of any size, the dilapidated earthworks offered some hope of delaying the Prussian advance. But the Prussians had already captured the bridges leading into Sedan and destroyed the railroad impeding escape by rail. As at Beaumont, the encirclement had already begun.

Shellfire ripped the town asunder, setting houses on fire. Billowing smoke rose into the morning sky while French marines and civilians battled the encroaching Prussians and their Bavarian and Saxon counterparts. Casualties increased as combatants bludgeoned one another in the narrow, corpse-littered streets.

Jack skirted Sedan, pushing the mare northward toward the town of Floing beside the low-lying Meuse valley. He'd assumed that he would encounter no enemy forces if he kept on the Meuse-Sedan road, but within minutes he could hear the thunder of German guns. The possibility of a French counterattack, much less a breakout, was becoming impossible.

Explosions rained down around Jack, and a shell struck an ammunition caisson, exploding with a blast that tore apart the gun and its crew.

Jack held his mount with a tight rein as it shied from the blazing eruption. Pieces of men and caissons littered the ground, and an eye-stinging pall engulfed him. Struggling to calm the horse, he heard choked voices in the smoke. The words were in English.

"Run! Run! Uhlans! They're all over!"

Covered in dust and emerging from the pall, Jerome and Marcel rushed madly through debris, pursued by Prussian cavalry. They were no more startled by the sight of Jack on the black mare than were the three Germans, lances already lowered for the kill.

"Jack!" shouted Jerome. "Get back! Go!"

Drawing his pistol, Jack stared at the closest uhlan whose lance swung toward him, his horse charging forward, closing the distance. Two shots rang out, barely audible in the surrounding din, and the Prussian fell forward, his lance ripping into the chest of Jack's mount. The animal screamed and toppled, throwing Jack against the remains of a wagon. His pistol flew from his hand. Dazed, he watched as the uhlan's horse reared up. The lance, ripped out of his wounded mount, fell to the ground.

Jerome and Marcel ran toward him. An officer followed, saber in hand, while two other uhlans charged through the smoke.

Wearing dark blue uniforms and metal spiked helmets, they came on, the steel tips of their lances glinting in the sun. To the right and left swarmed more Prussians, intent on targets of their own. The remaining French, firing madly, retreated, regrouped, and retreated again.

Dust and smoke swirled about as Jack tried to rise. His dying horse kicked out, sending him sprawling against the barrel of a splintered gun. His arm twisted, his pistol and chassepot spun away, he could only stare up as Colonel Albrecht von Brandenburg raised his saber and spurred his horse toward Marcel.

"The lance!" shouted Jack as his brother came to a halt, eyes focused at the huge form bearing down upon him.

"The lance, get the lance!" Jack again blurted, the words torn by a ragged cough.

Suddenly comprehending, Marcel grabbed the lance. He lifted it high and slammed it down on Brandenburg's arm. Face red, mouth opened in a scream, Brandenburg dropped the saber and, with his one good arm, tugged hard on the reins. The obese man, his balance suddenly shifting, plunged off his gelding and fell heavily to the ground.

Marcel snatched the gleaming saber and ran it into the Prussian's chest. For the briefest moment he stared at the man who, eyes rolling back, clutched at the steel that had impaled him.

Marcel stumbled back and tripped over Jack's chassepot. The third uhlan, spurring his horse, leveled his lance and aimed at Jerome. Arms flailing, stumbling over dead men and debris, Jerome turned to face the rider, and the lance ripped through his arm and came out the other side. The uhlan turned in the saddle and, gripping the strap, yanked hard to extract his weapon. Screaming in agony, Jerome fell to the ground.

Marcel snatched up the chassepot. With a strangled cry he sprang forward, aiming and firing the rifle, then sliding back the bolt and firing again even as the uhlan threw up his arms and pitched from his saddle.

Marcel, followed by Jack, ran over to where Jerome had fallen. Jerome's face looked drained of blood. Jack knelt beside and handed Marcel a tattered strip of a French flag, pulled from beneath the wheel of a caisson. "Wrap it around his arm and make it tight. You have to stop the bleeding."

His hands shaking, Marcel bent to his task until the flow became a seepage.

"Hurts, hurts," groaned Jerome, as Marcel lifted him to his feet. Jerome's knees buckled.

"You'll pull through. The bleeding will slow." Jack turned to Marcel. "We can't stay here. There will be another wave."

"Where do we go?" asked Marcel, helping Jerome to his feet again.

"Those woods on the hill. I saw some houses, it's not far."

"I know that place," said Marcel. "But you have to help me with Jerome."

As the three men struggled up the hill past dead horses, splintered wagons, and dead men, they finally came to an abandoned position just below the forested crest. Jack and Marcel laid Jerome against a tree while Marcel rummaged through a soldier's kit to find a clean bandage. He extracted a length of cloth and a whiskey flask, then removed a pair of binoculars from a dead officer.

"I didn't think the French liked whiskey," said Marcel, "but it should help prevent infection."

"I'll do the pouring; you hold him down. It's going to hurt. He may pass out." Jack unwrapped the blood-soaked cloth.

Blood poured from the wound, and Jerome screamed as the liquid ran into the gaping hole. Moments later the new bandage was tightened and Jerome, ashen-faced, slumped back against the tree.

In the distance, the thunder of Prussian guns continued to decimate French troops as they tried in vain to repel advancing infantry.

"There," said Jack, looking toward a rise above the town.

"French cavalry, whole squadrons," said Marcel.

Two generals were conferring and peering through binoculars while horsemen formed up in two long lines, lances held aloft. One of the officers rode forward a thousand yards to assess the situation but almost immediately returned, his jaw shot away. Upon seeing the bloody wound, a shout of *"Vengez-le!"* arose from thousands of throats. They began at a walk, then roared into a screaming, seemingly unstoppable charge downhill, tearing through the forward elements of Prussian infantry. Those who were not immediately impaled ran in desperation. Jack and Marcel watched the advance as the lancers rode over the retreating line. But just as suddenly they encountered an entire Prussian corps supported by artillery. The guns roared, and the magnificently attired ranks of horsemen were shattered, their bodies ripped open, their horses screaming and wildly bucking as rank after rank pitched forward. The survivors wheeled and sped toward the woods, the Bois de la Garenne, but the shellfire didn't slacken.

"What's happening out there? asked Marcel, as Jack peered through the binoculars.

Jack stared into the distance and saw a group of mounted officers and a cavalry troop in close order behind a single rider. One of the men carried the tricolor, another the flag of the emperor.

"It's Louis Napoleon," said Jack. "I think he's trying to rally the troops."

"There are no more troops. I think he's trying to get killed."

"That's a real possibility."

Marcel squinted toward the assemblage. "It looks like some French troops are trying to form up, but others are stopping them."

"The whole debacle is ending," said Jack. "Napoleon has halted, and there's a white flag. Prussian guns have stopped. Some of their officers are moving toward him. There! He is surrendering!"

Over the next few hours, thousands of French troops were rounded up, deprived of their weapons, and taken into captivity. Hospital wagons moved onto the field, and the wounded of both armies were loaded on board. French troops who could still walk formed up into long, dispirited lines. Escorted by Prussian cavalry, they began the march toward collection points near the Meuse and in Prussia beyond.

When it seemed safe to do so, Jack, having discarded any trace of uniform, helped Jerome to his feet.

"I can walk," said Jerome.

"But not very far," replied Jack. "There's a little village up ahead. We can stop there for the night. I have some money, maybe enough to buy a wagon and horses."

"And maybe some whiskey or a few bottles of wine." Marcel grinned. "For medicinal purposes, of course."

***

"Will I be like Shelby?" asked Jerome that night. They lay sprawled on the floor of an abandoned house.

"Not unless the wound turns gangrenous," said Jack. "But the spear point looked fairly clean, and there wouldn't be any rust. No uhlan would tolerate that. I think you'll get to keep your arm."

"More wine?" said Marcel. "I found a few bottles in the basement. I just love France."

"What's left of it," said Jack.

"They're going to lose some territory, I guess. Alsace, maybe Lorraine. I imagine they're celebrating in Berlin about now."

"They would feel quite righteous about it," said Jack. "Almost every king of France rampaged through Europe. Now they got a whuppin', and a lot of people think they deserve it."

"So, what's going to happen now?" asked Marcel.

"Depends. Besides destroying the army of Versailles and capturing Napoleon, Paris is the prize. It also has to surrender."

"The emperor is finished. Isn't the capitulation of Paris automatic?"

"Not necessarily. The Guard Mobile is there and Paris is rather well defended. The Prussians may not be sipping wine at French cafés for a very long time."

An almost preternatural silence had fallen over the land. A fire glowed in the house, and the wine took its toll. For a time, only Jerome's snoring broke the stillness.

"He'll need some real medical attention," said Marcel. "I know you tried to comfort him, but the arm doesn't look good. I suspect there's infection."

"The train tracks may be in good condition from Charleville, just north of Sedan. If we get him on a train, Paris is only a day or two away. Then Charlotte can see to him."

Marcel took a long slug of wine. "I'm sure you thought you would never see war again. I certainly never thought I would be in one."

"The world is full of strange events. Who'd have thought that you would run a saber through Albrecht von Brandenburg?"

"What? Brandenburg?"

"You didn't know?"

"I certainly didn't recognize him, not in that silly helmet. I was just angry, and ..."

"And became an instant soldier. You saved both me and Jerome. You redeemed yourself, at least in my eyes."

Silence again seeped into the house. Marcel took another drink and stared at the ancient ceiling. "Jerome and I would have been dead now if you hadn't been there. You can't imagine how surprised I was to see you. We had been running from one burning house to another with explosions all around us. I'd never been in a war zone before."

"Well, now you have. A little bit of hell, isn't it?"

"But why were you there?"

"To find you two. Charlotte got a letter from Jerome saying that the Prussians were already attacking Metz. I thought you'd need some help. I went to your house near the cathedral. But I couldn't find either of you, and with each defeat I had to move farther away. I actually gave up on finding you. I could only hope that you got out in time and made it back to Paris."

"That's what we intended, but the roads were clogged and the Prussians kept cutting us off."

"I doubt anything will be in our way now. But I'm curious. What were you and Jerome doing in Metz before the war?"

"Besides hiding? I worked in a cafe. It paid, but not like before. I didn't have a chance to tell you. I'm not Marcel anymore. I'm Steven. If they're looking for a Marcel, they won't find him."

"Logical, as long as someone doesn't recognize you as Marcel. What about Jerome? What was he doing?"

"It was rather ingenious. He went to the cathedral, met some ladies who wanted to learn English. He started teaching in people's homes and made some money. I think he fell in love with one of his students. But he was running scared, looking over his shoulder all the time."

"He had good reason to be scared. He was running guns with Abraxas, guns for some damned revolution. Jabari nearly killed him. Charlotte was very worried about him."

"He didn't say anything about the guns. Why was Jabari trying to kill him?"

"Jerome came to his senses and decided that the whole thing was too damn dangerous. He wanted out, and Abraxas assumed he would go to the authorities."

Jack thought for a moment. "Did you ever see Abraxas after the night at the salon?"

"Once. I knew that he was involved in something suspicious and wanted money. I wanted nothing to do with it. I was in enough trouble. Then I lost track of him, not that I ever want to see him again."

"You won't. He went underground."

"The sewers of Paris?"

"A grave. I killed him."

Steven stared at Jack. "How?"

"He came to Charlotte's house looking for Jerome. A bad mistake. I heard that the police found him dragged by his horse. There were a couple of bullets in him."

"Well, now that's two suspects out of the way," said Steven. "By the way, Jerome speaks very highly of you. He places you in the pantheon of gods."

"I'm not sure I want to be in their company. Some are pretty unsavory. The only one I would worship is Charlotte."

"My, my, who would have thought?"

"Now you sound like Shelby."

"So, you are in love?"

"Indeed, I am, brother."

Steven passed the wine bottle to Jack. "I'm going to grow a beard. A luxurious beard. What do you think?"

"A disguise. Why not? Most men have beards." Jack studied the bottle in his hand. "Something still bothers me. Jerome mentioned that he was delivering guns to a woman who seemingly ran a revolutionary cell. Abraxas only played a minor part. This anonymous woman appears to live in the shadows, almost a phantom, a specter. I presume she's still out there. Jerome told me a little about her during one of his less delirious moments after he was hurt. He said that he remembered seeing her in one of the cafés. He thought that she was a grisette. You know a lot of women, Steven. You went to the cafés. Do you know her?"

"A grisette who becomes one with the night and frequents the cafés? A revolutionary? Perhaps I did. But as you said, I knew many women in all parts of Paris. Including some rather unsavory places."

"Did this woman care for you?"

"I suspect she did. Perhaps quite a bit. So did many others. I had a way with them. But I think that's all changed now."

"A lot of things are going to change. Mummies and mystical stuff may be quite out of fashion in Paris."

Steven stared into the fire and shrugged. "I'm not interested in mummy talks anymore. It was getting tiresome. But, Jack, do you think they're they still looking for me? Do I still have to hide?"

"I don't know. Inspector Gustave is a single-minded man. So is his boss, Arseneau. Then again, their world is in turmoil right about now."

"But there are two fewer suspects," said Steven. "Abraxas and Brandenburg. You know, I never liked that Prussian, but I hardly thought he would be in the thick of battle."

"He was a soldier at heart. Shelby asked me to go to Prussia before the war, determine their capabilities, and Brandenburg showed me around. He was pompous, authoritarian, imperious. A true Prussian. He showed me the siege guns, the ones they didn't use and probably won't have to. But the guns made me sick, and he gloated over them. He even suggested that I should be an observer on the Prussian side and watch the decimation of the French army. He said Moltke and Bismarck had it all figured out. Prussia would take over Germany and they would all become, in mentality, Prussia. A military state. Then and there I realized France didn't have a chance. Not even with their chassepot or their vaunted mitrailleuse with its fifty barrels."

"It's still inconceivable. France, at one time the mightiest power in Europe, completely defeated in a matter of weeks. So many men killed."

"It's not the first time, nor will it be the last," said Jack. "'Paths of glory lead but to the grave.' Thomas Grey, eighteenth century."

"I guess the French didn't read his poetry."

"I don't think it would have made any difference. For France it was all about glory. Probably still is. All they will want is *revanche*."

"Will they get it?"

"Probably. In time. But that doesn't mean they will win."

***

The train chugged into Paris crowded with wounded men and a few able survivors who had escaped the encirclement and surrender. Jack, Steven, and Jerome encountered incredulity in the city, above all else. Upon finding a wagon, Jerome was taken to the American Ambulance and placed in a tent to await the arrival of a doctor.

"Where are *you* going?" Jack asked Steven.

"I'll skulk around. Likely in Montmartre where the living is cheap."

"I'm going to see Charlotte today. I'll ask her if she'll let you stay at her place."

"That would be intruding, Jack. No, I'll look out for myself, but I'll be in touch. Shelby usually knows where I am."

"Fine, but remember, you're good in my eyes." Then with a touch of mirth he said, "Maybe I'll write to the War Department on your behalf. I'm sure they need competent soldiers in Apache country."

"Don't even think about it! Those people are damned dangerous, and I'm not fit for any violence. At least not any more."

***

Jack held her more tightly than ever before, and their kisses and sighs lasted long into the night. They were safe, wrapped in the joy of being together again. The bottles of wine had been drained, the gleeful and tearful reunion hours past. They whispered their hopes as though nothing else in the world mattered.

Jack shivered. Charlotte pulled another cover over them and said, "I was hoping that we would never see war again. I still have nightmares from before, what I had to do to save those boys. Now the French are suffering. And I guess many Prussians too. I'll go to Jerome tomorrow. I imagine they could use another nurse."

"I'm sure they will be most welcoming."

"Will he live?"

"He will. He told me that he wants to see the girl he taught English to in Metz. He wanted her to come with him when he and my brother fled. But her father wouldn't let her go. She may have lived if she found a cellar in the city. She would likely have died if she left."

"I hope he gets to see her again." Charlotte covered Jack's hand with her own and in the quietest voice said, "Was it as bad as the last one?"

"Yes, just as savage, just as brutal. Men butchered, unbelievable anguish, helplessness, death, dismemberment. The French couldn't break out. For all the blood shed on those fields, they couldn't save France. They couldn't save themselves, they just could not."

"But it's over now, isn't it?"

"Only if Louis Napoleon speaks for all of France. If not, well, I cannot envision what may come next."

"I am hardly religious, Jack. But tomorrow I will pray. And maybe you should, too."

CHAPTER 34

Paris

Late September

A sense of disquiet and apprehension had settled over the city. The Prussians, having defeated the French army at Sedan, immediately began to move toward Paris. Moltke wasn't concerned about the large force still concentrated at Metz because it was completely surrounded, with breakout virtually impossible. Berlin recognized that far too many of the French felt that the war was not over, despite the surrender of eighty-three thousand men and the deaths and wounds of another seventeen thousand.

With the capture of the emperor, the Second Empire collapsed on September third, to the joy of many Parisians. Louis Napoleon, though treated respectfully, languished in a pool of dejection. Empress Eugénie fled to England, according to titillating talk, barely escaping through a back door of the Tuileries Palace.

At the Hôtel de Ville, the Third Republic was announced with the words *"Vive la république!"* followed by thousands of voices raised to the sounds of the Marseillaise. After seven weeks of war, the old order existed no more.

Steven, having grown a full beard, sat with Shelby, Jack, and Charlotte in the Café de Bade. Some minutes later they were joined by Manet, who appeared somber and drawn. They picked at the cheeses Shelby had ordered and drank wine with little interest. Despite the elation two months earlier, the café did not resound with the usual clamor of voices, each overriding the other with witticisms or ribaldry.

Charlotte watched customers come and go with unsmiling faces. "I had hoped that it was all over, but the Prussians don't think so. I guess you were right."

"They're demanding Metz, Strasburg, Alsace, and part of Lorraine. That's not acceptable to the French," said Jack. "The Germans want to see France humiliated and are determined to fight until it is. Moltke wants to march into Paris and expects the surrender of the protective forts outside the wall. The Parisians will never agree to that."

"They may have to," said Shelby. "I heard from a colleague in Berlin that Moltke ordered two armies to encircle Paris. The army of the Meuse has been ordered to the right bank of the Seine and the Third Army to the left. That's two hundred and fifty thousand men and seven hundred pieces of artillery."

"Not counting the siege guns, the ones I saw in Prussia," said Jack.

"I thought that the ambassador said they wouldn't invade Paris," said Charlotte with alarm.

"I don't think they will," said Shelby. "They would be smart to lay siege to it. Cut off communications, supplies, and any chance to be reinforced by armies still in the field. Then what have you got?"

"Starvation," said Steven.

"But that will take months," said Manet, coming out of his stupor. "Surely Prussian supply lines can be cut, and there may even be guerrilla war. Remember how devastating that was for us in Spain during Bonaparte's time. And there are at least one million people who can be mustered from cities all over France."

"Where do they get the weapons, the trained officers, the organization to coordinate an effective resistance?" said Jack. "All that was with the regular army, and you saw what happened at Châlons and Sedan. Guerrilla war may seem patriotic, but the Germans will be ruthless. There was talk of guerrilla warfare in the Confederacy after Appomattox. Lee refused to hear of it. The carnage would have been too great, and the hatred would have lasted forever."

"Yes, yes, I understand, but the army in Metz hasn't surrendered. There is also the army of the Loire, which hasn't capitulated," said Manet. "In fact, it's sworn allegiance to Louis Napoleon. They can be a real threat to the Prussians surrounding Paris."

"Not by themselves," said Shelby "They're separated by hundreds of miles, and the Prussians are keeping them that way. Neither can come to the aid of the other. The big question for the Germans is with whom can they negotiate the surrender of Paris. Louis is powerless but hasn't formally abdicated, and the Council in Paris wants to continue the war."

"Isn't Paris well defended?" asked Charlotte.

"There are two hundred and fifty thousand of the Garde. They may deter a frontal attack, but they're helpless against those siege guns. The forts and walls will mean nothing if the Prussians bring those within range," said Jack.

Manet leaned back in his chair and sighed. "None of you are French citizens. There is absolutely no reason for you to remain in Paris and suffer whatever is going to happen. If I were you, I would go to England or even Normandy until this is over. It may be six months or a year, but Paris will always be here. Come back when it's over. Then we'll all meet again."

"It would seem that we are abandoning the city, but perhaps you're right," said Jack. "But what about you?"

"I know how to shoot, and I will be at the wall. I am a Frenchman. *Vive la France!*" he said, raising his glass.

"*Vive la France,*" replied the others, draining theirs.

***

"*L'ambulance Américaine en avant!*" shouted the captain on his bay gelding, waving people aside to make way for a wagon filled with wounded soldiers. The wagon came to a halt on the Avenue de l'Impératrice halfway between the Arc de Triomphe and the Bois de Boulogne, and the men were carried into long white tents whose sides had been partially lifted for ventilation. Over two hundred beds stood on the two-acre plot of what had previously been weed-strewn ground. Money collected from concerned citizens and the hospital's founder, the American dentist Thomas Evans, had transformed the site into the most efficient hospital in Paris.

On two tall poles flew the American flag and that of the Red Cross. Flowerbeds, tidy walkways, and newly planted shade trees along with colorful shade awnings contrasted sharply with the dismal interiors of medical establishments in the rest of the city.

A piano was being played by an American volunteer, and within the tents were caged birds all chirping at once. In the center of the compound were kept a number of cows whose milk added to the soldiers' diet.

Charlotte and Jack walked beneath an awning toward one of the dozen tents and watched as a second wagon tore down the avenue, pulled by sweating horses and driven by brash Americans lustily singing "Marching through Georgia." Charlotte, wearing a gray navy cap and an armband with the insignia of the Geneva cross, stopped short upon hearing the words.

> Hurrah! Hurrah! We bring the jubilee!
> Hurrah! Hurrah! The flag that makes you free!
> So we sang the chorus from Atlanta to the sea
> While we were marching through Georgia.

"That's appalling!" she said. "Why in the world would they sing that?"

"I think it's very melodious," replied Jack with an impish grin. "Kind of stimulates the blood, don't you think?"

"It's stimulating my blood, that's for damn sure!" Charlotte stomped off to the hospital tent.

"I'm sorry, I just thought ..." said Jack, sounding very much amused as he followed her inside.

"I know what you thought. I love you, Jack, and maybe I'm overreacting, but some things are still very painful. Maybe they always will be. I hope you understand."

Thirty wounded soldiers lay on beds in two lines with a walkway between. A warm breeze wafted through the tent and a nurse, removing scalpels from a pot of boiling water, turned to Charlotte. "Thank goodness the boxes of soap finally came in," she said with a southern drawl. "I put a few bars beside the pan of water over there."

"Good" replied Charlotte. "There are new wounded coming in."

"Yes, we have to make room for them. I heard that one of the French positions defending the city has been overrun. I reckon there'll be many more wagons."

"You look tired. My shift is just starting—why don't you get some rest. I'll be here all day."

A short doctor with wavy blond hair walked briskly out of the tent, muttering to himself. Another doctor with a thin face, short black beard, and large spectacles followed close behind. Charlotte heard raised voices, though she couldn't make out what they were saying. A few minutes later, the second doctor returned, shaking his head. He stopped when he saw Charlotte.

"Oh, Nurse Stuart, good to see you. We can use your expertise today. So much to do." The man looked at Jack and thrust out his hand. "I'm Alexander Silver. New York. Miss Stuart told me about you. A promising artist, I understand."

"I'm not so sure about promising, and I'm not working on any art right now. I don't imagine many others are, either."

"No, I presume not," said Silver. "Things are getting more tense every day."

"Tense, yes. It's not really my business, but that other physician seemed very upset," said Jack.

"I gave him a tour of the Ambulance. The French government has been unwilling to give us any support, and though the French know a great deal about medical techniques, their treatment of patients is barbaric. He was quite condemnatory about the sensitivity of American doctors to their patients, and certainly didn't approve of open-air tents. He became quite upset when I pointed out that we save four out of every five men while the French lose four out of every five. I doubt he'll return."

"Just as well," said Charlotte.

"Well, I have to get back to work," said Silver. "But I did examine your Jerome this morning, Nurse Stuart. He's a brave lad."

"How is he doing?" asked Jack.

"I'm afraid his fever has worsened. The lance that penetrated his arm must have had some infectious material. Thank God that we have a microscope here—I detected various bacteria, though we're not sure what all of them are. And we have a new drug that's quite progressive."

"The antiseptic?" said Charlotte.

"Ah, so you've heard about it. It should cut down on the number of amputations."

"Will it help Jerome?" asked Charlotte.

"That's the hope. I think we can save his arm, but he's quite weak."

"Can he be moved, taken to a safe place beyond the city?" asked Jack.

"Absolutely not. Moving him in an unsanitary wagon for a long journey will mean certain death. The Prussians won't attack a hospital. But out there ..." Dr. Alexander shook his head. "No. He needs attention right here. It will take at least a month before he can be safely discharged. That, I'm afraid, is the honest truth. But I'll attend to him as often as I can."

"A mitzvah," said Charlotte.

"A mitzvah," said the doctor, his eyes lighting up.

"Then we'll stay and help."

"Like so many other Americans," said Silver. "Did you know that the ambassador's son is tending to the wounded? A soldier died in his arms recently. Very sad."

"I didn't know you spoke any Hebrew," Jack said to Charlotte.

"A few words. There are many Jews in the South. Several thousand even fought for the Confederacy."

"I'll be damned. I thought they were all with the Israelite Brigade and the Second Mass."

"Not everything was on your side, Jack," she said with fire still in her eyes. How well he knew that look.

Jack found two chairs. He and Charlotte sat beside Jerome, who opened his eyes and attempted a wan smile. Charlotte held his hand.

"Dr. Silver says you're going to be fine. It'll take time, but we'll be here for you."

Jerome nodded. "There's a girl in Metz I want to see again," he said in a weak voice. "She's very sweet, very pretty. I think I want to marry her."

"Marriage is a dangerous matter," said Jack.

Charlotte gave Jack an exasperated look and checked the bandages. "We would love to meet her."

Jerome closed his eyes, then blinked them open. "Are we under attack? I heard some explosions a while ago."

"Nothing yet," replied Jack. "And the Prussians won't breech the walls."

"I'm sorry I was such a bother. You and Marcel saved my life."

"You do have a penchant for getting stabbed, but fortunately it's not contagious," said Jack.

Jerome offered a thin smile. "That, sir, is truly good news."

"As I told Dr. Silver, I won't leave," said Charlotte after Jerome fell asleep. "I can't leave him behind."

"I know," said Jack. "We'll make the best of it."

"And we're in this together."

***

It had been hoped that the new Government of National Defense would be able to conclude a peace treaty with Prussia. But that nation's demand for Alsace and Loraine was totally unacceptable to the governing council, and negotiations ended with Bismarck and Moltke committing to moving on Paris after destroying the remaining French armies. That gradually took place despite the intervention of motley guerrilla forces, who often wore outlandish eighteenth-century uniforms based on the three musketeers and the tri-corner hats of the French Revolution, along with volunteers from Argentina. General Giuseppe Garibaldi led a force of Italians, but the Prussians regarded most of these fighters as brigands and shot them on sight.

The surrender of Louis Napoleon did nothing to stop the fighting through the month of September and into October. Despite brave attempts to break out, with sickness and food supplies exhausted, the fortress of Metz surrendered. The French Army of the Rhine, with its 170 thousand soldiers, was marched into captivity.

The same fate descended upon the other French force. In the forest of Orleans the Army of the Loire made initial progress against the Germans but were eventually overwhelmed with great losses. They capitulated on December fourth.

The Prussians encircled Paris in that bitterly cold winter, but they could only stare at its thirty-foot walls, ten-foot-wide trench, and the remaining forts that surrounded the city. Parisians, in the meanwhile, put aside their political rivalries and vowed to defend the city to the last man. On September fourteenth, under the leadership of General Trochu, over a million sailors, civilians, and members of the Garde Nationale marched from the Place de la Bastille to the Arc de Triomphe. They ranged through the boulevards and down the Champs-Élysées under the watch of hundreds of thousands of delirious Parisians, all flying flags, singing, and shouting their defiance. Certainly, it was believed that any Prussian breeching the walls would be eviscerated by tens of thousands, each exacting revanche on a hated foe.

***

"Hurry, we're going to miss it," said Charlotte.

She, Jack, and Shelby struggled uphill toward the summit of Montmartre along with thousands of Parisians. Shouting, waving hats, scarfs, and flags, they watched on that seventh day of October as a coal-heated balloon gently rose. It carried mail, as well as minister of the interior Léon Gambetta and two Americans, out of Paris. Gambetta had every intention of raising a new army from the provinces to challenge the Prussian might surrounding Paris. As German troops fired upon them, sandbags were dropped, and the airborne contingent climbed to ten thousand feet.

"You know, balloons were used by Union armies during the war, entirely for scouting," said Jack as they watched the contraption rise into a cloudless sky.

"But only briefly," said Shelby, "and those were tethered. They never sailed off like this. Simply amazing."

Descending the hill, Charlotte said, "It looks like they got safely past the Prussian guns, but I wonder if Gambetta can really raise a new army."

"If Paris is besieged and starved to death, it won't make any difference. And there's already a food shortage," said Shelby.

"Should we start conserving food?" asked Charlotte.

"Maybe." Jack glanced at Shelby. "Have you ever considered being skinny?"

"Oh, perish the thought!"

***

It rained the next day as Jack and Charlotte made their way to Ambassador Washburne's dingy building. Parked in front were two heavy cannon and their crew.

"Signs of the times," said Jack.

They were met by Gratiot, who ushered them through the corridor packed with Americans, Germans, and people of a dozen other nationalities, all heavily dressed for the cold weather. The scent of damp clothing permeated the building as they entered the cramped office.

Washburne rose from his desk and shook their hands warmly. "Gratiot told me you were coming. I'm glad you're here. I get out so rarely that I tend to lose touch with the mood, the temperament of Paris. Just give me a minute and we can be alone. I really do need a break; these have been eighteen-hour days. I've been giving passes out of the city for these people who've been waiting so patiently."

The ambassador left his office and proceeded from one person to the next, indicating his signature on the official safe-conduct papers.

"Remember," he said to the soon-to-be refugees, "the train departs from the Gare du Nord at eight at night. Take only what you absolutely need. The train will be very crowded."

With enormous gratitude they shook his hand and filed out of the building.

"Gratiot," said Washburne upon returning to the office, "now that our business is done, you're free to go. They may still need you at the Ambulance."

"If not, I'll be at the Café de Bade. Good to see you again," he said to Jack and Charlotte.

"I heard that you were hit when bringing men back from the front. How's the wound?" asked Jack as Gratiot gathered his coat.

"Not too bad. Dr. Evans removed the fragments when they brought me in. It's healing well, but the leg still feels stiff."

"Everyone at the Ambulance thinks you were very brave to aid the wounded so close to Prussian lines," said Charlotte. "Perhaps the French will give you a medal."

"That would embarrass me; it was such a slight wound. But a lot of men there do deserve a medal." He leaned in close. "Don't tell my pa, but I stole a tin of his fruitcake. I thought I deserved it."

"I heard that," said Elihu Washburne, laughing. "Now go, and remember, those are my favorite."

When his son left, the ambassador said, "According to the drivers, he was really in the thick of it. Could easily have gotten killed. But he's a tough one."

"Like his father," said Charlotte.

Washburne shrugged. "Gratiot tells me that you're staying."

"We can't leave, not without Jerome," said Charlotte."

"So many people are trying to get out," said Washburne. "I've signed thousands of passes for Americans and other nationalities. Thirteen thousand of our countrymen were here until a few weeks ago. Now most are gone."

There was a heavy tread of hoofs on the street below, and Charlotte glanced out the window. "They're still bringing cattle in from the rural regions."

"Yes, they're corralling them in the Bois de Boulogne. They will eat everything. It'll take years for it to recover," said Washburne,

"Forty thousand oxen, two hundred and fifty thousand sheep, all crammed into the park," said Jack. "And I hear that fifty thousand horses will be sacrificed, if necessary."

"There won't be a cab in the city," said Washburne. "The government's stockpiled enough food for about eighty days; the great powers should intervene by then. I'm sure they won't let Paris starve. But who'd have thought the siege would last until winter, and yet, here we are."

"I pray we never have to eat the zoo animals," said Charlotte.

"Indeed. I don't think I'd care for elephant consommé or roast ostrich *à l'allemande*," said Washburne.

"I'm not sure about elephant or ostrich," said Jack, "but horsemeat is already selling for ten cents per pound. Perhaps, Charlotte, we should visit the zoo before the animals are all gone."

"It may already be too late," said Washburne as a llama was led down the street.

CHAPTER 35

Paris

Late November

Jack alighted in front of the Café de Bade from one of the very few omnibuses still running. He was nearly at the door when Étienne Daudet brushed past him wearing the uniform of a captain in the Garde, his right hand covered by a flesh-colored leather glove. When his eyes met Jack's, his expression turned to one of fury.

"You think you destroyed me? Oh no, monsieur. I am ambidextrous, and I've been learning to paint with my left hand. I am still an artist. But you, I surmise, will never be."

"You are a pompous ass, Daudet. Favor me with a second duel and I will happily remove the other hand. But I suspect that you have concerns other than art. Fighting with the Garde is quite dangerous nowadays. I pray that you can shoot better with your left hand than you could with your right. Good day, sir."

With a self-satisfying smirk, Daudet strode across the street. Before Jack could enter the café, Yvette Maillard, eyes brimming with tears, walked out and almost ran into him.

"Oh, Monsieur Volant, please excuse me. I must look a sight," she said in a frail voice. "I have had to sell everything

—my jewels, my horse. I have even lost the flat. Monsieur Daudet refuses to pay the rent. What will become of us?"

"I'm sure you will find a way to survive, mademoiselle. You are still a beautiful woman."

"I am no longer a demimonde. No salon will invite me, and even wealthy men aren't spending money on things of the heart."

"Or the flesh."

She sighed. "That detective, Monsieur Gustave, found me the other day. He's still looking for the murderer of Camille Lapin, would you believe. He even suspects me. I told him that he should be looking for another woman, a dangerous one he likely will never find."

"And you know who she is," said Jack in a hard voice.

"I suspect so. But who it is, I won't say. No, I believe you should speak to Monsieur Marcel," she said, her eyes lighting up. "That might be productive."

When Jack didn't reply, the former demimonde said, "I never did get to thank you for defending my honor. I do so now, Monsieur Volant."

"Actually, mademoiselle, I was defending mine. But I thank you anyway, and I wish you all the best. I'd stay away from Monsieur Daudet if I were you. But of course, he may get himself killed before all this is over."

"You missed all the fireworks," said Shelby as Jack finally sat at the table with him, Manet, and Edgar Degas.

"Let me guess. It was between Yvette Maillard and the great artist Étienne Daudet."

"Very perceptive. How did you know?"

"I saw both of them leaving here. I resisted shooting Daudet—he is, after all, a patriot in full uniform—although I did have a few words with him. And the fine lady was rather distressed. What did I miss?"

"The entire show. She practically accosted him. Wanted money for the apartment and said that he owed her for unspecified forms of companionship. He said that he had no money to give her and that his interests were only in the defense of France. Anything else would be horrifically unpatriotic. Their voices were, well, a bit strident. In these despondent times it offered a bit of theatrics if not amusement."

"I think the word is hypocrisy," said Degas, looking glum.

"You heard the news?" asked Manet "I mean, about Bazille."

Jack shook his head

"He was killed in Beaune-la-Rolande by a sniper on the twenty-eighth, the last day of the war. A terrible shame. He was a true patriot, and now we have lost not one but two of our finest artists. My friend, the equestrian sculptor Louis Cuvelier, was killed at Malmaison. He was in the francs-tireurs, the sharpshooters brigade."

"Irreplaceable," added Manet, his usually infectious *joie de vivre* totally absent. "But we must continue the resistance. I am stationed at the wall, and we're praying the Prussians attack. They'll be decimated. And then we will charge out in the thousands and liberate France."

"That's nonsense," said Degas.

"Why? We have five hundred thousand men."

"Most of them are untrained. They won't get past the German lines. Even now we're being shelled every day. And the Prussians haven't even brought up their great siege guns yet."

"There's a real schism," said Shelby to Jack. "Auguste Ducrot, the general leading the men at the wall, demands revenge and wants to attack. General Trochu, head of the government, doesn't want to see thousands more dead and wounded. And he's in Versailles, not Paris."

"Ducrot is right," said Manet. "Last month fifteen thousand people stood at the lobby of the Hôtel de Ville screaming, 'No armistice, resist to the death.' They took over the government here, vilifying Trochu."

"Yes, they were shouting, '*Vive la République, vive la Commune!*'," said Degas hotly. "Then it all evaporated. But the rise of the commune, the poor, the anarchists, now that will be more dangerous than the Prussians. The civil strife will tear Paris apart, Frenchmen firing on their fellow citizens. We are on the cusp of disaster. Mark my words, Manet."

"We're a long way from that," said Shelby. "But smallpox has broken out, and over four hundred have died. And the government has turned off two-thirds of the street lamps for lack of fuel. Maybe Manet is right—a full-out assault may be the only solution."

"And if it fails?" said Jack.

"Then there will be thousands of dead and Paris will see the senselessness of further resistance. It will be over. So have your damn assault, Manet. And I will help bury the dead."

Degas stood and stormed out of the café.

***

The indiscriminate shelling began at night. With increasing fatigue, nerves were strained and tempers grew short. In a further attempt to wear down the populace, German guns began firing during daylight hours. Hundreds of shells fell around the perimeter of the city as well as the Left Bank, striking the once vivacious Latin Quarter and the Sorbonne University. Amid plumes of smoke, Parisians huddled in their houses as shell fragments fell about them. French guns fired back, adding to the incessant noise.

"You're looking as haggard as I am," said Jack as he sat with Shelby at Galignani's. "This is bringing back unpleasant memories."

Shelby nodded, and Jack saw his friend's deep fatigue.

"There were days, weeks, during the war when I was too tired to get on a horse," said Jack. "But we were soldiers and became used to the cost of battle. But these civilians have never experienced what we have, and now they're going to see the elephant. I'm afraid for them."

"I think more will die from hunger than bullets. They'll be eating horses before it's all over. This siege is a very serious matter and it's only going to get worse."

"You're probably right. I have to get back to Charlotte." Jack moved toward the door, then turned back. "Are you going to stay here?"

"No, I'm going to the wall. I think it's safer there."

"Maybe, but I don't think anyplace will be safe for long."

***

Their home was well outside the city center, and the cannon fire had seemed distant, but now shells rained down in a field beside the property. It was, thought Charlotte, as if the Prussians needed more targets and had to generate more fear.

Again, like years before, she felt her world collapsing. Her once promising career and the appreciation of her art had imploded with the downfall of the empire and the flight of the empress. Chipping away at stone seemed a futile act, small and irrelevant.

At least she had Jack. Holding her tightly in his arms he had tried to reassure her, spoke of the future and how as artists they would persevere. But it now felt like a hollow promise as the land was shredded and the ground shook both day and night.

346

***

Jack arrived to see flame rising from the barn. An explosion had struck it, collapsing the roof and setting hay on fire. Charlotte led her terrified horse from the inferno and struggled to saddle it as more shells ripped into a hill beyond.

Jack grabbed the lead rope. "I'll saddle her, but we have to get away."

"It was so sudden, and I didn't know when you would be home," she said as she rode beside Jack.. "The house is gone, walls have fallen in. I couldn't get anything out. Where can we go?"

Weeks earlier it might have been possible to slip past the farthest walls, but Prussian forces had sealed that escape. Jack scanned the hills as more shells fell.

"There are the sewers, they're shell proof."

Charlotte shuddered. "I don't want to go there. It's foul and so dangerous. Shelby said that there are entire communities in there—and lots of felons. And there are the catacombs. No, somewhere else."

They rode quickly, passing refugees, mostly on foot and some pushing carts containing frightened children and household belongings. Explosions erupted every few minutes. A great pall of smoke and flying debris was followed by screams and shouts.

Coming upon a partially ruined stone building, Jack said, "This one may have a basement. I'll take a look."

"I'm coming with you." Charlotte dismounted and tied their horses to a nearby tree.

They stepped into the remains of the structure. Jack was about to say that there was no basement when a shell exploded fifteen yards away, throwing them to the ground.

"Oh God!" said Charlotte when the smoke cleared, "The horses, they're dead!"

***

By late afternoon, covered in dust, they sat on a collapsed wall.

"Do you know where Steven lives?" Charlotte said. "Maybe we could go there."

"He never told me. For all I know it may have been burned to the ground."

"And Shelby?"

"He's at the wall. Galignani's is too dangerous."

"Should we go there?"

"The Prussians might break through."

"Then where?" said Charlotte, watching the stream of refugees, most not having any idea where to seek shelter.

"To the embassy. But we have to get there before dark."

***

"I'm so glad you're safe," said Elihu Washburne as he slid papers into his diplomatic pouch. "One place that hasn't been shelled yet—at least as far as I know—is the Hotel de Ville. An American couple, the Sherlocks, rented two rooms for the season, but they left for England weeks ago. They were terribly frightened and left without saying anything to the staff. I don't think they trusted them. When I gave them the passes for the train, they gave me the keys. The rooms, I assume, are still vacant, and now they are yours. I'm terribly sorry to hear about your house."

"We'll rebuild it," said Jack, "but not until the war is over."

"This shelling will continue until Paris surrenders," said Washburne.

"Do you still get foreign news?" asked Charlotte.

348

"The Prussians respect diplomatic pouches, but they aren't letting anybody out of the city, and Trochu isn't, either. He thinks it's bad for morale. Now, do you have any food?"

When Jack shook his head, the ambassador turned to Gratiot. "Get these folks a load of tins, won't you?"

"The fruitcake?"

"Of course the fruitcake. How much of it do you think I can eat? And the chocolate. Bring them a good store of it." He turned to Jack and Charlotte. "The French have suddenly discovered American canned food. They now consider it a delicacy. *Vive les Etats-Unis.*"

Washburn sighed. "There have been negotiations with the Prussians who have occupied Versailles, but food, or the lack of it, is the tip of the spear. Their strategy is starvation instead of assault."

"But they're still firing those cannons at us," said Charlotte. "If it's a matter of starvation, why bombard Paris?"

"That was a matter of contention between General Moltke and Bismarck. Moltke thought it would only result in the strengthening of French resolve, but Bismarck won out. So, we now have both starvation and shelling."

***

There were only a dozen tins of food left when Charlotte ventured to the ramshackle food stalls on Rue Rochechouart for government-rationed meat. Heavily clothed crowds pushed against display tables evaluating dog carcasses hanging from hooks.

"Have you any horsemeat left?" she asked the harried butcher.

"Long gone, but I do have horse blood for pudding and cat fillet. It's tastier than dog but more expensive."

Charlotte counted her coins. "I'll take the dog meat," she said with resignation.

Beside her a young girl clutched her mother's hand and pointed to a tray of decapitated rats.

"That one is nice and fat," said the girl.

The mother turned to Charlotte. "Do you think it's fresh?"

Sniffing, Charlotte said, "It doesn't smell rancid. I think it's safe."

"Very fresh," stated the butcher while wrapping Charlotte's side of dog. "You can make rat pâté or fricassee. And I might have monkey tomorrow. From the zoo, you know."

Charlotte shivered and walked away while the woman eyed the rats in the blood-smeared tray. She hadn't seen a live poodle in a month.

***

Jack and Shelby joined Manet at the wall on the last day of November. It was a bitterly cold morning as they peered into the distance where General Ducrot's corps, part of a one-hundred-thousand-man force, moved forward to break through the German lines. Days earlier a carrier pigeon from Tours had landed in Paris containing a message saying that General D' Aurelle had won a battle at Coulmiers. That a non-Parisian army had defeated a Prussian force offered encouragement not seen in months.

Citizens overjoyed with the thought of a *sortie torrentielle* raved, saying, "What could possibly stop such an army?" Most assuredly it would pierce the German front and, after combining with Aurelle, charge through the Forest of Fontainebleau to the south. Then, it was said, nothing would impede it.

"Where's Charlotte?" asked Shelby. French gunfire erupted as the offensive began.

"At the American Ambulance. They're preparing for casualties. Washburne and his son are there, too. He says it's the final push, the last throw of the dice."

"This entire operation was supposed to happen two weeks ago," said Manet, "but everything was delayed. All four hundred guns had to be repositioned, all brought through the streets of Paris."

"I heard that the French and German pickets have gotten along quite well. There's been a brisk trade of Prussian food for French information," said Shelby. "The Prussians know exactly where the attack will be. I'm sure they're ready."

There was a lull in the shelling, and Charlotte and Jack returned to the American Ambulance which, miraculously, had not been hit. On the second day Charlotte tapped Jack on the arm and said, "A wagon driver was kicked by a horse and is in the Ambulance. There are six nuns, all nurses, who want to volunteer, but they're stranded at Notre Dame."

"I'll drive the wagon, and I'll bring Shelby. He doesn't want to stay at the wall any longer. People are freezing to death there."

Later that day an orderly called out, "Wagon coming in!"

Charlotte and two other nurses stepped out of the tent and saw a wagon bouncing over the pock-marked road. Charlotte watched in amazement as the nun's habits fluttered in the cold wind and Jack and Shelby, with all the lung power they could muster, sang, "Look away, look away, Dixie land!" With each stanza lustily belted out, Charlotte and her Southern assistants laughed until it hurt.

"It was Shelby's idea," Jack told her as she led the frazzled nuns into the Ambulance.

"You two looked unbelievably silly, but I liked it more than 'Marching through Georgia.' Just don't look so amused."

***

The initial French assault gained ground, and the immense push seemed unstoppable. The troops silenced Prussian positions, but reinforcing units were stalled, and the Germans stiffened their resistance. After three tortuous days, the attack came to a bloody halt. At the end, despite unyielding courage, Ducrot ordered a retreat across the frozen ground.

It was as Washburne had thought, the final role of the dice.

Parisians abandoned the boulevards. They spoke of nothing but food. But there was no thought of capitulation to the Prussians who delivered pain upon what was once the City of Light.

***

Late in the day, Steven laboriously hauled himself out of bed. A one-room hovel abandoned by a soldier in Montmartre's Rue Pigalle had become his cocoon. Montmartre had been an art colony where both Monet and Renoir, with rent paid by Bazille, had once lived. Now, like a sodden blanket, perpetual dimness hung over the district. Venturing beyond one's door required the faith of a martyr.

The only heat on this miserably cold day was a cooking pot of glowing coals into which Steven had placed an iron cup filled with the last dregs of coffee. Fully dressed and wrapped in a greatcoat, he shivered as he slid out of bed and dipped his finger into the cup. The water was tepid, the coffee tasteless, but he drank it, then warmed his hands over the coals.

Nearly penniless, Steven had resisted the thought of appealing to Jack, and the tins of food he'd gotten from the embassy had long been devoured. Returning there would be an embarrassment, though Washburne had been kind and sympathetic, offering words of encouragement. But it would be a long walk to the Rue de Chaillot near the Champs-Élysées, and the man might not even be there. A fruitless venture, he determined.

At the start of the siege, when he still had money, Steven could visit the Café de la Paix at the corner of Boulevard des Capucines. But none of the women who frequented the place would be there now, nor could he afford whatever food the café had—if they had any at all.

Collecting the last of his remaining coins, he made his way to the Dîner de Paris on Boulevard Montmartre where, in earlier times, breakfast had only cost two francs. He passed two men carrying a body from a tenement. It wasn't an unusual sight, with four thousand dying per week from starvation.

The diner had an unusually large crowd, considering the weather, and the mass of bodies gave heat to the interior. A sign outside gaily advertised dandelion soup, pumpkin, and a concoction made from mugwort, chickweed, and thistle. Candles illuminated the gloom within, the gas having been turned off.

She looked in his direction, but she didn't recognize him. He bought coffee and a biscuit and sat at a table, all the while watching her. Petite, frail, she still had those dark, penetrating eyes, that sybaritic, sensuous energy which demanded that men follow her, hunger for her.

But it had been a very long time since he'd dared venture into her realm, the mysterious, dangerous streets where she moved in darkness. It seemed forever since she had wrapped her thighs about him, demanded his very soul and, with those lancinating eyes, promised vengeance if he betrayed her. Which he had.

Furtive knots of men and women gathered around. She stood on a chair, holding them in rapt attention. Steven was hardly surprised. Her words, impassioned, revolutionary, came out like a hiss of steam. Her audience leaned forward, not daring to miss a word.

"Comrades! We, the poor, the starving, the dispossessed have had our blood sucked dry, our very souls extinguished by the callous, indifferent aristocracy and the bourgeoisie. How long has it been since a single one of them has spoken on our behalf? How long since we have had the slightest relief?"

"Never!" shouted a gaunt man.

Her voice became strident. "We are beaten for sleeping in the street. They ignore our ceaseless pain and the deaths of our children. Do they care? They do not! Never do they look upon us, for their guilt is too much. Comrades, their days, their lives, will shatter like broken glass. We, the indigent, the slaves of the leeches will rise up and build a new Paris. No, a new France! They will die in their feathered beds, in their churches dripping with gold and hypocrisy. It is time! To arms!"

They were mesmerized, committed, and angry. They were resolved. She was a siren who would lead them to victory. Or certain death, when the time came.

She would have pulled the lanyard on the guillotine, carried the tricolor in the siege of the Bastille, and beheaded the king himself had she lived decades earlier.

Her indictment complete, she silently accepted the crowd's accolades of support. Steven heard the muttered words "guns, rifles, swords, and bayonets." She put a finger to her lips and looked around. The Trochu government was in power; the left supported him, but they were not the Commune. The time of the Communards, of anarchy, would come, she vowed, and it was clear that they believed it with all their heart.

Finally, she headed for the door. She probably had scheduled another tirade against everything sacred to the establishment. Her eyes met Steven's as she passed. For the briefest moment she halted and furrowed her brow, then swept out of the café.

Steven had options. He owed her no allegiance, not now. He finished his coffee, rose, and slowly trod back to his flat. He had seen her and knew where she might be found. But then what?

He lay awake much of the night. What was she worth to the authorities? Or to himself? He pondered that as fitful sleep overtook him at last.

***

The first of the day's four hundred explosions began on January fifth. It had taken far too long, Bismarck believed, for the great Krupp siege guns—seventy-two in all—to be placed, manned, and aimed at the people of Paris. The general staff had feared the cri de coeur of appalled governments, all invoking diplomatic and humanitarian pleas. But suspending operations without the absolute defeat of France wasn't a consideration. The bombardment began in earnest on the one hundred and ninth day of the siege.

Moltke had hoped that capitulation would come with starvation. Time was of the essence, however. While the huge artillery Jack had seen before the war belched shells at civilians as well as any military targets, there was far less damage than anticipated by either side. Many explosions ripped great holes in empty fields or crashed into buildings with little effect.

As the shelling continued without ceasing, the citizens began to develop a studied, resolute nonchalance. The resistance would not collapse because of Prussian guns. It would stop when there was nothing more to eat, nothing more to warm oneself with in the most bitterly cold winter in memory.

Taking a break from their work at the Ambulance, Jack and Charlotte walked back to the embassy. They watched as dozens of women and children ripped at branches brought into the street from the Bois de Boulogne.

"They're taking it all," said Washburne as they looked out the window of the embassy. "It was to be used for charcoal, distributed by the government."

"But no one was defending it," said Charlotte.

"The government's broken down along with the army," said the ambassador. "It's just as well, those people can't be allowed to freeze to death. As you could see when you came up the stairs, I turned the bottom floor into a dormitory for over a hundred men, women, and children. Almost all of them German, believe it or not. They can't get out of the city, and they would be murdered on the streets. I sent a cable to the secretary of state saying the American Ambulance is filled and there are French troops at the wall, frozen to death. To avoid the shellfire, some people are living in the tombs where the heroes of the Revolution lie in their crypts. This year is truly *l'année terrible*."

"And French regiments from the provinces are still in the field, still battling the Prussians," said Jack.

"Guerillas and franc-tireur forces. The Germans have carried out horrific reprisals against them and anyone else who dares oppose them," said Washburne. "There have been many violations of the rules of war—even the British are objecting to the growing atrocities. What was a war respectful of noncombatants has devolved into an orgy of murder and hideous retribution."

He rifled through several newspapers on his desk and held one out. "Then there's this, a statement by our General Sheridan. He's been an observer with the Prussians."

"What does he have to say?" asked Charlotte.

Washburne placed a finger in the middle of the page and read aloud. "The proper strategy consists in inflicting as telling blows as possible on the enemy's army, and then causing the inhabitants so much suffering that they must long for peace, and force the government to demand it. The people must be left nothing but their eyes to weep with over the war."

"What a brutal man. It's hard to imagine that this whole catastrophe began over the succession to the Spanish throne," said Charlotte.

"I think it's much more complicated than that," said Washburne. "What this has come down to is a war between two religions, two kinds of people: the organized, exacting Teutonic Prussians with their Lutheran solemnity versus the Roman Catholic French, boisterous, freethinking, and revolutionary. They don't mix. There's no room for compromise. If queried now, I think the French would be incredulous over the idea that the Spanish throne was adequate cause for war."

"When will it end?" asked Charlotte, her face drawn.

"Like Sheridan said," Jack sighed, "when the food is gone and the French can take it no more."

"I am saddened to think it," said Washburne. "But I hope it's soon."

CHAPTER 36

Jack, Manet, and Shelby sat around a table at Galignani's, thankful that it had not been shelled. They scanned a French translation of the *Berliner Börsen-Zeitung*, which proudly announced the rise of the new German nation. In a regal event it had been proclaimed that Germany, led by Wilhelm I would become one and indivisible. To the dismay of all France the great ceremony to finalize the joining of Prussia and Germany would take place in the Hall of Mirrors in the Palace of Versailles.

Otto Von Bismarck, standing beside King Wilhelm, read the decree before the assembled representatives of the military and officials of the previously independent provinces. Bismarck, upon the completion of the proclamation, led the magnificently attired assembly in the words "His Majesty, Kaiser Wilhelm," which was repeated enthusiastically three times amid great jubilation. This was followed by a parade of troops around Versailles singing *"Nun danket alle Gott"* (Now we thank God).

"So, now we have the ascendancy of a German potentate," said Manet.

"They could have had the ceremony in Berlin," said Jack, "but the entire Prussian elite has been at Versailles for months. I guess Bismarck thought it was a good time, since all the major French forces have been defeated."

"Now all of the German states are under Prussian control," said Manet. "This is an ominous thing. Prussia is a warring state. Always has been."

"I think they considerate it their destiny, and nobody can do anything about it," replied Jack.

***

During the third week of January, the Germans increased their bombardment of the city in a final attempt to bring capitulation. Negotiations continued in Versailles between Bismarck, Moltke, and the French representatives, and it was suddenly announced to the relief of most that a truce and the cessation of the bombardment would occur on January twenty-eighth, the one hundred and thirty-first day of the siege.

Charlotte was still treating the wounded at the American Ambulance the day prior to the surrender when Ambassador Washburne arrived, handing out invitations to the entire staff.

You are invited to the Voisin on Rue Saint-Honoré
for an elegant dinner on behalf of the American Embassy

went the handwritten note.

That evening, honored guests, both French and American, descended upon the restaurant.

It seemed eerie to Jack. Not a gun fired, not a single shot ripped into Paris. It was only a truce, but it was expected to hold unless the city's most rebellious continued the war.

Over one hundred hungry souls looked over the elaborate menu prepared by Étienne Choron, one of the city's most prominent chefs.

There was laughter and gaiety as waiters in black ties, white aprons, and gloves scurried about filling orders. Charlotte raised a piece of paper in the candlelight. "Jack, it's a poem."

She read it, then handed it to him, giggling.

Kind patrons and friends,
You smile at this food,
But never 'til hungry
Can you tell what is good,
Remember I pray you,
Of these kinds of meat,
We were eating to
Live, not living to eat!

Jack smiled, pulled Charlotte close, and kissed her. "So, what's on the menu?"

"Well," said Charlotte, squinting, "there's terrine of antelope, wolf with deer sauce, fricassee of rats, filet of ostrich à l'allemande, roast filet of horse with cabbage, horse broth soup with toast, potatoes with elephant consommé, and elephant trunk. There's also mice—*à la chinoise*."

"Delightful. I guess the elephants were Castor and Pollux from the zoo," said Jack, peering at the menu. There was still plenty of wine, and it was being poured liberally.

"There's also hippo," said Jack.

"No hippo for me," relied Charlotte. "I won't have the lion or tiger, either."

Jack continued to peruse. "Now this is novel: 'Donkey head with sardines, slowly glazed in congealed fat, carved and stewed.' Then there's kangaroo minus the pouch. I'm going for the antelope, the soup, horse filet, and a slice of hippo, nicely roasted. What about you?"

"Jack, I know it's costing Washburne a fortune, but this is the most sickening menu I've ever seen."

"Perhaps, but there are hundreds of thousands in Paris who'd kill for a dinner of lion or elephant."

"I know, I shouldn't complain ..."

"We don't know when the Prussians will allow food to come in. It may be weeks. There were twenty thousand rats in Paris, and now they're gone. One hundred grams of meat per day and a slice of bread is the daily fare." Jack covered her hand with his. "I think you'd like the roast filet of horse. It's a delicacy, after all."

From time to time, Jack glanced out the window to watch the few people who ventured onto the streets peering through the restaurant's windows. After they ordered, Jack saw a figure staring at him. She slowly waved a hand. The woman, drawn and fragile, dressed in a heavy coat that was wrapped around her like a coffin, looked familiar. Indeed, he'd seen her months before at the Café de Bade. But then Yvette Maillard had still looked sensuous and beguiling. He stared back and raised a hand. A hesitant smile appeared on her frozen face.

Jack was tempted to invite her in, to have her share in the abundance of the feast, but it would require the consent of the ambassador, who was in serious, deliberate conversation with Trochu. It wouldn't be proper to interrupt that. And what would he say about inviting a demimonde, this demimonde, to sit beside them? No, it wouldn't do. And then she was gone.

Later that night when he wrapped his arms around Charlotte, she murmured, "When will we be married, Jack? I cannot bear being away from you."

"Soon, when this is all over, when in the bright light of day we can invite all of our friends to the wedding. I love you with all my heart. It's just a matter of time."

Then, with a puzzled look, she said, "You waved to a woman outside the restaurant. I didn't recognize her. Who was she?"

"The demimonde who frequented the salon where Steven performed. She was once the favorite of Daudet. "

"Oh, yes, I remember. The duel. Now she looks so destitute."

"So many do," Jack said. "Now go to sleep. I think I drank too much wine."

"Will you please me in the morning?"

"Just the thought will keep me awake."

***

Paris

Early March, 1871

For the previous month the citizens of Paris had waited with trepidation for the arrival of the Prussians and the terms of surrender. All resistance had ended, but none of the captured French army had yet been released from captivity.

Efforts had begun to clean up the bombarded streets, but a sense of ineptness pervaded the city.

Jack and Charlotte stood on the sidewalk of the Champs-Élysées with hundreds of others across from the Arc de Triomphe, through which the Prussians stridently marched. Suiting the mood, a dull, overcast sky lay like a pall over Paris. Eventually the clouds blew away and the day began to warm, but that provided little respite. Despite the absence of any official proclamation, no stores or cafés opened their

362

doors, no conveyances moved down the street. It was as if the entire city had died. Charlotte pulled her shawl closer. "Jack, more are coming now. What do you think they're going to do?"

It had been hours since the first Prussian cavalry had warily entered Paris and ridden down the boulevard, weapons at the ready. Except for a few taunts, there was nothing for them to fear. Charlotte's question was answered when several dozen troops with bayoneted rifles positioned themselves around Napoleon Bonaparte's great monument to his victories. Now the victories were German. Sullen crowds watched the immaculate but silent Prussians with stoic awe. By late afternoon entire battalions from the Third Army had paraded down the street, and that night, with no gas for lamplights, the city remained dark and silent.

Two days later, with utmost correctness and abstaining from vengeance upon the population, most of the Germans departed the city. They had made their statement and thoroughly humbled France. But within hours of their departure, the streets came back to life. Food and donations poured in, much of it from America, and the trains began to run again. And, quite amazingly, there began a strange comradeship between the French troops and the few Prussians remaining in the city.

***

Several days later, Jack sat again with Shelby and Manet at Galignani's.

"According to *Le Monde*, the Germans are getting Alsace and a big chunk of Lorraine and a pot full of francs—one million, five hundred thousand, to be exact," said Shelby.

"And there are still fifty thousand German troops in France," replied Jack. "But they're leaving Versailles to make room for Louis Thiers's government."

"But the French government is not in Paris," said Manet.

"No, things are too unsettled here," said Shelby. "With the concern about possible riots, the Germans have released forty thousand French troops with their weapons."

"That many are needed?" asked Jack.

"The new government thinks so. There's still a lot of anger in Paris. The middle class, the elite, will reestablish Paris as we knew it, but the status quo is despised by many.

"So, what's your prediction?"

"I think it's going to get ugly. With the war over, you might want to get out of Paris," said Shelby.

"That's not going to happen. Charlotte doesn't want to leave. She hopes to rebuild if we can find the money."

They watched as crowds reappeared. There were still a few horses to pull the omnibuses but virtually everybody walked.

Manet sipped a glass of wine and leaned back in his chair. "I was so foolish, thinking the war would be a short, glorious thing. So, now that that it's over, what have we gained? What was it all for? Honor, glory?"

"Only if you think it was worth one hundred and fifty thousand wounded and dead Frenchmen. And nearly one hundred and twenty thousand Germans," said Shelby. "And, of course, the end of the Second Republic."

"Do you think the third will be any better?" asked Jack.

"I think it's off to a very rocky start, Lieutenant, sir."

***

"I want to thank you for coming on such short notice," Ambassador Washburne said, offering Jack a chair.

"Charlotte was wondering why I alone was invited here. She enjoys speaking with you."

"And I with her. But this is a matter between me and you; I didn't want to unnecessarily involve her."

Jack frowned. "It sounds serious."

"Perhaps, but perhaps not. Two detectives from the police prefecture visited me yesterday afternoon. Messieurs Gene Gustave and Gaspard Desvaux. They said that there is reason to believe that a certain Marcel Cheval, purportedly an American, might have been involved in the murder of a courtesan before the war. For some reason, somewhat inexplicable to me, they suspect that you know of this person and his whereabouts."

He raised his hands slightly. "Unless it's a matter of confidentiality or a situation of extreme embarrassment to the United States, I'm generally required to cooperate with the French investigators. So, I told them that I would speak with you."

"The person you're speaking of is my brother. He's since changed his name back to Steven Volant. I would have reported directly to you if I thought he'd been involved in a capital crime. He wasn't, though some of his business dealings prior to the war were of a dubious nature. But why didn't they ask me directly?"

Washburne put two fingers to his temple and looked over his reading glasses. "Probably because they thought you might not acknowledge that Steven is your brother. Apparently they only know him as Marcel. I presume he's not making himself known to them."

"No, because, though innocent, he assumes quite correctly that if recognized, he would be arrested and falsely accused as an accomplice. If not the murderer."

"I see. Is he still in Paris?"

"I believe so. He's changed his appearance, grown a beard. I haven't seen him for some time, and I don't know where he lives. But I do know that he's frequented the less savory areas of Montmartre. Perhaps he's engaged with some of the people there."

"And, if I may ask, what duplicitous activities was he involved with before the war?"

"The unwrapping of mummies and the sale of fake scarabs and such. It was in a salon where he performed that the murder took place. But he wasn't there when the crime was committed. There were a number of suspects, some now deceased. In fact, one of them was an Algerian criminal wanted by the police, but he is no longer alive. Steven killed another suspect in the battle at Sedan, a Prussian officer named Colonel Albrecht von Brandenburg, the husband of the lady who ran the salon."

The stoic ambassador could not suppress a smile. "I presume you have told Charlotte all about this."

"Like all honorable men, I tell her nearly all of what she needs to know. We all have our little secrets, some more embarrassing than others. I certainly have my share."

"None of us are saints," said Washburne.

"The French believe that *you* have achieved sainthood. Probably some Germans do, too."

"It's my job to do what I can. After all, I represent the United States. My behavior must be beyond reproach. I'm not sure if the detectives are still interested in your brother, but I advise that he turn himself in. If he chooses to do so, I'll write on his behalf. The French will appreciate that he fought bravely against Prussia. My official letter should carry some weight."

Jack shook the ambassador's hand and had turned to leave when Washburne asked, "Is your brother still in the same business?"

"Egyptian mummies? Not anymore. He's seen enough dead bodies."

***

Jerome, now fully recovered, joined Jack, Manet, and Shelby at Galignani's in mid-March as Louis Adolphe Thiers, leader of the French Third Republic and the Republican conservatives, attempted to moderate tensions and restore order in the city. It was an impossible quest. Although most of the French army had been relieved of their arms, the Garde Nationale, all within the confines of the city, weren't required to give them up. They marched to a different drummer: the commune and the popular cry for *la République démocratique et sociale!*

"Things are moving very quickly," said Shelby. "Thiers was here before but fled to Versailles. Sources tell me he's trying to marshal eight hundred thousand troops, his original forty thousand regulars, plus another forty thousand released by the Prussians."

"How many men do the Communards have?" asked Jerome.

"On paper, about three hundred and ninety thousand. In reality, perhaps twenty-five thousand. But they do have artillery," said Shelby.

"Maybe four hundred bronze cannons. But most of them are obsolete muzzle-loaders," said Jack. "About one hundred and seventy of them were taken to Montmartre. The Thiers government, the regular army, tried to take them away, but there were no horses available and a soldier in the Garde was killed. That led to a huge crowd surrounding the regulars. The soldiers were ordered to fire on the crowd of Communards. They joined them instead.

"Then the Communards captured and shot two government generals. One was General Clément-Thomas, the siege disciplinarian That was followed by the Communards' assault on the Hôtel de Ville, where they mistakenly thought they'd find Thiers and the national government. They were wrong, but a red flag's been hoisted above the building."

"Charlotte said that she saw perhaps twenty thousand of the Garde camped outside the Hôtel, all ready to fight if the French army attacked the city," said Jack.

Jerome shook his head. "Until I was released from the American Ambulance I had no idea things had gotten so bad."

"Well, they have," replied Jack. "I'd better get back to Charlotte. Things can turn bloody if the Garde opposes Thiers."

"Speaking of which," said Shelby, "the Garde crossed the Seine this afternoon. They captured the Place Vendôme and the Ministry of Justice, and that's just the start."

"I hope they realize they'll be opposed by the Army of Versailles, the one the Prussians defeated and imprisoned," said Manet. "Those men will insist on reclaiming their honor, their glory. They'll want no part of the Communards. I think it's going to become very ugly."

"Perhaps so, but the army will need a respected leader. Has Thiers appointed someone?" asked Jerome.

"Marshal MacMahon," said Jack. "He's popular and fought well during the war."

"He's no one to fool with. That man will have no mercy," said Shelby.

"That word will be deleted from the dictionary," said Jack.

"What about murder?" asked Manet.

"That one will be in bold print," said Jack.

Shelby turned to Jerome and said, "Considering that the matter of stolen guns hasn't been settled, I think you should get out of Paris while you can."

"I'm not going. My loyalty has always been to the poor, the destitute. I sympathize with the people of the Commune and I will fight for them."

"That could be quite dangerous," said Jack.

"Perhaps, but it the righteous thing to do."

"I hope you reconsider," said Shelby. "Their quest for glory may end very badly."

CHAPTER 37

Paris
April 1871

"I was nearly shot," said Renoir as he met Jack, Manet, and Shelby at Galignani's. Visibly shaken, he waved away a glass of wine and slumped back in his chair.

"By whom?" asked Jack. Cannon fire was audible from as far away as Porte Maillot and the Arc de Triomphe, where huge barricades had been thrown together.

"The Garde Nationale. Foolishly, I was sketching a scene at the Seine—the river, houses, and such. Soldiers saw me and accused me of spying for the army of Versailles. It didn't matter what I said in my defense. With bayonets at my back, I was marched to a firing squad where corpses were being dragged away. There was no trial, no one to defend or speak for me. I was thrown against a wall."

"But you weren't executed," said Shelby.

"No. It's so surreal, I still can't believe it." Renoir dabbed at his forehead with a napkin. "Many years ago, there was a man, Raoul Rigault, who was running from the police. This happened in the forest of Fontainebleau where I was painting. He begged me to help him. At first I was hesitant. I saw this sinister man, thick black beard, wild eyes, with a malicious sort of smile. I could have been charged with aiding a possible fugitive if discovered. I would have been imprisoned or worse."

"Is this the same revolutionary who's in charge of the Communard's police and the executions?" asked Manet.

Renoir nodded. "Back then I gave him a smock, a palette, and disguised him as an artist. When the gendarmes appeared, I pointed toward a field and they rushed past. I hid him, and they never found him. And then today, when I was about to be shot, he suddenly appeared. He came up close and stared at me, and I said, 'Raoul, it's me, Renoir.' He told the guards to lower their guns. He embraced me and ordered my instant release. Another three minutes and I would have been dead."

"You are damn lucky," said Shelby. "Hundreds have been rounded up and imprisoned on the orders of the Central Committee."

"When was this?" asked Manet.

"You didn't hear? It was during the Garde's attack outside the fortifications against the army of Versailles a few days ago. Of course, it was repulsed, and captives were summarily shot. In response, the Commune issued the Decree of Hostages in which a special jury will shoot three army soldiers for every Garde Nationale prisoner executed."

"So it's really begun," said Jack. "I picked up this, a proclamation by the Committee. They're all over Paris." He handed it to Shelby, who read it aloud.

"'Citizens, the hour for revolutionary war has struck! You will rise up as one man. Citizens, your leaders will fight and, if necessary, die with you but in the name of glorious France. The Commune is counting on you, count on the Commune!'"

Shelby handed the proclamation back to Jack and sighed. "Censorship even more rigorous than during the Second Republic is ratcheting up. Any newspaper not supporting the Commune is being shut down, including *Le Gaulois* and *Le*

Figaro. But there are dozens starting up that support it, like *Le Cri du Peuple* and *La Nouvelle République*."

"Do you think *The Messenger* will be shut down?" asked Manet.

Shelby shrugged. "It's only read by Americans and British, and most of them have fled. In any case, I've tried to steer a middle course, but I did write a column about the Communards and the Church. I expect that I'll hear about that."

"The Church is really their main enemy," said Renoir. "All Church property is being confiscated, and the archbishop of Paris has been arrested by Rigault. He also imprisoned twenty priests in Mazas Prison. It's a monstrous place."

"So I have heard," said Shelby. "The hatred against the Church is deep."

"Ambassador Washburne's tried to get Rigault and the priests released, but no luck so far," said Jack.

"It only gets worse," added Manet. "I heard that orders have been issued to burn down Notre-Dame and the Louvre as symbols of the Second Estate, its myths and superstition."

"Not surprising," said Renoir.

"But the common people built the cathedrals and supported the church for centuries," said Jack.

"That was before," said Renoir. "Now they view the Church as the bulwark of the status quo. It supports a medieval mentality, using its wealth and fear of excommunication to maintain the supremacy of the aristocracy. That's why the Communards want a separation of Church and State and the secularization of schools."

"Still, it wasn't the symbols that oppressed those people," said Jack. "Losing Notre-Dame and the Louvre would be a tragedy."

"I don't support the burning, but I understand it. Unless you're French, you cannot feel the depth of hatred and contempt that the underclass has for the Church. To them it's a syringe that sucks the life out of everything."

More shelling ensued, and several hundred of the Garde rushed past to stiffen the support of a barricade. Behind them a cannon was pulled by a dozen civilians, and Jack could see another gun in the distance from the window.

"It's not the first time the Church has been under attack," said Shelby, his attention turning away from the Garde.

"I doubt it'll moderate its dictums, and it's too entrenched to be toppled by a few thousand anarchists," said Jack. "The Army of Versailles and General MacMahon will see to that if they take Paris."

"It's not 'if.' It's 'when,'" said Shelby.

***

Steven and Jack crossed the bridge on foot and entered the Prefecture of Police on the Île de la Cité. There was a sense of anxiety in the air as staff members sorted through files and placed papers in boxes. Crates were being loaded from a wagon into the rear of the ancient building.

A plainclothes officer approached and brusquely announced, "I am Monsieur Gaspard Desvaux, a senior detective. We are quite busy here. What business do you have with the Prefecture?"

Before he could receive an answer, Desvaux turned to another officer. "Gustave, have you heard anything more about that mob?"

"I have not, monsieur, but I do believe our informants." Seeing Jack and Steven, he handed a file folder to an underling and approached them as well.

"Who are these men?" asked Gustave.

"I do not know," replied Desvaux with a hint of disdain.

"I am known to you as Marcel Cheval," said Steven. "And I have a letter for Chief Inspector Monsieur Ambroise

Arseneau. A letter that will clear my name and end any further investigation."

"A letter? From whom?" said Desvaux as Steven handed him the envelope.

"From the honorable Monsieur Elihu Washburne, the American ambassador to the French Third Republic."

"And it supposedly exonerates you?"

"It does, based on the testimony of this man, Jack Volant, an American like me."

An exceedingly short man with an extremely long beard moved through the disheveled room. "What is this? A letter for me?" he said in a commanding voice.

"Indeed, Chief Inspector," said Desvaux.

Arseneau opened the envelope and quickly read the letter. "Neither the assailant nor accomplice, but a hero of France, having fought bravely at Metz in the war against the forces of Prussia."

The chief inspector, standing two feet from Steven, peered through his monocle. "I do not recognize you, monsieur. This letter from the esteemed ambassador claims that you are innocent of some crime. A crime in which he provides no details. Perhaps you might educate us regarding the event."

"There was a murder before the war of a courtesan named Camille Lapin at a salon, Chez d' Chantilly."

"Ah, the one owned by Madame Marguerite Couture. I know this-this case well." Gustave turned to Arseneau. "This man was a performer, a charlatan who unwrapped mummies at the salon. He is most assuredly a suspect."

Arseneau sniffed. "Not according to the ambassador, but —"

"I am innocent. If I were guilty, would I appear before you?" said Steven. "And would someone as prestigious as the ambassador to France write that letter? You can ask him yourself if you don't believe me."

"May I add," said Jack, "that although the ambassador didn't mention it, Monsieur Cheval shot and killed a Prussian colonel in the war. It was, in fact, the oberst married to Madame Couture."

"And exactly who are you and how do you know this?" said Desvaux.

"Because I was at that battle and witnessed it. My name is Jack Volant, and this man saved my life. I was the target of Colonel Brandenburg."

"Even if you are innocent, Monsieur Cheval, there is still a murderer out there. And, having an intimate knowledge of the salon, surely you have a theory of who it might be," said the chief inspector, one of his myopic eyes greatly enlarged by the monocle.

"Several suspects come to mind."

"Well?" blurted Desvaux, "Who is it, we haven't all day."

"Besides the maid—"

"They're coming!" shouted a gendarme, bursting through the door. "The mob. The Communards. Hundreds of them, some with torches."

"To arms! To arms!" shouted Arseneau, thrusting the letter at Marcel. "We'll deal with this later. Report back here when these rodents are destroyed!"

Jack and Steven pushed their way past the dozen police who drew their weapons and rushed outside. Nothing, however, impeded the Communards; they threw the police aside and stormed into the building. Hurrying from the confrontation, Jack and Steven put as much distance as they could between themselves and the shots and screams.

"Where to?" asked Steven.

"Charlotte said she's going to speak with Washburne. I'm going to the embassy."

"I should go, too. I want to thank him."

"Fine, but he doesn't need a courtesy call right now."

"I'll just stay a minute. By the way, Jack, are you carrying your gun?"

"I have for a very long time."

"I think I need one, too."

"Under normal circumstances I would dissuade you. But these times are not normal. You'd better find one. Also, do you have a passport?"

"Yes, thanks to Washburne."

"Keep it close. The French like us. Being an American could save your life."

***

"He's still writing laissez-passers for all the people trying to get out of Paris. I'll take you to him," said Gratiot. "I'm packing all the diplomatic papers. My father hopes to leave here in a few hours."

"Are you leaving Paris?" asked Jack.

"No, we've found an apartment in Fontainebleau that can serve as the embassy. It'll be safer there. We aren't sure of what the Communards think of us, but I do know what my father thinks."

"What's that?"

"The city will burn."

"Last time I saw him, he looked very tired," said Jack.

"He travels to Versailles almost daily to speak with Adolphe Thiers. It's some twenty miles. He is tired, and not at all well."

Jack, Steven, and Gratiot squirmed through a crowd of several hundred people, all hoping to receive passes before the Communard barricades were complete.

"Is Charlotte here?" asked Jack as they headed up the stairs.

"She left an hour ago. My father told her to go back to the Hôtel de Ville. She's expecting to see you there. I wouldn't dally here long."

Jack introduced Steven to Elihu Washburne, who said, "Oh, yes, I do remember you. The tin cans and the letter. I must commend you for your gallantry against the Prussians. I only wish that I might hear of your exploits, but time is of the essence. Perhaps when this idiocy is over."

There were explosions in the street below. A ragtag cluster of people with red kerchiefs shouted, *"Vive la Commune!"*

"You hear that?" Washburne signed another pass. "This is a city with no protection, no law, no authority except disorganized mobs. They think their venom can defeat the army of Versailles. But slogans aren't reality. Now they issue decrees. I took this one off a telegraph pole."

Jack read it and handed it back. "So, as of tomorrow, no one will be permitted to leave Paris, and all able-bodied men are to take up arms."

"And all rail service has ended. Shells have been landing on Avenue de l'Impératrice just a stone's throw from my house."

"I heard that the Communards want to tear down Bonaparte's Vendôme Column, and they've already trashed the home of Thiers," said Jack.

"Most unfortunate," replied Washburne. "Not that I'm a great admirer of Napoleon, but it's a famous monument."

He ran a hand through his graying hair. "I sent another dispatch to Secretary Fish at State about the deteriorating situation and especially about the archbishop. I was allowed to visit him, you know. He's a fine man and doesn't hold a grudge against the Communards even though he's jailed in a cell the size of a closet. The Communards want to exchange him for a raving mad revolutionary named Auguste Blanqui. I pleaded with Thiers to do it, but to no avail."

"How much longer do you think this will last?" asked Steven.

"I have no idea. Paris, the 'City of Light,' is now one of darkness. I don't know when the light of sanity will be restored."

***

The sound of artillery woke Jack. He scooted from bed and stared out the window.

"Are the explosions close?" asked Charlotte, pulling the covers over herself.

"Not very. I see smoke somewhere near the Bois de Boulogne, maybe around Porte Maillot."

"In that case, why don't you come back to bed. It must still be early."

"I was thinking of speaking with Shelby. He said something about a weakness in the fortifications."

"Mmm. I think you should stay here. We can snuggle some more."

"A wonderful idea, but Shelby also mentioned Jerome and said that he might be in danger."

"Jerome?" Charlotte sat up groggily. "What sort of danger?"

"Shelby thinks that he's at the barricades."

"Well, I want to find him," she said, getting out of bed and dipping her hands in a washbowl.

"You should stay in the room, it's dangerous out there."

"It's dangerous everywhere, Jack. And I don't take orders from damnyankees."

"Charlotte, that's—"

"Oh Jack, just put on some clothes before your important parts turn blue."

***

"I was right, Jerome has joined the—" A shell exploded on the Rue de Rivoli, two hundred yards from Galignani's. "—the Communards," said Shelby.

"Where is he?" asked Jack, his eyes straying to a squad of Garde soldiers carrying away the corpse of a legless man.

"Most likely in Montmartre. I spoke to him only briefly. He said that he was going to assist a number of women building a barricade at Chaussée Clignancourt in the eighteenth arrondissement."

"I want to speak with him."

"It's a long way and no omnibuses are running."

"Was Jerome with anybody else when you spoke with him?" asked Charlotte.

"There was a young woman waiting outside. She wore a red bandana. I only got a glimpse, but she seemed tense and exceedingly agitated"

When Jack and Charlotte arrived, thirty men and women were hurling furniture from windows and piling them on overturned carts across the wide boulevard. Others hauled in shattered masonry, adding to the six-foot barricade. Behind it, unkempt people waited with guns. Jack and Charlotte approached the defenses where rifles and barrels of gunpowder were being placed. On the hills of Montmartre near where the balloons had been launched now stood one hundred brass cannons, their barrels glinting in the dull morning light.

"There he is." Jack pointed toward a wagon upon which Jerome stood amidst a load of stone.

"I think these should go in front of the barricade," Jerome said to a slight woman with hands on her hips.

"Yes, but we'll need fifteen more loads. We have to leave spaces open for three cannons. The Versailles must not be allowed to storm the hill."

"What if they get past us?"

"Don't worry, they won't." She looked beyond the barricade. "Those people are watching you. Do you know them? Are they spies?"

Jerome turned, saw Jack and Charlotte, and waved. Descending from the wagon, he hugged Charlotte and shook Jack's hand. "It's going to be much larger, sturdier," he said, nodding toward another wagon hauled by two horses.

"Who is that woman, the one supervising this?" asked Jack.

"That's Jeanne. We're all divided into ten-person cells. She's the head of the one I'm in."

"What's her last name?" Charlotte said, seeing the woman's petulant frown.

"I don't know. We just call her Jeanne. She's from Montmartre, an organizer for a long time."

"A revolutionary," said Jack.

"For the people, yes," said Jerome cautiously.

"Can we speak with you?" asked Charlotte.

"Just for a moment. We have work to do."

"We won't take much of your time," said Jack as a cannon was rolled toward the barricade.

Half a block further on, Jack said, "Just what the hell do you think you're doing? That conglomeration of junk won't last five minutes against the Versailles. I don't have to tell you that, you've seen what artillery can do. We were nearly killed by it. And those cannon on the hill, they're obsolete, probably not even rifled. They would've been obsolete during the Civil War. Only trenches will hold anyone back, and no one's digging up asphalt to make those. This is suicide, and it's not your fight."

"Jack's right," said Charlotte decisively. "You're an American, and the United States is neutral in all this. The ambassador despises the Communards. He'd be furious, knowing you've joined them. He would order you to immediately desist."

She put her hands on his shoulders. "My dear Jerome, I beg you. Come away. This is going to become a morgue. Jack and I have seen war, and so have you. That army out there, the real French army, may not have the ideals you do, but they will stamp out rebellion and all who support it." Tears welled up in her eyes. "You are a good man and have a fine future. Yes, in France, particularly in France. But even if you survive this, you'll be marked and sent away. We may never see each other again."

Jerome remained quiet for a long moment.

"Charlotte, I was born a slave. You were good to me, but I lived as a slave. These people live in abject poverty. It's slavery of a different kind and there's no manumission, no compassion, and the elite have no interest in making it any better. If I can help, even if it costs my life, I will do it."

"But things will change," said Jack. "Circumstances make things change. We did so in America. It's bound to happen. And Charlotte and I need you. We must rebuild the house, and I cannot do it alone."

Jerome smiled wanly. "I want to help you, both of you, but I am with the people of the Commune. The common people who have no voice. I have to remain here. There's nothing more I can say. But I wish you all the best in the world."

Jack lowered his head. "In the war at home, soldiers would pin a piece of paper to their coats with their name on it. It was the only way we could identify them days after the battles. I suggest you do that. We would want to give you a proper burial. I was hoping I wouldn't have to say that, but I know how this is going to end. And so do you."

He shook Jerome's hand again, gripped his shoulder, and waited while Charlotte gave him a final hug.

"Jerome, the truth," said Jack as they were about to leave. "Who is that woman? Is she the one who stole the guns? Was she in with Jabari Abraxas?"

"She's a revolutionary. She's one of the people. And so am I."

CHAPTER 38

Paris
The third week of May
"La semaine sanglante"
(The Bloody Week)

"It seems so long ago," said Jeanne Virot. She lay naked beside Steven, having slipped into the Hôtel de Ville after midnight. She traced a line with her fingers down his chest and kissed him gently. "Was I insane, Marcel? I wanted to hold onto something, someone, so badly. And then when I saw you with her, how much you desired her, fawned on her, well ..."

"Camille was a passing fancy. A tasty treat, like many others. I have always had an insatiable need for beautiful women. I should have told you that Camille was only one of many. Perhaps it would have made a difference. But I was shocked, I must tell you that. To make love to a living, breathing woman and then see her dead. The horrific finality of it all."

"But you didn't know who did it, so you still sought my affections, my treats. But after Camille, I wanted nothing of you. I already had a different lover, one that captured my imagination, my entire being."

"The revolution."

"Yes, the revolution," she said. "A passion for people like me, the poor, the wretched debris of Paris, of all France. It's become an inferno. Its heat, like your lust, it's unquenchable."

Steven kissed her breast. "And it will consume you, devour you, as I did. But you survived my passion. You won't survive this. I'm sure you know that."

"Of course, my dear Marcel. I'll be dead in a day or two. I care not."

"You know that I tried to find you in those stench-filled alleyways in Montmartre. It was frightening. I knew that I was being watched."

"I know. I saw you from the shadows. I thought of coming to you, but it would've ended badly for me and for you. Love, jealousy is like that. There was another man I considered killing. An Algerian who ran guns with me. He wanted me, would have raped me, but I was a specter. He never knew where I would appear and in what guise. That terrified him."

"Abraxas is dead. My brother killed him before the war."

They lapsed into silence.

"Abraxas wasn't only wary of me. Strangely, he was troubled by a young man, a colored, who's joined the Communards. I think the boy is dangerous though he pretends to be so innocent. Yet I enticed him, seduced him, played upon his sense of justice. But it saddens me now. And he will die too."

"Jerome."

"You know him?"

"He was with me during the war at Metz and Sedan. I had to run away, you know. I was a suspect in the murder."

Jeanne Virot sighed. "Did you ever love me?"

"Love? I knew desire, lust, compulsion. You've been a siren's song, a magnet I could never pull away from. Last night I remembered a poem and thought of you."

"What poem?"

"*La Belle Dame Sans Merci* by Keats." Slowly, he recited:

> "I met a lady in the meads,
> Full beautiful, a faery's child;
> Her hair was long, her foot was light,
> And her eyes were wild."

Virot laughed. "A faery's child? That's silly. Surely you know something else, something that speaks of me, of our time."

"Then there's this:

> 'To every man upon this earth
> Death comes soon or late;
> And how can man die better
> Than facing fearful odds
> For the ashes of his father
> And the temples of his gods?

"It's by Macaulay, an Englishman."

"I've never heard of him. And the only god I worship comes from the barrel of a gun."

"That saddens me."

"Well, I've come back to you. That should please you, but it's the last time."

"And it's the last pleasure for you?"

"No, that will be at the barricades. Too bad you won't witness my last testament, my final defiance. It will be magnificent, the scream of ultimate desperation. And then the last act will be over and the curtain will fall."

"It doesn't have to. I can hide you. You can survive this, go on, do other things."

"No, living is for those who know how to live. I don't anymore. I gave everything away, all the money I stole, the jewelry, everything except the knife, which I'll keep for the last killing. Everything else I gave to my mother. She deserves it. She knows everything and said nothing. Not even about Camille. She is the only one who knew."

"Are you speaking of Madame Couture? She is your mother?"

"Of course. You didn't know?"

"How would I? Tell me about her. She always appeared so aristocratic."

Virot laughed. "Aristocratic? Hardly. At thirteen she was raped and I was the result. Too poor to raise me, she abandoned me on a church pew. I was raised by the nuns. But at twelve I ran away and began a different life. I saw my mother from time to time, but I kept my distance and so did she."

"Is she still in Paris?"

"No, she got out. She isn't one for revolution. She detests the Communards and only wants her old life back. But not with Brandenburg. You said he was killed?"

"Yes, I killed him in the war."

"That pleases me."

"Will your mother come back? The salons been destroyed, you know."

"Of course she will. It's her life, she has nothing else. She'll rebuild with the money I gave her. And you?"

"I won't unwrap mummies there anymore."

"You'll find something else. Maybe something a little less deceiving, Marcel."

"That's not my real name. It's Steven."

"So many secrets. My name isn't Jeanne."

"What's your real name?"

"It doesn't matter. Remember me as Jeanne. After all, what do we really know about each other?"

"Hardly anything, except that I will miss you."

"And I will miss you. But I won't miss the grand finale. And then there will be a new Paris."

"You think so, Jeanne?"

"Someday. When there is, there will be—what do you Americans say? 'Liberty and justice for all.'"

***

Jack hurried from the Hôtel de Ville to Galignani's and stood beside Shelby. Together they watched hundreds of men, women, and children rush past carrying any stone they could carry.

"I was in the hotel when the Central Committee ordered that all the barricades be manned," said Jack. "Particularly the one at Place de la Concorde—that's where all those people are going."

A lieutenant in the Garde stopped beside Jack and observed his platoon rushing past.

"Monsieur, has the barricade been breached?" asked Shelby.

"Regretfully, yes. The tricolor is flying from the Arc de Triomphe; the army of Versailles has broken through. They came in at Porte de Saint-Cloud yesterday afternoon and marched on the right bank of the Seine. Amazingly, they weren't detected and took us by surprise. Then they routed the garrisons at Porte Maillot."

"So, what can your men do now?" said Jack.

"We can just try to hold the remaining barricades. I can only imagine the chaos at the Hôtel de Ville. There may be another headquarters somewhere, but I don't know where."

The lieutenant was joined by a major, who said, "Get your men to the guns on the hill. We've lost our positions at Pont-du-Jour. Everything is completely open."

"Sir, what of MacMahon?" asked the lieutenant.

"He has sixty thousand troops in the city, and they brought their artillery."

Both the lieutenant and his superior hurried off.

"I can't help but feel for them, the people of the Commune; they're so damn determined," Shelby said. "But they're doomed and they know it. I wonder how many will sink to their knees and pray for mercy."

"And it won't be enough," said Jack.

They were surprised to see Steven arrive ten minutes after they reentered Galignani's. They listened as bells rang throughout parts of the city not already taken by the Versailles. Steven handed Shelby a sheet of paper. "This was pasted on a pole outside the hotel."

"Another proclamation," said Shelby, who scanned it and handed it to Jack. "This one's from Communard delegate Delescluze, the minister of war:

> In the name of this glorious France, mother of all the popular revolutions, permanent home of the ideas of justice and solidarity which should be and will be the laws of the world, march at the enemy, and may your revolutionary energy show him that someone can sell Paris, but no one can give it up, or conquer it! The Commune counts on you, count on the Commune!

"And there's this one," said Steven, sliding the proclamation onto the table. It's from the Committee of Public Safety." It read:

TO ARMS! That Paris be bristling with barricades, and that, behind these improvised ramparts, it will hurl again its cry of war, its cry of pride, its cry of defiance, and its cry of victory; because Paris, with it barricades, is undefeatable ... That revolutionary Paris, that Paris of great days, does its duty; the Commune and the Committee of Public Safety will do theirs!

"This is the stuff of desperation," said Jack.

"Well, I share their desperation," said Steven. "I can't stay in the Montmartre district any longer. The Versailles are moving closer and shells are flying everywhere. Everyone is being marshalled by the Communards, and I'm not in their fight. I really don't know what to do."

"I wish you had gotten out with all the other Americans. You had that chance," said Jack.

"I know, but I didn't think it would come to this."

"You could get a white handkerchief and throw yourself on the mercy of the Versailles."

"I considered that, but the Communards are confiscating all white fabrics. They'll shoot anybody who tries to surrender." Steven tapped their bare table. "You see, even here, all the white tablecloths and towels are gone. Burnt."

"There's a maid's room next to ours at the hotel. It's vacant—she ran off with the Communards. It has a bed, table, and chair, but not much else. I think it's the best you'll be able to find. Shelby, I think you'd better come, too. We'll find you a nice closet."

"A big one. My girth, you know."

***

May twenty-third was the second day of battle against the Communards. News filtered in to the Hôtel de Ville all day since it was still the command post. Garde soldiers and frantic civilians brought messages from arrondissements still under Communard control. But the reports were becoming more ominous by the hour.

Shelby and Steven knocked on the door, and Jack ushered them in.

"You two look exhausted," said Charlotte as she poured cups of tea.

"We've been out," said Shelby. "I'll be writing about this when it's over, providing we survive. I wanted to learn firsthand what's going on. It's bad. Yesterday there was a big battle on the Quai d'Orsay and the cemetery at the Madeleine as well as on the grounds of the Tuileries. There are now about eighty thousand regulars in the city. That's four times the Communards."

"I was under the impression they'd enlisted more," said Jack.

"A few days ago, perhaps, but hundreds have been captured and shot. Men, women and children. Trials are short and predetermined. In reprisal, the Communards are cutting off the hands of captured Versailles. They've also set fire to buildings on the Rue de Rivoli and Rue Saint-Florentin, and they've torched the Tuileries Palace. The place is an inferno," said Shelby.

"They tried to burn the Louvre," added Steven. "But the fires were put out."

"Not entirely," said Shelby. "The Richelieu library, the one connected to the Tuileries, has been torched."

"Why the Louvre?" asked Charlotte. "All those paintings, priceless work."

"Because many of the paintings celebrate the Church along with the royals and their wars," said Jack.

"The Communards can't hold this place much longer," said Shelby. "Maybe we should find a cellar or the sewers."

"Oh please, not the sewers," said Charlotte. "Anywhere but the sewers."

***

Allied with the Versailles government and protectors of the status quo, hundreds of gendarmes fought to retake the burned out police prefecture. Chief Inspector Ambroise Arseneau stood by the ruins and assembled his staff.

"This is an abomination! The apogee of lawlessness. And it will be punished! We'll assist the army and destroy the thieves and murderers manning the barricades at Montmartre."

Addressing Gaspard Desvaux, he said, "I order you to find Raoul Rigault, the self-proclaimed chairman of the Committee of Public Safety. It was he who set fire to this. I want him executed."

"Monsieur Terrier, he's already been shot. The army found him after he murdered four of his captives, all Versailles."

"Very well. He got what he deserved. Now we shall eliminate the filth of our city. You will follow me."

***

Communard crowds watched with cheers of approval as the Vendôme Column came crashing down and *pétroleuses*, women hurling bottles of incendiary liquid, set fire to the homes of supporters of the Versailles. Throughout the night, screams filled the streets. Hundreds, then thousands were executed by the Versailles. Their opposition did no less. With blue-checkered handkerchiefs tied around their foreheads, Communards fought like banshees, screaming their defiance. Ragpickers, prostitutes, common workers, and even middle-class merchants struggled ferociously against the well-organized and effectively led French army.

As insurgents were apprehended, hands were searched to see if they had been stained with black powder, and those who failed the test were summarily executed. Many innocent people who decried the executions were also shot, as well as children handing out leaflets in defense of the Communards. By the afternoon of the twenty-third, the River Seine was red with blood. The combined hatred of the Versailles and the Communards overran the abyss of insanity.

The skies were clear on the twenty-third, but a drenching rain fell on Thursday, the next day. At the barricades fronting the slopes of Montmartre, Communards waited as the army obliterated one obstruction after another. Nearly all nine hundred barricades burned brightly as their defenders were shot or captured. Prisoners, soaked by the rain and vilified by those who had not joined the Communards, understood their fate. The executions continued apace in the Luxembourg Gardens, in prisons, and on the grounds of the Louvre.

"They are coming! To arms, to arms!" shouted Jeanne Virot as the army came into view. The Communard artillery commenced a horrific fire, and for a moment the Versailles troops staggered and fell back. Officers regrouped their men, and with a bugle's blast the assault regained momentum. Pushed onto the boulevard was the government's artillery, and quick-firing rounds exploded amongst the Communard guns. Artillery carriages and gunners were blown skyward as the shelling mounted with increasing effect.

Behind the barricade, Jerome aimed a chassepot, fired, loaded, and fired again. A sudden blast tore into the breastwork. Furniture, wagons, rock, and wooden beams were shredded. A dozen insurgents with arms, legs, and heads severed were flung off the ramparts. Screams and shouts and ineffectual commands contended with the eruption of barrels of gunpowder.

Many Versailles rounds were directed at buildings on either side of the barricade from which gunfire had erupted. Entire walls crumpled, showering defenders with shards of brick and stone.

With the silencing of the Communard batteries, the Versailles troops intensified their attack. Amongst them were gendarmes and, incongruously, a gnome of a man with a long white beard who brazenly waved a large pistol.

"Forward!" bellowed Ambroise Arseneau, who was flanked by Desvaux. Intent on leading the charge, they sprinted in front of the battalion, firing madly at any figure that dared rise above the shattered barricade. A few paces behind them, Gene Gustave put another round in his revolver and hurried forward.

"Don't stop shooting!" Jeanne Virot shouted, hastening between Communards with extra ammunition, a long, curved knife unsheathed in her belt. Upon reaching Jerome she pointed to the assembling Versailles. "There, the gendarmes, the old one with the beard."

He stared through the smoke. "That one, the leader?"

"Yes, the midget. Kill him!"

Jerome trained his weapon on the diminutive figure, whose short legs propelled him like a steam engine. With amazing speed, Le Terrier rushed forward, his beard singed, his face a reddened mask. A sudden volley of Versailles artillery ripped into the barricade, collapsing it and killing dozens.

Thrown from his position high on the barricade, Jerome fell yards in front of the flaming debris. Rising to his knees, he saw Jeanne raise her jambiya and fling herself at Arseneau.

"It's her! The leader!" shouted Desvaux, pointing at Virot.

For a brief second Arseneau stared at the woman and the knife she held poised above her. "You," he screamed with unbridled hatred, "you will die!"

Three times the chief detective fired. The woman twisted, lurched forward, and fell at his feet as a final blast from a Communard gun exploded amongst them, halting the assault.

The headless torso of Arseneau and the arms and legs of Jeanne Virot rained down amid paving stones, shattered weapons, and bits of clothing.

A tall, gaunt man, his arms ripped by shrapnel, suddenly stumbled and fell over Jerome.

Gasping and writhing with bloodied hands, the man stared into Jerome's eyes. His coat was ripped open, and a glint of metal peeked out. The troops, infuriated, resumed their advance, shooting and bayoneting Communard survivors. Two soldiers, seeing the wounded man, rushed forward.

Hoping to be spared, Gene Gustave roared, "The badge, show them the badge!" as a soldier aimed his rifle.

Terrified, Jerome ripped the shield from the detective's coat and shouted, "We are gendarmes! Gendarmes!"

The soldier wavered, finger on the trigger, and peered at the badge.

"Can't you see?" said Gustave. "Get us help, we're hurt. Just do it!"

The soldier nodded, motioned to an orderly, and hurried on. Gustave lay back on Jerome and closed his eyes. "It's good I didn't shoot you."

"Will you?" asked Jerome.

"Probably not. But you are *not* a Communard. Do you hear?"

"I am not a Communard."

He looked toward a shell crater and saw the body of a woman.

"Who is that?" asked Gustave, following Jerome's eyes.

"The leader."

"Well, she isn't anymore," said the detective as a corpsman emerged from the smoke.

CHAPTER 39

Paris
The following day

The wind was howling, and the drought of the previous month had made everything tinder dry. Dawn crept in like pestilence from the Old Testament. Great columns of black smoke rose through the morning sky as flames consumed the Palais Royal, the Palais de Justice, and dwellings facing the Rue de Rivoli. The unceasing rain did little to extinguish the flames while women with cans of oil did all they could to set more fires. Buildings not ignited by them were set ablaze by artillery rounds as the battle continued.

The army of Versailles held three-fifths of the city, including the Latin Quarter. But strong pockets of insurgents fought on, and an intense battle was waged by fifteen hundred of the Garde Nationale against three brigades of government troops in the thirteenth arrondissement. Yet there was no coordination, no plan of organized defense among the Garde, and it began to disintegrate.

Jack rose early and put on his old Union greatcoat and slouch hat with the gold braid. He reached into his carpetbag and took out his passport and, after a moment's reflection, an American flag, both of which he tucked into a pocket of his greatcoat.

Charlotte opened her eyes. "Where are you going?"

"Down to the first floor. I want to talk to Shelby about the position of the Versailles. But I think you'd better get dressed. We may have to leave here quickly. This may become a target."

"I can't imagine the French army destroying a landmark like this."

"They may not, but the Communards will."

Pushing his way through the crowded corridor and down the stairs, Jack passed wounded soldiers, one with a chest wound with a blood-soaked bandage. The man feebly raised a hand. "Can you find me a doctor?"

"I'll try," replied Jack.

"There are no more doctors here," another soldier said. "They've all run off."

"Then, monsieur, please find me something else to wear, maybe just a shirt or a hat," said the wounded man. "The Versailles are shooting everybody in Garde uniform."

He coughed up blood, closed his eyes, and laid his head down. A whisper came from his lips, then nothing.

"Don't bother," said the other soldier. "He's dead and he wouldn't have been able to get out anyway. We have to leave; this will be an inferno."

Bedlam reigned as men hastily tore off uniforms and clothed themselves in whatever civilian garb they could find.

"What's happening? I hear people running in the hallway," said Charlotte when Jack returned.

"The Garde is running away. At least the ones that can."

"Then they won't be defending the hotel," said Charlotte, a worried look in her eyes.

"No, they hope to merge into the loyal population. Shelby says that the Garde has only about nine thousand left.

They're holding out at La Roquette Prison, the Rue Haxo, and the heights of Buttes-Chaumont. I ran into Steven, and he said that the Communard barricades at Montmartre have been wiped out."

"Oh Lord. Poor Jerome." Charlotte sank onto the sofa. "Do you think he's been killed?"

"I have to presume so. The Versailles are not in the mood to take prisoners, especially ones defending the barricades."

"I want to give him a proper burial when this is over."

"If we can find his body, Charlotte, but ..."

She was silent for a time.

"I hear the cannons. They seem much closer now."

"We should have gone to the sewers or found a cellar somewhere," Jack said. "It's my fault we stayed here so long."

"I don't blame you. It seemed safe, and we've been able to stay together. I just want us to be together. Even if we're facing the end, I want us to be as one. I'm sure there's a priest somewhere in this building. I mean, with all the wounded and dying, there must be one giving last rites. Let's find a clergyman—I don't care what faith he is. Let's do it."

Jack took a deep breath. "Charlotte, dear, I didn't see any in the building. The Communards hate religion. They wouldn't tolerate a priest anywhere near here. In fact, they'd likely shoot him. I love you, you know that, but getting married right now, today, or any time before this is all settled... I mean ..."

There was a change in her demeanor, a gathering storm. She stiffened and gave him a peculiar look. He went to put his arms around her, to comfort her but she backed away, shaking her head. "Settled? Oh no. I've heard enough of your delays. First it was money. How much would we need? Five thousand francs? ten? twenty? It wouldn't matter if we only had a hundred. In your mind you will never make enough.

I've tried to put aside your past, tried to put your reasoning in perspective, but not anymore. I've been alone before, and I can damn well be alone again! You don't want to marry me, do you Jack? What has this been, all these months? A charade, a—"

"Of course not. We'll marry. I promise—"

Someone knocked rapidly on the door.

"There's a woman in front of the hotel," said Shelby. "She recognized me from Galignani's and asked me to give you this note. She's waiting down there and hopes that you'll meet her. She says you know her. I'm going back down. The Versailles are very close, and they're setting up artillery."

"We'll just pack a few things," said Jack. It was one hell of a time for an argument with Charlotte. "Tell Steven and see if there are wagons hitched up down there. We may need one. And get a pistol off one of those dead soldiers."

Jack closed the door and read the note. "I'll be right back. I know this woman. I won't be long."

Charlotte snatched the note from his hand and scanned it. "How dare she! Of course you know this woman—a prostitute—and you're going to her when we might be killed this very hour?" She looked at the scrawled note again, her hand shaking, voice quivering. "Yes, oh yes, the exquisite, the so elegant Mademoiselle Yvette Maillard. The one whose honor you defended and who nearly got you killed. And just how well do you know her, Jack? Perhaps far better than I ever thought!"

"It's not that way at all! I just wanted to—"

"No! You won't marry me, but you'll go out there and console a strumpet, a trollop who suddenly appeals to your demented sense of honor. This charade is over, Monsieur Volant. Over!"

Shots shattered the window. A heavy blast struck a corner of the building, and someone screamed.

Jack moved toward Charlotte, but she grabbed her coat and pushed him away. "Go see her, Jack. Yes, go to her, comfort the poor lass, but stay away from me!"

She slammed the door, descended the stairs, and tore through the reception hall. Infuriated but heedless of danger or direction she hurried on, pelted by the drenching rain.

"Where did she go?" asked Jack when he came upon Shelby.

"Charlotte? I saw her for just an instant. She's out there, with the Communards. Why is she running, where is she going?"

"I don't know. *She* doesn't know. She's going to get herself killed."

Steven found Jack and Shelby and pointed to smoke rising from the building. "The hotel is on fire, Jack. The Communards are lighting it up."

"That's not my concern. I've got to find Charlotte."

"We'll go with you," blurted Shelby. He and Steven pushed ahead while shells ripped into the Hôtel de Ville.

Pressing forward, they passed Yvette Maillard. Upon seeing Jack, she raised one arm, but slowly dropped it when he ignored her, then pulled her coat over her head and cowered beside a wrecked caisson.

"There! I see her," said Steven as a wagon approached. Its panicked horses pawed the air as Versailles troops fired with steady aim. Bullets ripped into the wagon's driver, who toppled from his elevated seat.

An artillery round disintegrated a wall and threw Steven to the ground. The explosion covered him in stone and dust while shards ricocheted all around.

"Steven!" Jack shouted turning back.

Steven groaned and attempted to rise. His arm flailing, he managed to push a beam aside, but another held him fast.

A second explosion struck yards away, throwing Jack to the ground. Half blinded, he groped toward his brother and with desperate effort shoved the beam aside. Steven, with blood seeping from his arm, shakily stood.

"You're hurt," said Jack.

"I'll be all right. You have to find her, Jack. Just find her!"

Acrid smoke filled the air. Amid cries from the wounded, Jack heard a woman moan ten feet away. She lay sprawled on the pavement, a leg twisted at a strange angle and an arm pierced by a splinter of wood. He lifted her and turned to Shelby. "That wagon, get the wagon!"

Shelby grabbed the reins, leading the terrified horses forward. Jack laid Charlotte on the wagon's floor beside a child, its body stiff, its eyes unseeing.

"Stay with Charlotte, stop the bleeding," Jack commanded as Shelby hoisted himself onto the wagon. A Communard, seeing the wagon, reached for the reins, but Jack drew his pistol and fired. The man clutched his face, screamed, and fell away. Another shell struck the remains of a barricade, showering them in a cascade of debris.

"Are we going to the American Ambulance?" asked Shelby as the wagon bounced over stones and planks littering the Rue de Rivoli.

"Too far. The Hôtel-Dieu hospital is closer."

"But it's on the bank of the Île de la Cité, and we have to cross at the Pont au Double. That's in the hands of the Versailles. What about the Lariboisière?"

"No, we'll just take our chances. Tell Charlotte she'll be all right and take this, wave it over your head," said Jack, handing him a colored rectangle of cloth.

Gunfire from the Communards and the army of Versailles cracked overhead as Jack sped the wagon past ruined barricades and soldiers scrambled out of the way. Turning the horses onto the bridge, he saw a platoon coming on fast with fixed bayonets. It would be impossible to pass without being shot. "Shelby, wave the flag!"

The flag fluttered as smoke roiled past. Jack stopped the wagon, reached into his greatcoat, and pulled out his passport. The platoon having halted, a lieutenant approached, pistol in hand.

"*Je suis américain! Américain!*" Jack said, holding out the document. "My wife, in the wagon, is hurt. I must get to the hospital or she'll die."

The lieutenant snatched the passport, studied it, and peered into the wagon. Shelby pointed to the dead child. "Monsieur Lieutenant, this was her daughter. *S'il vous plait!*" He held the stars and stripes with both hands. "Américaine. Oui, Américaine."

"Make way!" shouted the officer, handing Jack the passport. The platoon parted and Jack resumed the rush, the hospital looming closer, its entrance teeming with orderlies, nurses, and wounded men. Two soldiers took the reins as the horses came to a halt. Jack carried Charlotte through a bloodied crowd, followed by Shelby. Once inside, they pushed their way down a corridor until they found an empty bed.

"Shelby, stop that doctor." Jack laid Charlotte on the bed. He held her hand, and she looked up at him. "It hurts, Jack. Will the doctor come?"

The doctor, an imperious look on his face, attempted in vain to brush Shelby's hand off his shirt sleeve.

"Monsieur Doctor, I think we should go to him," said a nurse carrying a tray of instruments. "A woman is on the bed. I saw him bring her in; she needs attention."

"They all do!" retorted the doctor as orderlies made way for him. He stood angrily before Jack. "You must wait your turn! Soldiers first, women come last."

Jack's hands balled into a fist. Shelby said, "I suggest you look at the woman. Her husband is a dangerous man."

The doctor pivoted and stared coldly at Jack. "Move her onto her back. The splinter must be removed."

Jack leaned over to reposition Charlotte and hesitated, trying to figure out how to do it without hurting her.

"I said turn her. This way!" The doctor grasped her arm, and Charlotte screamed in pain. Jack slammed him against the wall, his pistol inches from the man's head.

"I've shot twelve men and you will be next," Jack hissed, one hand around the man's throat, the other pulling back the hammer of the Remington.

The doctor's eyes grew wide as blood stained his shirt. "Monsieur," he said, staring into the barrel. "I am ..."

"Jack! Put down the gun. There's another doctor. He's coming."

"Oui, monsieur, another doctor," said the nurse. Her tray of instruments had fallen to the floor. "See, he comes now, please, let the doctor go."

Jack released his grip. The physician allowed himself to be led away as the other doctor hurried toward them. He studied Jack and glanced indifferently at the gun. "Shooting him will improve the morale here but it will make things a little less antiseptic, Mister Volant," he said in a New York accent. "Ah, I forgot—Lieutenant, yes, with the Seventh Michigan. I met you at the American Ambulance. Perhaps you remember. Now, let's take a look at Nurse Stuart."

***

Early June

"I spoke to Washburne yesterday, and he said that he's going to remain in Paris," said Jack as they walked past the Hôtel de Ville, now a burned-out ruin. "The secretary of state must be very proud of him, since his tenure would have been over in May."

"Shelby told me that he was at the archbishop's funeral at Notre Dame," said Charlotte, still unaccustomed to the engagement ring.

"He was. He said that it was a very moving tribute. He had first gone to La Roquette Prison to see where the archbishop had been executed. Washburne met him there in May and was impressed by the man's humility. He would have been very comforting to the wounded and dying, especially toward the end."

"Shelby said that the worst of the battle was on that Friday, twenty-eight May."

"It was the last day of the fighting, and the Garde made a final stand at the cemetery at Père Lachaise with about two thousand men. When it ended, the last one hundred and fifty Gardes were lined up and shot. Later, about thirty-five hundred more were captured. Shelby thinks that in all, some twenty thousand Parisians were killed."

"How terribly savage," said Charlotte.

"True, but as far as the government's concerned, it was like scouring a pestilence, a pox on the city."

"I think they were both infected," said Charlotte. "Shelby wrote that the city is dead and all is ash."

"I hate to say it, but my old friend is wrong. There are thousands of stone workers repairing the damage, and many others are cleaning away the debris."

"Speaking of damage, I can help you finish the roof. I'm pretty good with a hammer if you recall."

"You're very good with a hammer, but I completed that while you were relaxing in the hospital. I completed the downstairs bedroom and front parlor, but the upstairs will take time. Jerome said that he'll help, but he ran off to Metz to see that girl."

"That sounds like Jerome. And I was not 'relaxing' in the hospital. It was awful."

"You should've asked my brother to unwrap a mummy for you while you convalesced. He's quite the showman, you know."

Charlotte laughed. "Actually he was quite charming and had lots of stories to tell."

"Ah, brother Steven, a wily fellow and a survivor. But he'll likely stray into shadowy dealings unless, of course, he finds some woman of repute who will thrash him if he gets out of line."

"I know just the right woman," Charlotte said with a gleam in her eye. "It so happens that she's coming to Paris. But I'm not going to tell him. I think it will be a most interesting surprise."

Jack grinned. "Will this mystery woman be here before the wedding? I've already decided on the date."

"You have? You didn't tell me. Exactly what date did you have in mind?"

"The fourth of July."

"Jack! How could you?"

"With all the Americans coming back, it will be a great day. Lots of celebrations, and the French absolutely adore us. I think it's a splendid idea. And my parents are coming too."

"I would love to meet them, but must it be July fourth?"

"How about Lincoln's birthday? That's on the—"

"The fourth of July is just fine, Jack."

"Shelby said that there should be fireworks."

"I don't think so, Jack. Enough of Paris has already burned down."

CHAPTER 40

Paris
Mid-June 1871

The buxom, matronly, white-haired woman pressed an envelope into the hands of the gendarme standing guard outside the Prefecture of Police.

"Monsieur, please give this to your commanding officer. It is of the greatest importance, a matter of supreme interest to him."

The policeman glanced at the envelope. "And what is your name, madam?"

"It is of no consequence," said Marguerite Couture. She slipped into the crowd heading back from the Île de la Cité.

The officer, choosing not to pursue, entered the office and handed the envelope to the chief inspector.

"Who gave this to you?" asked Gene Gustave.

"She wouldn't give me her name. An elderly woman, well dressed and likely of some stature."

Gustave dismissed the guard and, adjusting his spectacles, opened the envelope and extracted a single sheet of scented paper.

Dear Monsieur Gustave,
I wish to put to rest questions regarding an investigation
involving your office which concerns a most unfortunate
incident prior to the late war. I write in part to ...

"Monsieur Chief Inspector," said the guard, suddenly reappearing before Gustave's file-laden desk. "There is a man outside who wishes to speak with you. A young lady is with him. He says that you know him and it's rather important."

"Is everything so important?" said Gustave, vexed at being interrupted. "Well, show them in, but tell them that I am quite busy." He gestured toward the stack of files.

The chief inspector had only a minute before an elegantly dressed young man and a girl of Mediterranean complexion, not more than seventeen, stood before him.

Gustave knitted his brows. "Do I know you? I certainly don't recognize you, monsieur."

"I'm sure that you wouldn't, Chief Inspector. After all, you only saw me for a few seconds during a most difficult time. But I do believe you might remember the words you said."

Gustave removed his reading glasses and with a curious look said, "And what were those words? Don't play games with me."

"No, monsieur. They were 'The badge. Show them the badge.'"

Gustave stared, rose, and rushed around the desk to embrace Jerome.

Furiously shaking his hand, he said, "Mon Dieu! It's you, the one I collapsed onto. I was hoping that you lived, and I would see you again."

"That you happened to arrive at just that moment, that you remembered the badge, saved us both," said Jerome.

"It was most certainly propitious, and you acted so quickly. But you were with the Communards, no? Of course," said Gustave in a discreet voice, "this I will never mention, now that that business is all over. A sad thing indeed. So many perished, including colleagues of mine and the former chief inspector."

Still clasping Jerome's hand, he looked at the young woman. "And who is this beautiful young lady?"

"My fiancée, Mademoiselle Marie Freycinet. She's from Metz. Her father agreed to our forthcoming marriage when he learned that I am studying law. I wish to be an attorney."

"A splendid idea. But now, besides the pleasure of your arrival, I must ask, is there something else you wish to communicate? Perhaps something dealing with the law?"

"I have come to learn through various sources that there is an elderly woman of perhaps feeble mind incarcerated in prison. As part of my legal training, I wish to intercede on her behalf. She was duped and taken advantage of."

He handed Gustave a formal appearing statement. "Perhaps you might look into the matter. It would be, in my humble opinion, a miscarriage of justice if she were to be imprisoned much longer, or executed following a trial. With all the turmoil of the last year, she has languished, and her health is now failing."

"Compassion and knowledge of the law is a worthy thing. I promise to look into it at my first opportunity."

They bid one another adieu. "I wish to say, I'm glad that you have come here. I know many people in the legal profession," said Gustave. "Return here when you achieve your credentials. I will write on your behalf."

Gene Gustave watched the couple from his window. What a strange turn of affairs, considering that many former Communards were still facing trial and, in numerous cases, execution. But whatever revolutionary motive once propelled the young man, it all seemed distant, replaced with the prospect of matrimony and an honorable career. But then he mused, nobody really wanted to think of the siege, the communards or for that matter, even the war.

He returned to his desk, put on his spectacles, and once again began to read the letter.

The matter of which I speak regards the demise of one Mademoiselle Camille Lapin, a courtesan associated with the salon Chez Chantilly on the Rue Saint-Honoré in the 1st arrondissement.

It has been brought to my attention that the presumed assailant, a Mademoiselle Jeanne Virot and a leader of the Communards, was killed in the final days of the conflict. And indeed, Mademoiselle Virot did violently attack Lapin, wounding her seriously. But (and I say this to clear my conscience if that is indeed possible) she wasn't the one who, with hatred and overwhelming jealousy, fired the weapon that ended her life. I am the lethal assassin.

Thus, it is no longer necessary for you to investigate the possible involvement of any other suspects. As for me, I am no longer living in France, and I will never be found or judged by the French legal system. Only God will be my judge, and I duly await my sentence when that time comes.

With time, the desire for vengeance of that proportion eventually passes. I do regret the dastardly act I committed, and I will have to live with its burden for the remainder of my days. That is my sentence for which no penitence shall be granted.

The other assailant,
Mademoiselle Yvette Maillard

***

The driver in livery, seated on his high perch, drove an elegant barouche decked out with gas lamps and bunting, trailing a clattering of tin cans. It was followed by a procession of landaus, the horses' tack adorned with bells and feathers. Bystanders cheered the newlyweds while Charlotte waved and Jack doffed his silk top hat. They proceeded from the reopened gardens of the Tuileries where the nuptials had taken place, down the Avenue du Général-Uhrich, previously known as Avenue de l'Impératrice, then on to the superb Café Foy on Boulevard des Italiens. On this, the fourth day of July, French and American flags graced the oldest restaurant in Paris.

Weeks earlier Jack had telegraphed his parents to say that he was to be married. They offered their enthusiastic congratulations, saying that they were seeking passage on the fastest steamship bound for France.

To Steven's delight he received a telegram again thanking him for his assistance years before and looking forward to a happy family reunion.

All Les Refusés had already arrived, and Jack hoped that the ambassador and his wife, Adele, would soon join them. Jerome and Marie sat at the same table as Jack, Steven, and their parents. Around them, wine was poured amid the gaiety spurred on by their close friends.

Gathering her long white train, Charlotte took Jack's arm and, along with Shelby and a coquettish young woman, took seats at the specially arranged table. Monet, having returned to Paris, stood and raised a glass. "To the future great artist and his lovely wife, the esteemed sculptor, a toast to their happiness and success!"

"And to the memory of our dear friend Bazille, who gave his life for the glory of France," added Manet.

Charlotte chatted with Jack's father, who hadn't been in Paris since the revolution of '48. He was impressed by all the changes made by Haussmann but saddened by the ruins of the Tuileries Palace and the Hôtel de Ville, as well as the loss of life during the siege and its aftermath. During a lull in the conversation, Charlotte nudged Jack and glanced at Steven, who was staring unabashedly at the young lady sitting beside her.

"Did you introduce them yet?" asked Jack.

"I was waiting for the right time."

"You might as well do it now, before he faints and falls off his chair."

Interrupting Steven's reverie, Charlotte said, "Allow me to introduce my cousin Annabelle Beauregard Simpson from the Commonwealth of Virginia. She has come to Paris to pursue her antiquarian studies—especially those of ancient Egypt and Mesopotamia."

Steven stood, bowed, and shook the lady's hand.

"I am honored to make your acquaintance," he said in his most charming manner. "I presume that you will be staying for some time."

"Indeed. Charlotte tells me that you have a passing interest in those subjects."

"I do, but I have only a smattering of knowledge, nothing terribly academic. But perhaps you might instruct me in such things. I am a fast learner."

"Steven!" said Charlotte, a warning shot over the bow.

"Well, I did do some study, a while back." Steven grinned sheepishly, then said, "I am struck by your interesting name."

"Well, my daddy liked the poem about Annabel Lee by Edgar Allen Poe."

"'For the moon never beams, without bringing me dreams / Of the beautiful Annabel Lee,'" said Steven.

"Oh, you know it," said Annabelle with a radiant smile.

"I do love poetry," replied Steven ingratiatingly.

"And, as you most assuredly know, I am distantly related to the great Confederate general Pierre Gustave Toutant Beauregard, hence my middle name."

"Oh, my heart goes pitty-pat," said Shelby, "A true daughter of the South."

"I remind you, good sir," said Jack, speaking just over the din, "that the esteemed general lost his entire division at Gettysburg."

"Mere details," replied Shelby with a dismissive sniff. "The lady has excellent breeding."

"Indeed," said Charlotte. "I would not introduce our dear Steven to anybody of lesser repute. And," she added, holding Annabelle's hand, "Steven is really a splendid man and exceedingly versed in great literature. In fact, he so kindly read to me when I was in the hospital. I'm sure that with a bit of encouragement and dedication, you can make him into a truly respectable citizen."

"There is that possibility, but it will be, to use Wellington's phrase at Waterloo, 'a near run thing,'" said Jack with an impish smile.

"I am respectable. Well, basically," said Steven with an exaggerated sign of distress.

"He certainly looks respectable," said Annabelle, her luminous blue eyes appraising the distinguished and expensively attired gentleman.

"See there," said Steven.

"Yes, in fact, he looks quite French. Perhaps he should adopt a nom de plume like Pierre Georges or Jacque or Cheval. I think the latter is quite fitting, don't you, Monsieur Steven?"

Monsieur Steven sputtered in reply.

"I do declare," said Annabelle, "perhaps we might even get to know one another a little better. Who knows what might result from that."

"That's an inviting statement, something you should consider, brother," said Jack.

"Annabelle always says what she thinks," said Charlotte. "And Steven, as they say south of the Mason-Dixon line, you just may be happier than a six-legged pig in the sunshine."

Steven put two fingers to his temple and studied Annabelle, ten years his junior. He reached out and took her hand. "Six-legged pig or not, I think we'll do quite well in the sunshine."

An hour later, after several bottles of wine, Jack and his bride mingled with Manet, Renoir, Degas, Pissarro, and Sisley, all of whom were in serious conversation over the prospect of artistic success.

"I think we should honor Bazille's idea and do our own exhibition. The Salon des Arts be damned," said Monet.

"I agree," said Pissarro. "It might take a few years to accumulate enough work, but Cézanne, Sisley, and even Degas think it's the only way we can show our paintings without scathing reviews by the jurists. And I know just the right place on the Rue des Capucines."

"I won't do it," said Manet. "It's best to try the Salon. There's a new director, Louis Blanc."

"He only likes the old masters," said Pissarro.

"I don't care what he likes."

"Well, I want to be accepted by the Salon," said Manet. "And for now, I'll do what will get me in. So, I'm painting a canvas I named *Le Bon Bock*. It's of an old fellow sitting at the bar with a beer. I hope to get a medal and make some real money. And become famous, of course."

"Then you may be the only one," replied Degas, a dour expression on his face.

"But we should still stick together," injected Sisley. "We're all doing fine, imaginative work—unique pieces defying the old norms. Someday we may be famous."

"After we're all dead," said Jack tartly.

"It's about the art," said Charlotte. "You do it because creativity is in your soul, your very being. Perhaps the art world isn't ready for you, but does that really matter?"

"As long as we don't starve," said Monet.

"But who will buy your work?" asked Manet.

"Everybody who can afford it in fifty years. So I think we should pour another glass and make a toast," said Pissarro with unexpected enthusiasm.

"To what?" asked Jack.

"To the future, and to the most bizarre artists of the Third Republic. To the City of Light and to us, Les Refusés!"

"To the City of Light and to us, Les Refusés!" they joyously agreed.

***

"Have you given any thought to babies?" asked Charlotte as the barouche approached the house.

"Those little things that cry and wake one up in the middle of the night?"

"Exactly, dear husband. I think children will be a wonderful addition, and they do eventually grow up."

"It takes a long time, Mrs. Volant."

"You have survived horrendous things, Monsieur Volant. A daughter will be an unimaginable joy. She may even become a great artist."

"I guess it's worthy of consideration," said Jack. "I mean if he—"

"She. If *she* becomes a fine painter like Marie Cassatt."

Jack put his arm around his wife. "It is a rather intriguing idea. I'm sure *he* will become a fine artist like his father."

"If you insist. But either way, we should begin as soon as possible. We're artists, after all. We live to create."

"Mon Dieu, what a spectacularly insightful woman," said Jack.

"I'm glad you approve. Now ask the driver to go faster. I'm in a very romantic mood."

THE END

Author's Notes

The following personalities in the book are an invention of the author: Jack, Charlotte, Jerome, Steven/Marcel, Shelby, Daudet, Abraxas, Brandenburg, Marguerite Couture, Camille Lapin, Jeanne Virot, Yvette Maillard, Eliza Breton, the detectives (except for Eugene François Vidocq, the father of modern forensics), François Regnard, and Jacquet Lapieux. For the historical characters, I employed their own words where possible to convey their personalities.

"Refusés" was a term given to the Impressionists in 1874 by art critic Louis Leroy upon viewing Claude Monet's landscape *Impression, Sunrise*. Leroy said of it, "The panting is just an impression." The name "Refusés" was adopted by the Impressionists. For literary purposes I used the term at an earlier date.

All paintings mentioned in the novel were completed on or before 1871, the year the story ends. The derision of the works by the French jurists and public is accurate, and popular opinion remained quite negative until late in the nineteenth century. Only a few of the artists' works were accepted by the Salon.

An excellent source of information regarding the gods of ancient Egypt can be found in *What Life Was Like on the Banks of the Nile: Egypt 3050–30 BC* by Time-Life Books.

Impressions of the Battle of Gettysburg were gained by the author from his cavalry reenactment experience at the site during the one hundred and twenty-fifth anniversary of the battle. The heat and humidity in July 1993 was much the same as one hundred years before. The action was spirited and as accurate as possible, but thankfully there was no bloodshed. The reenactment was close to but not on that hallowed ground; yet the bugle calls, the pounding hoofs of horses, the shouts and the sound of the guns gave us all a very lasting impression.

It has been estimated that over twenty thousand Communards were killed during "the Bloody Week" ("La Semaine Sanglante").

The actual menus provided for the dinner given by ambassador Elihu Washburne following the siege are shown on the web.

Thousands of passes were issued by the ambassador for passage out of Paris during the siege. He was idolized during and after the siege by the people of Paris and in appreciation of his noble service the U.S. Department of State extended his tenure in Paris as he requested. The simple interior of the American embassy is as described.

The artist Frederick Bazille was killed by a sniper in the last days of the Franco Prussian war.

The demimondes Cora Pearl and La Païva were real courtesans.

The poem "On a Bulbous Root" was written by Martin Tupper.

All street names were in effect before the fall of the Second Empire. Many have been changed numerous times since 1871.

Count Émilien de Nieuwerkerke was in charge of determining which paintings would be displayed at the Salon des Beaux Arts.

Galignani's bookstore where *The Messenger* was printed is real and still exists in Paris today.

The Hôtel de Ville was the site of the last stand of the Communards and was not rebuilt for ten years following its destruction. Reconstructed, it still exists.

THE REFUSED

The Prussian heavy artillery that Albrecht von Brandenburg showed Jack was constructed by the Krupp Gun Works and utilized during the Siege of Paris.

The American Hospital existed as described, and ambulance drivers really did sing "Marching through Georgia." Washburne's son Gratiot volunteered at the hospital.

All cafés mentioned existed in real life, and many were frequented by the Refusés.

The description of conditions in the morgue and the practice of gawking at the deceased is accurate, as is the use of the Guillotine during the period described.

Prostitution during the Second Empire of Louis Napoleon was legal, and marriage customs existed as described.

Empress Eugénie was largely responsible for encouraging her husband to declare war on Prussia. She, along with Louis, fled to England following the French defeat. She was assisted in her escape by the American dentist Dr. Evans.

The Prussians did release and rearm eighty thousand French prisoners of the Army of Versailles to put down the Communard uprising in support of the Thiers government.

The coronation of Kaiser Wilhelm did take place at the Versailles Palace and it was there that Germany was united under Prussian domination.

The poem Charlotte read regarding food eaten at Washburne's dinner at the end of the Siege of Paris is actually documented.

Pierre-Auguste Renoir was nearly executed by the Garde Nationale during the siege and was saved by the Communard Raoul Rigault. Rigault was killed shortly after by the Army of Versailles.

"Mummy Mania," the unwrapping of mummies, was a popular activity in Paris salons, and thousands of pounds of wrappings were shipped to America as described. There was a flourishing market for fake mummies and Egyptian artifacts.

French medical practices existed as described. The advances in antiseptics are as mentioned.

Baron Georges-Eugène Haussmann, the "Demolition Artist," was awarded the contract by Louis Napoleon to redesign Paris with paved streets and magnificent boulevards that are seen in the city today.

All battle sites during the war between France and Prussia are as described.

It should be noted that one of the reasons World War I occurred over forty years after the Franco-Prussian War was the annexation of Alsace and Lorraine by Germany following the 1870–71 conflict. During the ensuing decades, both France and Germany prepared for the "Great War" through the development of strategy, weaponry and alliances. Although the Franco-Prussian War is largely forgotten, its ramifications directly shaped the tumultuous events of the twentieth century and beyond—events that those involved could not have possibly imagined.

Any historical errors are the sole responsibility of the author.

ABOUT THE AUTHOR

RON SINGERTON

After graduating from California State University at Long Beach in 1965 Ron Singerton joined the U.S. Army Security Agency and spent his overseas time in Asia.

The subsequent twenty-five years were devoted to teaching history and art in Southern California High schools, where he developed a particular love for writing and historical research.

During the early 1980s, he authored a series, *Moments in History*, of some thirty mini books on famous people and events ranging from Columbus to the moon landing. The books were adopted as supplementary teaching material for the State of California and approved by the Los Angeles School board as a teaching aid. Published by Santillana Publishing Company, the original ones are considered collector's items.

An avid horseman and saber fencer with a special interest in the American Civil War, he "heard the bugle and the sound of the drums" and became a re-enactor, riding with the Union cavalry in dozens of engagements from California to Gettysburg, Pennsylvania.

Always interested in an exciting but obscure story, his historical research meandered from the nineteenth and twentieth centuries back to the ancient world. Singerton once said, "Technology of the past often appears elementary to us; the emotions do not." For a writer, the thoughts of peoples long past, as well as civilizations now little more than sand-pitted ruins, still evolve into a pageant of love, intrigue and dire conflict. "It is nothing less than a shadowed mirror of our own world."

Through the writings of Plutarch, Pliny and Julius Caesar he uncovered an epic event that would take him from Rome in the last days of Republic to the Great Wall of China. After years of research the tale became the gist of a two-volume novel: *The Villa of Deceit* and *The Silk and the Sword*.

In his third historical novel, *A Cherry Blossom in Winter*, Singerton turns to the tumultuous opening years of the Twentieth Century with a stirring novel of the Russo Japanese war of 1904.

Ron is also an award winning artist, with artwork in glass, stone, paint and bronze sold and displayed online, in galleries, and numerous art shows.

IF YOU ENJOYED THIS BOOK

Please write a review.
This is important to the author and helps to get the word
out to others
Visit

PENMORE PRESS
www.penmorepress.com

All Penmore Press books are available directly through our
website, and internationally.

Villa of Deceit
BY

Ron Singerton

Action Adventure, Crime, Mystery,

Rome, 70 B.C.E.

A house in turmoil: a controlling father, an adulterous mother, and an angry son made reckless by a forbidden love. Young Gaius defies his father Toronius, fleeing with a slave girl whom he marries, only to see her die in childbirth. Disinherited and grieving, Gaius leaves his infant son Tacitus behind with a trusted aunt and devotes his life to the sword.

On the battle field Gaius is trained and tempered into a hardened veteran of war. His leadership and bravery in campaigns earn him respect and the rank of Senior Centurion. But his greatest challenge is returning home to face his son Tacitus, now grown to a wild, undisciplined youth. Gaius forces the errant boy against his wishes into the army that he may be molded into a man.

Like Gaius before him, Tacitus must fight to become his own man in defiance of his father. But together as Legionnaires, they must survive an invasion mired by betrayal and confront the fury of war.

PENMORE PRESS
www.penmorepress.com

Silk and The Sword
BY

Ron Singerton

Action Adventure, Crime, Mystery,
Roman History

Young Tacitus, torn from the girl he loves and accused of defiling his late mother's temple, is dragooned into the Roman army by his father Gaius, a bitter and unbending Centurion. With his father and seven legions, he joins General Marcus Crassus in an ill-fated attack on the sprawling Parthian Empire. After the Roman forces are decimated at the Battle of Carrhae, Tacitus, Gaius, and four hundred survivors venture eastward on the fabled Silk Road to find a river beyond a wall that will lead them back to Rome. Tacitus becomes the soldier he never wanted to be while battling bandits, trekking through frozen mountain passes, and dealing with a formidable foe on the other side of the world. But his greatest challenge is a personal quandary: should he return to Rome for his long-lost love or seek the hand of a princess in the mysterious land beside the Great Wall?

"A tour de force of Roman military survival across a long and arduous trek through the Parthian empire, the silk road, and into the celestial kingdom

PENMORE PRESS
www.penmorepress.com

A CHERRY BLOSSOM IN WINTER
BY
RON SINGERTON

As the 20th century dawns, Japan is a rising power at odds with determinedly expanding Russia. In Moscow and St. Petersburg, aristocrats advance their political interests and have affairs as factory workers starve. Young Alexei Brusilov, son of an ambassador, accompanies his father to Japan and there falls in love with the daughter of a Japanese war hero. Despite threats and warnings, he pursues this forbidden romance, delighted to discover that Kimi-san returns his affection, until disaster overtakes them.

Amid the rising storm of revolution at home, Alexei returns to St. Petersburg to become a naval officer. A deadly rivalry with another cadet, a dangerous family secret, and friendships with revolutionaries imperil his career – and his life. Years later, Alexei finds himself aboard ship as the rusting and badly out of date Russian fleet is sent half way around the world to fight a modern and determined Japanese Navy. Will Alexei live to see his love again, or die under the blazing guns of the fast moving enemy cruisers?

"This is a sweeping work about the clash between Western and Eastern cultures, pretended morality, and grand passions struggling against heavily ritualized matrimony.... The author's observations about Russian society and his grasp of its good and bad points would likely have gained an approving nod from Tolstoy. This is first-rate storytelling!" —John Danielski, author of The King's Scarlet and Blue Water Scarlet Tide

PENMORE PRESS
www.penmorepress.com

THE REFUSED

Blossom In The
Ashes
By
Ron Singerton

1941: Two Brothers, One Woman, One War

Tad, elder son of Russian-born political refugee Alexei and Japanese-born Kimi, flies planes for the U.S. Navy; his brother, Koizumi, is a fighter pilot in the Imperial Navy of Japan. When Koizumi visits his family in Hawaii, he is accompanied by the beautiful Sayuri. To Koizumi's dismay, she and Tad begin a passionate romance, only to be torn apart when she and Koizumi are ordered back to Tokyo.

All too soon, Tad discovers that, if being estranged from a brother for 25 years is bad, seeing him in your gun sights is worse. And as American bombs fall on Japan, Tad fears that he will never see Sayuri again.

Commitment, terror, compassion and unswerving loyalty comprise *A Blossom in the Ashes*, a story of unyielding nations in a world gone mad.

"*A riveting novel that is a new twist on family relationships during World War II. Singeron's characters are interesting, the story engrossing and fast-paced. It's a must read for those who like this genre.*" — Marc Liebman, author of award-winning novels *Forgotten* and *Inner Look*, and *Big Mother 40*, a top 50 war novel.

The sequel to award-winning *A Cherry Blossom in Winter*

PENMORE PRESS
www.penmorepress.com